A QUIET LIFE IN THE COUNTRY

T E Kinsey

For my family and friends.
For all the missing evenings and weekends.
Thank you for your love, patience, help and indulgence.

ONE

The Body in the Woods

A quiet life in the country, that was what my mistress had wanted when she moved us from the smart apartments in London to the newly-built house just outside Littleton Cotterell in the summer of 1908. Life in Gloucestershire, she had said, would be peaceful and uneventful. Bristol was just a short train journey from the nearby market town, she had promised, so we'd not be cut off entirely from civilization, but she had also assured me that there would be calm after the years of adventure (and occasional terror). She would finally be able to relax. And to rest. To take it easy. No more rushing about.

And so it was that we were up shortly after dawn on our third day in the village, walking the lanes and the fields, energetically exploring our new home. We'd already met Toby Thompson, the scarlet-faced, curly-haired, barrel-chested dairy farmer. His curiosity at seeing a "lady from up London" striding across his lower pasture with her lady's maid in tow had caused him to stop driving his herd towards the milking shed and come over to speak to her. The cows, indignant at this interruption to their routine, began lowing irritably. Some plodded towards their usual morning destination, drawn on by the promise of the relief of milking, while the others milled around, leaderless and lost. Mr Thompson was oblivious, keen instead to make the acquaintance of his new neighbour.

Greetings and pleasantries were exchanged but my own attention was entirely held by the confused and disgruntled cows so I heard nothing of their conversation until I saw him pointing to the woods about half a mile distant and saying, in his unfamiliar West Country burr, 'I reckon they woods'll be a nice walk this time o' the mornin', m'lady. It's a beautiful day. I often goes into the woods for a bit o' peace and quiet of a summer's mornin' once the milkin's done.'

'Thank you, Mr Thompson,' said Lady Hardcastle, 'I believe I shall do the same.'

'Right you are, then. You 'ave a good day, m'lady, and don't forget to drop by if you needs anythin'. Our ma'd be ever so pleased to meet you, I'm sure.'

Lady Hardcastle expressed her delight and thanks and we set off across the pasture towards the dense stand of trees.

As we entered the woods, I looked back across the field we had just crossed at our tracks through the dew-damp grass. I had a sudden jolt of panic at leaving such an obvious trail, but just as quickly I remembered that we no longer had to worry about such things. No one had wanted us dead simply for being English for a number of years now. Indeed, here in Gloucestershire "English" was rather a desirable thing to be, but "old habits..." and all that.

Ahead of me, Lady Hardcastle stepped nimbly over a patch of mud and turned back to me. 'Keep up, Armstrong,' she said with a smile, 'and watch out for the mud.'

'Yes, m'lady,' I said in my best approximation of the local accent as I hopped across the miniature mire. I checked behind us again as we made our way farther into the dimness of the wood.

'For goodness' sake,' she said, 'do stop acting like a blessed bodyguard, you'll upset the natives. You've been looking for pursuit since we left the house.'

'Sorry, my lady. It's just...'

'I know, dear.' She reached out and touched my arm reassuringly.

The morning sun was struggling to have much of an influence on the world beneath the canopy of rich green leaves. The dark ground beneath our boots was soft and damp and the air was surprisingly chill; I began to wish I'd thought to put on a jacket, or at least to have brought my shawl.

Lady Hardcastle resumed her enthusiastic descriptions of the local plant and animal life. She had a passion for the natural sciences which she never tired of trying to share with me, but I confess that despite her best efforts I was still unable to tell a beech tree from a beach hut. There were the obvious difficulties one might have in getting into a bathing costume in a beech tree, of course – at the very least there would be issues of balance and of being poked by errant limbs. Though thinking about it, an errant limb can be a problem in a shared beach hut, too. My laugh brought a questioning look and I was was about to share my observations when we broke through into a beautifully sunlit clearing.

'And in the centre of the clearing, my dear Armstrong,' she was saying, without apparently having broken her conversational stride, 'we have... I say.'

'A dead body, my lady?' I said.

'I was going to say, "a magnificent English oak",' she said, somewhat distractedly, 'but the body is definitely the more arresting sight.'

We stepped forward to take a better look. There, in the centre of the clearing, was a magnificent oak tree; a rather old one to judge from its girth. Hanging by its neck from one of the elderly tree's lower limbs was the body of a man.

We approached. It was a youngish man, perhaps in his late 20s, dressed in a neat, dark blue suit of the sort that might be worn by a clerk. And he was most definitely dead. Even without Lady Hardcastle's scientific education I knew that being suspended by the neck on a length of sturdy rope wasn't conducive to long life.

A log lay on its side beneath his feet and I immediately had the image of the poor despairing fellow teetering on it with the rope around his neck before kicking it aside and bringing an end to whatever troubles had tormented him.

Lady Armstrong interrupted my thoughts. 'Give me my bag, dear, and hurry back to the village. Rouse the sergeant and tell him we've found a body in the woods,' she said, calmly but firmly. 'We're not too far from the road,' she said, pointing. 'That way, I think.'

I took the canvas bag from my shoulder and passed it to her. 'I'll be as quick as I can, my lady,' I said as I struck out in the indicated direction.

Lady Hardcastle was right, and the road back into the village was just a few hundred yards through the trees. My sense of direction has never been the best but I managed to make the correct choice when I reached the road, turning right and heading at a brisk trot down the hill.

Perspiring gently, and slightly out of breath, I reached Sergeant Dobson's house within just a few minutes. The large, cast iron knocker on the dark blue door made a pleasingly loud bang as I rapped it firmly, and soon there were sounds of activity f rom within.

Village life had proved quite a contrast to the bustling anonymity of London, and between our arrival at lunchtime two days ago and retiring for the night on the previous day, just about every inhabitant of the village, rich and poor, had paid a call on Lady Hardcastle. They had come to introduce themselves, to offer their services and, most of all, to goggle at the lady from London. The local landowner, Sir Hector Farley-Stroud, seldom had visitors it seemed, and a lady from London was by way of an exotic curiosity, especially once rumours about her past had begun to circulate. All of which meant that not only did I already know exactly which of the little houses on the village green belonged to the Gloucestershire Police, but also which one served as both the village police station and the home of Sergeant Dobson. It also meant that I was known to the portly sergeant who recognized me as soon as he opened the door. His gruff rebuke for disturbing the constabulary slumbers died on his lips when he saw me standing there.

'Why, Miss Armstrong,' he said solicitously, 'whatever's the matter? You look all of a pother.'

As succinctly as I could, I told him what we had found and within just a few moments he had fetched his hat, finished fastening his tunic and was leading me to the door of the smaller cottage which adjoined his own.

'Young Hancock will be fast asleep like as not, so just you keep knocking till he wakens. Tell him what you told me, then say I said he's to fetch Dr Fitzsimmons. They're to come up to the old oak in Combe Woods in Dr Fitzsimmons's carriage so we can bring back the body. Begging your pardon, miss.' He blushed slightly at speaking of such things in front of a woman, then turned hurriedly away and mounted his black, police-issue bicycle.

He turned and waved as he rode off towards the woods, and I began knocking on the door.

It was, as Sergeant Dobson had suggested, something of a task to awaken the sleeping constable and almost five minutes had passed before a bleary-eyed young man in a long nightshirt opened the door.

'What the bloomin' 'ell do you–' Once again coherent speech was extinguished by the sight of a slightly unfamiliar woman at the door. 'Sorry, miss, I thought you was... No matter. Miss...?'

'Armstrong,' I said, 'I'm Lady Hardcastle's lady's maid.'

'So you are, so you are,' said the tall young constable, yawning, and scratching at his beard. 'What can I do for you, miss?'

'Lady Hardcastle and I were walking in Combe Woods and we found a man hanging from the old oak in the clearing.'

'Dead?'

No, I thought to myself, he was in remarkably fine spirits, actually, despite the rope round his neck. His face was purple and his breathing a little... absent, but he seemed frightfully well, considering. I decided not to say that, though. Be polite, Flo, I thought.

'Yes, constable, quite dead. Sergeant Dobson asks that you fetch Dr Fitzsimmons and bring him and his carriage to the clearing. He wants to bring back the body but I imagine the doctor might want to certify death, too.'

'He might at that,' he mused. He stood awhile in thought before making up his mind what to do, then stepped brightly out of the door. But when his bare feet touched the cold, dewy grass, he became suddenly aware of his state of dress. 'Oh. Oh,' he said, slightly flustered. 'Give me a few moments to make myself decent and I'll be with you.'

'Thank you. Might I prevail upon you for a lift back to the woods? It was quite a run to get here.'

'You ran?'

'I did indeed.'

'But you're a...'

'Yes, I'm one of those, too. It's remarkable the things we can do when we think nobody's looking.'

He looked briefly puzzled before hurrying back inside and slamming the door. I heard his footsteps running up the stairs and waited patiently for his return.

Dressed, behelmetted and ready for duty, Constable Hancock reappeared at his front door a few minutes later and we made our way across the green to Dr Fitzsimmons's house.

'Might I ask you a question, Constable?' I said.

'Certainly you may, miss.'

'This seems like a very small village to me; why does it have two policemen? And such luxurious accommodation?'

Hancock laughed. 'We're not just here for Littleton Cotterell, miss, this is just where we have our headquarters. We serve several villages for miles around.' He seemed to inflate with pride as he said it. 'It's quite a responsibility, and one that the boys in the towns tend to underestimate.'

'Well I'm glad we have you to ourselves this morning. I don't know what I should have done if I'd had to get all the way to Chipping Bevington for help.'

'You'd'a been disappointed when you got there, an' all, miss,' he said, 'them's idiots over there. You could have used the telephone, mind. We've got one now.'

I'd been wondering about that. We took the telephone for granted in London, but I had no idea if such conveniences had made it all the way out here. It seems that the police stations had them, at least.

We reached the doctor's house and knocked at the door. It was answered very promptly by a middle-aged woman dressed from head to toe in black.

'Hello, Margaret, is the doctor in?' Hancock said.

'Whom shall I say is calling,' she asked.

'It's me, Margaret, Sam Hancock.'

'I know who you are, you fool, don't be so impertinent. But the... lady?'

Hancock was losing his patience. 'Is he in or not? We are here on urgent police business and I don't have time for your tomfoolery. I've a good mind to—'

A well-dressed, elderly man – tall, balding, and with quite the longest nose I've ever seen – appeared behind the snobbish housekeeper. 'Thank you, Mrs Newton, I'll take care of this.'

Margaret reluctantly shuffled back into the hall and went about her business.

'My apologies for the welcome, Constable. How may I help you?'

Hancock introduced me and I ran once more through my brief account of the finding of the body.

'I'll get Newton to harness the horse and we'll be off in no time. Do come in in the meantime. Can I offer you anything while we wait? Tea, perhaps? Have you eaten, Constable? I'm sure Mrs Newton could find an extra helping of something.'

We both accepted the offer of tea and sat in the doctor's waiting room while Margaret's husband prepared the carriage.

By the time we reached the clearing, more than an hour had passed since we'd made our grisly discovery. Dr Fitzsimmons's horse had been tethered by the side of the road and we'd walked to the clearing to find Lady Hardcastle deep in conversation with Sergeant Dobson some way from the dangling body. They seemed to be looking at some sketches.

'Look at this, Hancock,' the sergeant said with glee, 'Lady Hardcastle has sketched the scene for us.'

Hancock inspected the drawings and nodded gravely with what he imagined was professional approval. 'Very good,' he said. 'Very good indeed.'

'They'll be a great help at the inquest, Lady Hardcastle,' said the sergeant. 'Thank you. Oh, and where are my manners? Lady Hardcastle, may I introduce Dr Fitzsimmons.'

'We met yesterday, thank you, Sergeant. How are you, Doctor? It's a shame our second meeting couldn't be under more pleasant circumstances.'

'It is indeed, my lady, it is indeed. Now what have we here? A suicide, it seems. Do we know who it is?'

'Not quite yet, sir, no,' said Dobson. 'I've got the queerest feeling I've seen the gentleman before somewhere, but I just can't place him. I can't quite reach his pockets, neither, or else I'd have seen if he had a letter or something that might have identified him.'

Constable Hancock had been staring at the body. He didn't look too comfortable and I wondered if he'd seen many bodies in circumstances like this rather than laid out neatly in a coffin ready for the last respects of their loved ones.

'I knows him,' said Hancock, slowly. 'That's Frank Pickering. He's from over Woodworthy but he plays cricket for us since their club folded last season. Or "played", I should say. He worked in Bristol. It cost him to get in on the train every day from Chipping Bevington but he always said he'd rather that and live out here than live in the city. Nice bloke.' His voice drifted off as he looked on, still mesmerized by the body.

'That's it, young Hancock,' said the sergeant with a jolt of satisfied recollection. 'Well done, boy. Yes, I seen him playing against Dursley a week ago last Sunday.'

'Was he a melancholy fellow?' the doctor asked Hancock.

'No, sir, that's just it. He was the life and soul, he was. Bright and bumptious, always had a joke.'

'It can often be the way that a jovial exterior masks the pain within,' mused the doctor. 'Shall we cut the poor fellow down? Then we can take the body back to my surgery and we can make the arrangements for the inquest.'

Lady Hardcastle had been slightly distracted throughout all this. She was looking at the ground beneath the body and checking it against her sketches. 'Might we test one or two of my ideas before we do, please, gentlemen?'

'If we can, m'lady,' said Dobson. 'What troubles you?'

'Would you say the ground was soft, Sergeant?' she asked.

'Passably soft, m'lady, yes.'

'And so one might expect that this log, which had borne the weight of quite an athletically hefty man, should have left an impression in the ground beneath the tree.'

'That seems reasonable, m'lady.'

'And yet...' She indicated the ground immediately below the body. It was trampled and bore one or two odd impressions, but there was no obvious, large indentation from the end of the log. 'I wonder if I might trouble you to stand the log on its end, Constable, just as it would have been before poor Mr Pickering met his unfortunate end.'

'Certainly, m'lady,' Hancock said, stepping forwards and lifting the log. He positioned it on its end with its top some six inches below the toes of Frank Pickering's boots.

We looked at the newly-created tableau for a few moments before constable Hancock slowly said, 'Wait a moment, if his feet don't touch the log, how can he have been stood on it before he topped hisself?'

'Upon my soul,' said Dr Fitzsimmons.

'Well, bugger me,' said Sergeant Dobson.

'And there, gentlemen, you see what's been troubling me,' said Lady Hardcastle. 'I'm not an expert in these matters, but I'd say the odds were somewhat against this being suicide.'

'It does seem unlikely,' said Fitzsimmons, looking up at the body.

'But how the devil did they get him up there? He's not a featherweight, is he?'

'Cruiserweight at the very least,' said Dobson, appraisingly.

'They could have just hoisted him up,' said Hancock.

'I thought that,' said Lady Hardcastle, 'but take a look at the rope. See where it's wrapped around the branch there? If one had hoisted him up from the ground, how would one then manage to wrap the rope five times round the branch and tie it off so neatly? It was made to look like Mr Pickering had prepared the rope before standing on the log, and if he'd been hauled up, the rope would have to be tied off down here somehow, by someone standing on the ground.'

'But,' said Hancock, still trying to puzzle things out, 'why would he be out here in the woods in the middle of the night? And who would have wanted to kill him?'

'Luckily,' said Dobson, 'that's soon to be someone else's problem. We need to get him down, get him to the surgery, and then telephone the CID in Bristol. Murder makes it their case.'

'Just one more thing I noticed before we go,' said Lady Hardcastle. 'There are ruts in the ground running from the road to the tree, along the line you all walked to get here. Maybe two inches wide, about a yard apart. My guess, and I don't want to be seen to be interfering in any professional work here, is that they might be from some sort of hand cart. It would be an ideal way to get a body here.'

'If he were killed somewhere else, you mean?' said Hancock.

'As I say, gentlemen, none of this is within my area of expertise and I wouldn't want to step on any toes.'

''Course not, m'lady, and we appreciates your help,' said Dobson.

'You're most welcome, I'm sure. Gentlemen, it's been quite a morning for me, would you mind awfully if I excused myself? You know where to reach me if you need me.'

'Certainly, m'lady. You get yourself home and get a nice cup of hot, sweet tea for the shock. We'll take care of things from here.'

'Thank you, Sergeant. Come along, Armstrong, let's get home.' And with that, she strode off towards the edge of the clearing and I followed. Once we were on the road and safely out of earshot she said, 'Hot, sweet tea, indeed! We shall have a bracing brandy and the devil take the blessed tea.'

We set off for home.

* * *

The next few days passed peacefully enough, though busily. There was a lot to do to get Lady Hardcastle settled into her new home and I spent my days arranging things just so. Clothes needed to be unpacked, furniture polished, curtains hung, rugs beaten and placed. And that was on top of my regular daily duties.

I'd been working for her for nearly fourteen years now. Fourteen years. I was just seventeen years old when she and her husband had tempted me away from my parlour maid's job in London. They'd lured me with promises of travel and adventure. Promises upon which, as it turned out, they made good. There had been some terrible times during the adventures of those fourteen years but I wouldn't have swapped a moment of that time for anything in the world. Now, though, I confess that I was more than ready for some peace in the countryside.

It wasn't going to happen.

We had found Mr Pickering's body on Wednesday and had both been interviewed by the detective in charge of the case on Thursday afternoon. It was now the following Monday and we'd heard nothing more of the murder from official sources in the intervening days. That's not to say we'd not been asked to talk about it, mind you.

Sir Hector Farley-Stroud from the big house on the hill, The Grange, had invited Lady Hardcastle to dinner on Saturday evening, ostensibly to welcome her to the village. But she had been under no illusion about his true intention which had been to get a full account of the deadly goings-on, and she told me next day that she'd spent the evening being cross examined by Sir Hector, Lady Farley-Stroud, and their friends. Evidently they had been almost indecently excited by the idea of a real crime in their midst and had been determined to hear everything in the most scandalous detail possible.

I, meanwhile, had been closely questioned by every shopkeeper and tradesman we did business with. The butcher and baker had both kept me talking while I placed Lady Hardcastle's orders, and if there'd been a candlestick maker in the village I'm sure he'd have done the same. As it was I had to make do with being interrogated by Mrs Pantry who ran the grocer's shop. She did sell candles, though, so I decided that was good enough. It was a pity the conversation was so strongly biased towards violent crime, though; I was desperate to find out if Pantry was really her late husband's name or if she'd changed it for business reasons, but the moment to ask passed before I got the chance, and now I may never know.

But back to Monday. I'd finished helping my mistress dress and was just beginning to clear away the breakfast things when the doorbell rang. It was Constable Hancock.

'Good morning, Miss Armstrong,' he said, amiably. 'Is Lady Hardcastle at home?'

'She most certainly is, Constable,' I said. 'Won't you come in, and I'll tell her you're here.'

'Thank you, miss, Most kind.'

The drawing room opened off to the left of the entrance hall and I invited him to make himself comfortable in there while I went upstairs to find Lady Hardcastle. The house had been built recently by a friend of hers in preparation for his own family's return from India. Business matters had compelled him to stay in the Subcontinent at least another year and so when he discovered that she intended to move out of London he had offered to rent the new house to her. This meant that a widow and her maid were living in a house built for a family of six, but even so "finding Lady Hardcastle" didn't involve a lengthy search through a labyrinth of rooms and I found her exactly where I expected to: in her bedroom.

She turned from examining her clothes in the wardrobe. 'Hello, pet,' she said. 'I don't seem to own anything that isn't black. Do you think I ought to branch out a little, invest in something more fashionably colourful?

'Black suits you, my lady.'

'Thank you. I sometimes worry that people might think I've spent altogether far too long in mourning.'

'My understanding was that you wear black because you imagine you look magnificent in it. Which, if I'm to be properly truthful, you actually do. And you always wear red corsets. They're frightfully jolly.'

She laughed. 'Well, yes, but I can't really offer either of those as mitigation to the oh-so-solicitous ladies about town who insist I should brighten myself up lest I never find a man.'

'No, my lady, I don't suppose you can.'

'Ah well,' she sighed, closing the wardrobe. 'I shall worry about that another day. Who's that at the door?'

'Constable Hancock, my lady. He'd like to see you.'

'Oh, how exciting. Do you think there's news?'

'I'm not sure, my lady,' I said. 'To be honest, he looks as though there's something troubling him.'

'Then we mustn't keep him waiting an instant longer. Lay on, McArmstrong, let us meet the steadfast watchman and see what's bothering him.'

I led the way downstairs where we found Hancock standing in the drawing room, inspecting the bookcase.

'My dear Constable,' said Lady Hardcastle over my shoulder as I opened the drawing room door for her, 'what a delight to see you. Has Armstrong offered you tea?'

'Good morning, m'lady. No, I didn't give her the chance, but I must say tea would be most welcome.'

'See to it, dear, would you?'

I bobbed the little curtsey I used whenever we were in company and bustled off into the kitchen. I left the doors open, the better to hear their conversation as I boiled the kettle on the stove and prepared the tea tray.

'Well then, Constable, to what do I owe the pleasure of this unexpected visit?'

'It's something of a delicate matter, m'lady,' said Hancock, somewhat hesitantly. 'I don't really know how to broach it, to be truthful.'

'Just be bold, dear boy. Out with it and hang my sensibilities. I've seen more than you'd credit in my long life; little shocks me.'

'Oh, it's not that it's delicate in that way, m'lady. It's more of a matter of it p'raps not being quite appropriate to be talking to someone outside the Force about it.'

'Something to do with the murder of Mr Pickering?'

'Exactly so, m'lady. See, the thing is, I don't know you or nothing, and I wouldn't dream to presume, but you seemed like a lady who knew what was what and I don't know who else to talk to.'

'Something is wrong?'

'I think there very well might be, m'lady. It's the detective from Bristol. Inspector Sunderland. You met him, I believe.'

'I did. He seemed intelligent enough, but not very... interested. No, that's not quite fair. But he gave the impression of having more important things to be getting on with.'

'He gave me that feeling too, m'lady. He started interviewing people on Thursday after he'd spoken to you and Miss Armstrong.' He paused for a short while as though still unsure whether to proceed, but then a look of resolution suddenly came over him and his thoughts tumbled out as though tipped from a bucket. 'He went straight to the Dog and Duck and talked to old Joe Arnold there. It seems Frank Pickering had been in the pub on Tuesday night and got in a fearful row with Bill Lovell, one of the lads from the village, about a girl they was both sweet on. Seems Frank had been sitting there with some of his cricketing mates and this lad had come over and started a terrible to do. He said he was engaged to Daisy Spratt and how dare Frank be taking her out for a walk. And Frank said he could walk out with whoever he liked and Lovell could go hang. And Lovell had said he'd be the one who got hanged if he had anything to do with it and stormed out.'

'Sorry, Constable, let me just check. Lovell was engaged to Daisy. Pickering walked out with Daisy. Lovell found out and threatened violence?'

'That's how it seemed, m'lady, but I knows them both and I knows it was just young lads squaring up to each other. You knows what it's like. They might let fly with feet, fists and elbows if they had a chance for a good set to on the green, but there'd be no murdering. But that's not how Inspector Sunderland sees it. He's arrested Bill Lovell for murder and he's holding him in a cell down in Bristol.'

'Gracious me. Did he speak to anyone else?'

'No, m'lady, that's just it. Clear case of jealous murder, he says, and lays him by the heels.'

'And you're not convinced?'

'No, m'lady, not by a long chalk. See, old Joe Arnold called me back in. He was right agitated. He says the Inspector didn't give him a chance to tell him everything. He says there was another row that night. A row between Frank Pickering and Arthur Tressle, captain of the cricket team.'

'What about?'

'Something and nothing as far as I can make out. But he didn't reckon Lovell had it in him to murder no one neither, and he says it could just as easy be Arthur as Bill.'

By this time, the tea was ready and I brought the tray through. I set it on the low table and stood to one side, not wanting to miss anything.

'It all seems a bit perfunctory on Inspector Sunderland's part, I must say,' said Lady Hardcastle at length. 'Is there anything I can do? Would you like me to speak to your sergeant? He seemed like a reasonable man.'

'No, m'lady. I spoke to him myself but he says there's nothing we can do. But would you mind sort of helping me get to the bottom of it all. Even round here where they've known me for years people puts up the shutters when they sees the uniform. That's why the detectives get so much out of them, I reckons, but the detective in this case doesn't seem like he cares overmuch.'

'I say,' said Lady Hardcastle. 'Detective work. How exciting. Isn't it exciting, Armstrong? You can be Watson to my Holmes.'

'But without the violin and the dangerous drug addiction, my lady,' I said.

'As soon as the piano arrives from London that will make an admirable substitute for the violin. And I'm sure we could both have a tot of brandy from time to time to grease the old wheels, what?'

Hancock seemed slightly nonplussed by Lady Hardcastle's sudden flight of whimsy.

'What do you know about the victim, Constable. Who was Mr Pickering? What did he do? Who were his friends? Where did he work?'

'I can't say I knows much about his private life, m'lady, 'cept to say he was a fine and well-liked fellow. Calm and quiet for the most part, jovial company and a demon on the cricket pitch. Finest pace bowler the village has ever known, by all accounts.'

Lady Hardcastle and I exchanged confused glances.

'Sorry, m'lady, I forgets not everyone enjoys their cricket. He could bowl the ball very fast. Very useful for taking wickets.'

'Thank you, constable. Roddy – Sir Roderick, my late husband – used to talk about cricket all the time and I tried so hard to be interested, but the game lacked excitement for me, I'm afraid and I never really picked up the argot.' She paused in wistful contemplation as she often did when something reminded her of her husband. And then, just as suddenly, she came back to herself. 'I'm so sorry, do carry on.'

'Yes, m'lady. I made some enquiries, spoke to a few people and it seems there weren't nothing remarkable about him apart from that. He grew up at Woodworthy, about three miles east of here, and when he left school he got hisself a job with a shipping agents at Bristol: Seddon, Seddon and Seddon. He moved on down to the city and found hisself cheap diggings nearby the office. He worked hard. Damn good at his job, they say, and he done very well for hisself. But he was homesick, see, so when he got his latest promotion last year to Chief Clerk, he come back out to Woodworthy to be with his friends and family, like. Like I said t'other day he rode his bicycle into Chipping Bevington every morning and caught the train into the city.'

'He sounds like an admirable fellow,' said Lady Hardcastle at length. 'I think the least we can do for the poor chap is to find out the truth of his murder.'

'Would you be willing to help, then, m'lady?' he said. 'I mean, I don't like to impose and it's all highly irregular, but apart from Dr Fitzsimmons you're the cleverest person I knows. They say you went to university. And I can't see a lad from the village hanged for shouting the odds in a pub just because a city detective thinks as how he's got more important things to do.'

'It sounds like exactly the sort of fun I've been missing, Constable,' she said. 'But we need to be discreet. If I start asking the locals all manner of questions I'll draw unwanted attention and possibly even get you into trouble. Would you allow Armstrong to help, too? She can be my eyes and ears around the village. No one notices a lady's maid, they're invisible.'

'It all sounds grand, m'lady. If you don't mind, miss?'

'No, Constable, I don't mind at all,' I said. 'I'd be delighted to help.'

We chatted inconsequentially while the constable finished his tea and he left looking much more at ease than he had been when he arrived.

'Gracious me, Flo,' said Lady Hardcastle once Constable Hancock had gone, 'we seem to have become embroiled once more. What a pair we are.'

She would never have dreamed of calling me anything but "Armstrong" in company, but alone in the house she tended to call me by my first name. Somehow, though, I could never quite bring myself to call her anything but "my lady". I think I only ever called her Emily once, in China, when we were sure we were about to die.

'We do seem to be something of a pair, my lady,' I said. 'At the very least, you're a one. I distinctly remember being promised a quiet life in the country, and yet here I am about to equip myself with thumbscrews and cosh and slink into the murky village underworld on your behalf.'

'"Murky village underworld" indeed! You do have an overdeveloped sense of the melodramatic, Flo. And when have you ever needed a cosh to protect yourself?'

'It's just for show, my lady, just for show. But are you serious? Shall we really investigate this murder? I really thought we'd left all the skulduggery and intrigue behind us. And, be honest, what do we really know of detective work? It's not as though we have any experience. We were always involved in more... direct action.'

'It's true, it's true, but I really think we need to get involved and try to do something to help. Neither of us would be happy to see a lad hanged for something he didn't do.'

'Surely it would never come to that,' I said. 'Surely the truth will come out during the trial, at least. And if we mess things up, we might make it worse for him. Or for constable Hancock. We don't really want our first act in Gloucestershire to be to upset the Bristol Police Force.'

'Oh, we shall be most circumspect, pet, don't worry. I'm sure that Inspector Sunderland will come to the truth in the end, but just in case, let's have a dig around and see what we can come up with. What can it hurt? And poor Constable Hancock is so sweet, how can we refuse him?'

'Hmmm. Very well. Let's imagine, then, that we really are detectives and that we have even the first idea how to conduct a murder investigation. Where shall we start?'

'We need to be methodical. We must start at the beginning, we must start with our victim. We need to find out all that we can about him—'

She was interrupted by the ringing of the doorbell.

'Excuse me, my lady,' I said, and went to answer it.

It was the boy from the local Post Office with a telegram.

'Telegram for her ladyship,' he mumbled quickly, holding it out for me to take.

'My lady doesn't sail,' I said.

He looked blankly at me.

'She doesn't have a "ship",' I tried to explain. 'She's a knight's widow so she's "Lady Hardcastle" or "my lady".'

'Eh?' he said, bewildered.

'Never mind,' I said. 'Thank you for bringing it.' I made to close the door.

He stopped me. 'I'm to wait for a reply,' he said.

'Very well. Wait here and I'll see if there is one,' I said and took the telegram through to Lady Hardcastle who was sitting at the dining table, sketching.

'What is it, Flo?' she asked. 'News?'

'Telegram for you, my lady,' I said, handing it over.

She opened it and read it. 'Aha,' she said excitedly, 'and here is our chance to take that first step. You remember my dinner with Sir Hector on Saturday? Two members of the local social set were unable to attend, but it seems they're as keen to be in on the gossip as everyone else. They've invited me to lunch with them at their home in Chipping Bevington tomorrow. Their names... are James and Ida Seddon.'

'Of Seddon, Seddon and Seddon, the shipping agents?'

'I rather expect so, yes. Our Mr Pickering's employer.'

'Which Seddon is he, do you think?' I asked.

'The second one, I should imagine.'

'How can one tell, I wonder?'

'I believe they have it stamped on the bottom. But anyway,' she said. 'Tomorrow I am to pay a call on the Seddons where I might learn more about our victim, and you shall accompany me.'

'I shall?'

'Of course you shall. I need to win them over and impress them if I'm going to get anything useful from them, and nothing impresses the commercial classes more than a title and turning up to lunch with a personal servant in attendance. It'll give you a chance to snoop around and talk to his own staff, too.' She scrawled a reply on the form and gave it to me with some change for the boy.

He was kicking stones on the path and looked up guiltily when I opened the door. I handed him the reply and the money.

'The ha'penny's for you' I said. 'Don't spend it all at once.'

He grinned and scampered off towards the village. 'Tell her ladyship I says thanks,' he called over his shoulder as he disappeared from view.

I could put off the laundry no longer and so Tuesday morning was spent soaking, washing, wringing, mangling and hanging. It was perfect drying weather – sunny and with a good breeze – and the work went well, even pleasantly. By eleven o'clock everything was done, there was tea in the pot and I still had an hour to make myself presentable for Lady Hardcastle's lunch at the Seddons'.

Lady Hardcastle appeared at the kitchen door. 'There is a trichological crisis of disastrous proportions,' she said.

'I beg your pardon, my lady?'

'My hair, Flo, my hair. Look at it.'

I looked at the wispy mess of long dark hair, inexpertly piled on top of her head. 'It does look a little... untidy,' I suggested.

'It looks as if squirrels are nesting in it. Squirrels, Flo!'

'If you'll forgive me for pointing it out, my lady, it's your own fault for being so impatient. I did say I'd help as soon as the laundry was done.'

'Hang the laundry. Can't we get someone to do that for us? There must be a laundry nearby.'

'We're not in London any more. But I've finished now and we have plenty of time to make you beautiful for your appointment.'

'I'll settle for "presentable", but thank you. But where are my new stockings? And have you seen my small handbag? And are my patterned boots clean? And–'

'I'll take care of it all, my lady. Sit down, drink this tea, and I'll be with you as soon as I've changed into something less... domestic.'

She sat at the kitchen table, heaved a great, frustrated sigh, and drank her tea.

By five minutes to twelve we were both dressed for lunch and ready to go. That's to say, Lady Hardcastle was dressed for lunch and I was dressed in my smart "going out" uniform – I'd get lunch with the servants if I was lucky. I was helping her with her hatpins.

'It strikes me, Flo, that this fashion for huge hats might have its advantages. What do you think of hiding a Derringer in there?'

'A pistol, my lady? In your hat?'

'Quite so.'

'Wouldn't that open you to the danger of shooting yourself accidentally in the head?'

'I had a sort of holster in mind,' she said, 'concealing the gun inside, perhaps covered by a flap.'

'I see. And wouldn't that open me to the danger of you shooting me accidentally in the head as I walked beside you?'

'You could walk a pace or two behind like a proper servant and then you'd be well clear.'

'I could indeed. Do you think you need a Derringer?'

'A lady should always be prepared for any eventuality.'

'Like the Boy Scouts, my lady?'

'Similar, but with skirts on.'

'I don't think the Boy Scouts are allowed to wear skirts, my lady. Perhaps some female equivalent of the organization should be formed.'

'Most definitely it should,' she said. 'As long as they would always be prepared.'

'One would certainly hope they would. I doubt they would allow them to carry small calibre pistols, though.'

'It would seem rather reckless,' she said, thoughtfully.

The doorbell rang.

'A timely interruption, my lady. I believe you're ready, and I'll wager that's the car.'

I answered the door and there on the step was a handsome young man in a chauffeur's uniform of fine grey wool. Behind him, on the road, was a similarly grey, similarly handsome Rolls-Royce Silver Ghost.

'I'm Daniel, miss,' said the chauffeur, 'come to take Lady Hardcastle to Mr Seddon's house.'

'Thank you, Daniel,' I said. 'I'm Armstrong and my mistress will be with you presently.'

'Shall I wait in the car, Miss Armstrong?'

'Thank you, that will be fine. She'll be a minute or two longer, no more.'

'Yes, miss.' And with that he turned smartly and returned to the beautiful car.

I made to return to the kitchen but Lady Hardcastle was already on her way into the hall. 'Ready, my lady?' I said as she inspected herself in the mirror.

'I believe I am, pet, yes. Let's go snooping.'

I locked the front door while Daniel helped Lady Hardcastle into the car and then clambered in beside her while Daniel settled into the driving seat.

It was a perfect driving day as well as a perfect drying day and the half-hour journey was exhilarating and all too short. The Seddons lived in a grand Georgian house on the main road into Chipping Bevington and as the Rolls scrunched onto the broad gravel drive, Mr Seddon himself appeared at the door to greet his guest.

'My dear Lady Hardcastle,' he gushed as Daniel helped her from the car. 'How wonderful of you to come.'

'Good afternoon, Mr Seddon. It was charming of you to invite me.'

Daniel was sweet enough also to help me while this pantomime continued and I was out of the car in time to see Mrs Seddon greeting Lady Hardcastle with equal effusion. Daniel winked at me.

'Leave the car there, Daniel,' said Mrs Seddon, brusquely, 'and take Lady Hardcastle's maid...'

'Miss Armstrong, madam,' said Daniel, quickly.

'Quite. Take Armstrong to the kitchen. Cook has some lunch for her, I believe. Does that suit, Lady Hardcastle?'

'That will be fine, Mrs Seddon,' she said. 'Enjoy your lunch, Armstrong. I'll ring through to the kitchen if I need you.'

'Yes, my lady,' I said with a slight curtsey and followed Daniel round to the rear of the house where I was warmly invited into the kitchen by the cook, Mrs Birch.

I was led to a large, oak table which had been set for a lavish lunch. I was treated as the guest of honour and was seated at one end of the table, in a wonderfully comfortable chair.

In private Lady Hardcastle and I usually ate well and had shared some splendid meals, but when she was staying away from home and I was dining with the household servants, the best I could usually hope for was "hearty and satisfying". "Meagre and grudgingly served" was more common, but this lunch was utterly magnificent. Pies, cold meats, poached salmon, scotch eggs, fresh salads, fresh breads... all prepared with exquisite skill. It was like the most wonderful picnic. There was even a bottle of champagne.

The kitchen was spacious and well equipped and the atmosphere friendly to the point of rowdiness. To my immense surprise I was welcomed as a fellow professional by the staff and was taken immediately into their confidence as one after the other the cook, valet, lady's maid, housemaid, kitchen maid and chauffeur each shared with me their joy at meeting the servant of a "real lady" and their dismay at the their own arriviste employers.

'Blimmin Lady Muck and her airs and graces,' said Mrs Birch through a mouthful of pie. 'She was a shop girl when she met him. A blimmin shop girl. And now she swans round here like the Duchess of Blimmin Lah-di-Dah, treatin' us like the dirt on her shoe. That's not proper class. She don't know how to behave.'

The others nodded their agreement. And one by one added their own descriptions of their employers' shortcomings. I wasn't completely sure that any of this was appropriately professional, but I also got the feeling that I was providing an important service as a sort of safety valve. I'm not at all sure I would ever have complained about my employer to anyone, much less a complete stranger, but as they told their tales of extravagance, rudeness and generally gauche behaviour, I realized that they felt besieged and just needed to tell someone that might understand. I let them talk and carried on eating.

Mrs Birch had noticed my surprise at the extravagance of the meal. 'We might as well treat ourselves, my dear. She don't know what goes on, nor care overmuch, I'm sure. She don't deign to come into the kitchen and talk to the likes of me; I gets summoned to her study to discuss menus, then sent off to crawl back to my proper place. She pays the bills without looking at them. I overheard her talking to one of her friends once. "If one has to worry about the bills," she says, "one can't afford them anyway." So if that's the way she sees it, I makes sure to slip a little treat in for us now and again. Nothing too much, mind – I i'n't no thief – but a nice treat once a month is only what we deserves after putting up with her.'

As our eating slowed in pace and the savoury course drew to a natural close, the bell from the dining room rang and the housemaid slipped out, carrying a tray of cakes and pastries.

They asked me about Lady Hardcastle, where we'd come from, how we were settling in, and what we were up to now. I answered truthfully as much as I could, but not fully. I did let them know we were trying to find out about the murder of Frank Pickering, though.

'Ah, yes,' said Langdon, Mr Seddon's valet. 'Poor Mr Pickering. He worked for Seddons, you know. A fine young man. More of a gentleman in manner than his employer if you ask me.'

'You met him?' I asked.

'Yes, once or twice. I usually accompany Mr Seddon on business trips and Mr Pickering was sometimes there or thereabouts. He came to the house once.'

'To the house? Isn't that a little unusual.'

'It was, rather. It was quite recently, too.'

'Have you any idea why?'

'None at all, I'm afraid. Sadly this is quite a robustly built house and opportunities for eavesdropping aren't quite what they were in some of the houses I've worked in. Thick walls and doors, you see. But he didn't seem in the best of spirits when he arrived and he saw himself out, slamming the door as he went, so I can't presume it was a joyful meeting.'

I was about to try to press him for more details when the bell rang from the dining room again.

'I expect that'll be for me,' he said, getting up. 'Please leave me a piece of trifle if you can spare it. I'm rather partial to trifle.'

He went off towards the dining room and our conversation lightened once more, turning to stories about the antics of the younger servants. We were still laughing at a story told – with actions and comic voices – by Doris the kitchen maid, when Langdon returned. He came over to my chair and spoke discreetly in my ear. 'It was for you, actually, my dear. Lady Hardcastle asks if you'd take her her pills.'

'Of course. Thank you,' I said, rising from my chair. 'Please excuse me, everyone. Duty calls.'

I found my bag and rummaged inside. Lady Hardcastle didn't take "pills" but she clearly wanted me in the dining room for some reason. I carried a box of aspirin which would suffice and I took out two of the little pills and went towards the door I'd seen Langdon use.

'Straight up the passage, turn right and it's the second door on the left,' said Mrs Birch. 'Follow the sound of self-important bragging and you won't go far wrong.'

The others laughed and I made my way out.

* * *

The panelled passageway was hung with watercolours of ships, and the harbour at Bristol, interspersed with polished brass nameplates. There was a binnacle beside the dining room door, complete with compass, with a brass ship's bell mounted on a shelf above it. If I'd been asked to identify the theme of the décor I should definitely have plumped for "nautical".

The door was ajar and I slipped quietly inside and looked around. The room was large, high-ceilinged and decorated in fashionably pale shades of blue. Around the wall were more items of nautical memorabilia: polished portholes; another bell, this one slightly dented; framed bills of lading; an intriguingly asymmetrical display of blocks and lines from a ship's rigging; more paintings of ships; and there, in pride of place above the fireplace, a large portrait in oils of Mrs Seddon in regal pose.

The dining table was large enough to seat ten but there were only five for lunch. Mr Seddon sat at the head of the table with his wife to his right. Lady Hardcastle sat opposite her, with a portly, red-faced gentleman I didn't recognize to her left and a similarly plump lady that I presumed was his own wife opposite him. Mary, the housemaid, was pouring tea. Their lunch, the remains of which were piled on the sideboard, appeared to have been a more modest version of the one I had just enjoyed. I smiled.

'Ah, Armstrong,' said Lady Hardcastle beckoning me over. 'Thank you so much.'

I gave her the aspirins and she swallowed them down. She thanked me again and waved me away but instead of leaving, I made full use of the mystical powers of invisibility possessed by all household servants and slipped unnoticed to the corner of the room.

'You poor thing,' said Mrs Seddon. 'Are they for nerves? It must be the shock of talking about that terrible business.'

Mrs Seddon was in her early 30s, I judged, slim of figure and blonde of hair. Pretty, I thought, but not truly beautiful, while her clothes were on the gaudy side of elegant, but undoubtedly expensive.

She spoke again. 'We were simply horrified to hear of his death,' she said. 'How much more awful it must have been to actually find his... body. Was it suicide do they think?'

Her accent was hard to pin down. She seemed to be trying hard to sound like a lady, but traces of her Bristol accent poked through the veneer, making her sound like a music hall artist playing a lady for a satirical skit.

'That's certainly how it was intended to appear,' said Lady Hardcastle, 'but the police weren't convinced. They've arrested a local man for the murder.'

'Murder? Did you know about this, James?' she asked her husband sharply before turning back to Lady Hardcastle. 'He used to work for James, you know,' she explained.

'I... er... yes, my dear. I think I heard something about it,' he stammered, nervously.

'You never said anything.' Her tone was distinctly icy by now.

'I... I... didn't want to vex you unduly, my sweet. Nasty business. Nasty.'

Mr Seddon might have been the senior partner of a successful shipping agency, but it was becoming clear who was the senior partner in the Seddon household.

'Don't want to speak ill of a chap when he's lying on the slab at the mortuary and all that,' said the red-faced man, slightly drunkenly, 'but it's dashed inconvenient his dying like that. Left us in the lurch, what?'

'Oh, Percy, don't,' said the unknown lady. 'You speak as though he got himself murdered on purpose.'

'Unless he was the victim of a lunatic, m'dear,' he said, 'he must have upset someone. Could say he brought it on himself, what?'

'No, one couldn't,' she replied, sternly. 'And I think you've had altogether quite enough to drink.'

There was an embarrassed silence during which everyone but the red-faced man sipped at their tea; he mutinously carried on with his wine. The silence dragged on for almost a minute before Mrs Seddon said, 'Oh, my dear Lady Hardcastle, you do look quite ill. Are you sure you're all right? Should I call a doctor?'

Lady Hardcastle looked absolutely fine to me, but it was an elegant way of giving her a reason to excuse herself early. She took it. 'Thank you, Mrs Seddon, I'm sure I'll be fine. But might I impose upon your generosity a little further and ask your chauffeur to drive me home?'

'Of course you may, of course,' said Mrs Seddon with barely concealed relief. 'Mary, please go back to the kitchen and tell Daniel to ready the Rolls. You can clear this up later.'

'Yes, ma'am,' said Mary and made for the door.

As unobtrusively as I could, I followed her out and we walked to the kitchen together. As soon as I thought we were safely out of earshot, I said, 'That all got a bit frosty.'

'It had been heading that way for some time, miss, that's why your mistress sent for you, I reckon; wanted to get out of there. The missus don't like being shown up, see, and what with the other Mr Seddon being a little tipsy and him and our Mr Seddon joking about, then all that talk of Mr Pickering, our Mrs S was just about ready to knock some heads together. There's going to be skin and hair flying when the guests have all gone, I'd put money on it.'

By now we were back in the kitchen and Mary indicated to James that he was required.

'Do they fight often?' I asked as I put on my hat and gloves.

Mrs Birch laughed. 'Now "fight", dear, that's a tricky word. See, for a fight you needs two, and their fights is a bit one-sided. She screams and shouts and throws things and he stands there meekly and takes it.'

'Crikey,' I said. 'Well, I hope we've not made your lives any worse by our coming. Thank you so very much for your hospitality, that was quite the most enjoyable lunch I've ever had.'

'It was our pleasure, miss,' said Langdon. 'And I hope we have the pleasure of your company again soon.'

Everyone gathered round to shake my hand and I followed Daniel out of the back door and round to the car. I sat inside while he started the engine then he rang the front doorbell to let them know that the car was ready.

Mr Seddon showed Lady Hardcastle to the door and shook her hand as they said their goodbyes before Daniel assisted her into the car.

'That, my dear Armstrong, was quite a luncheon,' she said as we drove off.

'Mine was rather splendid, too,' I said with a smile.

'You'll have to tell me all about it when we get home. But for now, Daniel, please tell me all about your magnificent motor car. I really must get one of these for myself.'

Daniel puffed with pride as he described the car and all its many features and we were home before we knew it.

* * *

'Well, pet,' said Lady Hardcastle as we took off our hats and gloves in the the hall, 'That was... bracing.'

'An unusual experience, to be sure,' I said.

'Disappointing not to get anything helpful about Mr Pickering. And lunch was lacklustre.'

'That's a shame, my lady,' I said with a smirk. 'Still, it does mean we're home somewhat earlier than planned. Perhaps I should use the opportunity to try to talk to some people in the village? Fetch out those thumbscrews?'

'A splendid notion. From what Constable Hancock said yesterday, I think your first task will be to get to the Dog and Duck and speak to... what was his name... "old Joe Arnold" and see what he's got to say for himself. But first I want a cup of tea; there'll be time for thumbscrews later. And you must tell me everything you found out from the Seddons' servants.'

I told her about the delicious lunch, and Mrs Birch's reason for it.

'You got champagne, you lucky thing? I didn't get any flipping champagne. I had to make do with an indifferent white burgundy.'

I went on to describe the servants' general contempt for their employers and Mrs Seddon's stern ruling of the Seddon roost.

'I definitely got the impression that he's slightly in awe of her,' said Lady Hardcastle. 'She has a taste for the more expensive things in life, too, I noticed, white burgundies notwithstanding.'

'Not perhaps the most elegant or refined things, though,' I added.

'Oh, Flo, you snob,' she laughed. 'But yes, you're right. Opulence without elegance seems to be her motto. I'm glad to know the "shop girl" history, though. Her accent is atrocious.'

'Who's the snob now, my lady?' I said.

'Touché.'

'What happened before I arrived?'

'Nothing of note. They twittered on about people they knew, dropping names and titles at such a pace that even I couldn't keep up, and then as soon as I mentioned Pickering's death, the whole mood of the table changed. Mrs Seddon feigned an air of delicately swooning propriety, but it was more like she was trying to avert a scandal.'

'She does seem the type that wouldn't want that sort of attention. Not quite the elegant sophistication she aspires to.'

'Not at all,' she said. 'To be fair, I don't think any of them wanted the firm to be dragged into a murder investigation. Understandable, I suppose. Reputation is everything in the business world.'

We drank our tea together in the kitchen and it was with some reluctance that we left the table, with me still feeling far too full from lunch. But we hauled ourselves up, put hats and gloves back on and walked the half mile into the village together. I left Lady Hardcastle to call upon Constable Hancock to find out if there were any new developments while I made my way round the green to the village inn.

To judge from the architecture, the Dog and Duck had been serving food, ciders, ales, wines and spiritous liquor to the people of Chipping Bevington for at least a hundred years, possibly longer. It was a small country inn with a yard to one side filled with barrels and crates awaiting the drayman's next visit. There was also a stout handcart, tipped up and propped against the wall of the building.

I went into the snug and coughed delicately to attract the attention of the landlord. Old Joe Arnold was, indeed, rather old, but he was spryly alert and fairly skipped across the bar to greet me.

'I was wondering when we might see you in here, my love,' he said, toothlessly.

'Good afternoon, Mr Arnold, it's a pleasure to meet you.'

'And you, m'dear. What can I get you? A nice glass of sherry? A small cider? On the house, of course. It's not often we get new folk in the village and you and your mistress are the talk of the town.'

'You're very kind, Mr Arnold, very kind. What a charming inn. Have you been here long?'

'Family business, my love. My old dad ran it afore me and his dad ran it afore him, back four generations.'

'You must see all the village life in here. Everyone must come in sooner or later.'

'We're the heart of the village, miss. The very beating heart of it. I'n't that right Daisy?'

Daisy, the young barmaid, was wiping the public bar with a dirty rag. 'The beating heart, Joe,' Daisy agreed, with only the tiniest trace of weary sarcasm.

I recognized the name. 'Daisy Spratt?' I asked.

'That's right,' she said suspiciously. 'How'd you know?'

'You're engaged to Bill Lovell.'

'What if I am?'

'It's just that I'd heard both your names recently. What with the... er... the goings on.'

'I bet they're all talking about us now. Well, he didn't do nothing and neither did I and don't you go thinking we did. He didn't do for Frank. Not my Bill.'

I hadn't fully thought through how I was going to go about questioning Mr Arnold but both bars were empty so it seemed as good a time as any for my interview. I still wasn't sure quite how to broach the subject, but with Daisy there too, I thought I might have an opening. I didn't want to create false hope but I wondered if I might start with a little bit of openness to see if I got any in return.

'Would you both mind talking about that night a little?' I asked. 'Lady Hardcastle and I don't think Mr Lovell guilty, either, but Inspector Sunderland is going to need a little more to convince him than the opinion of a newcomer and her lady's maid.'

They looked briefly at each other before Mr Arnold said, 'I never seen a copper in such a hurry to get gone. We usually has to chase old Sergeant Dobson out with the brush and bolt the door behind him to get him to stop talking once he gets going, but this feller from Bristol was in and out afore I could tell him anything. He heard what he wanted to hear and was off to collar young Bill afore you could say ninepence.'

Mr Arnold's toothlessness made it very difficult for him to convincingly say "ninepence" at all, but I suppressed my smirk. He led me over to a table in the corner of the bar and beckoned to Daisy to join us.

As we sat, he continued talking. 'See, I told him about the argy-bargy 'tween Frank and Bill, but that weren't the only row Frank got into that night.'

Daisy interrupted. 'No, it weren't. Arthur Tressle near started actual fisticuffs right there in the Public,' she said, indicating the other bar.

'What about?' I asked. 'Was Mr Pickering walking out with his fiancée, too?'

Daisy glared at me. 'No one,' she said, indignantly, 'was walking out with anyone, most 'specially not me, and I'll thank you to keep your insinuations about my character to yourself. Frank was sweet on me, that was all, and I walked out with him once – in public, mind – to set him straight about me and Bill.'

'My apologies,' I said, 'I didn't mean any offence. But your Mr Lovell got to hear about it?'

'Well, yes. He's protective is all. He just wanted to set Frank straight. He wasn't even going to hurt him, much less kill him. He just has this way of talking. He can be a bit...'

'Fiery?' I suggested. 'Hot tempered?'

'I s'pose you could put it like that. But he didn't do for Frank. He wouldn't. He wouldn't.' She was close to tears.

Mr Arnold looked slightly embarrassed and carried on quickly, trying to defuse the situation. 'Arthur, see, he's the captain of the cricket club. They was all in here that night for a meeting and Arthur, well he's a prickly sort, and he's got it in his head that young Frank was trying to take over. He was only a fair batsman, was Frank, but he had a fast ball as could take a man's arm off. He was keeping that team going, I reckon, and Arthur had taken a notion that he was angling for the captain's cap.'

'And was he?' I asked.

'Couldn't say, my love. All I can tell you is that they squared off in the public bar and I had to get a couple of my regulars to separate them.'

'They threatened each other?'

'No, young Frank was one of they gentle giant types. Calm as you like normally. He could stand his ground, mind, but he wasn't the sort to go shouting the odds. No, it was Arthur. Seething, he was, fair ready to boil over. Said he'd never let Frank do it. Said he'd do for him if he tried it.'

'All that over a cricket team?' I asked, incredulously.

'We takes our cricket very serious round here, my love, very serious.'

'Then what happened?'

'I was trying to calm Arthur down and Daisy saw to Frank.'

'There weren't much for me to see to, to be honest,' said Daisy. 'I went over to him and asked him if he was all right. He said he was, then he gets out his watch, takes a look at it and says, "Yes, well I'd probably best be going anyway," and walked out.'

'And what time was it?' I asked.

'Just 'fore eleven, I think,' she said.

'And that was the last you saw of him?'

'Last time I ever spoke to him,' she said with a sniff.

'And what about Arthur? Did he stay?'

'He sat back down with his mates and they finished their drinks,' said Joe. 'They didn't stay long, mind, maybe another quarter of an hour. They was the last in here so I shut up after that, sent Daisy home and went to bed.'

'Did you see anything on your way home, Daisy?' I asked.

'I saw the cricket lads on the green, still larking about.'

'But nothing else?'

'No,' she said. 'I walked straight home. I lives with my ma and dad round the corner. Our dad's the butcher.'

'Yes, I've met him. You live above the shop?'

She looked affronted. 'We most certainly do not. We've got a house up near the church.'

'Ah, I beg your pardon,' I said. 'What about you, Mr Arnold? Did anything else happen here?'

'I should say it did, my love, but I can't see as how it's connected. Must have been getting on for half past when I hears this commotion outside in the yard. Banging and crashing and laughing. Our bedroom's round the back and I looks out the window but I couldn't see nothing, so I puts on me boots and a coat and goes down in me nightshirt to see what's what. They'd had me bloomin' handcart away, 'a'n't they.'

'Who had?'

'Cricket lads, I reckon.'

'But it's back there now. I noticed it when I arrived.'

'That it is, my love, that it is. We found it next morning over by the cricket pavilion, and Arthur Tressle asleep inside on the dressing room floor.'

'Sleeping it off?' I said.

'Or hiding out, racked with guilt,' said Daisy, venomously.

'You think he murdered Frank Pickering?' I asked.

'Well, it certainly weren't my Bill. There's no way he could do an awful thing like that. No way on earth. And that Arthur Tressle's a nasty piece of work, you mark me. Nasty and spiteful. I wouldn't put it past him at all.'

We chatted for a few moments longer with both of them vehemently proclaiming Bill Lovell's innocence but not really saying anything new. After listening for a polite length of time, I thanked them for their help and said my goodbyes.

Mr Arnold showed me to the door and I walked off towards the main road and home. I'd gone a few yards before I had a sudden thought and went back to the yard to take a look at the handcart. It was old and weathered, but sturdy enough, with large, iron-bound wheels about two inches wide and set about a yard apart. It was about six feet long, easily big enough to accommodate a dead body, but it showed no obvious signs of having carried one recently. To be truthful, I wasn't sure what form such signs might take – a fragment of torn cloth, perhaps, or a smear of earth from the victim's shoe – but I thought it only right and proper that I take a look and report my findings, or the lack thereof, to my mistress.

I set off once more for home.

Lady Hardcastle had been home for just a few minutes by the time I arrived and was in the hall, taking off her hat when I opened the front door.

'Ah, splendid, it's you,' she said.

'It is I indeed, my lady,' I said, closing and bolting the door.

'I do wish you'd relax a little,' she said. 'I'm quite sure there's no need for bolts and bars out here.'

'One can never be too careful, my lady,' I said, unmoved. 'When I'm certain there's no danger, then I'll leave all the doors and windows open as much as you like. Until then, the simple act of sliding a bolt will make me feel much safer and will cause inconvenience only to those who would be ill mannered enough to attempt to open the door and enter without invitation.'

'Very well, have it your way. But come. Make tea. Tell all.'

Removing my own hat and gloves I went through to the kitchen and began to make a pot of tea. As I worked I recounted my conversation with Mr Arnold and Daisy Spratt as closely as I could.

'You're terribly businesslike,' said Lady Hardcastle when I had finished. 'No small talk? No gossip? No servants' chatter to tease out the sordid secrets of the village? I thought you'd have been hours yet.'

'No, my lady. I'm not completely sure they trust me yet. But I thought I was under instructions to collect facts, anyway.'

'Facts, dear, yes. But what about your impressions? Who are these people? What do they think? What are they like? Can we rely on their testimony? Are they hiding anything?'

'Well, then. From her manner, I suggest that Daisy is a flirty little tease who had been stringing Frank Pickering along and is devastated to have been caught out. I don't trust her farther than I can spit your piano – is there any word on when that's being delivered, by the way? – but beyond desperately trying to cover her tracks and make out what a pure and virginal girl she is, I don't think she's hiding anything important. Her belief in Bill Lovell is genuine.'

'Gracious. Remind me never to ask you for a character reference.'

'"Emily, Lady Hardcastle, is a bossy, overbearing, yet flippant woman with a fine mind, a remarkable education, a breathtaking talent for music and drawing, and absolutely no common sense, nor any sense of self preservation, whatsoever. Without me to look after her she would have long since starved to death, been strangled by her own corsets (the fitting of which continues to baffle her, despite her advanced years), or have been set upon by thugs, footpads and garotters as she made her giddy way about town." Will that suffice, my lady?'

'You're a cheeky wench and I shall have the carpet beater to your backside,' she laughed. 'And what of Joe the Publican?'

'Mr Joe Arnold,' I continued in the same style, 'is a charming and toothless old soul of indeterminate years. He's honest, hardworking and rather too fond of the locally brewed cider which is the preferred tipple in these parts. He likes to avoid arguments when he can and is slightly intimidated by women, most especially Miss Daisy. I suspect there's a Mrs Arnold waiting upstairs of whom he is inordinately fond and profoundly afraid. He seems to have a keen sense of justice and, like Daisy, is steadfast in his belief that Bill Lovell is not the murderer.'

'No, indeed, they both seem to favour this Arthur Tressle fellow.'

'They do, and I'll allow that the case against him is stronger than against Bill Lovell. But I can't quite shake the feeling that they're charging in as blindly as Inspector Sunderland. They don't want it to be Lovell so they're pointing the finger at the next person they can think of. But there doesn't seem to be any proof for either of them beyond a bit of shouting.'

'I say, you do seem to have picked up something of the scientific method, my girl. My giddiness hasn't prevented me from passing that on, at least.'

I curtseyed and she smiled a wicked smile.

'That handcart,' she went on, 'seems to be just the sort of thing to have made those tracks in the clearing. And the cricket lads seem like just the sort of fellows to have pinched it for a lark.'

'I'd not be out on the street proclaiming their innocence if they were banged up for that, my lady. But pinching a handcart and doing a chap to death are two completely different matters. Joe and Daisy don't seem to have linked any of the goings-on to the handcart, though. I just got the feeling Joe was aggrieved that it had gone briefly missing.'

'Then we shall have to see what proofs we can come upon.'

'Even if that means proving it was Bill Lovell all along, my lady?'

'Even so. I'm more than happy for a guilty man to hang, but as yet I remain as unconvinced as Constable Hancock that Bill Lovell is guilty of anything more than being humiliated by that strumpet Daisy.'

'Did the constable have any more news?'

'Not really. We talked about the events of that night in the pub as he understands them. I came to much the same conclusion as you did about Daisy; she's well known around the village for being something of a flirt. I expect she thought she might be able to paint herself in a more flattering light to a newcomer. She just hadn't reckoned on meeting such a shrewd newcomer.'

'Anything else?'

'I confirmed my initial impression that Constable Hancock is an absolute poppet.'

I laughed. 'Yes, I suppose he is.'

'Like a big, eager puppy.'

'You could keep him in a kennel in the garden and he could guard the cottage for us. Maybe that would make you take security seriously.'

'I'll keep you in a kennel in the garden, my girl. But I had a delightful little chat with the good constable; he's been quite diligent in his researches.'

'Anything more of our victim? Any rivals? Any other romantic entanglements?'

'I say, Flo, you're rather getting into the swing of this, aren't you. No, sadly, despite his heroic efforts he knows nothing more.'

'We're really not very good at this, are we, my lady.'

'We have to be, Flo, we have to be. But let's leave it for now. I confess I'm not really in the mood for dinner. Would you be a dear and make some sandwiches?'

I made the sandwiches and we ate them together in the drawing room, reading until bedtime.

On Wednesday it rained; a beautiful summer downpour that made me thankful I'd had time for the laundry on the previous day and saw me instead rearranging the freshly stocked pantry. Thanks to the mischievous whim of whatever malevolent gods are responsible for the security of bags of flour, one had split just as I was transferring its contents to my flour jar and I was covered in the stuff when the doorbell rang. Wiping my hands on my pinafore and trying to brush the worst of the mess away, I went through to open the door to find a man in overalls and cap.

'Begging your pardon, miss. Is this the right house for...' he said, consulting the scrap of paper in his hand, 'Lady Hardcastle?'

'It is,' I replied.

'Bloomin' 'eck – begging your pardon, miss – but you're hard to find. We've got a delivery for you.'

'A delivery of what?'

'A piano and a blackboard, miss. You starting a school?'

'Starting a school?' I said, incredulously. 'Why on earth... We're expecting a piano, but–'

'It's all right, Armstrong, it's for me.' Lady Hardcastle had appeared silently behind me. 'Bring them in, would you. I want the piano against the back wall in the drawing room and the blackboard by the fireplace in the dining room. Would you care for some tea? And there's cake. I should expect delivering things is quite thirsty work.'

'Tea would be most welcome, madam, yes. Thank you. I'll get my lad to start shifting a few things in here if you don't mind – give us a bit more room to get the piano in.'

I looked outside and parked in the lane was a large wagon, pulled by quite the most enormous horse. A young boy of about fourteen sat on the wagon's driving seat, and on the bed of the wagon, covered by an oiled tarpaulin, was – I presumed – Lady Hardcastle's new piano.

I went back to the kitchen and set about making tea while the delivery man and his "lad" began shifting furniture in the drawing room to make way for the new upright piano. Lady Hardcastle joined me. 'I'm so glad it's here. I've been missing having a piano in the house terribly.'

'I know, my lady. It'll be nice to have some music in the house again. But was I dreaming or did he also say something about a blackboard.'

'Ah, yes, that was an idea I had yesterday. After I'd finished talking to the constable I prevailed upon him to let me use his telephone to contact the music shop to complain about the absence of my new piano. The nice man told me it was just being loaded onto a train bound for Bristol and that he'd arrange for it to be delivered today. I explained that it really wasn't good enough and that I'd been in my new home for over a week without it, despite the fact that I'd placed the order over a month ago. He apologized profusely and asked if there was anything he could do to make things right, and I said that if he managed to get a large blackboard and easel onto the train with the piano we'd say no more about it.'

'You made him go out and buy you a blackboard?'

'No, silly, they sell them. For music teachers. I bought it, but I made it clear that my goodwill and continued custom were contingent entirely upon the safe arrival today of both piano and blackboard.'

'And so now you have a blackboard.'

'And a piano.'

'Why?'

'It's for making exquisite music. Obviously.'

'No, my lady, the blackboard. Why do you have a blackboard?'

'Oh, yes, of course. Well, you see, I rather got used to using a blackboard for working things out when I was at Girton. Helps me to think, d'you see? So I thought perhaps if I had a blackboard, it might help me to think about this murder business.'

'The murder.'

'Quite so. I thought if I could make notes, draw diagrams, perhaps even pin up little sketches of the people involved, it might help me to make sense of all the information about the murder and perhaps find a solution.'

'And so for this one case, you now own a blackboard.'

'And chalk. And a duster. And a box of tacks.'

'Tacks?'

'Thumbtacks. For pinning things to the blackboard.'

'Won't that make holes in it?'

'Oh, Flo, you do worry about the most inconsequential things. Take the tea out to our horny-handed sons of toil and rejoice that we finally have a piano.'

'You have a piano, my lady. I play the banjo as you very well know. You also have a blackboard.'

'Yes. Yes I do. Now feed and water the nice men who own the cart that brought it.'

I took tea and cake to the delivery man and the boy that I had by now established was his son, and supervised the rearranging for the furniture in both rooms to accommodate the new items. Less than an hour after they had first rung the bell, everything was safely in place and we had tipped them handsomely and sent them on their way.

I returned to the floury chaos of my kitchen.

With everything finally in order I set about preparing dinner while Lady Hardcastle continued her sketching in the dining/investigation room.

We dined early and while we sat at the table afterwards sipping some of Lady Hardcastle's excellent cognac – one of her few vices – she explained the "Crime Board" as she had christened the new blackboard which stood in the alcove beside the fireplace. While I'd been preparing our meal, she had been busy pinning up sketches of the victim, Mr Pickering, together with blank outlines of our two main suspects, Messrs Lovell and Tressle (she'd not yet met either of them so she had no idea what they looked like). Another chalk line linked him to a sketch of Mr Seddon standing outside a building with a sign above it reading, "Seddon, Seddon & Seddon, Shipping Agents".

There were notes under each sketch outlining what we knew as well as some speculation about motives and connections. She also had one of the sketches of the body in the tree and of a cart rather like the one in the yard at the Dog and Duck.

'After all that, though,' she said, sitting back down, 'I'm no nearer solving the case than I was before. We've got two men who might have a reason to kill Mr Pickering if their jealousy of him were strong enough. Both of them seem to have an opportunity to do so. Mr Tressle seems to have had access to a handcart that would be perfect for transporting the body to fake the suicide, but Mr Lovell could easily have taken it from outside the cricket pavilion where the rowdies left it. But we still have no proof that either of them did it nor any idea how they might have managed to get the body up into the tree. I fear we're getting nowhere, Flo.'

'We know more than Inspector Sunderland already.'

'Perhaps. But let's leave it for now, I feel the spirit of Chopin coming upon me.'

'I love it when that happens,' I said.

'Then come, servant, let us repair to the drawing room and I shall play.'

'I'll tidy these things away and make some cocoa.'

'Very well. But hurry, the spirits are restless and dear Frédéric might be elbowed out of the way by Franz Léhar at any moment.'

'Léhar is still alive.'

'He is? That hardly seems fair. Well such is the sickly power of his sentimental spirit that even life cannot stop him. Hurry, girl, or it'll be "The Merry Widow" for you, and that never ends well.'

'One merry widow in the house is quite enough for me, my lady. I shall be as swift as I can.'

The piano turned out to be a charming instrument and only slightly in need of tuning after its journey. It was nearly midnight by the time we retired.

Thursday morning saw us both engaged in mundane domestic matters, with me continuing to organize our household and Lady Hardcastle catching up with correspondence at her desk in the small study.

I had prepared a ham pie for lunch which we shared at the kitchen table. Lady Hardcastle declared it the most delicious pie of the day and we were toasting my success as Queen of Pies when the doorbell rang.

It was Constable Hancock. He snapped smartly to attention as I opened the door.

'Why, Constable Hancock,' I said with a smile, 'what a pleasant surprise. I trust we find you well?'

'Passing well, miss,' he replied, touching the brim of his helmet with his right index finger. 'I wonder if I might have a word with Lady

Hardcastle.'

She had, once more, arrived silently at my shoulder. 'You may have whole sentences, my dear constable,' she said as I opened the door wider to allow him in. 'Do come inside and tell us your news.'

He took off his helmet and placed it on the hall table.

'Tea, constable?' she said, genially. 'We were just finishing lunch; perhaps you'd care to join us in the kitchen? I hope you don't mind but I don't want Armstrong to miss anything and if we all gather in there, she can make the tea while we talk.'

'That would be most agreeable, m'lady,' he said, and we walked through to the kitchen together.

She bade him sit at the large kitchen table and sat opposite him while I busied myself with the kettle, teapot and cups.

'I gather you two have been asking a few questions, m'lady,' he said once he was comfortable.

'Not nearly enough, it seems,' said Lady Hardcastle, dejectedly. 'I had such high hopes. I thought it was all going to be so easy. But since your visit on Monday we've managed to speak to just two witnesses. Or Armstrong did, at least, and they told us nothing much of interest. We wasted yesterday playing with my new crime board–'

'Your what, m'lady?' he interrupted.

'Oh, yes, sorry. I'll show you later. We also had a frankly bizarre luncheon with the victim's employer which I thought was going to give us some important background but which actually turned out to be just a mediocre meal with some social-climbing snobs.'

'My meal was excellent,' I said, smugly.

'Well, at least someone enjoyed herself,' she said. 'And here we are two days later, no nearer the truth and no idea where to go next.'

'Ah,' said Hancock, slightly uneasily. 'Then my news won't come too welcome.'

'Oh dear,' said Lady Hardcastle. 'What's happened?'

'The coroner's court reconvened today, m'lady. The police surgeon's evidence showed that Mr Pickering had been strangled first with something broad and soft, perhaps a scarf, and that the body had only then been hung up by the rope we found. Based on Dr Fitzsimmons's measurements – whatever they might be – they put the time of death at around midnight. I'm still not quite certain how they knows that.'

'Body temperature and the ambient temperature at the scene,'

Lady Hardcastle interrupted. 'The body cools at a known rate once a person is dead so it's possible to estimate how long ago that was. Then there's *rigor mortis*, of course, but that doesn't set in for about twelve hours. Since we found him the following morning, that wouldn't have helped.'

Constable Hancock seemed impressed. 'I knew you was the lady for the job. Anyway, they weighed all that up and brought a verdict of wilful murder. Inspector Sunderland has charged William Lovell and he'll be up before the magistrate tomorrow. Most likely they'll refer the case to the next assizes.'

'And when are they?'

'That's the problem, m'lady. Assizes is nearly upon us. Judge is due on Monday and depending on how many cases there is, Bill might be up before him by the middle of next week.'

'Oh dear lord,' said Lady Hardcastle. 'That poor man. And we've done nothing to help.'

'Not exactly nothing,' he said, trying his best to console her. 'No one else was doing nothing at all. At least you tried to find out something.'

She sat a while in dejected thought but then snapped up, suddenly resolute. 'Not "tried", my dear constable, "are trying". We're not going to give up. He won't be on trial for his life until the middle of next week and we're going to find something. Armstrong, we're redoubling our efforts.'

'Yes, my lady,' I said, pouring the tea.

'Redoubling them,' she said.

'Consider them redoubled,' I said, joining them at the table.

Constable Hancock was trying to suppress a smirk.

We sat quietly for a few moments.

'We're back to the beginning, then,' I said at length.

'We are. But perhaps that's a good thing. Let's get back properly to the beginning. Constable, would you care to accompany us to the dining room?'

'Er, certainly, m'lady. Whatever you wish.'

I put the tea things onto a tray and followed the others through to the dining room.

'You see, Constable,' said Lady Hardcastle, indicating the blackboard, 'this is my crime board. I thought it would help me think,

39

but mostly it's been a diverting way of procrastinating while I draw pictures.'

'I see,' said Hancock, closely examining the board and reading the notes. 'Forgive me, m'lady, but why do you not have sketches of all the suspects?'

'I've not met either of them. I don't know what they look like.'

'Either of them, m'lady? I counts three suspects.'

'Three?' she asked, somewhat perplexed.

'I'd been wondering about that myself just this morning,' I said. 'Surely Daisy is a suspect, too. She has a quick temper and one could conceive of reason enough for her to want to do away with her unwanted suitor. Her reputation around the village is shaky enough without him causing trouble.'

'I'm so stupid,' said Lady Hardcastle. 'Of course she's a suspect. Does she have a scarf?'

'Most people have scarves, my lady,' I said. 'I don't think we're likely to get a fresh arrest based on ownership of a scarf.'

'I suppose not,' she said, defeatedly.

'So that's one more suspect for the board,' said Hancock. 'You haven't spoken to Arthur Tressle, you say?'

'No, we...' she trailed off.

'It hadn't really occurred to us,' I said. 'Are we even allowed to speak to suspects?'

'Not sure as he's a suspect as far as the police is concerned, miss. You can talk to whoever you likes far as we're minded.'

'Then perhaps we should go round to him now,' said Lady Hardcastle. 'Find out what his side of the story is. Where in the village does he live?'

Hancock chuckled. 'He don't live in the village, m'lady. He lives down in Bristol.'

'Bristol?' she exclaimed. 'Doesn't anyone involved in all this actually live here? I thought he played for the local cricket team.'

'That he does, m'lady. He grew up round here, went to the village school over Woodworthy, but soon as he got hisself a job he moved down to the city. Been down there near ten years. He comes up here for cricket matches. Loyal to his old club, see. It was unusual for him to be in the village on a week night but they had their special club meeting or whatever it was.'

'Do you have his address?' she asked.

'I'm sure I could find it for you, m'lady.'

'Thank you, constable.' She turned to me. 'Is it worth speaking to Daisy again, do you think?'

'Not unless you've got something solid to confront her with, my lady,' I said. 'Her "I a'n't done nothing" routine is well rehearsed and very steadfast. She'd just irritate you, I think.'

'Very well. Constable, you'll get the address for Mr Tressle. Armstrong, you'll take my note to The Grange asking Sir Hector if we can borrow his motor car and chauffeur to take us into Bristol. We must go this evening and catch Tressle after work, there's no more time to waste.'

'Yes, m'lady,' Hancock and I said together. We laughed and got up from the table.

Sir Hector hadn't been at home when I called but Lady Farley-Stroud had been only too delighted to oblige Lady Hardcastle with a car and driver once she read the note and realized what it was wanted for. Jenkins, their butler, had shown me to the garage where I waited beside the car for Bert, the chauffeur.

The car was much less luxurious than the Seddons' but no less practical, and after a brief stop at home to pick up Lady Hardcastle we were on our way into Bristol.

It took the best part of an hour to reach the terraced street on the outskirts of the city. There were children playing in the street as we drew up outside the address Hancock had given us and they came rushing over, noisily exclaiming over the gleaming motor car and bombarding poor Bert with a cacophony of questions about it. Fortunately for us, this meant that the lady and her maid in the back were of no interest at all and we slipped quietly out, and then up to the front door of the small house.

The door was answered by a small woman of late middle age wearing a housecoat and headscarf.

'Yes?' she said suspiciously. 'What do you want?'

'Is Mr Tressle at home?' asked Lady Hardcastle.

'What if he is?'

'I'd like to speak with him if I may.'

'I don't allow my lodgers no lady visitors. This is a respectable house.' She made to close the door.

Lady Hardcastle took a card from her silver case and handed it to the landlady. 'Please give him my card and tell him I'd like to speak to him. Tell him it's about... the Littleton Cotterell Cricket Club.'

The fearsome woman took the card and glanced at it. Her manner changed instantly. 'Oh. Oh, come in your ladyship,' she gushed. 'Cricket club, you say? Please wait in the best parlour and I shall tell Mr Tressle you're here. Can I get you something? Tea, perhaps? Or something a little stronger?' She grinned a gap-toothed grin.

'Thank you, no. You're very kind but I've only recently had some tea. Just fetch Mr Tressle for me, please.'

We followed the woman into the house and she showed us into the tiny front room, then she hurried out and clumped up the stairs.

A few moments later, a neatly dressed young man with thinning hair appeared at the door. He squinted through grimy spectacles at the calling card he'd been given.

'Lady Hardcastle?' he said, looking at each of us.

'That's me,' said Lady Hardcastle. 'This is my maid, Armstrong.'

'Pleased to meet you both, I'm sure. Mrs Grout said you'd come about the cricket club. You haven't come about the cricket club, have you?'

'No, Mr Tressle, I haven't. Shall we sit down?'

They each sat on one of the two overstuffed armchairs while I stood beside Lady Hardcastle.

'Is it about... you know... Frank Pickering?' he asked.

'Yes, it is. You know that Bill Lovell has been charged with his murder?' she said.

'I knew he'd been arrested.'

'But you knew he didn't do it?'

'I didn't think he could have, no.'

'Because you knew who it was? Was it you, Mr Tressle?'

'Me? How dare you come in here and say such things.'

'I know that you and he had a fight about him taking over the cricket club in the Dog and Duck the night he was killed. You were heard saying that you'd not let him do it. I think you followed him out, strangled him with your scarf and then took his body to the woods using the handcart from the inn. How did you get him up into the tree, Mr Tressle? That's what's puzzling me.'

'I did no such thing. Who told you we argued about the cricket club? Daisy?'

'I spoke to her on Tuesday afternoon,' I said. 'Both she and Joe Arnold were adamant that you'd had a fight.'

'Oh, I didn't say we'd not had a fight,' he chuckled mirthlessly. 'Just not about the club, that's all.'

'About Daisy?' said Lady Hardcastle.

'That strumpet? I'd not touch her with gloves on. Have you considered it might be her? That she might be trying to divert the blame?'

'What was the fight about, Mr Tressle,' said Lady Hardcastle, firmly.

'It was a confidential business matter,' he said.

'Business? What business did you and Mr Pickering have?'

He looked slightly disbelieving for a second. 'We worked together, Lady Hardcastle. I'm a clerk at Seddon, Seddon and Seddon.'

We sat in stunned silence for a few moments.

'Why,' she said eventually, and with some exasperation, 'did no one think to tell me that before? Armstrong? Did you know?'

'No, my lady,' I said, deciding against my initial, more flippant reply.

'Please tell me,' she said when she had collected herself, 'exactly what happened that evening.'

'We had our meeting at the Dog and Duck and we all got a little drunk,' he began.

'What was the meeting about?' she asked.

'Arrangements for the club's annual supper dance,'

'Give me strength,' she said. 'I'd been given the impression it was some sort of coup.'

He laughed. 'No, nothing like that. With our business concluded, we settled down for a few more convivial drinks. That's when Bill Lovell comes and has a go at Frank.'

'Yes, we heard about that. What next?'

'Then Frank and I has our... our private discussion—'

'Your argument.'

'Things did get a little bit heated, yes. Then Frank leaves, and we stays to have one more before home time. We leaves the pub in good time but a couple of the lads gets into some tomfoolery on the green—'

'They stole Mr Arnold's handcart,' interrupted Lady Hardcastle.

'They did, yes. We ended up larking about at the cricket pavilion and by the time I looked at my watch I was too late to get to Chipping Bevington for the last train home so I kipped down on the dressing room floor. I've done it before and I don't doubt I'll have to do it again.'

'And you didn't see Frank at all?'

'Not after he left the pub, no.'

'What was your argument about, Mr Tressle?' she asked, kindly. 'I really must know. If it has anything to do with what happened to him…'

'Look, I can tell you if you think it will help, but when I say it's a confidential business matter, I mean it. It would ruin lives if it got out.'

'If it helps to save a man's life, it might have to come out anyway, but I give you my word that I shall keep it in the utmost confidence if I possibly can.'

He sighed. 'Very well. Frank was the senior clerk at Seddons and he'd taken it upon himself to review some of our bookkeeping practices. He had it in mind that we could increase profits if we kept better track of our receipts and payments. In his own time he'd been going through the ledgers – stacks of them. Weeks it had taken him.

'And then one day he starts looking anxious and distracted. Really in a state about something. So I asks him what's the matter and he says he can't tell me. It gets worse for a few days until he finally says he needs to talk to someone and would I meet him in a pub down by the Centre after work.

'So I meets him there and we're drinking our beers and he suddenly says, "We're in trouble, Art." And I says, "What do you mean, trouble? What kind of trouble?" And he says, "It's Seddons. I've found something in the books. Someone's embezzling. Hundreds. They've covered their tracks, or they think they have, but nothing adds up. The firm's almost bankrupt, Art." And I says, "Blimey." Well, what else could I say, really? So I says, "Blimey, have you spoken to Mr Seddon about it?" And he says, "No, do you think I ought." And I says, "Well you've got to, a'n't you. You've got to say something if we're about to go under." And he just sits there looking like he's been poleaxed. Then he says, "You're right, Art. I'll go round his house tonight. Drink up and I can get the next train." And then off we goes.'

'Langdon mentioned that visit,' I said. 'He said he didn't think it went well.'

'Mr Seddon's valet? Nice bloke. No, it didn't go well. Next day me and Frank found somewhere private to talk and I asked him what had happened. He says, "I told Mr Seddon what I'd found and he just looked at me blank like he didn't want to believe it. Then he tells me not to breathe a word to anyone. So I asked what we were going to do and he said it was none of my concern and how dare I come to his home in the middle of the evening and start questioning how he runs his business. And I said I was only trying to help and he says I've helped quite enough thank you and tells me to get out. So I got out."'

'Slamming the door as he went, according to Langdon,' I said.

'I shouldn't be surprised if he did. So then I says, "Well what's next, Frank?" And he says, "I've got to go to the police, a'n't I?" And I says, "But if it all gets out, the firm will be ruined and we'll all be out on our ears." And he says, "And what if it gets out and they find out I knew and didn't say anything. I i'n't going to gaol to cover up for no embezzlers." I begged him to sleep on it, and to his credit he left it a few days, but when we met up at the Dog and Duck that night he says he's made up his mind and he's going to the police next day. That was the row. I lost my rag, I can't deny it. I knew if it all came out I'd lose my job, and who's going to employ a clerk from a firm that collapsed through embezzlement? I told him not to do it.'

'And threatened him,' said Lady Hardcastle.

'We all say things like that all the time. If everyone who ever threatened to kill someone actually went through with it, you'd be pretty lonely, I reckon. Most of the people you'd ever known would have been murdered and the rest hanged for killing them. But then he grabs me by the shoulders and leans in and says all quiet like, "I know who did it. I worked it out. I'm going to give them one last chance to come clean then I'm going to the law and neither you nor they can stop me. Support me, Art," he says. "Back me up. You're my oldest friend there. We've got to do the right thing." Then some of Old Joe's mates step in and pull us apart. So Frank sits down, then that dizzy trollop Daisy comes over, then he looks at his watch like he's got an appointment and that's the last I saw of him.'

Lady Hardcastle looked at each other in silence.

She finally spoke. 'Mr Tressle, would you like to free an innocent man from gaol?

'If I can,' he said.

'It may mean the financial collapse of your employers.'

'Now I've come to tell the story to someone else, I can see he was probably right. But how will it help free Bill Lovell?'

'You, my dear Mr Tressle, have just told us who the murderer is. Armstrong, tell Bert to turn the car around. Mr Tressle, fetch your hat. We're going to pay an unannounced call on Mr Seddon.'

Once we were out of the city the roads were clear and Bert was overjoyed with the opportunity to drive the car as quickly as it would go.

'Lady Farley-Stroud is a bit nervous of the motor car,' he called over his shoulder. 'She doesn't like me to drive this quickly.'

'This, my dear Bert,' shouted Lady Hardcastle over the noise of the straining engine, 'is a matter of life and death. To the Seddon house in Chipping Bevington and don't spare the horses.'

As we careered along the Gloucester Road, Lady Hardcastle gave Mr Tressle and me our orders and it wasn't much longer before we were almost there. When we were about a hundred yards from the house, Lady Hardcastle had Bert stop the car and let her and me out.

'We'll wait here for fifteen minutes,' she told him, 'and then go in. You two hurry back to Littleton Cotterell and fetch Sergeant Dobson and Constable Hancock. Bring them back to the house as fast as you can.'

We stood hidden behind a large tree beside the road, with Lady Hardcastle consulting her wrist watch every few moments. At last she nodded, and we walked to the gates of the Seddon house. We walked across the drive, then I made my way round the side of the house to the servants' entrance, leaving Lady Hardcastle to ring the front door bell. I hurried towards the kitchen.

A very surprised Mrs Birch let me in.

'I'm so sorry to intrude, Mrs Birch. The game, as they say in the stories, is afoot. Might I impose upon the hospitality of your delightful scullery for a few moments until the time comes for me to play my part?'

'Of course, dear,' she said, wiping her hands on her apron. 'But what the deuce is going on?'

'All will be explained in the fullness of time, Mrs Birch, I promise.'

I stood by the door that led into the main house, listening to what was going on in the entrance hall. As Langdon had already said, it was difficult to hear much from other parts of the house, but I was certain I'd heard Langdon announcing Lady Hardcastle and, after a brief exchange in the hall, their footsteps as they went into one of the rooms. I gave it a few moments more to make sure the way was clear and then slipped out.

'Thank you, Mrs Birch,' I whispered over my shoulder. 'I'll explain everything as soon as I can.'

I tiptoed along the passageway, listening carefully for sounds of conversation. As promised, Lady Hardcastle had made sure her confrontation was in the dining room and I stood quietly outside the partly open door, listening. Mr Seddon's voice bristled with indignation.

'...mean by bursting in here unannounced?'

'I didn't think it could wait,' said Lady Hardcastle, coldly.

'Didn't think what could wait. What on earth are you doing here?'

'Oh come, Mr Seddon, let's stop playing games. I know you were stealing from the firm. Why was that? To try to keep up with your wife's vulgar taste in clothes? I know Frank Pickering knew, too. I know he confronted you. I know you lured him to a meeting late last Tuesday night. I know you strangled him with your scarf. I know you carried his body to Combe Woods on a handcart you found near the cricket pavilion. I know...'

I missed what else she knew because I was somewhat distracted by the distinctive click of a revolver being cocked and the all-too-familiar feel of its barrel being thrust into my ribs. Even through the sensation-deadening embrace of my corset, I'd never forget that feeling.

'I think you'd better join your mistress,' hissed Mrs Seddon, 'don't you?' She jabbed the revolver into my ribs again, propelling me through the door and into the dining room.

'Look what I found in the hall,' she said to her husband, all traces of the upper class veneer disappearing from her voice. 'Lady Muck's lackey doing a bit of snooping.'

She waved the gun to indicate that I should join Lady Hardcastle by the dining table.

'Oh, Ida, what have you done now?' said Mr Seddon, despairingly.

'Just another bit of tidying up after your mess. It seems I has to do everything round here.'

'Everything?' said Lady Hardcastle. 'You mean you–'

'You think that wet rag could do anything practical?' she sneered.

'He manages to run a successful shipping agency.'

'He managed to run it all right. But he didn't have the sense to take what was his from it. "Investing in the future," he says. "Rewarding loyal service," he says. "That's where the profits go," he says. Well what about my future? What about my loyal service? You think I married into this carnival freak show of a family for love? Sharing a marriage bed with that feeble oaf? You think I did that out of passion. I wanted my just rewards. I earn everything I get.'

'So you bullied him into stealing from his own firm?'

'Bullied, dearie? He'd do anything for what I can offer him.' She crudely hoisted her impressive bosom.

'And when Mr Pickering threatened to cut off your funds by reporting the theft to the police...?'

'Yes, your lady-hoity-toity-ship, I got rid of him. Choked the interfering life out of him with a very expensive silk scarf from Paris and then strung him up in an oak tree. All carefully planned it was. Nothing could go wrong. Not until you started poking your beak in.'

'Excellent work,' said Lady Hardcastle. 'Apart from tying him too high so his feet couldn't reach the log. Oh, and not leaving an impression in the ground from the log. Other than that, an exemplary effort.'

'Details. The police would never have noticed anything like that. You're an interfering snooper too, i'n't you. And I reckon you know now what happens to them.'

'I believe so, yes. But satisfy my curiosity. Even when I realized who had killed poor Mr Pickering – and I confess I wasn't quite sure which of you it was until I got here – I couldn't for the life of me fathom how you'd managed to get the body into the tree. Even from the handcart it was quite a feat.'

Mrs Seddon looked up at the memorabilia on the wall and Lady Hardcastle followed her gaze. 'Of course,' she said at last. 'The block and tackle. That display isn't asymmetrical by design, it's because there's a piece missing. We should have noticed that, Armstrong.'

'I noticed, my lady,' I said, shifting my weight slightly and balancing on the balls of my feet. 'I thought that's why you wanted your meeting to be in here.'

'Did you, indeed? Well done. Well done. And so it was. And what happened to the block, Mrs Seddon? And the scarf? Why couldn't we find those?'

'In the coal hole till things had quietened down. But I'll have two bodies to dispose of after tonight, so I'll probably get rid of them then.'

'You're a very clever and meticulous woman, Mrs Seddon. I congratulate you on the thoroughness of your planning. Isn't she good, Armstrong?'

'Very accomplished, my lady,' I said.

'And you, Mr Seddon? You had no part in this?' said Lady Hardcastle.

He sighed. 'No. He came to me and told me he knew, but I thought I'd dealt with it. I thought he was going to be a gentleman about it and that we could sort things out without anyone being any the wiser.'

'You pathetic worm,' spat Mrs Seddon. 'I swear if I didn't need to keep up appearances I'd be finding a hole big enough for three. You're a usel—'

Her rant was interrupted by the creaking of a floorboard outside the door.

The next few things happened in something of a blur. The listeners at the door realized that they'd been tumbled and began to make their hasty way inside. Mrs Seddon turned towards them, levelling her pistol. She fired at Sergeant Dobson but at the instant she pulled the trigger, my right foot connected with her wrist with a satisfyingly loud crack of breaking bone that could be heard even over the report of the gun. Dobson fell to the ground, unhurt but wisely getting out of the way of more shots, while I grabbed Mrs Seddon's broken wrist, wrenching her towards me and smashing my open palm into her nose. Blood gushed. She collapsed. And Constable Hancock said, 'Ida Seddon I am arresting you for the murder of Mr Frank Pickering. Oh. Well, I'll be sure to tell you again when you wakes up.'

It was all over in an instant.

'I say,' said Mr Seddon, rather gormlessly. 'That was most incredible. Where on earth did a little thing like you learn to do that?'

'China,' I said. 'It's none too easy in this dress, either. Thank you for noticing.' I curtseyed.

'I say,' he said, blushing.

Sergeant Dobson was back on his feet. 'James Seddon I am arresting you for theft and embezzlement and for aiding and abetting Ida Seddon in the murder of Mr Frank Pickering.'

Mr Seddon was handcuffed and our policeman friends made ready to take him and his groggy, blood-soaked wife outside.

'Wait a moment, Sergeant,' said Lady Hardcastle. 'I believe there's a telephone on a table by the front door. Do you think you should place a call to Inspector Sunderland and get Bill Lovell released?'

'Yes, m'lady,' said the sergeant. 'Hancock, you get these two into Sir Hector's motor car and I'll place that call.'

By now the household servants were all very much aware of what was going on, but I went into the kitchen to explain more fully. There was consternation, of course – they were all probably about to become unemployed – but I very much felt a sense of relief, as though much that had been wrong in their lives was at last being put right.

'I said she was a wrong 'un,' said Mrs Birch. 'And him not much better. Good riddance to them both, I say.'

Lady Hardcastle had joined us and gladly offered her assurance that she would do everything she could to find them employment elsewhere, offering to write references and make whatever introductions she could. They were clearly pleased and began talking about what plans they might make for the future.

She asked them what they intended to do in the meantime, and Langdon decided that, for the moment at least, they should be free to remain. It was, after all, still the Seddons' house and they were all still, officially, in the Seddons' employ. We couldn't help but agree.

At length we said our goodbyes and Langdon offered Daniel's services to take us both home in the Rolls Royce. We gratefully accepted and left them to discuss their new lives.

I slept well that night, and next morning Lady Hardcastle and I were up bright and early to make our statements at the little police station in the village.

Constable Hancock was effusive in his praise and showed us a note from Bill Lovell, thanking us both for our efforts and pledging his undying service in return for saving his life.

When we had finished, we set off to walk towards home, but the sun was shining and it promised to be another wonderful summer's day, so Lady Hardcastle suggested instead that we take a walk.

We crossed Toby Thompson's field and stopped briefly to pass the time of day. He congratulated us on catching the killer and I marvelled at the efficiency of the village news service which had already spread details of events which had occurred several miles away only the night before.

We crossed the lower pasture where I didn't look back even once, then carried on into the woods where I remembered which tree was an elm and spotted hedgehog droppings on the track. The clearing was beautiful, with the sun catching the rich green leaves of the oak and I couldn't help feeling that we were home. We were safe, and we were home in this charming part of Gloucestershire.

'I think we stumbled through that pretty well, don't you, Flo?' she said as we crossed the clearing and made towards the road.

'Pretty well for a couple of bumbling old biddies with no idea what they were doing,' I said.

'You speak for yourself.'

'I should have thought, though,' I said, 'that after everything we've been through over the years, all the things we've survived, all the baffling situations we've become embroiled in, all the difficulties we've overcome... I'd have thought that after all that, two women as experienced and resourceful as us would have made a much more impressive fist of catching a lack-witted greed monkey like Ida Seddon.'

'"Lack-witted greed monkey"? Flo, you do make me chuckle. Detective work isn't nearly as easy as the stories make out, you know, we've a lot to learn.'

'We certainly have,' I said.

'There's a lot we should have done differently. One thing in particular...'

'What's that, my lady?'

'I could really have done with a Derringer in my hat last night.'

I laughed. 'I can see you now, fumbling and snatching at it, it going off by mistake, shooting a hole in that ghastly portrait...'

'I'm going to get one, you know.'

'No, my lady. No you're not.'

'I bally well am, and there's nothing a slip of a thing like you can do to stop me.'

'You'd be a danger to yourself and others, my lady.'

'No, my mind is made up. I shall make an appointment with a hatter in the morning.'

'Foolish and irresponsible.'

Down the lane we went, bickering amiably, and on into the house. I even left the front door unlocked once we were inside.

We took tea in the dining room while I helped Lady Hardcastle clear up the "crime board".

'Not such a bad idea, this,' she said. 'Needs a bit of work, but it might come to really help us.'

'Help us, my lady?'

'Oh, you know, future cases.'

'There will be cases in the future?'

'Oh, Flo, I do hope so. Don't you? Tell me that wasn't absolutely the most fun.'

'That wasn't even slightly the most fun, my lady.'

'Oh, you.'

We were interrupted by the ringing of the doorbell.

I left her unpinning her sketches and went to the door. It was the boy from the Post Office.

'Telegram for her ladyship, miss.'

'My lady hasn't got a... oh, never mind. Is there to be a reply?'

'No, miss. Morning, miss.' And he scampered off.

I took the telegram through to Lady Hardcastle. She tore it open and read it, her face turning white. She dropped the paper on the table and hurried from the room.

I picked it up. It was from her brother Harry in London.

HONEST - MAN - NO - LONGER - WHERE - YOU - LEFT - HIM - STOP - SEEN - THIS - AM - IN - LONDON - STOP - YOUR - CURRENT - WHEREABOUTS - STILL - UNKNOWN - TO - HIM - STOP - STAY - OUT - OF - SOCIETY - PAGES - STOP - WILL - CONTACT - WHEN - HAVE - MORE - NEWS - STOP - LOVE - HARRY

The "Honest Man" was their name for a German killer called Günther Ehrlichmann, and Lady Hardcastle had left him in a the hallway of a rented house in Shanghai with a bullet through his heart in 1898. We had believed him dead these past ten years and thought that we were safe at last. So what made Harry so sure he was alive and well and once more posing a threat? And why the admonition to stay private? Was he after her? If he was, then things didn't look good for a woman whose name was due to be in tomorrow's newspapers as the daring detective who saved an innocent man from the gallows.

TWO

The Circus Comes to Town

'Emily! Darling girl! What the devil are you doing here?' called the handsome man as he strode across the village green to greet Lady Hardcastle.

'George?' said Lady Hardcastle, equally surprised.

'Of all the... fancy meeting you in a place like this,' he said, kissing her cheek in greeting.

'I could say the same about you. How are you, my darling?'

'Passing well, mustn't grumble.'

The whole village had been abuzz for the past week because...

The circus was coming to town.

On the previous Tuesday, the village had awoken to discover that posters had appeared over night on the church hall noticeboard, on trees, on lampposts, on, indeed, pretty much anything that stood still long enough to have a poster pasted to it. They had all proclaimed that, "On Monday, the 20th day of July, for five nights only, Messrs Bradley and Stoke will present their most magnificent, most spectacular, most incredible circus and carnival on the village green at Littleton Cotterel. Come one, come all!" The posters further promised, "Lions, Elephants, Dancing Horses, Acrobats, Jugglers, Clowns and featuring Abraham Bernbaum, England's Strongest Man." How could we not be excited?

The first wagons had begun to arrive on Saturday morning, some of them absolutely enormous, and by nightfall the green had become a giant entertainment encampment.

We had risen early on Sunday as usual and Lady Hardcastle was trying to decide how most profitably to spend the day, when my pestering about the circus finally overcame her. We could hear the roaring of the lions even from as far away as our house and so, of course, I was desperate to investigate. Breakfast plans were abandoned and we had dressed in walking clothes and set off to be nosy.

With Lady Hardcastle's customary casual disregard for the rules of polite conduct, we had slipped under the rope cordon and were just beginning to explore the site when an athletic, dark-haired, handsome but decidedly angry-looking man in khaki shirt, riding trousers and boots came striding towards us to intercept us and, presumably, to eject us from the camp. It was only as he drew closer and recognized Lady Hardcastle that his expression had changed to one of surprise and pleasure and he had greeted her with the warmth of an old friend.

'What an absolute delight,' said Lady Hardcastle, holding both his hands in hers and looking appraisingly at him. 'You're looking frightfully well, George dear.'

'You too, old girl, you too. But what are you doing here? I say, you're not staying with the Farley-Strouds are you? You poor thing.'

'No, silly, I live here. Just up the road. Jasper Laxton's house. You remember Jasper? Manages a tea plantation in Assam. Got stuck out there another year and let me have the house.'

'Well I never. Last I saw you, you were in London. That was, what, four years ago? And the time before that... must have been Calcutta.'

'Good lord,' she said. 'Do we really only see each other every four years?'

'The fates seem determined to keep us apart,' he said, holding the back of his hand to his forehead theatrically. 'And is that the lovely Florence I see there, trying her damnedest to remain invisible?' He stepped over and hugged me.

'Lovely to see you again, Major,' I said.

'Major no longer, my dear girl,' he said. 'I attained the dizzy height of Lieutenant Colonel before I finally managed to retire. Still officially on the strength, too, don't you know. So just you be careful and salute when I pass by.'

I offered him my best impression of a military salute and he rolled his eyes.

'But what,' asked Lady Hardcastle, 'are you doing here?'

'I, my dear Emily, am the manager of this spectacular

entertainment,' he said, gesturing expansively to indicate the sprawling chaos of the circus camp.

She laughed delightedly. 'A circus manager? How enchanting. But what of Messrs Bradley and Stoke? The posters promise that this is their circus, not yours.'

'The Walrus and The Carpet Bag? They're more by way of being producers, directors and figureheads, really. Someone has to get on with all the day-to-day drilling and marshalling, and that pleasant duty falls to yours truly.'

'The who and the what?' said Lady Hardcastle, laughing again.

'Mr Aloysius Bradley is an immensely fat man with simply gigantic moustaches who takes care of the business side of things, while his business partner Mr Philbert Stoke is the flamboyant showman, given to dressing in garish suits that look as though they're cut from Persian rugs, and he looks after artistic matters. Together they are The Walrus and The Carpet Bag.'

'But not to their faces.'

'Crikey, no, I should say not. But I'm so thrilled to see a familiar face so far from home. And that it should be yours of all the most welcome faces...'

'It's wonderful to see you, too, George, darling. But are we interrupting? I do hope we're not keeping you from your work.'

'My work at the moment seems to consist mainly of keeping inquisitive townies off the camp until the fence goes up.'

'Sorry,' she said, sheepishly.

'Ah, but for you there's always an exception. But you're right, I should be getting on. The lion tamer says his cages are too close to the fence, the trapeze artists are complaining that their costumes have gone missing, one of the Chinese acrobats has an upset stomach, and you don't even want to know about the matrimonial dispute between the fat lady and the dwarf. And I need all that sorted out in time to get the parade ready for Chipping Bevington this afternoon. Can't have a circus without a parade through the local big town.'

Lady Hardcastle laughed again. 'You've more than got your hands full, then, poppet; we'd better go. I say, would you care to join me for lunch? We could have a proper chat. Flo cooks a devilishly good ham pie.'

'No can do I'm afraid, old girl,' he said, sadly. 'Got to stay on the site today; lots to do before we open tomorrow night. But perhaps you could both join me for dinner instead. It'll be plain fare, served at benches in our mess tent, but the company will be convivial and the beer plentiful.'

'That sounds absolutely marvellous. Thank you, George, we'd be delighted. How does one dress for dinner in the circus?'

He laughed. 'Nothing fancy, old thing. Riding togs would be least conspicuous, but anything other than an evening frock will be fine.'

'Riding togs it is, then, dear boy. When shall we arrive?'

'Dinner is served prompt at nine. We should have the perimeter fence up by then – keep trespassing townies like you out – so I'll leave word with the box office that you're expected. Come about eight and I can show you round before it gets too dark.'

'Eight o'clock then, darling. We'll see you then.' They kissed their goodbyes and we sneaked back under the rope and went home for breakfast.

Back at the house I prepared a lavish morning feast which we ate together at the kitchen table. Lady Hardcastle was the brightest I'd seen her for a while; she had been anxious and subdued since the news of Ehrlichmann's apparent resurrection a few weeks before. Her brother Harry had said nothing more since the alarming telegram, but she had convinced herself that it was only a matter of time before he tracked her down again. He was a deadly figure from the past, involved in the murder of her husband, Sir Roderick, and until he was safely locked away, or properly dead, she knew she would always be in danger.

'Fancy dear George working for the circus,' she said, helping herself to another poached egg.

'It does seem rather an eccentric career move,' I said.

'Oh, he was always wild and impetuous like that. I always imagined him running off to join the circus.'

'Wild, impetuous and devilishly handsome.'

'All of those. I had quite a crush on him when we were younger. Dashing young army officer and all that.'

'I find out new things about you every day,' I said. 'Did nothing come of it?'

'Sadly not. I'm not his type.'

'You, my lady? Surely not.'

'How shall I put this delicately? My, ahh... my coat buttons up the wrong way.'

'Gracious me, I would never have guessed. He keeps it well hidden.'

'It's the safest way. But alas it meant that my passions were unrequited.'

'You poor old soul.'

'Cheeky wench. But he's been a loyal friend despite not desiring me as he should have. I feel simply awful that I see him so infrequently.'

'I've always liked him,' I said. 'And I'm not sure what we'd have done without him in Calcutta.'

'Indeed.'

'And now we get dinner at the circus,' I said.

'We do indeed. And what do you intend to do with your day off until then? I shall be catching up with some correspondence, I think.'

'I have no special plans, my lady. A day of indolence and sloth seemed most appealing.'

'Very good. I shall leave you to it. Perhaps we might meet here for a light lunch at about one o'clock?'

'That would be splendid, my lady.'

At a quarter to seven that evening we convened once more in the kitchen. There had been a certain amount of conspiratorial chuckling while we chose our outfits earlier in the afternoon, but now that the moment had come to set off, it didn't seem like such a clever idea.

Lady Hardcastle had taken Colonel Dawlish's dress code somewhat more literally than I should have and had decided that "riding togs" meant jodhpurs, loose blouses and riding boots. I had no riding clothes of my own (I was, and remain, thoroughly terrified of horses) but Lady Hardcastle had spares. The difference in our heights made things a little interesting, but her second-best boots hid the excess length in the jodhpurs and the rolled-up sleeves of the blouse gave me something of a raffish air, so I was declared to have passed muster.

I opened the front door and peered out, trying to make sure that no one would see us dressed in so unladylike a fashion, but Lady Hardcastle was in more mischievous mood and gave me a hearty shove to get me out onto the garden path. She locked the door behind us and we set off down the lane to the village.

We passed no one on the lane, but my relief at having gone unnoticed was short-lived. The usually tranquil village green had been transformed in just the few hours since we'd last seen it and there, where the most excitement one might usually expect on a Sunday evening would be the dying moments of a genteel cricket match, was the brash excitement of a travelling circus. A fence, six feet high and formed of colourful canvas panels stretched taught between tall poles, surrounded an encampment that filled almost the entire green. Brightly coloured pennants flew from the fence poles with bunting fluttering between them. There were glimpses of tents and cages within, but the enormous Big Top dominated the encampment, red and white striped and bedecked with yet more bright pennants and bunting.

As we approached we could hear cheering from the other side of the green as the parade marched back inside the enclosure. We were just in time to see the elephant make its stately way in through the main gate and to hear the last boom of the band's bass drum before the villagers, chattering excitedly, began to disperse.

The village was crowded with locals out enjoying the warm evening air, and visitors from all around come to see the circus on the green. Old Joe was already doing a brisk trade in food and drink at the Dog and Duck and the mood was buoyant.

There was, I realized, no chance whatsoever of us not being noticed and so I decided that there was nothing for it but to be brazen. Together we strode towards the circus entrance, our hair flowing loose down our backs and the mouths of the villagers falling open one by one as we passed. I heard a matronly, 'Well I never,' from someone I thought I recognized as Daisy Spratt's mother and at least one, 'Shameful,' but by and large the reaction was rather pleasing. Several young men doffed their caps and bowed as we passed and there was a loud, 'Wah-hey,' from a lad in a small group that contained Arthur Tressle – obviously the cricket team.

The local police had been on hand to maintain order, though their presence was scarcely necessary in such a good natured crowd. Constable Hancock caught sight of us and came over to bid us good evening.

'I say, ladies, don't you look...'

'Delightful?' suggested Lady Hardcastle.

'I was thinking more along the lines of "surprising", m'lady, but there's delight to be had, that's for certain.'

'You're very charming, constable.'

'Are you dressed up for something special, m'lady?' he asked, obviously trying hard not to look anywhere he felt he shouldn't.

'We're having dinner with a friend of mine from the circus,' she said with a grin.

'Are you? Are you indeed? Well I hope you have a most pleasant evening, m'lady.'

'Thank you, constable.'

'And you, too, Miss Armstrong.'

'Thank you, constable,' I said and curtseyed.

He was about to stammer something else when Sergeant Dobson appeared.

'Ladies,' he said, touching the brim of his helmet with his finger.

'Good evening, sergeant. I trust we find you well,' said Lady Hardcastle.

'Very well indeed, m'lady,' he said.

'They're going to dinner in the circus, Sarge,' said Hancock.

'Then you'd better let them get on with it, hadn't you,' said Dobson. 'And put your tongue away, lad. I'm sure they don't want to see you drooling.' He winked at us and led the mortified constable away.

Laughing, we carried on to the main circus entrance.

A red, wooden arch bearing the legend "Bradley & Stoke's Carnival & Circus" in golden lettering marked the gateway to the wonderful otherworld within. The walkway beneath it led to an ornate wooden structure with another red and gold board above it reading, "Admissions". Two ticket windows were each manned by a smiling old woman of more than seventy years in red tunic with gold trim. As we approached, it became apparent that the women were identical.

'Good evening,' they said in unison.

'Er,' said Lady Hardcastle, looking from one to the other. 'Good evening.'

'Welcome to...' said the first.

'...Bradley and Stoke's...' said the second.

'...Carnival and Circus,' finished the first.

'How may we...' said the second.

'...help you?' asked the first.

'I'm Lady Hardcastle.'

'Ah yes...' said the first woman, consulting a piece of paper on the counter before her.

'...Lady Hardcastle. Colonel...' said the second.

'...Dawlish is expecting you. Please...'

'...wait a moment and...'

'...I'll let him know...'

'...you're here.'

Lady Hardcastle and I exchanged glances.

'Thank you,' she said. 'That will be...'

'...splendid,' I finished. 'It's a lovely...'

'...evening.'

The two old ladies laughed and clapped delightedly. Then the first took a whistle from the counter and blew it sharply three times.

'I'm Milly,' she said, putting the whistle down. 'And this is my...'

'...twin sister Molly.'

'It's a pleasure to meet you, ladies,' said Lady Hardcastle. 'And this is my... my good friend Florence Armstrong.'

I raised an eyebrow but her look said, 'Play along.'

'Good evening, ladies,' I said.

'It certainly seems to be a magnificent circus. Have you been with it long?' she asked.

'Sixty years this...'

'...November,' they said.

'Young girls we were then,' said Milly. 'We were...

'...acrobats,' said Molly.

'Oh, how wonderful,' said Lady Hardcastle. 'What a life you must have led.'

'We had our...'

'...moments,' they said.

'Alas,' said Molly, 'time passed and our...'

'...joints stiffened,' said Milly. 'And so now we're here...'

'...selling tickets and welcoming...'

'...the world to meet our...'

'...wonderful family.'

I was very much warming to these two old charmers and was keen to find out more about them and their lives in he circus, but another charmer had appeared.

'Emily! Emily,' said Colonel Dawlish. 'You came.'

'But of course,' she replied.

'And you brought... but wait, who's this with you? Surely that's not Florence Armstrong, lady's maid and all-England Mazurka champion? In rational costume?'

I bowed.

'Why the devil,' he asked, laughing, 'are you dressed like that?'

'You distinctly said, "riding togs",' said Lady Hardcastle. 'Didn't he, Flo?'

'He did, it's true,' I said.

'I suppose I did at that,' he said with a grin. 'Well done, you. But where did you get...?'

'I shall tell you the full story one day, dear heart, but it shall suffice for you to know for now that I had need of a disguise at Kidderminster in 1904.'

'I'd like to meet the man who would be fooled by the sight of that behind in those jodhpurs and give him the address of my optician,' he said. 'But in truth you look fantastic, the pair of you. Just right for the circus. Come on, I'll show you round.'

We offered our thanks to Milly and Molly for their hospitality and took our leave.

The walkway led from the box office, forming a short avenue that led to the entrance to the magnificent Big Top. About halfway there, it branched to left and right at a small crossroads, with an oversized road sign at its centre pointing to "Big Top", "Mysteries" and "Wonders". We took the left turn to the mysteries.

The meandering path took us past a series of small tents, each with a sign above. There was "The Great Sandino – Magician" and "Pierre Marron – Mind Reader".

'How wonderfully exotic,' I said, longing to go inside and see a show.

'Leonard Sanderson from Ipswich and Peter Brown from Salford,' said Dawlish. 'Lovely chaps, great showmen.'

There were smaller tents for clairvoyants, palmists, and mediums and then as the path rounded the corner, yet more containing, so said the signs, a fat lady, a tattooed lady and "Wilfred Carney – England's Seventh Smallest Man".

'Seventh smallest?' said Lady Hardcastle.

'So we boldly claim,' said Dawlish. 'To be honest, I doubt if he's in the top twenty, but, you know, "seven dwarves" and all that? Brothers Grimm?'

'Aha,' she said. 'Of course.'

There were more tents farther on, but we'd already turned back.

'You look quite giddy there, Flo,' said Lady Hardcastle.

Against all my instincts, I really was rather enchanted by the place. 'It's like the most wonderful little fantasy village,' I said,

'Very much like one,' said Dawlish. 'A greedy, hungry, messy, chaotic village with all the squabbles, rivalries, friendships and romance of the real thing. And when we've sucked a place entirely dry of all its spare cash we can pack it all up and move out in less than twelve hours to go and find somebody else to fleece.'

'You can't fool me with your sham cynicism, George Dawlish,' said Lady Hardcastle. 'I see through you. You love it.'

'The truth is, I really rather think I do. It's the camaraderie of the army without the shouting and shooting. Don't get me wrong, I do love to shout and shoot – there's not a man this side of the Shanghai docks who loves the army more than I – but there's something really rather splendid about this ragtag troop of misfits and outsiders. And although they'll happily relieve a chap of his last farthing, they offer him a belly laugh or a few moments' goggle-eyed amazement in return.'

By now we'd passed the crossroads and were heading towards "Wonders". Here we found larger tents for the acrobats and jugglers, the contortionist, the strongman and the prize fighter. We carried on through to a canvas wall and Colonel Dawlish lifted a flap and ushered us behind the scenes.

Part of me was disappointed by how prosaic the camp was beyond the public areas. The magic of the bright colours and cleverly-laid pathways that slowly revealed new delights to the wandering visitor gave way to an orderly array of tents and wagons very much like – as one might expect from something organized by Colonel Dawlish – an army camp. Sleeping quarters, a mess tent, an open area for meetings and rehearsals and, off to one side, rows of wagons for the wild animals and "stables" for the many, many horses. The circus was rare in that it didn't seem to have a menagerie, but I could see a lion cage as well as an enormous travelling cage for the elephant.

'I hope you're both hungry,' said Colonel Dawlish and led the way to the mess tent.

The tent was already filling up with high-spirited circus folk, many already sitting and eating, chattering noisily, and some still queuing for their bowl of stew. There was bread and fruit on the tables, and jugs of ale and water.

We waited in line behind Colonel Dawlish who introduced us to the cook, a mountain of a man with a prodigious beard and a ready laugh who seemed to be called Babble. He dolloped generous helpings of a delicious-looking vegetable stew into tin bowls and we carried them towards a table near the corner of the tent where there appeared to be a little space remaining.

'Did you say that man's name was Babble, Colonel?' I asked as we sat down.

'That's right,' he said. 'Babbling Brook: cook. It got shortened to Babble. His real name's Bert Smith but I don't remember the last time anyone called him that.'

We seemed to be joining a group of friends at the table and they shuffled along the benches a little to make room for us.

'Lady Hardcastle,' said Colonel Dawlish with formality, 'please allow me to introduce my dear friends and colleagues.'

He indicated the first, a fair-haired woman of average height, lightly built but with the appearance of a subtle strength. Even sitting down she appeared graceful. 'This is Miss Prudence Hallows, our trapeze artist.'

Next to her was a large, dark-haired man with an impressively luxuriant beard and an avuncular twinkle in his eyes. His shoulders seemed about to burst from his shirt and the forearms which emerged from his rolled-up sleeves looked to be thicker than my own legs. 'This is Mr Abraham Bernbaum,' said Colonel Dawlish, 'our strongman.'

'Next, we have Mr Jonas Grafton, our chief clown.' He was clean shaven and plain and might easily have been a chief clerk rather than a chief clown. Or even a clergyman.

'Mr Augustus Noakes, our lion tamer,' said Colonel Dawlish, indicating a red-headed man with an extravagantly curled moustache.

His attention turned to a beautiful woman will long blonde hair, and the ruggedly handsome man beside her. 'And then we have Miss Veronica Prentice and Mr Wilfred Carney.' Colonel Dawlish didn't mention their roles but it was obvious from their appearance that these two were the Fat Lady and the dwarf.

'Our lead juggler is Mr Hubert Parvin.' This was a mischievous-looking man in his 20s with a pointed goatee beard.

Next to him was a tiny girl, not yet 20 by the looks of her, who never looked up from her plate, but smiled nervously as Colonel Dawlish said, 'And here's Miss Adeline Rosethorn, the contortionist.'

And then all our attention was directed to the most exquisitely beautiful woman I had ever seen. Dark hair, cut and styled with exquisite care, the darkest eyes, and features that looked as though they had been painted by an artist as an example of physical perfection. 'Mademoiselle Sabine Mathieu, equestrienne extraordinaire,' said Colonel Dawlish.

'And then last, and by any measure least,' he said, 'we have Mr Mickey O'Bannon, pugilist.' The curly-haired man with a broken nose and a ready smile waved a greeting.

'Gracious,' said Lady Hardcastle, 'I promise to try my very hardest to remember all that, but please forgive me if I slip up.'

There were shouts of, 'Don't worry about it, love,' and, 'I can't remember any of their bloomin' names myself and I've been working with them for five years.'

'And next to her is Miss Florence Armstrong, Lady Hardcastle's—'

'My dear friend,' interrupted Lady Hardcastle.

'Indeed,' said Colonel Dawlish with an approving nod.

He sat down as the welcomes rang out around the table and we tucked in to our delicious food.

The conversation was loud and boisterous and the company, as promised, extremely convivial. The troop were the warmest, most welcoming group I've ever met and by the time the meal was drawing to an end I almost felt as though I were part of the circus myself. They had regaled us with stories of their triumphs and disasters, of audiences good and bad, and there was a warmth and comradeship between them that even their incessant teasing didn't seem to diminish.

As the beer mugs were refilled for the umpteenth time, Lady Hardcastle and I took our turn as the centre of attention as Colonel

Dawlish told stories about our time in Calcutta.

'...and then there's a flurry of knees and elbows and the robber is lying on the ground, spark out, and Flo here is standing over him with his own knife in her hand.'

'Well done, girlie,' said Mickey O'Bannon appreciatively. 'Where did you learn that? China?'

'I did, Mr O'Bannon,' I said. 'You know the Chinese arts?'

'Mickey, please,' he said. 'I know of them, at least. I met a Chinese sailor once in Cork who fought like that. Placid fella he was, but you wouldn't want to go picking a barney with him.'

'Perhaps we should put her in the ring, Mickey,' said Prudence. 'Give your poor weary old bones the night off.'

'I'd certainly like to see you fight, girlie, I truly would,' said Mickey.

I was about to demur when Veronica suddenly said, 'Oh!' and dropped her spoon noisily into her bowl.

Wilfred, who was sitting next to her, jumped in surprise and flung out his arms, knocking Hubert's beer from his hand.

'Bravo!' said Jonas. 'A new juggling trick for your act, Huey.'

With an ironic bow, Hubert got up and went in search of a cloth to wipe himself and the table.

Veronica was still all of a twitter.

'Whatever is ze matter?' asked Sabine.

'I just counted,' said Veronica. 'We're thirteen at table.'

I expected them to dismiss it as silly superstition but instead a worried murmur ran round the table as they each made their own hasty count. Colonel Dawlish leaned in close and whispered, 'Superstitious lot, the circus fraternity. Don't scoff, but don't let them spook you.'

The fuss quickly died down, but the merry mood had been broken and the conversation became more subdued. At length Colonel Dawlish raised a questioning eyebrow to Lady Hardcastle. She nodded in reply, and he put down his beer mug with a thud.

'Well, my dears,' he said, standing up. 'I promised my friends here a tour of the circus and we still have a few things to see so we'll take our leave. Don't stay up too late. I want a safety inspection tomorrow morning at nine o'clock sharp, and a technical rehearsal at eleven. Abe, can you tell the blessed band that that means them as well, please.'

'Yes, sir!' they all chorused, saluting sloppily.

'Scallywags,' he said, laughing, and we rose to join him as the party said their goodbyes and bade us enjoy the rest of our evening.

As we left, I could hear Veronica saying, 'Oh. Oh! The colonel was the first to leave the table. Ill will befall him before a year has passed.'

'Don't let them spook you,' said Colonel Dawlish. 'I left first on purpose so they weren't stuck there all night.'

'Actually,' I said, 'It was the juggler... Hubert? He got up to get a cloth when he spilt his beer.'

He grimaced. 'Oh lord, don't tell them that.'

Outside the mess tent, Lady Hardcastle checked her watch by the light of a lantern hanging from a pole.

'Actually, it's getting a little late,' she said. 'It's been the most marvellous evening, George dear, but I feel we mustn't keep you up, either.'

'It's been entirely my pleasure, darling girl. But you're right, there's still much to be done. Come on, I'll show you out.'

He led us back through the flap in the canvas and down the winding path towards the circus entrance. The way was lit with yet more paraffin lanterns making the sideshows seem even more beguiling.

Presently we reached the now empty ticket office and said our farewells.

'Thank you again,' said Lady Hardcastle.

'Yes, thank you,' I said. 'This is quite the most magical place.'

'It's been my pleasure to show off for you, ladies,' he said. 'You'll be coming to the show, of course.'

'Of course we shall,' said Lady Hardcastle.

'Splendid. You're on the guest list already. Just speak to Milly and Molly when you arrive.'

'"Guest list"?' said Lady Hardcastle.

'Of course. You don't expect I'd let my oldest friend pay for her own tickets, do you?'

'You're very kind, George dear. Now off you go and get some sleep. I want you bright of eye and bushy of tail for your safety inspection tomorrow. Nine o'clock sharp.'

'Yes, ma'am,' he said, saluting a good deal more snappily than his circus friends.

He kissed us both goodbye and waved us off as we set off back to the house.

I was in the kitchen doing some early morning chores when the doorbell rang. I had put the iron to one side and had my hand on the kitchen door handle when the bell rang again, followed by fierce hammering of the door knocker. I hurried through to the hall, unbolted the door and opened it to find Colonel Dawlish on the doorstep in a state of some agitation, looking up at the upstairs windows.

'Ah, Flo, thank goodness,' he said. 'Is Emily up yet?'

'I took her some tea about half an hour ago,' I said, 'but she's not been downstairs yet.'

'Here I am,' said Lady Hardcastle, fastening her dressing gown as she came down the stairs. 'Whatever's the matter, George? What's all the racket about? Can't a girl get some rest?'

'I've just come from the police station,' he said. 'Something awful's happened.'

'Well don't just stand there,' she said, 'come in and tell us. Flo, let the poor chap in.'

I stood aside and he swept in.

'Tea in the drawing room, I think,' she said, and led the way.

As quickly as I could, I made a pot of tea and prepared a tray. I took it through and found them deep in conversation.

'Ah, Flo, thank you,' said Lady Hardcastle. 'What? No cup for you? Fetch yourself one and join us; I think you'd better hear this.'

A few moments later I was sitting in an armchair sipping my tea while Colonel Dawlish retold his story.

'At about six this morning I was taking a walk around the camp, checking a few things, you know. I don't usually wander down through the animal cages – I'll be honest, those blessed lions put the wind up me a bit. Gus – that's Augustus, the lion tamer, he was with us at dinner last night – Gus says they're just giant moggies but I've never been comfortable. Anyway, they'd been unusually quiet this morning. Ordinarily there's a good deal of territorial roaring before breakfast but I hadn't heard a peep out of them. So I took a stroll down through the animal wagons and there they were, the pair of them, fast asleep at one end of their cage. There was a pile of rags at the other, near the door. I thought, that's a bit rum, someone leaving a mess there like that – you have to be dashed careful with these wild animals, you know, surprisingly fragile constitutions, some of them, doesn't take much to upset them – and I went over to take a closer look. It wasn't a pile of rags at all. It was Huey. Hubert Parvin. The juggler. Dead.'

'Gracious,' I said. 'How? The lions?'

'Yes, from the state of him I'd say he got into the cage for some reason and they mauled him to death.'

'Gracious,' I said again, vacuously.

'Obviously I had to tell the police and they got the local doctor in.'

'Doctor Fitzsimmons,' said Lady Hardcastle.

'That's the chap,' he said. 'So he and your Sergeant Dobson – he seems like a practical fellow, ex-army I'd bet – they said it looked for all the world like a tragic accident, but if I wanted to be sure I should talk to you two. Dobson told me a frankly astonishing tale about a hanged shipping clerk and the evil wife of a wealthy businessman. And now here I am.'

I was about to say, 'Gracious,' again but caught myself just in time.

'And why aren't you sure?' asked Lady Hardcastle instead. 'Why isn't it an accident?'

'Huey was in the cage. On his own. In the middle of the night. And the cage door was locked.'

'Could he have locked himself in?' I asked.

'He could in theory,' he said. 'The lock works from the inside as well as out.'

'But in practice?' said Lady Hardcastle.

'He didn't have a key with him. Nor was there one anywhere around. I looked most carefully.'

'Did you mention this to Dobson?'

'I can't.'

'Why not? He's already open to the possibility of it being murder, so why not confirm it and let him take it to the Bristol CID?'

'Because I imagined he'd want to close us down while the CID came in and investigated.'

'And...?'

'And we can't afford it. We're in the most awful trouble. Financially, I mean. We can't afford to close down while the police trample all over the place. We'd be ruined.'

'So it's all right to have a murderer on the loose as long as the circus stays open? Oh, George, surely you don't think that.'

'Of course not, Ems, that's why I've come to you. Can't you help clear it up? We can find out who's responsible and hand them over to the police and everything will be kushti.'

'Hmmm. Well. I'm not sure I'd do it for anyone else.'

'But for me, Ems? Please?' He looked so forlorn. 'Can't you help? I mean, I've helped the Provost Marshal with investigations in my time but to hear Sergeant Dobson and his man Hancock speak, you're like a West Country version of Scotland Yard all on your own.'

'Hardly, darling. We just did what the Bristol CID would have done if they could have been bothered. And more slowly, too. But of course we'll help. Whatever we can do, we shall.'

'Thank you. Thank you so very much.'

'Think nothing of it, dear thing. Now, first things first. One presumes that the first person we should suspect would be the lion tamer. "Gus", did you say?'

'Augustus Noakes, yes. He definitely seems the most likely,' said Colonel Dawlish.

'And would he have a motive?' I asked, trying to think of all the things we missed while trying to track down Frank Pickering's killer.

'Quite the strongest one I can think of: Hubert had an affair with his wife a few years ago, destroyed the marriage. She was one of the equestriennes. They thought they were being discreet, but of course everybody knew. She left Noakes shortly after and went to work at a riding school in Sussex.'

'Is Noakes the sort of man to bear a grudge?'

'I should say so. He was always having little digs at Parvin. Never let him forget it.'

'Well, it looks as though you don't need us at all,' said Lady Hardcastle. 'I'd say you've got a man with a strong motive for killing Hubert who very much had the means to kill him. I would wager that he intended to come back and unlock the cage after the lions had done their work and blame it on a drunken accident. He'd have wanted to leave the cage locked as long as possible to prevent the animals' escape, but if he timed it right they might only have to be unlocked for a few minutes before someone found the body. He was just unlucky that you decided to go that way on your morning rounds. You didn't usually visit the animals, you say?'

'Not usually, no. It was just chance,' he said.

'So it does all point to Augustus Noakes. But then again,' said Lady Hardcastle, thoughtfully, 'we've jumped to the obvious conclusion before and been wrong. Whom else might one suspect?'

'Well, there are the other one hundred and thirty-seven members of the circus. Everyone knows where the lion cage key is kept.'

Lady Hardcastle thought for a moment. 'But some would find it easier than others to arrange to meet him in the dead of night and somehow manage to get him into the cage. To trick him or lure him. An acquaintance might very well be able to do it, but a friend would have a much easier time of it.'

'I suppose you're right,' he said.

'So who were his friends? Who was part of Mr Parvin's inner social circle?'

'The nine others who dined with us last night were his closest pals. They're the senior members of the troop, my junior officers and NCOs if you like. They're almost always together.'

'Then those are our nine suspects,' she said, decisively. 'We shall start with them. Florence, set up the crime board.'

'Yes, my lady,' I said, rising from the chair.

'The "crime board"?' asked Colonel Dawlish with just the tiniest trace of amusement in his voice.

'The crime, as you so clearly heard, board,' said Lady Hardcastle.

'It's her special thing,' I said. 'Nod and smile and play along.'

'Set up my "special thing",' she said, sternly, 'and then come and help me dress. A detective, even a clumsy amateur who relies on her "special thing", must maintain an air of professionalism and I hardly think that conducting an investigation in my nightdress conveys the right impression. Help yourself to more tea, George dear, and if you're hungry I'm sure you can find something in the pantry.'

Colonel Dawlish smiled for the first time since he had arrived and Lady Hardcastle and I left the room together to prepare for the day's work.

The rest of the morning was spent in the dining room as Colonel Dawlish told us everything he knew about Hubert Parvin's friends.

Lady Hardcastle sketched each one in turn while I pinned the sketches on the board and made notes under each.

By noon we had images of all ten:

Hubert Parvin - Juggler, deceased

Augustus Noakes - Lion Tamer

Prudence Hallows - Trapeze Artist

Abraham Bernbaum - Strongman

Jonas Grafton - Clown

Veronica Prentice - Fat Lady

Wilfred Carney - Dwarf

Adeline Rosethorn - Contortionist

Sabine Mathieu - Equestrienne

Mickey O'Bannon - Prize Fighter

We knew already that Parvin had been mauled to death by lions and that he had had a none-too-secret affair with the lion tamer's wife a number of years ago. There were tensions between assorted other members of the troop, too, but his descriptions of the arguments and sniping seemed to me to be typical of a large group of friends who spent almost every waking moment in each other's company so I wasn't sure how significant they were.

We learned that Miss Veronica Prentice, the fat lady, was actually "Mrs Carney" and that she and Wilfred, the dwarf, were just about the most happily married couple that Colonel Dawlish had ever met, with a kind word for everyone and always willing to do anything they could to help. They were, he said, almost like parents to the group. We put them to the bottom of our list of suspects for now.

Colonel Dawlish was unable to think of any motive whatsoever that the remaining seven members of the inner circle might have for murdering Hubert Parvin. Niggles, teasing and petty jealousies aside, they all got on well as far as he knew. We'd already established that any member of the circus would have been able to open the lion cage – it was a matter of safety that everyone should know where the key was kept. And as for opportunity... even those in shared caravans or tents would have been able to slip away in the middle of the night without anyone knowing anything about it. In the stories, the detective would always be able to unpick someone's alibi, but after a hectic and exhausting day's work setting up the circus, "I was in bed asleep" would stand up to even the closest scrutiny; so was everyone else and who would gainsay you?

We had been talking for hours when to my immense relief Lady Hardcastle declared it to be lunchtime and sent me off to prepare something quick and light for us all to eat.

I returned with a large plate of sandwiches which we ate as we continued working.

'What about,' I said, enlivened by the renewed energy given me by my cheese sandwich, 'the possibility that someone wanted falsely to implicate Noakes in Parvin's murder? What if we're looking for motives for murdering Parvin, but that crime was just a means of getting Noakes hanged?'

'Why not just kill Noakes?' said Colonel Dawlish. 'Why not lock him in his own lion cage and let the lions get rid of him instead of leaving it for the hangman?'

'Because... er...' I had to admit I was stumped.

But Lady Hardcastle wasn't so quick to dismiss it. 'No, it's an intriguing notion. Execution is public punishment. The Crown points its judicial finger and says, "Guilty," for all to hear. Perhaps the killer was prepared to sacrifice Parvin in order to have Noakes suffer the shame and humiliation of public accusation before he was finally punished for whatever it was he had done.'

'It would take a deranged, sadistic mind to do that, Ems,' said Colonel Dawlish.

'Given the nature of the murder itself, I'd say sadistic derangement can be assumed as fact. This would just make it disturbingly calculating as well.'

'I suppose you're right,' he finally conceded.

'I so often am, dear,' she said and took another bite of her sandwich.

'So, then, Colonel Dawlish–' I said.

'"George", darling, please,' he interrupted.

'Yes, Colonel Dawlish, of course,' I said and he rolled his eyes. 'So what we're looking for is someone who might have felt themselves to have been wronged by Mr Noakes and who would have wanted them publicly humiliated and punished, if not for that, then for something else.'

'The only person I can think of, *Miss Armstrong*,' he said, 'would be our strongman, Abe Bernbaum. Did you see our posters?'

'How could we miss them?' I said. 'They were everywhere.'

'That was certainly the intention. Whose names did you see on them? Can you remember?'

'There was Mr Bradley and Mr Stoke,' I said.

'And Abraham Bernbaum,' said Lady Armstrong, 'Britain's strongest man. I remember it clearly because I wondered whether you had any evidence to back up such a bold claim.'

'To be truthful, we probably don't,' said Colonel Dawlish. 'But the point is that his is the only name on the bill. He'd been quite the draw in the London circus shows but the audiences were drying up a little. We were beginning to struggle too, so ours was a marriage of convenience. We offered him steady work, a decent wage and a place to stay, and he gave us a famous name for the bill. We all won.'

'It sounds like you did,' said Lady Hardcastle. 'But I presume all was not sunshine and flowers within the family.'

'Indeed no. Someone's nose was put quite seriously out of joint by the news that the new boy was getting top billing. Someone thought that if anyone should be getting top billing it was him. Someone thought that he and his lions were the reason people came to Bradley and Stoke's Circus.

'Now the finale of Abe's act is to lift a barbell above his head. Two enormous iron balls, it is, on either end of a long iron bar. He gets two men from the audience and asks them to try to lift it, you know, to prove how heavy it is. First one tries, then the other, then both together, and even between them they can barely lift the thing. One afternoon, as the show was being set up, someone removed the two enormous iron balls and the heavy iron bar from the trolley and replaced them with two papier-mâché balls on either end of a broom handle, all painted grey. The stage hands wheeled the barbell out on the trolley, just like always. Abe selected his two volunteers – big enough to look like they should be able to lift it, but never too big in case they actually could. He had the first one attempt to lift it, and of course it shot up into the air like it was made of paper and paste. Unluckily for Abe he'd picked a show-off, and this chap chucked the thing in the air, twirled it around, threw it to his friend... the audience were crying with laughter. They thought it was part of the act, but Abe was mortified.'

'He probably should have kept it in the show; it sounds marvellous,' I said.

'Actually, it was rather fun,' he said, 'but Abe didn't see it like that. And he knew exactly who was responsible. He knew that Gus had meant to humiliate him and never forgave him.'

'But, really,' I said, 'It's all a little convoluted. Murdering a man so that another man will be falsely accused of murder as revenge for a practical joke?'

'In my defence,' said Colonel Dawlish, 'I still think Gus killed Huey Parvin by locking him in the lion cage. Abraham Bernbaum is a charmingly gentle man who lost his temper a few years ago. It's you two who were trying to make things complicated; I just told you another everyday story of circus folk.'

'Very well, then,' said Lady Hardcastle, decisively, 'let's interview them both. Augustus Noakes the lion tamer is the bookies' favourite, and Abraham Bernbaum the strongman is the 100-1 outsider who may be worth an each way bet.'

'I never had you pegged for a gambling gal,' said Colonel Dawlish.

She took his face in both her hands. 'My poor, naïve little darling,' she said and kissed his forehead, 'there's so much you don't know about me.'

He laughed.

'Hurry, servant,' she said. 'Fetch hats and gloves, we are bound for the circus to speak to a lion tamer and a strongman. George, you need to do whatever it is you need to do if you want to open tonight; we'll make our enquiries as discreetly as we can.'

As we approached the circus entrance we could see that there was some sort of commotion within. We were met at the box office by a flustered Mickey O'Bannon.

'Thank the lord you've come, boss,' said the Irishman. 'Where the devil have you been?'

'I've been with my friends,' said Colonel Dawlish indicating Lady Hardcastle and me. 'Whatever's the matter now?'

'It's Gus, boss.'

'What about him?'

'He's dead, boss, God rest his soul.' He crossed himself.

'He's what?' exclaimed Colonel Dawlish. 'How?'

'Crushed, boss. We found him about an hour ago, backstage. He had one of Abe's barbells across his chest, pinning him down, and one of those iron weights he uses... crushed the poor fella's head, so it did. Burst it like a grape.'

'My god,' said Dawlish, obviously stunned. 'Who else knows?'

Mr O'Bannon swept his arm to indicate the hubbub and commotion inside the camp. 'Pretty much everyone, I'd say.'

'Right, we need to keep this on the QT. No one leaves the camp. No one says anything to outsiders except Lady Hardcastle and Miss Armstrong. Understood? Spread the word; it's a family affair. Then get me Abe. I need a word with him.'

'Really, George!' said Lady Hardcastle, angrily. 'Two suspicious deaths and you're going to keep it quiet? I can't be party to this, I really can't. You have to tell the police. I'm going to get Sergeant Dobson right this minute.' She turned to go.

'O'Bannon,' said Colonel Dawlish with a nod towards Lady Hardcastle.

The prize fighter took two steps towards her and went to lay his hand on her arm to stop her from leaving. But before he managed to touch her, I had seized his arm, turned it away and thrown him across my hip. Within moments he was face-down on the grass with my knee in his back and his right arm twisted painfully behind him.

'Please don't try to move, Mr O'Bannon,' I said quietly. 'It's a tricky hold and something might get broken.' I gave his arm a little tweak to emphasize his predicament.

'As I said, George,' said Lady Hardcastle, coldly. 'I'm going to fetch Sergeant Dobson. He's a sensible, practical man and I'm sure I can persuade him that discretion is of the utmost importance. But the police will be involved, and you and your staff will cooperate. I promised that I shall do everything I can to help you, George, and I shall, because that's what friends do. But what I shall not do is break the law. And I never expected a friend to ask me to.'

'For goodness' sake, Emily. You can't. You'll ruin us.'

'I can and I must. And you'll not be ruined, not if I can help it. You must trust me, George.' She looked at him sternly for a moment as he calmed slowly down. 'Now release Mr O'Bannon, Armstrong.'

I gently let O'Bannon's arm fall back into a more natural position and stood up, careful not to press my knee into his back as I did so. He got slowly to his feet, massaging his shoulder and took a step towards me. I readied myself for an attack but he held out his hand.

'Don't worry, girlie,' he said. 'My old da' taught me never to get into a fight I wasn't certain I could win.'

I reached out my own hand and he grasped it and shook it solemnly. He leaned in close.

'That was quite something, girlie,' he said quietly in my ear so that the others couldn't hear. 'I never even saw you moving. Now the colonel here, he's a nervous fella, and he sees disaster round ever corner. But me, I'm more of a philosophical sort. I don't trust the police as a rule – I've had more than my fair share of run-ins with them – but I reckon I'm a pretty good judge of character. I had a pint or two with your man Sergeant Dobson the other night and I reckon we can trust him. I reckon we can trust your mistress, too. I see things getting out of hand here and us getting into even deeper water if we try things the colonel's way, so you go with her to the police station and I'll calm the colonel.'

'Thank you, Mr O'Bannon,' I said, leaning back and looking him in the eye. 'No hard feelings?'

'None at all, girlie. And call me Mickey. You did what you had to do and no one can hold that against you. Just don't go telling anyone how easily you took me down or I'll be out of a job.'

As he let go of my hand, Lady Hardcastle turned and left the encampment, heading towards the police station. I followed.

'What did Mr O'Bannon say?' she asked me as she knocked on the sergeant's front door.

'He expressed his admiration for my abilities. He also said that he considers himself an excellent judge of character and that he trusts you.'

'So I should bally well think,' she said. 'I'm the most trustworthy person in the village. I've met the king, and everything.'

'You have indeed, my lady.'

'What else did he say?'

'That Colonel Dawlish is a nervous nelly but that he'll set him straight.'

'In so many words?'

'I might be paraphrasing slightly.'

'I think you probably might.'

Sergeant Dobson answered the door.

'Good afternoon, Lady Hardcastle, Miss Armstrong,' he said. 'What can I do for you two fine ladies?'

'Just so as we're completely clear, sir,' said Sergeant Dobson, 'you think your strongman, Mr Abraham Bernbaum, is responsible for these two murders?'

'Yes, sergeant. I believe he locked Hubert Parvin in the lion cage last night and then crushed Augustus Noakes to death just after lunchtime today.'

We were in Colonel Dawlish's tent, seated on camp chairs, as Colonel Dawlish and Lady Hardcastle explained recent events to the sergeant.

'And you agree, m'lady?' said Dobson.

'Let's say that I have no especially strong reasons to disagree at the moment, Sergeant,' she said, guardedly.

'That's not quite as unequivocal as I'd have liked, m'lady, but beggars can't be choosers. I'll get over to the Dog and Duck and arrest Mr Bernbaum straight away.'

'To where?' said Lady Hardcastle quickly.

'The inn, m'lady. He's been over there since about eleven this morning. I was in there... ah... having a bit of a chat with Old Joe. He came in, ordered a pint of ale and sat there reading a book. Been there ever since.'

'But, sergeant,' she said, 'we've already spoken to several people here, and Mr Noakes was alive and well and tending to his beasts at noon. Bernbaum can't very well have killed him if he was in the pub with you.'

'That's very true, m'lady, I don't suppose he could now you mentions it. So where does that leave us?'

'Blessed if I know, sergeant,' she said. 'I find both murders hard enough to credit without having to imagine that they're not the work of the same twisted mind. If Mr Bernbaum didn't kill Noakes, I can't really believe him guilty of killing Parvin, either.'

'As you say, m'lady,' said Dobson, stroking his beard thoughtfully. 'And a man as has been sitting in a pub all day under the very eyes of the local police doesn't seem to have a guilty conscience.'

'All day,' mused Colonel Dawlish. 'Is he fit to perform?'

'That I couldn't say, sir. I can't speak for his mental state but when I left half an hour ago, sir, he was still nursing the pint he bought when he got there. He's not drunk, sir, I think he just wanted somewhere to sit. Not sure he wanted the beer at all.'

'Then please be so kind as to send him over. We have a show to put on. Is there anything we need to do as regards the... other matter?'

'No, sir, I'll get that all squared away. Dr Fitzsimmons is on his way to take care of the body and I'll make sure all the correct forms are filled in. I should report the matter to the Bristol CID but I'll take the reprimand for that failing as long as we make some progress in the next day or so.'

'Thank you, sergeant, I'll not forget this,' said Colonel Dawlish, standing up.

'Right you are, sir,' said the sergeant, picking up his helmet and rising from his own chair. He bade us all good afternoon and left the tent.

Colonel Dawlish returned to his seat and we sat in contemplative silence for several minutes.

Lady Hardcastle was the first to speak. 'There's still a murderer at large, George.'

'Yes, I know,' he said.

'They've already killed twice and they might again.'

'I know,' he said, more impatiently.

'Our main suspect is dead, and our outside bet has an alibi.'

'I know,' he said sharply and slammed his hand on the table.

'And if you care that passionately about it,' she said, sharply, 'then stop snapping at me and bally well do something.'

'What, Emily? What? My experiences of killers are a great deal more straightforward: they tended to be wearing the enemy's uniform and pointing a gun at me. And I dealt with them by pointing my own gun back at them and shooting first. I have no idea how to track down a lunatic.'

'Nor do I, George, nor do I. But I strongly suggest that action trumps moping. Eight members of the group of friends remain. Do they take an afternoon break before the show?'

'They usually gather in the mess tent at about four o'clock for afternoon tea. I doubt they'll all be there today, though, not after what's happened.'

'Then it's up to you to make sure they are. It's something to do with that group, George, and I'd wager the killer is either among them or known to them. We need to get them talking.' She stood. 'Up you get, George. We'll take a stroll round the camp and meet you in the mess tent at four o'clock. Come on, Flo.'

We left Colonel Dawlish standing by his desk, tapping his fingers and looking as dejected as I've ever seen a man look.

Our tour of the circus brought us precious little new information. Both victims, as is so often the way with the recently deceased, were universally loved and admired. Circus folk, we found, are as superstitious and sentimental as sailors and we didn't hear a word spoken against them.

Of the rest, it seemed that Veronica and Wilfred, the married couple from the sideshow, were "a bit stand-offish, you know, keep very much to themselves" but for two people who earned their living as "freaks" that was scarcely a revelation. I'm sure I'd keep very much to myself if everyone I met was there only to gawp and mock.

Strongman Abraham Bernbaum was widely liked and respected, as much for his gentle wisdom as for his warm, kind sense of humour. He was the man people went to for advice and it was always freely given and gratefully received. He had, so the story went, begun training as a rabbi in his youth, but something happened and he had turned instead to the world of entertainment. "The synagogue's loss was our gain, I reckon," was the consensus.

Genial joker and clown Jonas Grafton divided opinion. Some saw him as quite the funniest and most loveable man they had ever laid eyes on, while others knew him as melancholy and given to sentimental brooding. It was widely known that he had a long-standing, unrequited infatuation with Sabine Mathieu and that was interpreted by some as the cause of much of the recent brooding. One person told us that he had written her some awful poetry, and had earned himself a fair amount of leg pulling from his friends when they found out. But all of that seemed to me entirely in keeping with the stereotypical image of the clown, so I for one didn't feel much better informed there, either.

Prudence Hallows, the trapeze artist, was elitist and a bit "hoity-toity" by some accounts, with "a vicious tongue on her when she's crossed", but those that knew her and her sisters – who formed the rest of the act – well, said that she was "an adorable, sweet little thing who couldn't do enough for you".

Pretty little contortionist Adeline Rosethorn was timid and shy, but was similarly kind and helpful and would, apparently, "bend over backwards to help anyone". We laughed politely and moved on.

Mickey O'Bannon we'd already met, and that left only the star of the dancing horse show, Sabine Mathieu. Beautiful women are seldom widely liked, and when they're also extremely talented and extremely French, they stand no chance at all. Sabine, we ascertained, was universally loathed. A native of Paris, she had that city's special talent for rudeness, which didn't help her, either, but there was, said everyone we spoke to, such an air of superiority and dismissiveness about her that, in the words of one of the stable lads, "I reckon if she met God himself she'd look down on him. And He'd be too frightened to say anything." Despite his obvious wariness of the woman, it was difficult to stop him waxing lyrical about her beauty and her skill on horseback once he got started.

It was approaching four o'clock so we left the stables and walked past the regimentally ordered living tents and caravans to the mess tent. Colonel Dawlish was already there and was pouring mugs of tea from a huge, ornate samovar for the four members of the gang who had already arrived. Veronica and Wilfred were sitting together, deep in some private conversation, with Mickey and Sabine opposite them, lost in their own thoughts. Lady Hardcastle sat down with them and I helped Colonel Dawlish carry the teas.

As we sat at the table sharing them out, the other four came in, led by Jonas. He and Adeline came to join us while Abraham and Prudence fetched four more teas and one of the plates of fresh buns that Babble had just brought out.

'It's been a hellish day,' said Colonel Dawlish once everyone was seated, 'but I don't need to remind you all how essential it is that we put on a good show tonight and get the punters talking about how magnificent, spectacular and incredible this circus really is. No matter how hard we've tried, news will already have got round about the murders so any of tonight's crowd that hasn't been frightened off will be here out of morbid curiosity. But who knows what might happen tomorrow; once the fuss has died down even they might stop coming.

But if we give them a show they can tell their friends about, we can have a full house for the week. You're the core of the show, you're my platoon leaders, I need you to spread the word, chivvy the troops. We can get through this if we stick together and do what we do best.'

'My girls, they are not affected by these things,' said Sabine, haughtily. 'They are the professionals. They will give the performance of their lives tonight. I guarantee it.'

The others nodded earnestly, but Jonas seemed lost in a world of his own and just gazed at the Frenchwoman with unconcealed adoration. Adeline had noticed Jonas's trance and nudged Prudence, who smirked. Her smile vanished instantly when Jonas came to himself and glared at her.

'The boys and I have been working on some new gags,' said Jonas, suddenly jovial once more. 'They need a little more work to get them perfect, but they've never been seen before so it might be worth trying them out tonight.'

'That's the spirit,' said Colonel Dawlish. 'Well done, you two.'

'The girls and I have been working on some new tricks, too,' said Prudence. 'I'm sure they're ready.'

'Wonderful, wonderful,' said Colonel Dawlish with boyish enthusiasm. I was sure he'd already forgotten why we'd wanted to get them all together, but it didn't seem right to try to disrupt this sudden burst of enthusiasm.

'I shall have one more bun, I think,' said Veronica. 'And try to continue to be fat,'

'And if I slouch I might pass myself off as Britain's sixth smallest man,' said Wilfred, reaching out and taking her hand.

The others laughed and for the briefest moment, the horrors of the day seemed to have been forgotten as the eight friends started planning an evening's entertainment. A burble of conversation erupted as more and more ideas occurred to them. Only Abraham looked forlorn. It was his equipment that had been used to kill Gus, and he was no doubt dreading having to go out and demonstrate his prodigious strength as though nothing had happened.

Suddenly, I had the most horrible feeling that we were intruding. Despite our promises to Colonel Dawlish to track down the killer, and despite our belief that he or she was somehow connected with this group, it suddenly seemed entirely wrong for Lady Hardcastle and I to be sitting with them while they tried to suppress their grief and save their circus. I caught Lady Hardcastle's eye and it was apparent that she had had precisely the same feeling.

Without saying a word, we rose from the table and left the mess tent. We walked home and it was only once we were safely inside the house that we began to discuss the day's events and to try to decide what we were going to do about our invitations to see the show that evening.

After much discussion, Lady Hardcastle and I had decided that we had no good reason not to go to the circus as planned. We joined the villagers and the visitors that mobbed the box office. Milly and Molly had been delighted to see us and had summoned a stable boy to show us to our seats in the area reserved for distinguished guests.

We sat with Sir Hector and Lady Farley-Stroud on one side and Dr Fitzsimmons on the other. I could tell that Lady Farley-Stroud was more than a little put out at having to share her exclusive spot with a servant, but I couldn't quite bring myself to care very much.

The show itself exceeded my expectations. The clowns, the elephant, the trapeze, the Chinese acrobats, and the wonderful dancing horses were even more magical than I'd dared hope. And the revelation of the evening was that Colonel Dawlish, in a tailcoat of hunting pink, wearing a silk top hat and addressing the audience through a polished brass megaphone, was the ring master. With jokes, outrageous exaggerations, and a line of patter of which I should never have dreamed him capable, he charmed the audience and whipped them into a frenzy of enthusiastic appreciation for each act.

By the time the show finished with the performers parading round the ring for their final bows, he was exhausted, but the crowd was enraptured. Even without the lion tamer and the circus's lead juggler, the show had been every bit as amazing as the posters had promised, and as we all made our way out into the warm summer's night, everyone was buzzing with the excitement of it all.

It was rather late by the time we got home and Lady Hardcastle had said that she had no intention of getting up at her usual hour and that a lie-in would be very much in order.

As is always the way when licensed slugabeddery has been offered, I was up with, if not the lark, then at least the lark's more lackadaisical cousin. Many a long-put-off chore had finally been completed and at least one cake baked by the time Lady Hardcastle rang from her bedroom.

I took her a tray with tea, crumpets and the morning post and soon afterwards she arrived downstairs in her dressing gown, still yawning, holding a letter in her hand.

'Harry has written,' she said. 'Ehrlichmann hasn't been seen in London for a few days, but his sources say that say he's been spotted in Portsmouth, probably trying to catch a boat back to the Continent.'

'So we shouldn't worry?' I asked.

'So Harry thinks.'

'I must say, it's something of a relief. Perhaps it's all over.'

'Perhaps, perhaps. But what's not over is this blessed business at the circus.'

'No. It was almost possible to forget about it for a while last evening, though, wasn't it. Tell me you didn't have the most marvellous time.'

'I confess it was rather more enjoyable than I had expected,' she said. 'Although I must say that slightly more enjoyable was your reaction to it all. I had no idea you were so keen on circuses.'

'Ever since I was little,' I said. 'I've not been keeping it a secret, it's just never come up before. What was your favourite part?'

She laughed. 'I enjoyed it all, but if I'm completely honest my favourite part was when the Chinese acrobat told that filthy joke in Mandarin.'

I grinned. 'Lady Farley-Stroud wondered what he was saying and I briefly considered translating for her, just to see which part of her exploded first.'

'You made a wise choice not to, I think. Although I do wonder if she'd have known what it all meant even if he'd told it in English. She doesn't look the type to go in for all that nasty, messy business, somehow.'

It was my turn to laugh.

'I think perhaps we ought to give some more thought to the murders, though,' she said. 'Perhaps more tea and crumpets and a look at the board, do you think? I'll get dressed while you ready the sustaining comestibles.'

A quarter of an hour later we were in the dining room revising the crime board.

'There just doesn't seem to be any reason for it all,' said Lady Hardcastle. 'I mean to say, what had those two men got in common aside from their membership of this inner circus circle? There must be some connection, don't you think? Or does that mean it must be someone from outside the group?'

'There's nothing I can see, my lady. I can see a reason for Noakes to kill Parvin, and for Bernbaum to kill Noakes. But Bernbaum was nowhere near the circus when he died and anyway that would mean two killers instead of one.'

'Hmm. How about–'

The doorbell rang.

It was one of the stable lads from the circus with a note from Colonel Dawlish. I gave the lad a ha'penny and took the note through to Lady Hardcastle who was still sitting in the dining room, staring at the board.

'He says, "Dearest Ems…" I do wish he'd not call me that. Emily's quite an easy name to say. Persephone, now that's quite tricky. I knew a Persephone when I was young. We called her Percy. Quite an unfortunately hairy girl. Married a clergyman, I believe…'

'"Dearest Ems",' I repeated, trying to get her back on track.

'Quite so, dear. "Dearest Ems…" Do you know, it's not like he's always done it. It's not like it's an old pet name from when we were younger. He's only started recently…'

'"Dearest Ems",' I said, slightly more firmly than perhaps I should.

'All right, pet, don't get agitated. "Dearest Ems, Thank you so much for coming last night and bringing such an enthusiastic local crowd with you. Box Office takings were our highest ever for an opening night and we've sold out for the rest of the week. I do hope you enjoyed yourselves. Would you both care to come over for elevenses and we can discuss your progress with the case before the rozzers start to get too overwrought? Shall we say eleven o'clock? That's when we usually have our elevenses. Perhaps that's why they're called that. There shall be coffee. And cake. Or perhaps biscuits. I'll speak to Babble. See you soon, love Georgie." There, now, you see, "Georgie", that's what I used to call him. I just don't know where Ems has come from.'

I looked at the clock on the mantel. 'It's a quarter-to already, my lady.'

'So it is. He doesn't give a lady much notice with his invitations, does he? Heigh-ho. Hats, gloves, and best feet forwards. I wish I hadn't had that extra crumpet now, I rather like Babble's cakes. It seems to be drizzling. Umbrellas will be needed.'

'Lady Hardcastle...'

'...and Miss Armstrong. How absolutely...'

'...lovely to see you...'

'...both.'

Milly and Molly were already working in the box office. I could just about see through the window that they were each doing something beneath the counter and went in for a closer look. They were knitting.

'Good morning, ladies,' I said. 'What are you knitting?'

'Baby...' said Milly.

'...bootees,' finished Molly.

'One each. It gets so...'

'...boring to have to knit...'

'...two of them.'

'They're for our...'

'...grand niece. She's expecting her...'

'...first in a few...'

'...months.'

Please pass on my best wishes,' I said. 'She's lucky to have such delightful aunts.'

'Great aunts,' they said together.

'Great indeed,' I said with a laugh.

'Colonel Dawlish is...' began Molly.

'...expecting you, he said...'

'...you know the way to...'

'...his tent.'

'We do, thank you,' I said. 'Enjoy your day, and try not to get too bored of your knitting.'

'We shall...' said Milly.

'...and we shan't,' finished Molly. It took me a second or two to work out what they meant, but they were clearly sharper than I gave them credit for.

We walked through the camp. Most of the performers and crew were still asleep so it was much quieter than we'd seen it thus far, but a few were beginning to stir and waved to us in greeting as we passed.

Colonel Dawlish was in fine spirits when we reached his tent and was already pouring coffee into tin mugs as we approached. He had tied back the flaps of the tent and everything within was in perfect military order.

Lady Hardcastle rapped on the tent pole with the handle of her umbrella.

'Come on in, Ems darling. Tent's open.'

'Thank you, dear.'

We ducked under the tent flap and sat in the comfortable canvas chairs he had waved us to. He brought the coffee and offered delicious-looking oatmeal biscuits from an enamelled tin plate.

He was boyishly excited. 'What did you think of the show?'

We gushed, gushingly. It really wasn't difficult to be very enthusiastic and complimentary. Lady Hardcastle told him the joke the acrobat had told.

When he had finally finished guffawing, he wiped his eyes and said, 'Those cheeky beggars. I always wondered what all that chatter was about. I thought they were explaining their great acrobatic tradition or something.'

'There was certainly an element of acrobatics involved,' she said with a grin.

He began giggling again and was about to say something further when there was a tap on the tent pole. We looked over and saw a grim-faced Mickey O'Bannon waiting to attract our attention.

'Ah, Mickey,' said Colonel Dawlish. 'Lady Hardcastle was just telling me what those blighters the Chinese acrobats are saying every night.'

'Filthy jokes in Mandarin, sir,' replied Mickey, flatly.

'You knew? Why didn't you tell me?'

'I was worried you might stop them, sir. I was rather enjoying them.'

'I see. Heigh ho.'

'Sorry, sir, but I'm afraid I've bad news.'

'Not today, Mickey. No bad news today, I forbid it.'

'Sorry, sir, but you'd better come. You, too, Lady Hardcastle. And Miss Armstrong.'

'What is it, Mickey?' asked Colonel Dawlish, his buoyant mood deflating rapidly.

'Just come, sir. The Big Top.'

Reluctantly, Colonel Dawlish put down his coffee and gestured for us to follow. We made our way in silence to the main circus tent and entered through a tied-back tent flap which led into the artists'... the artists' what? I wondered. It would be the green room in a theatre, I suppose; it was a sort of marshalling area where they readied themselves before stepping out into the spotlight to perform. We carried on through and I caught sight of Colonel Dawlish's increasingly anxious face as we passed a row of large mirrors. Presently we entered a canvas tunnel and emerged into the ring.

A small group of lads was clustered in a circle near the edge of the ring to our right. They looked round when they heard us enter and then shuffled aside to reveal something large and oddly glittery on the sand between them. As we approached I saw that it was a body in a black leotard with gold-sequinned trim. A few steps more and I realized with a shock that it was the large, muscular body of Abraham Bernbaum, twisted and broken, and very obviously dead.

Colonel Dawlish knelt by the body and touched the skin of his face. 'Who found him?' he asked.

'I did, Colonel,' said the young stable lad we'd spoken to the day before. 'I was just coming in to rake the sand for Sabine and there he was.'

Colonel Dawlish looked up at Lady Hardcastle. 'He's been dead a while, I'd say. His skin's cold to the touch.'

'The doctor will be able to get a better idea,' she said, 'but it doesn't help much. It just means he died in the middle of the night like Mr Parvin. It's unlikely anyone would have seen anything. Mr O'Bannon, have you sent for the police?'

'Yes,' said Mickey. 'I sent one of the lads off while I was fetching you.'

It seemed obvious that Abraham had fallen from a great height and I looked up to see where he might have been. Almost directly above the spot where he lay was one of the trapeze platforms.

'Ladies,' said Colonel Dawlish standing up, 'we need to talk privately. Mickey, take care of everything here. As it stands it looks as though Abe killed the others and topped himself out of guilt. Suggest strongly that this wraps things up but don't commit to anything. If the sergeant asks, we'll be in my tent, but don't volunteer it unless he actually does ask. I need to do some thinking.'

'Right you are, Colonel,' said Mickey.

We left the way we had come.

Colonel Dawlish had stopped at the mess to collect a fresh pot of coffee and was pouring it for us as we sat once more in his canvas chairs.

'What do you think, then, Emily? Suicide? Is he our man? Can we draw a line under all this?'

'It would be tragic but convenient, that's certain,' said Lady Hardcastle. 'He killed Parvin in the lion cage, stove Noakes's head in with an iron weight and then, overcome with guilt, took his own life by jumping from the trapeze. I know of an Inspector in Bristol who would be more than happy to close the case based on that.'

'But what do you think?' he asked.

'I'm still not happy with it at all. I don't pretend ever to know what goes on in the mind of my fellow man, but from everything I do know, murder is rarely without reason. Even the insane man kills according to his own private logic. But we have no reason to think that Abraham was insane, and I can see no sane motive for his having killed Parvin. If he bore any grudge at all – and the more I've heard about him over the past days, the less I believe him capable of even that – it was against Augustus Noakes, the lion tamer. We had our convoluted hypothesis about his trying to implicate Noakes in Parvin's murder, but I think that sank without trace when we found Noakes dead.'

Something about the murders was niggling at me, a half-understood idea that I couldn't quite place. And then, 'Oh!' I said suddenly, reminding myself of Veronica.

'Yes dear?' said Lady Hardcastle.

'Am I imagining it, my lady, or is there a pattern?'

'There are always patterns. Sometimes they're patterns we imagine, but there are always patterns. What's yours?'

'Well,' I said, trying to marshal my thoughts, 'The juggler was killed by lions. The lions were tended to by the lion tamer and the lion tamer was crushed with heavy weights. The heavy weights are part of the strongman's act, and the strongman was killed by a fall from the trapeze platform. The first two deaths are related to the second two victims. Do you see?'

'I think so,' she said, slowly. 'But how does that help us?'

'Well what if the trapeze lady... what was her name?'

'Prudence,' said Colonel Dawlish.

'Prudence, that's it. What if she were next? Did she have any grudge against Abraham?'

'Only of the vaguest sort. Prudence's brother was crippled in a fall from a poorly secured platform and the original story was that Abraham had been responsible for the accident by not checking the rigging as he had been supposed to. But the investigation found that there was a fault with one of the cables and that Elias Hallows had been too drunk to notice it when he went up there. It was nothing to do with Abe, but he was briefly blamed at the time.'

'Right,' I said. 'So Augustus Noakes had a reason to kill Hubert Parvin, and Abraham Bernbaum had a reason to kill Augustus Noakes. And now Bernbaum is dead and Prudence Hallows had a reason to kill him.'

'Hell's bells!' exclaimed Colonel Dawlish, jumping to his feet and going out to the walkway between the tents. 'Runner!' he shouted.

Within just a few moments a stable lad arrived.

'Find Mickey O'Bannon,' said Colonel Dawlish. 'Tell him to organize a search for Prudence Hallows. Immediately. I want reports every five minutes, and I want her found. Her life may be in danger.'

'Yes, Colonel,' said the lad and ran off as fast as he had arrived.

'I'm still a step or two behind,' said Lady Hardcastle. 'You're saying that the murders are forming some sort of bizarre chain of death?'

'Something like that, my lady,' I said. 'I think that the apparent motives for the murders are coincidence or smokescreen or something. I think it's the sequence that's important.'

'Then you're right to be concerned, George,' she said. 'We must find Prudence Hallows. And we need to find out who's responsible.'

'More than ever,' he said.

'Do you trust O'Bannon?'

'With my life,' he said. 'He was one of my company sergeants in Bengal.'

'And although I ought to suspect everyone, I can't seem to bring myself to think that it's you, so who does that leave us? The prize fighter is a trusted NCO, the juggler, the lion tamer and the strongman are all dead. The trapeze artist might be next. The fat lady and the dwarf could be in it together, but I'm beggared if I can think why. The clown seems more interested in the equestrienne than in anyone or anything else. The equestrienne herself is obnoxious but I suspect is more inclined to wound with harsh words than heavy weights. And the contortionist... quite the most charming and delightful little thing I've ever met. I know that doesn't rule the girl out, but she really is adorable. Don't you think, Flo?'

'She's the one I sat next to at dinner on Sunday?'

'That's the one.'

'Yes, she was very sweet. And tiny – I couldn't see her lifting that weight and dropping it on Noakes.'

'Quite so. But those are our suspects.'

'Then there are the one hundred and twenty-eight other members of the circus,' I said. 'We can't rule them all out. Then the people of this village. And Woodworthy. And Chipping Bevington. And strangers from anywhere the circus has ever visited who might have followed it here.'

'True, true,' she mused. 'But it's got something to do with this group, I'm sure of it.'

We sat in contemplative silence for a few more minutes and were interrupted by the arrival of the stable lad.

'Nothing to report, Colonel,' he said breathlessly. 'Mr O'Bannon says he's doing it systemagically but he's found nothing yet. He said to tell you that Sergeant Dobson has gone, too.'

'Thank you, Jimmy,' said Colonel Dawlish. 'Carry on.'

The boy disappeared again.

'If there's no danger of running into the sergeant and getting embroiled in official police doings,' said Colonel Dawlish once the lad had gone, 'we ought to join the search. You don't really think she's been done in, do you, Flo?'

'I don't think anything, sir,' I said. 'But if there really is a pattern, she's the next on the list.'

'I hope you're wrong, dear girl, I really do.'

'We all do, George, darling, but we'll never find anything sitting here. Where should we start?'

'Well,' he said, 'I imagine Mickey would have started from the Big Top and worked outwards, so we would probably go to one of the corners and work our way back in.'

'Then off we go. Servant, bring brollies.'

We got up to leave with Lady Hardcastle leading the way.

'Does she always talk to you like that?' asked Colonel Dawlish.

'Always, sir. Treats me awful, she does,' I said.

'You poor thing. Come and work for me in the prize fighting ring.'

'I can still bally well hear you,' said Lady Hardcastle over her shoulder.

We began our search in the corner of the camp we'd first entered on Sunday. When we'd seen it before it was just a collection of tents and caravans like any other in the circus but in the intervening days it had been transformed into a miniature, travelling Chinatown. Red banners, red ribbons, red bunting was everywhere. Golden letters embroidered on the banners proclaimed it to be the home of "Imperial China's Greatest Acrobats" with various other pictograms for prosperity and good fortune painted on panels and fluttering flags. Having sent me to squeeze between the farthest tent and the canvas fence in case there was anything there, Lady Hardcastle rapped her umbrella handle on one of the tent poles. There was no response from within so she poked her head through the flap.

'Storage,' she said. 'We'd better take a look inside.'

We duly followed and rummaged through the cases and duffels stacked neatly within. We found nothing, and as we emerged once more into the drizzle, we found ourselves face to face with the leader of the troop.

'Is something the matter, Colonel Dawlish?' he asked in accented English.

'Ah, Mr Liu, splendid to see you, dear boy. Have you not heard? We're looking for Prudence; we fear something may have happened to her.'

'What manner of something?' asked Mr Liu with concern.

'Abraham is dead and we fear Prudence may be next.'

'This is most...' he struggled to find the word. 'Vexing? We have been busy all morning with some new tricks, and I have heard nothing. I am saddened by the news of Mr Bernbaum. He was a kind and wise man.'

'Thank you,' said Colonel Dawlish.

'We didn't mean to intrude, Mr Liu,' I said in Mandarin, and his eyes widened in surprise, 'but if we're correct then Prudence is in terrible danger.'

'I'm sorry, my dear, but I don't think we have been introduced,' he replied in his own language.

'My apologies. I am Florence Armstrong and I serve as lady's maid to Emily, Lady Hardcastle. It is an honour to meet you.'

'And an honour to meet you, Miss Armstrong. I am Liu Feng. It is not often that I meet English people who are civilized enough to be able to speak Mandarin.'

'Lady Hardcastle and I spent several years in China. We first travelled there in 1895 and left in a hurry in '99.'

'You were there during the Boxer Rebellion?'

'We were. It was a dangerous time, but for other reasons. We fled inland when Lady Hardcastle's husband was killed by a European and then found ourselves having to hide from the rebels as we travelled overland to Burma and then India.'

'You are brave women to attempt such a journey alone.'

'We had the company of a Shaolin monk for much of the time.'

'Ah, and so you must be the lady I have heard about who threw Mickey O'Bannon to the ground.'

'I am,' I said with a smile. 'Our friend and guide taught me much on our trek.'

'So it would appear. I would be honoured if you would join my friends and I for dinner one evening before we leave. It would be wonderful to hear the story of your journey.'

'Thank you, it would be a pleasure.'

'Yes, Mr Liu, thank you,' said Lady Hardcastle, also in Mandarin.

'But stories must wait,' he said. 'Now we must find Miss Hallows. She is a great acrobat and she and her sisters have been good friends to us over the years. I shall get my troop to join the search.'

'Thank you, Mr Liu,' I said.

'Liu Feng, please,' he replied. 'I feel we shall be friends.'

'I do hope so,' I said, 'In which case you must call me Flo.'

'Thank goodness for that,' he said in English. 'I was wondering how I would ever manage to say Florence.'

We laughed as he bowed and went to fetch the rest of the acrobats.

'What was all that about?' asked Colonel Dawlish once he had gone. 'Did he tell you anything useful?'

'I just told him about our time in China,' I said.

'Oh.' He looked dejected. 'I thought from all the chatter that he was giving you some vital clue or other.'

'No dear,' said Lady Hardcastle, 'just chit-chat. I suspect they feel a little homesick. I think he was pleased to find someone who knew even a little of his homeland. He's invited us to dinner.'

'Has he, by crikey? And where's he gone now?'

'To fetch the rest of the troop,' I said. 'He seems very fond of Prudence and wants to help find her.'

'Then thank you for taking the time to chat, dear girl. Many hands, and all that.'

'Indeed,' said Lady Hardcastle.

Presently the rest of the troop arrived and we recommenced our own "systemagic" search of the camp. Liu Feng organized the acrobats and stayed with us, chatting occasionally as we looked through tents, opened trunks and peered into every nook and cranny.

'Something has been bothering me, Flo,' said Liu Feng in Mandarin. 'Were you at the show last night?'

'We were, yes,' I said.

'And you didn't happen to be outside, perhaps, getting a drink or a breath of the evening air while my troop and I were performing.'

'No, Liu Feng, we saw the whole thing.'

'Ah.' He blushed.

I laughed. 'Please don't worry. I'd never heard that one before. And it was quite an eye-opener. I never realized you could do that in a hammock.'

He blushed redder still.

'But I do hope we haven't caused any trouble,' I said. 'We told Colonel Dawlish and he seemed very amused. And Mickey loves them.'

'And I thought it was utterly delightful to be next to such prim old English ladies listening with such rapt attention to a speech that would have them spitting out their false teeth in horror if they'd understood it,' said Lady Hardcastle.

'I confess that's why I do it,' he said, with a mischievous twinkle. 'But I would die of shame if I thought I'd caused any actual offence.'

'None whatsoever,' I said.

'Gracious me, no,' agreed Lady Hardcastle.

He smiled and we continued our search.

Suddenly, there was a shout from our left and one of the younger acrobats waved frantically to us from outside another store tent. We broke into a run and raced towards him.

'In here, Colonel,' he said, holding up the tent flap.

We went inside and he led us to the farthest corner where there stood a beautiful mahogany steamer trunk. Gingerly, he lifted the lid and beckoned us closer. Inside was the grotesquely folded body of Prudence Hallows.

'My God!' exclaimed Colonel Dawlish.

'Who would do such a thing?' asked Liu Feng in English.

'A monster,' said Colonel Dawlish, furiously.

'But how did you know she was in danger?' said Liu Feng.

I explained the sequence of murders to him in Mandarin, as well as our thoughts about the group of friends who were at the centre of it all.

He nodded. 'That would mean that the next murder would be Adeline, the contortionist,' he said in English. 'And then you will have the set.'

'The set?' said Lady Hardcastle. 'What do you mean?'

'They were the five close friends from your group. The inner... clique, do you say?'

'Clique, yes,' she said.

'This is all news to me,' said Colonel Dawlish.

'When they were with you, George,' said Liu Feng, 'they were all one group, they were... united by your presence. But when you were not there, they formed different... alliances. The four victims and Adeline formed one faction. Then there is the married couple, Veronica and Wilfred. The other three are alone without the group. They are outside it when you are not there. Jonas tries to woo Sabine but she remains... aloof. Mickey keeps his own counsel.'

'Well I never,' said Colonel Dawlish. 'I've always prided myself on knowing my troops well, especially my junior officers. I feel quite ashamed never to have noticed.'

'There is no shame, George,' Liu Feng assured him. 'You knew what you needed to know to make the circus run smoothly and well. We have never worked in a better... atmosphere. You cannot know those things that they choose to conceal from you.'

'Thank you, Liu Feng. But we must take care of this poor girl. Can you send one of your troop to tell Mickey we've found her, and to ask him to inform Sergeant Dobson.' He turned to Lady Hardcastle. 'This has gone on long enough, Emily. I don't think I can insist on keeping the police out any longer. I should have listened to you sooner. These deaths are on my conscience.'

'You're not responsible, George, and we do need the authorities to be involved, but we might yet be able to catch the killer before anyone else has to die. By all means tell Sergeant Dobson and Dr Fitzsimmons, but our killer is still confident of getting away with it. If you close down the circus and get the CID involved now, he or she might just fade back into the background and we'll never hear from them again. There have been no real clues and no solid evidence that we can see, so we need to catch them in the act.'

'My lady!' I said, slightly shocked. 'You mean to use Adeline as bait? You'd put that poor girl's life in danger to catch the killer?'

'Flo makes a good point, Emily,' said Colonel Dawlish. 'It's a bit reckless to risk a girl's life to prove a point.'

'There needn't be any risk,' she said. 'You go to her now; I'd lay odds she's in her tent. Keep her chatting. Don't frighten her. But don't let her out of your sight until you hear from me.'

'And what will you be doing?' he asked.

'Armstrong and I will be having words with a sideshow attraction.'

And with that, she turned and left. I had no option but to follow.

'Where are we going, my lady?' I asked as I strode along beside her.

'What did you think of what Liu Feng said, Flo? About the group, I mean.'

'I'm not sure I thought anything very much. It's interesting the way that small groups of friends like that are made up of still smaller groups, but I don't really see...'

'What was it that the tuba player said about Mr and Mrs Carney? They're a bit stand-offish? They keep themselves to themselves? And why did we think that? Because they were always being mocked and bullied. And I'd bet that the bullies were the ones that formed the inner circle's inner circle. And now all but one of those bullies is dead.'

'You don't think...?'

'I'm certainly starting to. And that's why we're going to go and see Veronica and Wilfred.'

'Crikey,' I said.

'I just want to just stir them up a bit and see what happens.'

'And if you're right, they'll find my body in a ditch, shot through the head by a gun concealed in my hat.'

'And I'll be lying beside you, killed by withering sarcasm and a lack of proper respect.'

We had arrived at the caravan. Very few of the circus folk lived in caravans, most of them preferring the same sort of spacious tent that Colonel Dawlish occupied. But Mr and Mrs Carney were clearly caravan dwellers. And what a caravan. It was of the Romany type, covered in the most intricately carved, gold-painted designs. Even in the grey drizzle it was a magnificent vehicle but I imagined that in the sunlight it would glitter and gleam like a jewel.

Lady Hardcastle climbed the steps and tapped on the door with the handle of her umbrella.

Wilfred opened the door a crack and looked out suspiciously. When he saw it was us, he opened the door fully and motioned for us to come inside quickly. The caravan was surprisingly roomy on the inside and just as lavishly decorated as on the outside. I could see why they preferred to live there; it was a proper home.

Wilfred turned awkwardly and put something back behind the door as we entered. I thought I caught a glimpse of a cudgel in an elephant's foot umbrella stand as he took another look outside and quickly shut the door. I was on my guard immediately.

I wasn't much reassured when I saw that they were in the middle of packing to leave.

'Are you off?' asked Lady Hardcastle.

'Yes, my love,' said Veronica. 'We can't stay around here, not with all this going on. Three dead and Pru disappeared. Who knows who might be next?'

'Prudence is dead.'

Veronica let out a little scream, an oddly girlish sound from such a large lady. 'Oh no! How? No, don't tell me. No, I have to know. Was it as horrible as the others?'

'It wasn't obvious but I'd guess she was strangled,' said Lady

Hardcastle. 'But it's the way the scene was dressed that caught everyone's attention. She'd been quite brutally folded up – ligaments snapped and bones broken, I shouldn't wonder – to force her into a tiny space in a steamer trunk.'

Veronica whitened and sat heavily on a stool. 'Oh my goodness!' she said. 'Contorted. Where's Addie?'

'You tell me,' said Lady Hardcastle, coldly.

Veronica just sat there, mouth agape.

'Have a care, Lady Hardcastle,' said Wilfred, menacingly. 'You might be a Lady, and you might be a friend of Colonel Dawlish, but you can't come into our home and accuse us of murdering our friends.'

Lady Hardcastle turned to him. 'And yet your wife knows exactly who the next victim is expected to be.'

Wilfred laughed bitterly. 'It doesn't take a murderer or a Cambridge graduate to work it out, my lady,' he said. 'Pru was contorted. The next victim will be the contortionist. We're circus freaks, not idiots. And because we're not idiots, we're getting out before you find Addie with her legs chopped off to make her into a dwarf or stuffed to make her fat.'

Lady Hardcastle was clearly stumped. She had become certain of their involvement but that certainty was evaporating quickly now that she had actually confronted them. I had not been so convinced of their guilt, and I was even less sure now in the face of their seemingly genuine distress at being accused.

'May I sit?' she said, almost meekly.

Wilfred indicated a chair beside a small fold-away table.

'My apologies to you both,' she said after a moment's pause. 'I jumped to a conclusion. Perhaps more than one.'

'More than one, dear?' said Veronica, dabbing her eyes with an embroidered handkerchief.

'The victims so far,' said Lady Hardcastle. 'We've heard them described as "the inner circle's inner circle".'

'That would be about right,' said Wilfred. 'They were very tight, that lot.'

'It seemed logical to me that they'd been bullying you. We heard that you kept to yourselves. I thought it was for protection, to get away from them.'

Wilfred laughed. 'Not us. It's true that we keep to ourselves, but we like it that way. We enjoy the company of our friends, but we enjoy our own company just as much, don't we, Ron?'

'We do, Wilf, we do.'

They looked fondly at each other and I wondered if I'd ever seen a couple so much in love. It was an oddly touching moment in the midst of all the chaos and death.

'But they never bothered us,' said Wilfred.

'No, love, it was never us,' agreed Veronica.

'But they were picking on someone?' I asked.

'They were always picking on someone, dear,' she said. 'You know what gangs are like. Teasing the stable boys for getting things wrong, teasing the trumpeter when he fell off his chair...'

'You've got to admit that was rather funny,' said Wilfred.

'It was,' she conceded.

'But was there anyone specific,' asked Lady Hardcastle. 'Had they gone too far, made someone angry?'

'Well,' said Veronica, tentatively.

'What is it, my love?' asked Wilfred.

'The poems,' she said.

'Poems?' said Lady Hardcastle.

'The poems Jonas wrote for Sabine,' said Veronica.

'What about them?' I asked. I remembered someone saying something about poetry while we were asking around the day before.

'You must have noticed,' said Veronica, 'that poor old Jonas is absolutely smitten with Sabine. Really head-over-heels. He absolutely idolizes her. "Worships" might be a better way of saying it.'

'There is a certain obvious attraction there,' said Lady Hardcastle. 'He was certainly gazing at her rather longingly at dinner on Sunday night.'

'Longingly, love? Obsessively more like. He's been like it for months. Just took it into his head one day that she was the only girl for him and set about trying to woo her. But of course, she's the snootiest sort you're ever likely to meet. Heartbreakingly beautiful, and oh, you should see what she can make those horses do – well, of course you did, didn't you, you were at the show last night – but so difficult to get close to. She treated everyone like something the cat had sicked up.

'So of course, she just spurns his advances, tells him there's no way someone like her could ever love a "mere clown", and takes no more notice of him. But that just made him more determined. The gang, the... the... murdered ones,' she whispered the word "murdered", 'they took the rise out of him something shocking. Thought it was hilarious, they did. But he didn't seem to take any notice, he just tried to think of new ways to impress her.

'Eventually he decides that he has to prove he's serious, prove that he's not just some clown, and he starts writing her these love poems. Now I'm no judge of poetry, love. I like a nice sentimental music-hall song as much as the next girl, but I don't know about proper poetry. But when I heard some of what he wrote, even I knew they were awful.'

'How did you hear them?' I asked.

'That's what I was getting to, love,' she said. 'We usually eat breakfast in here. We've got our little stove and we make ourselves a little something and eat on our own. But on moving days we like to pack up all our things and leave it to the boys in the mess to clear up after us. So on Saturday morning when we were leaving Worcester, we got up early, squared everything away in here Bristol fashion and went to the mess together. We got there to find our usual table in an uproar. "The gang" were passing round sheets of foolscap, reading things out and laughing. Really laughing. Cruel, mocking laughter. When we got there we asked what was going on and Pru told us that they'd found the poems Jonas was writing to Sabine. Jonas was there himself. Sitting silently at the table. Almost catatonic he was, like he was in shock. He wasn't trying to stop them, he just sat there, letting them laugh at him.

'Of course, we tried to stop them. I tried to make them see what they were doing, but they wouldn't. Abe was doing his best, too, but you could see even he was amused by it all. We tried to take Jonas away, to get him out of there, but he wouldn't have it, he just sat there staring off into the distance like his mind had gone.'

'What happened then?' asked Lady Hardcastle.

'I couldn't stay, could I, Wilf? It was quite disturbing. So we got some bread rolls, and coffee, and some eggs, and sausages, and a few rashers of bacon, some mushrooms, a few tomatoes, and came back here to our own place.'

'And what happened to Jonas?'

'Next we saw him was when we were pitching here on the green, and he was right as ninepence. Never seen a man in a better mood. It was like it never happened and we forgot all about it.'

She lapsed into silence and we were all lost in thought for a moment.

'I really don't think that he did, though,' said Lady Hardcastle at length. 'I don't think you're in any danger, though. Please don't leave.'

They looked apprehensive.

'I had the beginnings of a plan to trap the killer when I believed it was you,' she went on. 'And now I have an idea how we can bring an end to all this once and for all. I need to speak to Colonel Dawlish urgently.' She paused. 'Would you be prepared to help?'

'Oh,' said Veronica. 'I don't think...'

'We must, my love,' said Wilfred. He looked up at me. 'I heard what you did to Mickey yesterday. Can I trust you to protect my lady as fiercely as you protect yours?'

'Upon my honour,' I said. 'Nothing will happen to any of you while you're with me.'

'That's good enough for me,' he said, and offered me his hand.

'Thank you,' said Lady Hardcastle. 'We must lose no more time. Colonel Dawlish is probably with Adeline in her tent. Can you take us there?'

'Come with me,' said Wilfred, and we followed him out of the caravan and back into the drizzle.

It was rather crowded in Adeline's tent by the time we'd all crammed in there. Adeline herself was sitting on her bed with her knees drawn up to her chin, looking even more childlike than usual. Colonel Dawlish was sitting in her chair, with the trusty Mickey O'Bannon perched on the table beside him. Lady Hardcastle, Wilfred, Veronica and I filled all the available floor space as Lady Hardcastle tried to explain her plan as clearly, but as quietly, as she could.

'The thing is,' said Mickey, 'he can't possibly not have noticed all the activity this afternoon. He must have known we were looking for Pru. Why isn't he just going to lie low and keep himself safe?'

'Because that would be the act of a rational man, Mickey,' said Lady Hardcastle. 'After the events of the past two days I think it's safe to say that he's no longer sane. Something inside him broke on

Saturday morning.'

'Then it's just as bad. If he's mad, he's not predictable.'

'I don't think so,' she said, thoughtfully. 'I think that now we know what he's up to, he's very predictable. He's working his way through his tormentors one by one and he thinks he's invincible. He has been careful or lucky, but not cautious so far. And he's in a hurry. I think he wants to finish the job as quickly as possible. That means that Adeline is next and I think we know how he intends to try to kill her.'

Adeline gave a little whimper and Veronica reached out a surprisingly delicate and gentle hand to comfort her.

'How on earth do we know that?' said Colonel Dawlish.

'If we're certain that Adeline is the last of his planned victims, then he'll have come full circle and he will use some method peculiar to the world of juggling, the talent of his first. If you were to kill someone in the manner of a juggler, George, what would you use?'

'I suppose an Indian club would be the most reliable thing,' he said. 'But I'm sure an inventive fiend could come up with lots more.'

'He possibly could,' she said. 'But somehow I think it would have to be that obvious. There has been nothing oblique or obscure about his methods so far, no doubt about whom he was trying to implicate.'

'Fair enough,' said Mickey. 'But how does he do it? How does he get them where he wants them? We haven't found any notes, have we?'

'No,' said Colonel Dawlish, 'nothing like that.'

'So how is he trapping them? He wasn't ever anyone's best friend, but especially not lately, so why would any of them just follow him to their death?'

'I confess I don't know,' said Lady Hardcastle. But I'm sure we'll find out. Is everyone agreed that this is our only course of action? The police could never convict him on what we can give them so far. He's left no clues, no evidence; all we have is two witnesses who saw him being teased. It's as I said before, we need to catch him in the act.'

Adeline whimpered again and Veronica snapped, 'Really! Must you talk this way? You're terrifying the poor girl.'

'I'm sorry, Adeline–'

'Addie,' said the girl, weakly. 'I never liked Adeline, not since the song, anyway. People kept calling me "Sweet Adeline".'

'I'm sorry, Addie, but you understand that it's our only course?

We'll all be on hand to protect you. We shan't let him harm you.'

'I understand,' she said, and hid her face behind her knees.

'Well, then,' said Lady Hardcastle. 'Where would he most easily be able to find Indian clubs, and where would be the most appropriate place to kill someone if one were killing in the manner of a juggler?'

'The sideshow tent,' said Colonel Dawlish. 'Huey had a set of clubs in his own tent but everything there has been packed away. There are stage clubs in the "Jugglers & Acrobats" tent.'

'Then I suggest that that's where he intends to strike. Mickey, will you take Veronica and Wilfred to the "Jugglers & Acrobats" sideshow tent and conceal yourselves inside. I shall join you presently. Armstrong, station yourself in the storage tent opposite this one and keep watch. Be prepared to defend Addie if she is in immediate danger, but otherwise simply keep her in view and let things play out. George, go to the village and summon Sergeant Dobson and Constable Hancock, we shall need them at the close. Bring them to the sideshow tent and conceal yourselves outside with a view of the entrance. Be prepared to enter as soon as I shout. Does everyone understand?'

'What do I do?' asked Addie, quietly.

'You, my dear, must wait here. Somehow Jonas Grafton will contact you and try to lure you to what he intends will be your doom. Go with him, but don't worry; Flo will be watching you all the time, and once you arrive at the sideshow tent, we shall all be there to protect you.'

'Very well,' she said, and returned to her ball of terrified silence.

Lady Hardcastle stood and went over to Addie. She reached out and tried to stroke her hair, but the frightened girl flinched away and instead she signalled to the rest of us that it was time to leave and take up our positions.

I had found myself a packing crate to sit on in the storage tent and had positioned myself to one side of the tent's opening, completely concealed from an observer outside the tent, but with an unobscured view of Addie's tent through a brass-bound eyelet in the canvas.

An hour had passed and the drizzle had finally given way to weak sunshine. The need to remain alert had fended off the potential boredom of such a lengthy vigil, but I was very much wishing I'd managed to find a cushion before I'd settled into my vantage spot.

Despite all the disruption, the circus was still busy and a few people had passed along this little side street but amid these comings and goings, no one had called upon Adeline. I was beginning to wonder if we were wasting our time, but then the most unexpected thing happened. Walking furtively along the path between the tents, in jodhpurs and riding boots, was the unmistakably elegant figure of Sabine Mathieu. She stopped at the entrance to Addie's tent and looked quickly up and down the path before ducking through the flap and disappearing inside.

I moved to the entrance to the storage tent and strained to make out what was going on opposite but I could hear nothing but the faint murmur of two voices within. Presently, the two women emerged, arm in arm, with Sabine chattering away with the warmest smile on her face. Addie looked less comfortable, but thankfully had the presence of mind not to look across to my hiding place. I let them get a little way ahead and then slipped out of the storage tent and followed.

As predicted, they made their way through the flap in the canvas wall and from there directly to the Jugglers & Acrobats tent where they disappeared in through the audience entrance. I went round to the back of the tent and slipped silently into the artists' "green room". I was surprised to see the small space in such a state of disarray with the table and chairs overturned and a water jug and cups flung haphazardly on the floor; that was completely out of character for a camp run by the Colonel who insisted on military levels of cleanliness and order.

I approached the canvas flap that opened onto the performance area and tried to find a way to see and hear what was going on within. There was a little hole in the canvas, clearly made so that performers could check on the state of the audience before they made their entrance, and I looked cautiously through it to receive my second shock of the evening.

In the centre of the performance area were not only Addie, kneeling and trembling before Sabine who was now armed with a small revolver, but also the bound and seemingly unconscious bodies of Lady Hardcastle, Veronica and Wilfred. And there, pacing manically about and armed, as predicted, with a colourful Indian club, was Jonas Grafton in full clown make-up and costume.

'Come, my pet,' said Sabine. 'Finish her off. Finish what you started. They mocked you and they had to die. Let me see. Let me see what you will do for me.'

'It was all for you, Sabine. They laughed at me. They laughed at my love. They couldn't be allowed to get away with laughing at my love for you. They were mocking you. They didn't deserve to live.'

'No, my pet, they did not. And these others, these fools, you will not let them live, either. You will not let them endanger the great Sabine with their petty morals and their childish interference.'

I heard the faintest rustle behind me and felt a gentle tap on my shoulder. Without thinking I turned quickly and grabbed my assailant's wrist. I had drawn back my other arm to strike him in the throat when I saw that it was Colonel Dawlish. I relaxed and he put his finger to his lips. But it was too late.

'Is that you, Miss Armstrong?' said Sabine from inside the tent. 'Please stop lurking out there and come and join us.'

There was nothing for it, I had to go. Colonel Dawlish put his finger to his lips again and indicated that he would be there, watching. I stepped through into the miniature circus ring.

'You think so much of yourself,' said Sabine, 'with your hiding and your sneaking about. You think that I did not see you following me? You think that Sabine Mathieu did not know what you were up to? You stupid woman.'

I walked slowly towards her.

'That is quite far enough,' she said, levelling the pistol at my chest. 'Do not think me as stupid as that Irish thug to let you get close enough to strike. You will watch with me while my pet snuffs out another pointless life and then we shall decide what to do with you, your owner and these two freaks. I am sure my pet can be persuaded to find suitably imaginative ways of ending you all.'

'It was you all along?' I asked.

'*Mon dieu*, you really are stupid, aren't you. No, of course it was not me. Sabine does not dirty her hands with such things. There are always others all too willing to act for her.'

'You manipulated him?'

'This creature here?' she said, indicating Jonas. 'Oh yes. A simple matter. He's quite insane, you know. He had been fragile before, but his mind snapped completely a few days ago when I "accidentally" allowed his "friends" to see all the laughable poetry he had been writing to me. He was very open to the idea of revenge.'

'And you helped him?'

'Someone had to lure those pathetic so-called "artists" to him,' she said. 'Hubert was easy. He thought to taste the delights of the Great Sabine and imagined that I was excited by the presence of the lions. Gus? He was terrified that he would be suspected and was so grateful to kindly Sabine when she offered to go with him to the strongman tent to listen to his worries. Abraham was suspicious, but that stupid, sentimental man came to speak to me anyway and then of course he couldn't resist trying to help poor Jonas who was so upset by what he had done that he was threatening to jump from the trapeze platform. And Prudence, dear, sweet Prudence. She just wanted to comfort poor, frightened Sabine and saw nothing before Jonas choked her with a cord. He's very strong, you know. Even I was surprised by how easily he snapped and folded her body into that trunk.'

'But why?' I asked, utterly incredulous.

'Why? Why not? To see them die, of course. To watch the light of life go out in their empty eyes. Who were those pointless people? They were nothing. Who would miss them? No one.'

'It strikes me,' I said, rather more boldly than I felt, 'that you're the insane one.'

'Have a care, servant girl,' she said, waving the pistol. 'I have not killed yet, but your life is worth less than even these animals. "Poor Sabine was defending herself against the violent servant. You all saw what she did to Mickey. Sabine thought her life was in danger. The girl must have been working with the mad clown all along." A bullet through the heart will not be as poetic an end as the others I have witnessed, but it will leave you just as dead.'

Throughout all this, Jonas had continued his pacing but now he had stopped and was looking blankly at Sabine.

'Do you love him?' I said.

'Love him? Love... that?' She laughed. 'How could a woman such as me love something like that? It is nothing, just a tool to be used for the amusement of Sabine. It makes me laugh even to think of such a thing. Love Jonas Grafton? Never!'

She didn't see the club until the very last instant. Jonas had swung it with all of his considerable strength, aimed directly at her temple. As she caught sight of the glittering shape coming towards her, she turned, and at the instant the heavy wooden club made contact with her skull, she fired the pistol. She collapsed instantly, blood-soaked and broken, the life smashed out of her. Jonas looked down at his chest, and examined the spreading blood with evident surprise. Slowly, he too collapsed to the floor of the ring and breathed his last with his head resting on the lifeless body of the object of his infatuation.

I was too shocked to move, and the next thing I was properly aware of was Colonel Dawlish taking me by the shoulders and leading me to one of the audience seats. Sergeant Dobson and constable Hancock had come in through the main entrance with Mickey and were untying Lady Hardcastle, Veronica and Wilfred and helping them to their feet while Mickey took care of Addie.

Once again we were back in Colonel Dawlish's tent. Veronica and Wilfred were side-by-side, hand-in-hand on the Colonel's bed, with Addie beside them, while the Colonel himself, Lady Hardcastle and I sat in the canvas chairs. Sergeant Dobson was standing by the table, having left Mickey O'Bannon and Constable Hancock to see to administrative matters in the Jugglers & Acrobats tent.

'I knows as how you've all had something of a shock,' said Sergeant Dobson, 'but I very much needs to get a few things straight before I calls headquarters and tries to explain myself.'

'Oh, Sergeant,' said Lady Hardcastle, 'I'm so sorry. Are you going to be in terribly hot water?'

'Tepid, I should think, m'lady. Luke warm at worst. But don't you go fretting over that; it was my decision and I'll take the consequences.'

'I'll speak up if you need me too, though, don't forget.'

'I shan't forget, m'lady, and I appreciates it. So as I understands it, this Jonas Grafton was the circus clown, and he went on a murderous rampage, killing four of his fellow performers, five if you include the French woman, and all because folk was laughing at him.'

'In a nutshell,' said Colonel Dawlish.

'And this French woman, this Sabine Mathieu, she was his accomplice?'

'Not as such,' said Lady Hardcastle. 'She was more the instigator, goading him on. She helped in that she lured his victims to him, but she was mostly just an enthusiastic observer.'

'This really is most disturbing,' said Dobson, scribbling in his notebook.

'We feared for our very lives,' said Veronica, still close to tears.

'I'm sure you did, madam, I'm sure you did. Well, obviously we shall be needing formal statements in the fullness of time and the full story will have to be told in the Coroner's Court, but I think I've got it clear enough in my mind that I can square things away with CID.'

'I very much appreciate all your... indulgence, Sergeant. Thank you,' said Colonel Dawlish. 'I understand that it was all highly irregular, but you've probably saved the circus and I'll not forget. If there's ever anything I can do for you, you have only to ask.'

'Well, sir, there was one thing,' said the sergeant, almost bashfully.

'Name it.'

'Well, the missus and I would have loved to have seen the circus – she loves the circus, does Mrs Dobson – but see I never got a chance to get no tickets and they's all sold out.'

'Then you must come as my guest,' said Colonel Dawlish, expansively. 'Can you make it tonight?'

'That would be handsome,' said the sergeant, grinning.

'Tonight, George?' said Lady Hardcastle in disbelief. 'You're opening again tonight? After everything? Six members of your company dead, and the show must go on?'

'I think it's what they would have wanted,' he said, defensively.

'I think,' she said, 'that what they would have wanted was not to have been murdered in the first place.'

'No, love,' said Veronica from the bed, 'he's right.'

'He is,' agreed Wilfred. 'It's our way. They'll be looking down on us, shaking their fists if they think we're going to cancel a show just because they're not here.'

'It'll be our way of honouring them,' said Veronica. 'They lived for the circus and ended up giving their lives for it. We'll put on another show and give the punters an evening's happiness in their name. It's right and proper.'

'My apologies,' said Lady Hardcastle. 'I hadn't thought. In that case, Armstrong, you and I had better get out of the way. Good luck to all of you.'

She rose to leave and I stood, too.

'Thank you for your help, dearest Ems,' said Colonel Dawlish. 'We owe you as much as we owe the sergeant for sorting out this mess.'

'Oh, pish and fiddlesticks,' she said. 'As always we did nothing more than simply be here while everything happened around us. If we'd thought more clearly and more quickly, more lives might have been saved.'

'Nevertheless,' he said, 'you helped me to hold things together and it was your plan that brought an end to it all.'

'Think nothing of it, dear boy,' she said, kissing him fondly on the cheek. 'May I return the favour and invite you for elevenses tomorrow?'

'That would be lovely, thank you. Eleven o'clock?'

'I believe that's when we have them, these days,' she said, and after saying our goodbyes to the others, we left for home.

The next morning I was up with the lark's more energetically conscientious cousin, taking care of domestic matters and attempting to outshine Babble with the quality and selection of cakes and pastries on offer, when Colonel Dawlish came to call.

Lady Hardcastle had joined me in the kitchen and was chattering inconsequentially as I worked. At exactly the moment that the hall clock began to chime eleven o'clock, the doorbell rang. It was our guest, Colonel Dawlish.

'I think George is a good enough friend that he won't mind if we stay in the kitchen, Flo,' said Lady Hardcastle. 'I'm growing rather fond of the informality of it.'

'I say,' said colonel Dawlish. 'Eating in the kitchen with the servants? How common. Whatever will our friends say?'

'Watch yourself, mush,' I said, 'or I might have to slosh you one.'

'She will, you know,' said Lady Hardcastle. 'She's a terror when her dander's up.'

'I can quite believe it. Calm yourself, my dearest Florence, we shall eat together as equals. I say, did you make all this nosh?'

We had arrived in the kitchen and he had seen the plates heaped with treats that I had spent all morning preparing.

'With my own, delicate hands,' I said, curtseying.

I served the coffee and we sat together at the oak table.

'How's the circus today, Georgie?' said Lady Hardcastle as I poured the coffee.

'It might take a while for us all to settle back to normal,' he said. 'But last night's show was another triumph and the troop send their warmest regards. With extra thanks from Addie for saving her life.'

'I think we rather endangered the poor girl's life,' she said. 'But I'm pleased she's well.'

'Ronnie and Wilf haven't said much since they left my tent yesterday afternoon, so I still don't quite know what happened. How did you come to be trussed up in the middle of the ring?'

'Oh, it was sheer stupidity. I was full of my own cleverness and sent Mickey off to scout round while we bowled merrily into the backstage area, imagining that we could conceal ourselves behind props or furniture before Grafton got there. It never crossed my mind for a moment that he might be working with someone else and would already be there. He heard us bumbling about and sneaked in while we were trying to hide. He managed to cosh Wilf and overpower me before Veronica fainted and we were out of the game. I presume Mickey wisely thought discretion the better part of valour and awaited reinforcements. I came to on the floor in the ring just as Sabine was pointing a pistol at Flo and dismissing the rest of humanity as worms beneath her Goddess-like feet.'

'Might I just point out,' I said, 'that this is the second time since you moved to Gloucestershire that a madwoman has pointed a revolver at me. I shall have to insist on a rise if this sort of thing carries on.'

'Duly noted, pet, duly noted. I'd wager my Derringer-in-the-hat idea is starting to look a good deal less risible now, though, eh? What?'

'Your Derringer what?' said Colonel Dawlish, laughing.

'Don't encourage her,' I said.

'Nuff said, my curiosity is duly stifled. Mickey, as you say, was waiting for us to get there rather than trying to take them on on his own.'

'Wise man. Have there been any official developments?' asked Lady Hardcastle. 'Is Sergeant Dobson all right?'

'He seems fine,' said Colonel Dawlish. 'I went to see him first thing and it looks as though he'll get a stiff talking-to from HQ, but with everything wrapped up so neatly he doesn't think the coroner will cause any further trouble. He did have some news, though.'

'Oh?' she said, raising an eyebrow.

'Yes, he told as much of the story as he could to Bristol CID and a chap there – Sunderland, I think he said his name was – made a few enquiries. There was a flurry of international cables overnight and it seems that the late Sabine Mathieu has been of interest to the French, German, Belgian and Dutch police for some years.'

'Gracious,' I said.

'Quite so. Apparently there have been several murders in circuses across the Continent while she was there. There was never even a hint that she had committed the murders, but after a couple of incidents in Germany people began talking and she acquired a reputation as an "angel of death". I told you that circus folk were a superstitious lot and though they never actually suspected her of anything, she found it increasingly difficult to get work in the European circuses. That was when she came over here and got the job with us. Your Dr Fitzsimmons was at the station and he said she sounded like a "psychopath" I think he said. Some sort of brain doctor word for stark raving barmy if you ask me.'

'Well I never,' said Lady Hardcastle.

'Still, it's all done and done with now,' he said. 'No point in dwelling. I say, Flo, these scones are quite the most delicious—'

There was another ring at the doorbell. I rose to answer it and it was the postman with two letters. One appeared to be a bill from Lady Hardcastle's dressmaker, and the other a letter from her brother Harry. I returned to the kitchen and handed them to her.

'Oh, it's from Harry,' she said, having discarded the bill with an impatient huff. 'Do you mind, Georgie? I wonder what he has to say. He's been writing rather a lot lately and I fear there are developments afoot.'

'Please, darling, go ahead. Florence and I shall indulge in one or two more of these delightful pastries.'

Lady Hardcastle read in silence.

'Oh that's a relief,' she said at last. 'I rather feel that things might be improving. He says that his contacts in the British embassy in Berlin report that Ehrlichmann has returned to Germany.'

'That is good news,' I said. 'You must be relieved.'

'I am, pet, I am.'

'Ehrlichmann?' said Colonel Dawlish through a mouthful of biscuit.

'Don't worry, dear,' said Lady Hardcastle. 'I'll tell you another time. You enjoy your cake.'

THREE

The Case of the Missing Case

Life had settled into a rather comfortable summer routine since the circus had left. We had had dinner with Liu Feng and his acrobats where we had enjoyed genuine Chinese cooking for the first time in many years. Colonel Dawlish had called round for lunch, too, before they all left, but all too soon they had packed up and gone from our lives.

We'd been tied up for a week or so with police interviews and other official matters and had presented our evidence to the Coroner's Inquest, which had then been adjourned pending the results of investigations by the police surgeon. We had received a stern talking-to from Inspector Sunderland of the Bristol CID for attempting to take matters into our own hands, but the Coroner himself had praised our efforts and had said that in view of Jonas Grafton's obvious mental instability there was nothing that we, Colonel Dawlish, the local police, nor even the Bristol CID had they been called in, could have done to prevent any of the deaths.

And once all that was over, there had been a blissful period of summery calm. Lady Hardcastle had been on a few trips to Bristol and had engaged the services of a firm of solicitors there to take care of assorted business and legal matters for her. There had also been a fair amount of shopping, and the house in Littleton Cotterell was finally beginning to feel like home.

Lady Hardcastle had been welcomed into village life. That was terribly important to her, I think. The story of the capture of the "Killer Clown" (as the papers had rather unimaginatively dubbed Jonas Grafton – I preferred "Perilous Pierrot" or even "Utterly

Terrifying Murderous Red-Nosed Madman", but perhaps that's why I never managed to get a job with the press) had spread as rapidly as any story ever did in a small village, and she was regarded with increasing awe and respect as a result. I fared similarly well, it should be said, and found that my trips to the village shops took much longer than expected for a while as everyone, shopkeepers and customers alike, pressed me for details on the case and congratulated me on my part in the adventure.

Summer walks in the woods and fields continued, complete with more nature talks from Lady Hardcastle and my continuing inability to tell the difference between male, female and juvenile Great Spotted Woodpeckers (it has something to do with the red feathers on their heads, but I'm dashed if I can remember what). Our own walled garden flourished, and we often enjoyed our afternoon tea in the shade of the apple tree there. Actually, when I say "flourished", I mean "ran wildly out of control", but Lady Hardcastle assured me that the fashion was for "natural" country gardens. It seems that what I thought of as something akin to the jungles of Burma – an impression aided by the abundance of wildlife that seemed to be living there – was actually quite the most fashionable plot in all of England. I begged her to employ a gardener.

Lady Hardcastle had even entertained once or twice, hosting visits from her London friends who were as enchanted as we were by the chance to get completely away from society and hide out in a small house in the country for a weekend.

But society could not be avoided completely and so when the engraved card had arrived from The Grange, inviting Lady Hardcastle to celebrate the engagement of Miss Clarissa Farley-Stroud and Mr Theophilus Woodfield, she had responded immediately. She wrote by return to Sir Hector and Lady Farley-Stroud, saying that she should be delighted to attend and asking that they convey her warmest congratulations to their delightful daughter and her charming beau.

Her enthusiasm was genuine – she had always been fond of parties – though her admiration for Clarissa (whom she regarded as a vacuous ninny) and Theophilus (who was equally witless and who was possessed of slightly less charm than a blocked drain), was entirely, if politely, feigned.

A few days later, another letter had arrived from The Grange which had caused a strange mix of amusement and irritation in Lady Hardcastle.

'Well, of all the...' she had said as she read it at the breakfast table.

'What is it, my lady?' I asked.

'Gertrude Farley-Stroud asks ever so sweetly, and if it's not altogether too much trouble, whether I might see my way clear to letting her hire your services for the evening of the party. She says she's having some minor, temporary staffing difficulties – which as anyone in the village will tell you means she hasn't got the chink to pay for all the servants she needs – and would be so terribly grateful if she could make use of my "most excellent lady's maid" – that's you, pet – as part of the serving staff, etc, etc. Oh this really is too much.'

'I don't mind, my lady. It's a chance to be at the party, after all.'

'Yes, but I mean, really. It was a chance for you to have a night off,' she said, indignantly.

'It's not as though I could go to the music hall or anything. Village life is wonderfully peaceful, but the nightlife is the Dog and Duck. I would just have been sitting here reading. This way I get to listen to the music, eavesdrop on the conversations, have a sneaky secret dance in the corridors when no one's looking. I really don't mind.'

'I wouldn't get your hopes up for a handsome fee, mind you.'

'Then I shall have to make sure I eat more than my fair share of canapés and swig a few glasses of champagne—'

'Cheap, sparkling wine, I should think. Poured in the kitchens so no one sees the bottles.'

'We shall see. But it'll be fun. And it'll help them out; they're not bad people.'

'They're not. Very well, you shall be hired out like some agency skivvy and I expect as much below-stairs gossip as you can glean.'

And so it was agreed. Lady Hardcastle replied at once and, over the next couple of weeks, the arrangements were made. My own uniform was deemed suitable ('Which means,' Lady Hardcastle had said, cattily, 'that she can't afford to have one of her own shabby maids' uniforms spruced up and adjusted to fit you') and I was to report to the kitchens by four o'clock on the day of the party.

The day of the party eventually arrived and I was dressed in my very best uniform, cleaned, pressed and generally dandified as I helped Lady Hardcastle with her own preparations for the evening. She wasn't the sort of lady who was incapable of getting herself ready without help, but it seemed a shame not to do a few maidly things for her before I left.

She had negotiated with Lady Farley-Stroud for her chauffeur, Bert, to come and pick me up and I was just putting the finishing touches to her hair when the doorbell rang.

'That'll be your carriage, pet,' she said. 'Run along. Be good, pilfer as much free food as you can and, most importantly, gather gossip. I want to know the real story of the Farley-Strouds.'

'I shall do my utmost,' I said, and went to the front door.

Bert had already got back in the car and was waiting with the engine running.

'Hello, Bert,' I said as I got in beside him. 'I hope this isn't too much trouble.'

'None at all, Miss Armstrong,' he said. 'Fact is, I'm glad to be out of the place for ten minutes. It's bedlam up there, it is. Bedlam. Everyone's running about the place, setting up this, tidying that, moving t'other thing. Cook's shouting at the kitchen maid. Jenkins is shouting at Cook, the footman and the parlour maid. The mistress is shouting at Sir Hector. Sir Hector is shouting at the dogs. Miss Clarissa is shouting at Mr Woodfield. And I was thinking I'd be next in the firing line if I hadn't had to pop over here to fetch you.'

'Then I'm both grateful for the lift and delighted to have been of some help,' I said as we set off.

'I don't suppose you needs to go over to Chipping Bevington to fetch something for your mistress? Bristol...? Gloucester...? London...?'

I laughed. 'We should get up to The Grange, Bert. Maybe an extra pair of willing hands will lessen everyone's need to shout quite so much. And perhaps they'll all be better behaved with a stranger in their midst.'

'Perhaps, Miss, perhaps. But don't let them bully you into doing more than your fair share. There's one or two of my fellow staff members who does as little as they think they can get away with and still complains about how hard done-by they are.'

'I shall do my share and nothing more, Bert, I promise.'

'I think you'll be all right anyway, miss. I reckon a few of them are a little bit frightened of you after all them things you did.'

'All what things?'

'Catching them murderers. And there's a story about how you threw that Irish prize fighter to the ground like he was a sack of straw. Did you really do that?'

'Well... I...' I stammered, bashfully.

'I knew it,' he said, with some triumph. 'So that's why them's slightly afraid. Little thing like you chucking boxers about. Make anyone nervous.'

I laughed again and he smiled back.

It was only a few minutes' drive to The Grange and we were pulling into the garage before I'd properly settled down to enjoy the ride.

'If you go in through there,' said Bert, indicating a door at the back of the garage, 'that'll take you into the servants' passage round the back of the house. Go down the stairs and follow the sound of angry screaming and you'll pretty soon be in the kitchen. I'll be out here... er... adjusting the carburettor... yes, that's it, I'll be adjusting the carburettor if anyone asks.'

'Righto, Bert. Thank you for the lift.'

'My pleasure, miss. Good luck.'

I left him to his skiving and set off in search of the kitchen.

His directions, though vague, were uncannily helpful. The passageway was easy to follow and the sounds coming from ahead were, indeed, the sounds of pots and pans being clattered about and of Mrs Brown, the cook, screeching invectives at the top of her formidable voice. Someone in the kitchen was not having a happy time of it at all.

I decided that any show of timidity, even polite deference, would most certainly be my undoing and would see me badgered, nagged, hounded, and generally put-upon for the remainder of the day. The strict hierarchy generally observed among household servants could be all too easily forgotten if one failed to assert oneself. With that in mind I stood a little straighter, breathed a little deeper and opened the kitchen door with a confident flourish.

'Good afternoon, everyone,' I said, in my most self-assured, take-no-nonsense, Lady's Maid's voice. 'How are we all today?'

Mrs Brown halted in mid-slam and stood with the pan in her hand, glaring towards the door as though her kitchen were being invaded. Rose, the kitchen maid, carried on with her chopping. She kept her head down and it was apparent that she was crying, but she glanced up and smiled gratefully at me for bringing her a moment's respite from the yelling.

'Oh,' said Mrs Brown, placing the pan on the range, 'it's you, Miss Armstrong. Come to join our merry band?'

'Indeed yes,' I said, breezily. 'I was told Mr Jenkins would need some help upstairs.' I had been told nothing of the sort, but I wasn't going to give Mrs Brown an opportunity to co-opt me into her downtrodden kitchen brigade. 'Is there somewhere I can leave my coat?'

'Rose!' she snapped. 'Show Miss Armstrong to Miss Denton's room, she can leave her coat there. Then come straight back here. No dawdling.'

'Yes, Mrs Brown,' said poor Rose, weakly, wiping her hands on her apron. 'Follow me, miss, I'll show you the way.'

As she led me through the warren of subterranean corridors, I tried to engage her in conversation.

'How long have you been working here?'

She plodded on forlornly. ''Bout two munfs.'

'It's early days yet,' I said. 'Things will get better.'

'Will they?' She was close to tears again. 'I never thought it'd be like this. I can't get anything right.'

'I rather think the problem is with Mrs Brown, not with you. She hasn't impressed me so far. I'm very much thinking of giving her a piece of my mind. All that shouting and banging. It's not on.'

'Oh, please don't make trouble, miss. You don't know what she's like.'

'I've met her sort before, Rose, don't worry. I know how to deal with the likes of her.'

She didn't seem reassured and when we arrived at Miss Denton's room she simply gestured at the door and scuttled off as quickly as she could manage.

I knocked on the door.

'Yes?' said an imperious voice from inside.

I opened the door and poked my head round. Sitting in an overstuffed armchair with her feet on a stool, was a plump woman with greying hair swept up in an unfashionable style. Her face was set in a scowl. 'Good afternoon,' I said, cheerfully. 'I'm Florence Armstrong, Lady Hardcastle's lady's maid. Mrs Brown suggested I might be able to hang my coat in your room.'

'Come in,' she said, more brightly, her face softening. 'I'm Maude. Maude Denton. Lady Farley-Stroud's lady's maid. Pleasure to meet you.'

'And you, I'm sure.'

'I half want to say no, just to prove that bossy old biddy wrong, but I can't take it out on you, my girl. Of course you can hang your coat in here. Join me for a cup of tea?'

'I should love to, thank you.'

'It's just brewing now. Fetch yourself a cup from the shelf over there, there's a good girl.' She indicated a shelf above the small gas ring. 'I gather you volunteered come over to help us with the party.'

'That's the plan, yes,' I said, reaching for a cup and saucer.

'What on earth possessed you to do something as silly as that?'

'Well, it was this or sit at home on my own for the evening. This way I might get to listen to the band, at least. And I'm not exactly a volunteer. There was talk about "hiring" me for the evening.'

She laughed. 'Don't hold your breath, m'dear. If any payment is eventually forthcoming it'll be grudgingly given and probably a penny or two short. Times is hard for the Farley-Strouds.'

'Ah well,' I said. 'I'm here now. Have you any idea what I'll be doing?'

'Hiding out here with me for a couple of hours is your first duty, m'girl. Then when the heavy work has been done we shall swan imperiously about the place doling out soggy canapés and cheap sparkling wine as though they were the food and drink of the Olympian gods.'

'That sounds like a workable plan,' I said. 'I don't suppose you have any biscuits?'

'Funny you should ask,' she said, reaching into a cupboard behind her. 'I happen to have snaffled a plateful from under Cook's eternally grumpy nose this very morning. Help yourself.'

It was going to be quite a pleasant day after all.

It turned out to be a most pleasantly relaxing afternoon. Maude, who revealed herself to be a game old girl, had been excellent company and had provided me with more than enough household gossip to keep Lady Hardcastle amused for weeks, but eventually we had been rounded up by Jenkins and assigned our party duties.

I was, as predicted, given the task of mingling unobtrusively with a tray of limp nibbles and warm fizz. Other than that we were to direct guests to the facilities if asked and to keep them out of the library, which had been given over to the band to use to store instrument cases and to relax during their breaks. It wasn't onerous work.

Clarissa had exhibited unaccustomed determination and had overridden her mother's original choice of string quartet, insisting instead that Roland Richman's Ragtime Revue be engaged – a London-based band of some repute – and had booked them herself at extremely short notice. Lady Farley-Stroud's disapproval had been loud and hearty, but she had eventually been persuaded that it was not, despite her firm belief to the contrary, *her* night and that the young people would prefer something a little more lively and up to date. I was grateful to Maude for telling me all this – it made Lady Farley-Stroud's loud exclamations of enjoyment and attempts to tap her feet appreciatively all the more entertaining.

Lady Hardcastle had made her customary unobtrusive entrance somewhere between the early arrivals and the stragglers and it wasn't until nearly nine by the hall clock that we spotted each other and she came over to ask how things were getting along.

'Not so badly, my lady,' I said, proffering my tray. 'Do help yourself to an over-salted snack and some champagne-style *vin de table*.'

'I see a career for you as head waiter at the Ritz with a line of patter like that.'

'Thank you, my lady. Have you been here long? Are you having fun?'

'Oh, you know how it is. I've been to better parties, but I've been to far worse. Oh, but Clarissa's London friends are quite fun. They seem to have adopted me as some manner of Eccentric Aunt figure so I'm not wanting for respectful admirers.'

'Not a racy big sister, then?'

'Sadly not. I think my Disreputable Aunt years are well and truly upon me. What of you? Have you knocked the staff into shape?'

'There's at least one I wouldn't mind knocking on her derrière, but all is generally well, thank you,' I said.

'Splendid, splendid. Oh, look out, here comes Captain Summers.'

'Bad news?'

'Frightful bore. Newly returned from India.'

'Ah, Lady Hardcastle, there you are. I thought I'd lost you,' said a suntanned, luxuriantly-moustached man of about my own age.

'What ho, Captain Summers,' said Lady Hardcastle. 'No, not lost, just mingling. Armstrong, this is Captain Roger Summers. Captain Summers, my maid, Armstrong.'

'Oh,' he said with some bewilderment. 'How d'you do.' He turned quickly away from me and back to Lady Hardcastle. I curtseyed slightly, but politely, and melted a step or two backwards, invoking the servants' mystical powers of invisibility.

'Is this what parties are like back in Blighty these days?' he blustered. 'Not sure I've quite got the hang of it yet. And this dashed awful music? American, isn't it?'

'It's quite the thing with the young people,' she said. 'Give it a chance, I'm sure you'll like it.'

'Bah. Give me a military band any day,' he said, dismissively. 'And this weather. So dashed cold.'

'Oh, you Raj types and your silly complaints. It's perfectly delightful weather.'

'You were in India, weren't you?' he said. 'Surely you noticed the difference.'

'I was in Calcutta for a year or two, yes.'

'What was your husband doing in Calcutta? Perhaps I knew him.'

'My husband died in China before I got to India.'

Captain Summers was embarrassed. 'I... er... I'm so sorry. I had no idea...' Sadly, though, he didn't quite know when to stop digging. 'But does that mean you were in India on your own? Gracious me.'

'Not alone, no. Armstrong was with me.'

'Well I never. Alone in India. I've never heard of such a thing.'

'Then this must be a very exciting evening for you,' she said, dryly.

'What? Oh. Well, I ought to circulate, don't you know. Got to put the old face about a bit. Try to be sociable and all that.'

'Cheerio, Captain,' she said brightly and turned to me. 'Insufferable oaf.'

'He's just a little out of his natural environment,' I said. 'He'll adapt soon enough.'

'We'll make a scientist of you yet, my girl. Yes, he might well adapt. Or become extinct. One can only hope.'

I was still laughing when Sir Hector came over with a gaudily dressed stranger. I melted into the background again.

'Emily, m'dear,' said Sir Hector, jovially. 'Are you having fun?'

'Enormous fun, Hector, yes. Thank you for organizing such a diverting evening.'

'Bah! Not me, m'dear, it's all down to the memsahib. I couldn't organize m'sock drawer, what?'

She laughed with seemingly genuine delight.

'But where are me manners? Lady Hardcastle, may I present Mr Clifford Haddock. Mr Haddock, this is m'good friend and neighbour, Lady Hardcastle.'

'Charmed, I'm sure,' he oozed in an unpleasant, nasal voice.

'How do you do,' said Lady Hardcastle, offering a hand which he kissed ostentatiously. As she withdrew her hand, I could see her mentally counting her fingers to make sure none were missing.

'Haddock's in antiques, don'tcha know,' said Sir Hector. 'Come to appraise some of me knick-knacks, what?'

Poor old Sir Hector had a charmingly naïve talent for indiscretion, and I could imagine Lady Farley-Stroud giving him her most terrifying Gorgon's stare for revealing their straitened circumstances.

'He's got some lovely pieces,' said the oily antiques dealer. He looked Lady Hardcastle up and down. 'And you look like a lovely piece yourself, my dear.'

Lady Hardcastle favoured him with a Gorgon stare of her own and Sir Hector, recognizing the danger contained in such a look, took him quickly by the elbow and began to steer him away.

'I'm glad you're having fun, m'dear,' he said, 'but I think we'd better circulate, what?' He led Haddock away in the direction of another small group of people.

'Another charming fellow,' said Lady Hardcastle as soon as they were out of earshot. 'Where on earth did they dig them all up? And why do they keep picking on me?'

'It's because you're such a lovely piece,' I said. 'You're bound to attract the nicer sort of chap.'

'Is a lady still allowed to flog her servants? I'm sure there used to be a law that said I could.'

'I couldn't say, my lady, but I think that might be frowned upon in this day and age.'

'Pity,' she said. 'Oh, I say, who's that chap?'

She indicated an elegantly-dressed young man of Indian appearance whom Haddock had engaged in earnest conversation.

'That, my lady,' I said, eager to show off, 'is Mr Bikash Verma, emissary of the King of Nepal and best friend of the prince.'

'Gracious,' she said, though whether she was impressed more by his exoticism or my own knowledge I couldn't tell. 'I never knew the Farley-Strouds were so well connected.'

'I believe he's an acquaintance of Miss Clarissa,' I said. 'Through one of her London friends.'

'Well I never. It might yet turn out to be an intriguing evening,' she said. She took a sip of her drink and grimaced. 'I say, be a love and see if you can't find me something nicer to drink. I bet he's hidden the good stuff somewhere. Have a scout round and see if you can find me a brandy. I shall turn quite green if I have to sip any more of this sparkling cooking wine.'

'Yes, my lady. I shall see what I can lay my hands on.'

The ballroom opened directly into the main entrance hall and I crossed to the corridor to the left of the grand staircase, on my way to the library. I had no real idea where to begin looking for brandy, but I wondered if the decanters full of the "good stuff" might be stashed in the one room where guests were expressly forbidden to go.

I arrived at the library door and reached for the handle and was startled to feel it pulled from my grasp by someone opening the door from within.

'Oh, I say,' said a strikingly pretty young woman. 'I'm so terribly sorry. Didn't mean to startle you. Just fetching something from my bag. Didn't expect there to be anyone about.'

'Please don't worry, madam,' I said, thinking frantically. 'I was just... checking that no guests had wandered into the library to interfere with the band's things.'

'It's all safe and well, thank you. We're being well looked after.'

And then I realized who she was. This was Sylvia Montgomery, the singer with the ragtime band.

'I'm pleased to hear it, madam. May I say I'm enjoying the music very much. You're very good.'

'Why thank you, you're very kind. I say, you couldn't do a girl another kindness and tell me where I might find some decent booze, could you? I'm absolutely parched and champagne gives me a headache.'

'Oh,' I said, somewhat disappointed. 'I'd been hoping to find something in there. I'm not actually on the staff here, I work for one of the Farley-Strouds' neighbours.'

'Come to steal their booze, eh? Don't worry, I'll not let on.'

I laughed. 'Yes, my mistress sent me in search of brandy. The sparkling wine isn't agreeing with her.'

'I know how she feels, but I'm afraid you're out of luck here, old thing. I turned the library upside down but there's not a drop to be had. He's got one of those old fashioned globe whatnots in there – you know the sort that opens up – but he's taken all the liquor out.'

'How very disappointing,' I said. 'Heigh ho, I shall have to continue my search elsewhere. The household servants are bound to know where I can find something.'

'Bound to.' She made to leave. 'If you manage to track any down – scotch, brandy, even gin at a pinch – see if you can't smuggle some onto the stage for us. We'll make it worth your while.' And with that she breezed off down the corridor, back towards the ballroom.

I walked in the other direction and went through the door that led downstairs to the servants' domain.

Miss Denton's door was shut, but there was a light coming from under the door. I knocked. There was a clatter of hasty tidying and then the imperious voice. 'Yes?'

I opened the door and poked my head in. 'What ho, Maude,' I said. 'Don't mean to intrude.'

'Flo!' she said with evident relief. 'You frightened the blessed life out of me. I thought you were old Jenkins come snooping.'

'You're hiding out?' I asked, not terribly impressed by the idea of hiding in the first place one might be expected to be.

'Just a quick break, don'tcha know,' she said, gesturing towards the half-concealed glass on the side table. 'A girl needs to wet her whistle.'

'She does indeed. Is that brandy, by any chance?'

'The very best,' she said, proudly. 'They hide it in here when they have guests.'

'Well that's a stroke of luck. I don't suppose you can spare a drop? My mistress is desperate for something to take the taste of the fizz away.'

'I expect we can sort her out, my dear,' she said, slightly slurred. 'They've not quite got round to marking the decanter. Not yet, at least. Fetch a glass from the shelf and we'll transfer it to something more elegant upstairs.'

I did as she asked and left her to her brandy-fuelled shirking, wondering if anyone actually did any work in this household. Perhaps Mrs Brown had a right to be angry after all if she were the only one of them doing her job.

I set off once more for the ballroom. I was wary lest I should be caught smuggling contraband cognac back to Lady Hardcastle in a servant's glass but I encountered no one. I had to check my step a little as I rounded a corner and heard the library door closing, but whoever it was was on their way into the room and I decided that it was none of my concern. It did remind me that I'd been asked to undertake a little more smuggling on behalf of the musicians, but I really couldn't face going all the way back to Old Ma Lushington and trying to snaffle some scotch from her secret stash. And when it came right down to it, she was responsible for the booze, and as idle as I was beginning to think her, I didn't really want to get her into any trouble by pinching it. The band would have to play sober. If they could.

'Armstrong!' proclaimed Lady Hardcastle as I approached. 'You're an absolute gem. A proper little darling wonder. A servant beyond compare.' Evidently, the sparkling wine's unpalatable flavour hadn't actually been inhibiting her consumption of it overmuch. 'What?' she said as I proffered the cheap glass filled with its expensive cognac. 'No brandy balloon? I take it all back. You're a slattern and an idler.'

'It was all there was, my lady. Expediency is all in matters of larceny. Now if you'll just stop hooting I shall find you some more elegant glassware and you can move onto "the good stuff".'

'Quite right. Quite right. Your reputation is saved.' She swayed slightly and I looked around for a suitable glass. There being none to hand, I tipped the dregs of her wine into a nearby aspidistra pot – to judge from the vinous aroma issuing therefrom, I don't think I was the first – and decanted the cognac into the empty glass.

She was loudly effusive in her thanks and appreciation of my attentiveness, and I left her singing my praises to a small group of Miss Clarissa's friends as I once more sought out my tray of drinks and nibbles and set about serving as unobtrusively as possible and listening to the band. I had found a suitable spot just as an instrumental number ended.

'Thank you very much, ladies and gentlemen. We're going to take a short break now, but we'll be back in the jiffiest of jiffies.'

And with that, they put down their instruments and stepped down from the low stage one by one. Just my luck.

The trumpeter disappeared, presumably off to the library, but the others milled about, chatting to each other and accepting the congratulations and admiration of the guests. Roland Richman had been buttonholed by Lady Farley-Stroud. She seemed to be at about the same stage of uninhibited merriment as Lady Hardcastle and from the snippets I could overhear over the chatter she seemed to be bombarding him with comically ill-informed questions about the music couched in girlishly flirtatious language which should have been mortifyingly embarrassing but actually made me warm to her a little. It was good to see that the flame hadn't gone out.

Sylvia Montgomery sidled up to me. 'I say, are you the girl I saw in the corridor just now?'

'I am, madam, yes.'

'Any luck?'

'I'm afraid not, madam. I managed to locate the stash but it proved more difficult than I had imagined to liberate more than a glassful for my mistress.'

'Not to worry, dear. Nelson "remembered" that he has a little scotch tucked away in his things. He's gone to fetch it.'

I smiled. 'A generous fellow. He's the trumpeter?'

'He is.'

'He's very good. You're all very good. I'm so glad I came.'

'Then I'm glad you came, too. Thank you. And thank you for trying to see us right. It's much appreciated.'

She turned away and went back to her friends.

The rest of the evening passed all too quickly and I found myself getting busier as the party slowly wound down. I heard little of the band, but they seemed a little less lively than they had earlier so I didn't feel I was missing too much.

I did as much of the clearing away as I felt was my proper share, probably a little more if truth be told. Maude had deigned to pitch in but she was working painfully slowly and although it galled me to make things too easy for her, I didn't want the burden to fall too heavily on the rest of the household. In truth, they were probably used to it, but it gave me a pleasantly self-satisfied feeling to lift some of the load from the junior staff.

By midnight I was dismissed with grateful thanks by Jenkins, who assured me that my assistance wouldn't be forgotten and that help was always available to me at The Grange if ever I should need it. I shook his hand and asked if perhaps I might take advantage of his kind offer immediately.

'Obviously Lady Hardcastle isn't staying at The Grange, but we don't yet have our own transport. Might I trouble Bert for a ride back to the house?'

'Of course, of course,' he said with a smile. 'I'll have him prepare the motorcar and bring it to the front of the house. He should be ready in ten minutes.'

'Thank you,' I said, and went off in search of Lady Hardcastle.

I found her in the ballroom, sitting on a chair in the corner and surrounded once more by Miss Clarissa's young friends, including the handsome Nepalese man, as though by a circle of adoring acolytes. I could hear the familiar end of one of her favourite anecdotes about her adventures in China and was gratified to hear that my own part in it had not been diminished by the repeated retellings. I waited until we were safely concealed in the ox cart and heading for the Burmese border before discreetly signalling that I wished to speak to her.

'Well, my lovely darlings,' she said, 'I fear the time has come for dear old Aunt Emily to make her grand exit. My maid – you remember her from the story? She's the chap that broke that ruffian's nose. My maid seems to require my attention. If I know her at all well, she'll have arranged transport home. She's an absolute poppet like that. It's been wonderful to meet you all.' She rose unsteadily to her feet, saying her goodbyes to the excitable youngsters. The Nepalese emissary kissed her hand with elegant courtesy and expressed his desire to hear more of her adventures.

She smiled. 'Thank you, Mr Verma, it's been a pleasure to meet you. Now then, the rest of you, do have fun, and if you absolutely must get up to wickedness, do please try not to make too much noise; it alarms the old folk.'

With that she left them and walked over to me with exaggerated care. She suddenly remembered that she was still holding a brandy bottle in her hand and turned to give it back to Miss Clarissa.

'Thank you so much for finding this, my dear,' she slurred. 'It's just the medicine Aunt Emily needed.'

I raised an eyebrow, thinking I could have heard a little more of the band if I'd not been off on my own, now seemingly unnecessary, brandy quest. 'Bert is bringing the car round, my lady.'

'You, Flo,' she said, linking arms with me, 'are an absolute poppet. Have I told you that? I don't know what I'd do without you.'

I led her to the front door. We passed Sir Hector and Lady Farley-Stroud on the way and she thanked them for a lovely evening, kissing them both on the cheek. I managed to steer her out the front door before she went any further – I once saw her kiss her host, a rather diminutive Earl, on the top of his bald head to the eye-popping alarm of his wife – and poured her into the waiting motor car.

Bert took us home.

I knew Lady Hardcastle wouldn't even be awake, much less up and about, until quite late the next morning so I'd taken rare advantage of the opportunity for a lie in. Or tried to. By eight o'clock the indolence was too much for me and I'd risen, washed, dressed and gone downstairs looking for things to do.

By half-past nine, there was bread proving beside the range and I was well into the mending when the doorbell rang. I put down my sewing and went to the door.

'Morning, Miss Armstrong,' said Constable Hancock as I opened it. 'Is your mistress at home?'

'Good morning to you, too, Constable. She's "at home" in the sense of actually being here, but "at home to callers" I couldn't say. She was at The Grange last evening and is still lying in.'

'I know she was, miss. You too, I understands. That's the reason I'm here, in fact. Would you mind terribly trying to rouse her? I rather needs to speak to her. To you both, in fact.'

'Of course. Is there something the matter?'

'There is, miss, but I'd prefer just to go through it the once if that's not too idle of me.'

'Not at all, Constable. Please come in, won't you. You know where the kitchen is? There's some tea in the pot, do please help yourself and I'll try to awaken Lady Hardcastle.'

'Much obliged, miss,' he said, plodding obediently into the kitchen.

I run upstairs and knocked on the bedroom door. There was no reply but I opened it and went in anyway. She was still fast asleep and it took quite a bit of shaking to awaken her.

'Oh, Flo, do leave off, there's a dear. Let poor Emily sleep.'

'No, my lady, you have to get up. The police are here.'

'The police?' she mumbled. 'What, all of them? Whatever do they want? I hope they wiped their feet.' Her eyes closed.

I sighed and shook her again. 'No, my lady, just Constable Hancock. But he needs to speak to us both and I think it has something to do with The Grange.'

'If it's about the missing brandy, tell him I'll buy them a case of the stuff and then invite him to come back tomorrow.'

'I really don't think it's about the brandy, my lady, and I really do think you need to get up. This instant.'

'Have I ever told you how much of a bully you are, Florence Armstrong?' she said, groggily. 'Can't a girl lie in bed with a hangover once in a while without puritanical maids and officious policemen intruding on her slumbers?'

'You tell me all the time, my lady. Please get up.'

'Very well, very well,' she said, sitting up at last. 'Tell him I'll be down presently. Make tea. And eggs. Scramble eggs for me. With toast.'

'Yes, my lady.'

I left her to get up in her own time and returned to the kitchen where I found Constable Hancock sitting at his ease and sipping tea. He made to stand up, slopping his tea slightly as he did so.

'Please don't get up, constable,' I said, waving him back down. 'Lady Hancock will be just a few moments.'

'Very good, miss. Thank you.'

I gave him a damp cloth and he dabbed at the tea stain on his jacket as I set about making some breakfast.

'I'm making some breakfast for Lady Hardcastle, would you like some eggs?'

'Thank you, miss, yes please. You're very kind. Is that fresh bread I smells?'

'It is, but it's still proving. I was hoping to have it ready for lunch. I have some left over from yesterday that will be perfect for toast, though. I do love to bake my own bread. Do you bake?'

He laughed the heartiest laugh I'd ever heard him give. 'Me, miss? Bake? You are a caution. Whoever heard of such a thing? No, our ma always used to make her own bread, mind.'

'Most professional bakers are men, are they not?' I said, mischievously.

'That they are, miss. But most professional bakers are not policemen. Quite aside from it being a woman's work to bake around the house, I doesn't have time for no baking shenanigans. Baking.' He chuckled again. 'I shall have to tell the sarge about this.'

'Unless he thinks it such a great idea that he has you baking bread for his breakfast.'

His cheery laughter erupted again.

'Gracious, you two seem happy,' croaked Lady Hardcastle from the doorway.

Constable Hancock jumped to his feet. 'Good morning, m'lady. I'm sorry to call so early.'

'Nonsense, constable, it's already...'

'Ten o'clock, my lady,' I said, nodding towards the large clock on the kitchen wall.

'Quite so,' she said. 'Plenty late enough to be calling. So what can I do for you, my dear constable?'

'It seems we only ever meets when there's bad news, m'lady,' he said, apologetically. 'There's a to-do up at The Grange.'

'Oh dear,' she said, accepting the glass of water I'd just poured for her. 'What sort of to-do?'

'Seems one of the musicians died, m'lady.'

'Oh no, how sad. Was he ill? Was it unexpected?'

'I don't suppose as how he expected to be clouted round the back of the head with something heavy, no, m'lady.'

She sat down at the table and sipped slowly at her water. 'Gracious me. Is there anything I can do?'

'That's more or less why I'm here, m'lady. Inspector Sunderland has already arrived and asked if I'd come and fetch you both so as how you could give witness statements and such.'

'Of course, of course.' She looked more than a little fragile. 'I don't suppose,' she began with unaccustomed tentativeness, 'you have transport of some sort.'

'I've got my bicycle,' he said with a wink in my direction.

'Oh,' she groaned.

'Only teasing, m'lady. Sir Hector sent me in his motor car. Bert's waiting outside.'

'Oh, thank goodness. You're a wicked man, Constable Hancock. I think Armstrong is a bad influence on you.'

'Me, my lady?' I said, setting out plates on the kitchen table for the impromptu breakfast party. 'I am a paragon of virtue, I'll have you know.'

Constable Hancock began to chuckle but looked suddenly embarrassed and busied himself with the teapot and cups I'd just set down in front of him on the table.

'Relax, Constable,' said Lady Hardcastle. 'I think we can safely say by now that you're among friends.'

He smiled and poured the tea.

We ate hastily together, the conversation turning completely away from the "to-do" at The Grange and focussing instead on more mundane matters of village life. There would be a time for dead trumpeters and head-walloping in due course.

'Lady Hardcastle,' said Inspector Sunderland, 'thank you for coming. I'm sorry to have to summon you so early on the morning after a party, but you can understand the urgency, I'm sure.'

Lady Hardcastle had taken Aspirin as well as sweet tea and her light breakfast, and was already more like her normal self. 'Please think nothing of it, Inspector. I'm only too pleased to help.'

'Thank you, my lady. And thank you, too, Miss Armstrong. I gather you were both here last evening.'

'Yes, Inspector,' I said. 'I arrived at The Grange just before four in the afternoon and spent most of my time below stairs until around seven o'clock when the guests started to arrive. Lady Hardcastle and I left together at around half-past midnight.'

'Seven? Isn't that rather early for a ball? I thought these things began around ten.'

'They do, Inspector,' said Lady Hardcastle, 'in fashionable society. But out here in the country they prefer an early start and early to bed. To be fair, it was more of a soirée than a ball.'

'I see,' he said, clearly still bemused by the antics of the privileged classes. 'And you, Lady Hardcastle? When did you arrive?'

'At around a quarter past eight, I should say.'

'The invitations say "Seven O'Clock".'

'They do, Inspector. But, really. Who arrives on time at a party?' She often played the dizzy socialite when she was unsure of people; she found it kept them a little off guard. Give it a while and she'd be giggling and calling him "darling" and he'd either dismiss her as a fool or be taken in by her warmth and give away far more than he had planned. I'd seen it many times before.

'Who indeed, my lady,' he said stiffly. He'd met her before and was clearly not taken in. 'Now on the off chance that Constable Hancock has been the soul of discretion and hasn't already told you all the confidential details of the case, I'd quite like to explain everything to you. You've been something of an irritation to us down at Bristol CID over the past few months, not to mention a reckless danger to yourself. But I can't deny that you have an able mind and it's obvious that you take some manner of pleasure in solving these little puzzles so I'd rather like to see if you can offer any help on this one, most especially since you were actually here.'

Lady Hardcastle seemed slightly taken aback. The Inspector had always been courteous, if a little stern, in his dealings with us, but neither of us had ever thought that he had anything but contempt for our "meddling" (as one of his superiors had called it).

'Of course, Inspector,' she said. 'It would be a pleasure and an honour to help.'

'Quite so,' he said. 'The facts of the case, then, are that Mr Nelson Holloway, the trumpet player with...' he consulted his notebook, 'Roland Richman's Ragtime Revue – whatever happened to a good old sing-song round the piano, that's what I'd like to know – Mr Nelson was found in the library this morning at about six o'clock by Dora Kendrick, the housemaid, when she went in to open the shutters and tidy the room which had been used by the band during the evening before. Thinking him still drunk, she went to rouse him but on approaching his recumbent form, she found him "stiff and cold" with a "deathly pallor" and "lying in a pool of blood" whereupon she screamed the house down and has had to be sedated by Dr Fitzsimmons.'

'Is she all right?' I asked. I'd not seen an awful lot of Dora the day before, but she seemed like a sweet girl.

'She'll be fine,' said Inspector Sunderland. 'Not so fine, though, is Mr Holloway. The "pool of blood" was actually a tiny trickle from a small laceration on the back of the scalp, but it was enough to frighten the girl. Dr Fitzsimmons and I are of the opinion that he was struck on the back of the head with some sort of heavy, blunt object which split his scalp causing the bleeding but which also did enough internal damage to the man's brain to kill him, though not instantly. The doctor suggests that he would have been unconscious and breathing when the assailant left him. Death would have occurred some time later, and he estimates that he actually passed at around four o'clock this morning.'

'So we've no idea when the attack itself actually happened,' said Lady Hardcastle, thoughtfully. 'But the intention was probably not murder.'

'Very good, my lady,' he said, impressed. 'No, a murderer would have made certain that he was dead. But as to the time, we might be able to narrow it down a little. We have statements from witnesses that Mr Nelson was last definitely seen alive at ten o'clock when the band took its break.'

'That's when I last saw him, too,' I said. 'Miss Montgomery – she's the singer – she said that he'd gone off to the library to fetch his secret supply of scotch.'

'Oh?' he said. 'And why would she tell you that, I wonder? Establishing an alibi, perhaps?'

'Possibly, Inspector,' I said. 'But it all seemed perfectly innocent at the time. I'd met her earlier, she'd been searching the library for booze, and she asked me if I could find some for her. She came over during her break to ask me if I'd managed it.'

'I see. Why you? Why not one of the household servants?'

'All servants look alike, Inspector,' I said, indicating my uniform. 'How would she know I didn't work here?'

'Quite so,' he said. 'And you didn't have any luck with your search, I presume?'

I hesitated.

'She found me a little brandy, Inspector,' said Lady Hardcastle. 'But the Farley-Strouds had hidden all the good stuff.'

The Inspector laughed. 'Always the way in these big houses,' he said. 'But anyway, that leads me to believe that Mr Nelson was attacked some time between leaving the ballroom at ten and when the band started again at half past. If he'd been able to return, he would have, I reckon.'

'Did no one try to look for him?' I asked.

'Only the band would have known he was missing, miss,' he said. 'And once they'd started playing, there wasn't much they could do about it. They were already a man short so they couldn't very well spare another to go searching for the trumpeter, even if he was bringing the scotch.'

'I suppose so,' I said. 'I thought they sounded a little less lively after the break.'

'That would be why, miss.'

'Were there signs of a fight in the library, Inspector?' said Lady Hardcastle.

'Aside from the dead body by the bookshelves, you mean? Some. The room was in some disarray as though it had been ransacked. My guess is that the killer was looking for something.'

'And Mr Nelson caught him at it?'

'Quite possibly. That would certainly account for his being knocked unconscious and left on the deck while the robber fled.'

'It would indeed,' she said.

'So that's my working hypothesis at the moment,' he said. 'And my next task is to try to establish where everybody was during the course of the evening. I need to know everything you can both remember: where you were, who you saw, when you saw them, and anything else you noticed, no matter how unimportant you might feel it. Can we start with you, please, Lady Hardcastle?'

'Of course. I arrived at about a quarter past eight, as you now know. Sir Hector's chauffeur, Bert, was kind enough to bring me up the hill. I greeted my hosts, who introduced me to Captain Summers – a frightful bore recently returned from India – and then left me to his oafish attentions. I stayed with him for as long as I thought polite and then slipped away while his eye was roving elsewhere, and circulated. I spoke to Miss Clarissa and her London friends, congratulating the happy couple and whatnot. I had a bit of a wander round, bumped into a couple of the Farley-Strouds' friends that I'd met at a dinner party when I first moved to the area, and then finally tracked down Armstrong. We chatted briefly, then I was buttonholed once more by Captain Summers whom I managed to outrage.'

'"Outrage", my lady?' said the Inspector, looking up from his notebook.

'I revealed that I'd spent some time in India "alone" after my husband had died. He couldn't quite grasp how a lady might do such a thing.'

'Plenty of ladies end up coping on their own in India after their husbands die,' said the Inspector, somewhat puzzled.

'But my husband died in China and I made my own way to India with Armstrong. And then stayed for a couple of years.'

'Ah,' he said. 'Out of the ordinary, but hardly outrageous.'

'Not to Captain Summers. He very quickly found someone else to badger. Which actually turned out to be a shame because that left an opening for Sir Hector to bring a rather unpleasant man over. An antiques dealer of some sort.'

Inspector Sunderland flicked back a few pages in his notebook. 'Mr Clifford Haddock,' he said. 'I've already wired Scotland Yard about him. He seems like a very fishy character.' He seemed very pleased with his own joke.

'Well, quite,' said Lady Hardcastle, raising an eyebrow. 'Then I sent Armstrong off for booze – the fizzy wine was quite undrinkable – and after that things got a great deal more merry. I ended up holding court with the youngsters and impressing them with my tales of derring do from Shanghai to Calcutta. Then Armstrong found me and, strongly implying that I was brandified, took me home.'

'You were sloshed, my lady,' I said.

'I was, as you say, all mops and brooms, but it's indelicate of you to point it out to the inspector.'

'It shall go no further,' said the inspector with a smile.

'You're most kind,' she said. 'And that was my evening.'

'Did you notice any unusual comings and goings at around the time

Mr Nelson disappeared?'

'No, Inspector, I'm afraid not. It wasn't the liveliest of parties, but it was a party nonetheless and people were coming and going all the time.'

'Yes, that's the problem,' he said, finishing off his notes. 'And you, Miss Armstrong, what did you see?'

I recounted the events of my own evening and was describing my meeting with Sylvia Montgomery.

'Miss Montgomery was coming out of the library as you were on your quest for brandy?' asked the inspector.

'Yes, that's right.'

'So this was during the break?'

'No, I don't think so,' I said. 'I think the band was still playing.'

'There were some instrumental numbers, I think,' said Lady Hardcastle. 'Perhaps it was during one of those?'

'Perhaps,' he said. 'Do you remember the time of this meeting?'

'I'm sorry, Inspector, I never wear a watch. I have no idea.'

'No matter. Please continue.'

I told him about my meeting with the tipsy Maud Denton.

'The lazy maid,' said the inspector. 'I'm so sorry, I meant to say lady's maid. What was I thinking?'

I laughed and continued. I described my sneaking back to the party with the illicit brandy and how I'd had to hide to avoid being seen by someone who was going into the library.

'Did you see this person?' asked the inspector.

'No, I just heard the door closing. When I peeked round the corner again there was no one in sight so I presumed they'd gone in rather than coming out.'

'Could it have been Mr Nelson?'

'No, the band was still playing when I got back to the ballroom and it was only after that that Mr Nelson slipped away and Miss Montgomery came over to ask about the scotch.'

'Interesting. So that could have been our man,' mused the inspector.

'Or woman,' said Lady Hardcastle quickly.

'True, true. Though a man is more likely to clout someone round the back of the head with something heavy. A woman would like as not try to talk her way out of it.'

'Have you met Armstrong?' she asked with a smile.

He turned to me. 'Your reputation precedes you, miss, but from what I hear you'd not need a heavy object to render someone unconscious.'

'No, Inspector. And he'd be able to get up and walk away with a headache when he woke up, too. It shows a considerable lack of skill to kill someone by accident when there are so many effective ways of simply incapacitating them.'

He looked faintly disquieted but carried on. 'And what happened when you returned to the ballroom?'

I told the tale of the rest of my evening but there was little else of any substance to offer him.

'Did no one go into the library while you were tidying up?' he asked when I had finished.

'No, we were told not to bother with it because the band members were still using it. That's why Dora was in there first thing, it was to be her job to get the room back in order before the band rose and came in to pack up their things.'

'They didn't pack up at the end of the party?'

'No, they finished their performance and left their instruments on the little stage. I didn't see what happened to them after that.'

'They cadged some booze from Miss Clarissa and went off to the rooms that had been set aside for them in the attic,' said Lady Hardcastle.

'Without looking for their friend,' said the inspector. 'They're a strange lot.'

'Oh, I think they wanted to. The one they called Skins was very keen to search for him, but Richman very firmly told him no and he seemed to drop it.'

'Skins... Skins...' said the inspector, leafing through his notebook again. 'Ah yes, Ivor "Skins" Maloney. The drummer. "Skins"?'

'Drum skins, one imagines,' said Lady Hardcastle. 'It's calfskin, I believe, scraped very thin and stretched very tight.'

'Is it? Is it indeed? Well I count it a poor day indeed if I don't learn at least one new thing, so today is looking up already. So Richman said no, eh? Very interesting.' He sat for a few moments reviewing his notes. 'Well, my lady, Miss Armstrong, thank you for your help. I'm going to have to give this one some serious thought. I just can't seem to get the timings straight. People seem to be in and out of the ballroom, and in and out of that damn library, but no one seems to know when anything happened.'

'It's almost as though they didn't expect to be witnesses in a murder investigation,' said Lady Hardcastle, dryly.

'You're right, my lady, of course. Heigh ho,' he said, snapping the little notebook shut. 'I shall have to think of some way of making sense of it all.'

'Might I suggest a little trick I've been using,' said Lady Hardcastle. 'I call it my "Crime Board",' and she went on to describe her use of the large blackboard in our previous investigations.

Bert and a footman called Dewi (who swore continually and colourfully under his breath in Welsh and didn't think anyone could understand him) had been called upon to bring down a blackboard and easel from the nursery and set it up in the large dining room which Inspector Sunderland had adopted as his base of operations. Meanwhile, Lady Hardcastle had been sketching guests and we'd both been trying to recall any details of the previous evening which might be helpful.

'To whom else have you spoken, Inspector?' asked Lady Hardcastle as she finished off a particularly accurate, if unflattering, sketch of Clifford Haddock.

'Just you and one or two of the staff so far, my lady,' he said. 'The majority of the guests left shortly after you and I didn't want to waken those that had stayed the night. I thought I'd let them lie in.'

I caught the wicked glint in his eye as well as Lady Hardcastle's own raised eyebrow.

'I trust you think I've been punished enough now for irritating you in the past,' she said.

'More than enough, thank you, my lady,' he said with a grin. 'Perhaps we might work together in the future instead of against one another.'

'In the future, Inspector?'

'Oh, come now. We both know that whenever anything happens in the village, you'll be first on the scene with your deerstalker and Meerschaum, hunting for clues and trying to solve the mystery before the clodhopping oafs in the Police Force get a look in. I'd just rather not be thought the clodhopping oaf, that's all. Perhaps you might consider me "that splendid chap from Bristol whom I really should speak to because he's a professional detective and it's his job to solve crimes".'

She laughed. 'I never considered you a clodhopping oaf, Inspector, though to be fair, you did arrest completely the wrong man in the Frank Pickering case. Would it have been entirely unreasonable of me if I had thought that of you?'

'Given what you knew at the time, no, I don't suppose it would. I was, however, dealing with a particularly sensitive case in the city which involved several children being abducted from the streets. They were about to be shipped off to eastern Europe somewhere for who knows what horrible purpose, and time wasn't something I could spare. I knew Lovell wasn't our man but I had to keep the gentlemen of the press quiet for a while, and arresting suspects always does the trick. I'd have caught the Seddons soon enough.'

'Oh,' she said, clearly crestfallen.

'"Oh" indeed, my lady.'

'But I'm still not clear on the subject of "in the future". I've moved out here for a quiet life in the country. I don't anticipate becoming embroiled in any further mysteries.'

'Well, now, my lady, that's the funny thing. How are you on the subject of statistics and probability?'

'I get by,' she said, breezily. 'I read Natural Sciences at Cambridge, but I like to keep up with new developments in mathematics, too, and I like to think I can hold my own if the subject should turn to statistics.'

'I rather thought you might. You see there's a funny thing about this part of Gloucestershire. There's those as would say that London would definitely be England's murder capital. Others are sure it's Birmingham, or Manchester, or Liverpool. Some even suggest my own home city of Bristol. There's a cluster of villages in Oxfordshire that regularly vies for the title, but have a guess where it really is.'

'I should suppose, given the devilish twinkle in your eye,' she said, 'that it's here.'

'It is, as you suggest, my lady, right here. There are more murders per head of population in this part of Gloucestershire than anywhere else in the country. A person is more than twice as likely to be murdered here than anywhere else. Did it not strike you that you've been here less than three months and you've already seen at least eight people killed? It is eight, isn't it?'

'It is now, Inspector, yes.'

'Most people go their whole lives without knowing of a single murder, and yet you've already seen eight since June.'

'I'd known more than my fair share before I even arrived. Perhaps it's me.'

'Yes, of course, my lady, there was your husband. I'm terribly sorry, I didn't mean to be insensitive.'

She waved a friendly dismissal. 'Please don't worry, Inspector. It was a long time ago now.'

He nodded and continued. 'But no, it's not you, it's what they call a statistical anomaly and it's centred on Chipping Bevington.'

'I see.'

'And so I think "in the future" the probability is very high that there shall be more and that you shall be somewhere at the heart of it, meddling and interfering and generally making a nuisance of yourself. But I hope that now you'll remember to call me, cable me, or even send a trusty carrier pigeon my way before you go trying to get yourself killed.'

'Right-oh, Inspector,' she said with a cheeky grin. 'I promise.'

'That's agreed, then. And for my part I promise not to send burly constables to your home when you'd probably rather be resting in bed nursing a hangover.'

'It was a rather nasty one.'

'I hoped it might be.'

I was beginning to warm to this Inspector Sunderland.

'Right then,' he said decisively. 'Let's just start working through them. It's a tiresome job, but I find thoroughness usually gets results.'

Lady Hardcastle looked at him as though about to remind him of his lack of thoroughness in the Pickering case, but she thought better of it when he returned her stare.

He flipped through his ever-present notebook. 'Miss Armstrong, would you do me a great service and get one of the staff here to fetch Miss Sylvia Montgomery. Let's see what she has to say about her visit to the library.'

Sylvia Montgomery was only slightly less stunning in her day clothes than in her stage outfit and she sat opposite Inspector Sunderland and Lady Hardcastle, regarding them coolly but without apparent hostility as they asked her about the events of the night before.

'...and then I slipped out to the library in search of something to drink. I'm not needed during the last couple of numbers in the first set apart from to sway around and look gorgeous, so I usually just nick off at that point. I had a good hunt around, looking in the globe, behind the books, under the chairs, in the window seats. Nothing. Not a drop. So I gave it up as a bad job and that's when I met you.' She looked over towards me. 'I went back in to the ballroom and stayed there until we'd finished. We managed to cadge some half-decent scotch from the birthday girl–'

'It was her engagement party,' the inspector corrected her.

'Was it, indeed? That chinless chap with the wispy moustache?'

'Mr Woodfield, yes. Heir to the Woodfield Engineering business.'

'Really? Good for her. If you can't land a looker, go for the money. Good girl. But anyway, we snaffled her scotch and went off up to the dingy rooms they'd begrudgingly let us have. We drank until about two and then called it a night.'

'Did none of you wonder what had happened to Mr Holloway?' asked Lady Hardcastle.

'At first, yes. Skins was all for looking for him but Roland insisted he'd probably found a doxy to canoodle with and we should leave him to it.'

'Was he the sort to "canoodle with doxies", miss?' said the inspector.

'He was a man, Inspector. The prospect of canoodling with doxies at parties was what got him to take up the trumpet in the first place.'

'Fair enough, miss. Understood. What did you all talk about?'

'When, Inspector?'

'While you were drinking. I presume you didn't all sit there in gloomy silence.'

'Oh, I see. Oh, you know, the usual. How the performance had gone, which numbers worked and which didn't, what engagements were coming up. That sort of thing.'

'I see, miss, thank you. My friends here,' he indicated Lady Hardcastle and me, 'haven't seen the library yet and I think it might help for us all to see it in the company of someone who saw it before the crime took place. See how things have changed, if you get my meaning. Would that be too distressing for you, miss?'

She favoured him with a withering look and he shrugged in response and stood. Together we trooped out of the dining room and headed for the library.

The library was a long, rectangular room with three large windows along one of the long walls and a large stone fireplace set in the centre of the other. Apart from that, every other inch of wall space was fitted with floor-to-ceiling bookshelves. There were four comfortable leather armchairs, one in each corner of the room, with the empty globe bar beside one of them and small tables set beside the other three. I could see the bloodstain on the polished wood of the floor near the fireplace and when I looked more closely I could see that there was also a bloody mark on the corner of the stone hearth.

'It looks like he hit his head on the hearth when he fell, Inspector,' I said.

'Very good, miss, very good indeed,' said the inspector. 'The doctor and I rather think that's what caused the fatal damage to the man's brain.'

I felt ever so slightly patronized, but part of me was also rather pleased with the praise.

At the other end of the room was a jumble of instrument cases. A double bass case lay on its side with its red velvet lining ripped out making it look like another bleeding corpse. Round cases of pressed cardboard, like oversized hatboxes, were strewn haphazardly about, lids and leather straps lying chaotically among them.

'Is that how you left your things, miss?' said the inspector.

'I should jolly well say not,' said Sylvia, walking towards the jumble of cases. 'Our instruments are our livelihood, Inspector, and we treat them with the utmost respect. Even the cases we keep them in.' She reached out to tidy them, as though the chaos were an affront.

'Please don't touch anything, miss. Our fingerprint expert hasn't been here yet.'

'Oh,' she said, pulling her hand back. 'Sorry.'

Until now I'd been puzzled by her reaction to the whole thing. The band all seemed to get along well and she'd not appeared to be in the least bit upset by the murder of one of her friends. Even the sight of the bloodstained floor had left her unmoved, but somehow this apparently unimportant mistreatment of the instrument cases had affected her, as though it were the worst violation of all. She looked shocked and anguished for the first time.

'Please sit down, miss,' said the inspector, taking her by the arm and leading her to one of the armchairs. 'I did try to warn you this might be distressing.'

'Yes,' she said absently, 'you did. I'm so sorry, Inspector, you must think me a frightful ninny. I suppose it hadn't really sunk in until I saw what they did to our things. It wasn't real somehow. Do you know what I mean?'

'I do, miss,' he said solicitously.

'Wait a moment,' she said, suddenly much more alert. 'Where's Nelson's case?'

'I beg your pardon, miss?'

'Nelson's trumpet case. Have you removed it?'

'No, miss, we've not touched a thing at that end of the room. Like I say, we're waiting for the fingerprint man.'

'I thought you detectives did all that sort of thing yourself,' she said, clearly having trouble maintaining her train of thought.

'Some do, miss. We're trying a new system, though. Specialists, if you get my meaning.'

'Oh, I see.'

'Mr Holloway's case, miss?' he said, trying to get her train of thought back on the rails.

'It's not there.'

'And it was there last night? He didn't leave it in his room, perhaps?'

'No, they unpacked in here. We warmed up here.'

'Warmed up, miss?'

'You know, ran through a couple of things, I did my voice exercises.'

'Ah, like sportsmen.'

'Just like that, yes. We need to loosen up, get ourselves prepared. And we did that in here. I distinctly remember Nelson getting his trumpet out of its case and putting it on top of one of Skins's drum cases.'

Inspector Sunderland stepped over to the jumble of cases and peered into them all. Then he cast around the room, trying to see under the chairs for any trace of the case.

'Hmm, that's most interesting,' he said at length. 'It's definitely not here now. It looks as though we might have found out what it was the thief was after. But why...?'

'An empty trumpet case?' said Lady Hardcastle.

'Certainly a trumpet case without a trumpet in it,' he said. 'But I doubt it was "empty" if it was worth clouting someone over the head for. Did you see anything else in there, Miss Montgomery?'

'In the case, Inspector? No. A trumpet, a mouthpiece. He usually had a cleaning cloth and little bottle of valve oil in there. Oh, and one of those stick things they poke into the tubes for cleaning. There might have been some brass polish. I saw him using all that sort of stuff at one time or another but I never really looked inside. It's not the done thing, you know, poking around in another musician's things. Not the done thing at all.'

'Fair enough, miss. Thank you. Now, I think the best thing for you would be to take some air.'

He rang the bell and a few moments later, Jenkins appeared.

'Ah, Jenkins,' said the inspector. 'I wonder if I might ask you to find Miss Montgomery here a spot in the garden where she might relax a while in the fresh air. She's had something of a shock. If you were able to find her a little brandy, I'm sure that would be most beneficial.'

Jenkins looked briefly horrorstruck at the thought of having to treat a mere musician – no better than a tradesman in his eyes – as an honoured guest, but a nod of agreement from Lady Hardcastle persuaded him that it was, after all, something he should just get on with.

'Yes, sir, of course,' he said emotionlessly. 'Will there be anything else?'

'No, Jenkins, thank you.'

He opened the door for Sylvia who went out into the passage. He made to follow her.

'Oh, Jenkins,' said Lady Hardcastle. He stopped at once and turned to face her. 'We'll be returning to the dining room presently. Be an absolute darling and have some coffee sent in, would you?'

'Of course, my lady.' He had no complaints about helping a proper lady. 'Luncheon will be served at one, my lady. In the garden since the inspector,' he paused and looked pointedly at Inspector Sunderland, 'has commandeered the dining room. Will you be joining us?'

'I don't think so, Jenkins. Would Mrs Brown make us a plate of sandwiches, perhaps?'

'I'm sure she'd be more than happy to, my lady.'

He closed the door behind him.

'Of all the uppity, stuck-up, hoity-toity...' said the inspector, viciously.

'Oh, come now, Inspector,' said Lady Hardcastle. 'He's just a little old fashioned.'

'I ask him to help a girl in distress and he's looking down his nose, you ask him to run around and bring you coffee and sandwiches and he almost trips over his shoes in his haste.'

'It's the accent and the title, dear boy,' she said with a wink, and he harrumphed to indicate that she had entirely proven his point. 'Oh, and...' she glanced down at her ample chest.

The inspector blushed the deepest scarlet and hastened from the room. I tried not to laugh and embarrass the poor man still further.

'You, my lady, are going straight to Hell,' I said as I followed him. She grinned.

We entered the dining room to find a bewildered Captain Summers looking forlornly at the empty sideboard.

'What ho,' he said, breezily. 'I seem to be a bit late for breakfast, what?'

'A little, sir,' said the inspector with a smile, his embarrassment almost forgotten. 'It's very nearly lunchtime. And you are...?'

'I might ask you the same question, sir,' said Summers pompously, eyeing the inspector's neat but unfashionable suit disdainfully.

'I do beg your pardon,' said the inspector. 'Inspector Sunderland of the Bristol CID.'

'CID, eh? Detective, eh? What are you detectin'?'

'There's been a murder, Mister...?'

'Captain. Captain Summers.' His face had whitened. 'A murder?'

'Yes, sir, last evening at the party. Are you quite well, sir? Do you think you ought to sit down?'

'I... er... yes. Do you mind, my lady?' He looked over towards Lady Hardcastle. 'I feel a little queer.' He sat on one of the dining chairs, still looking very pale. 'Funny how a chap can spend his life fighting for King and country – Queen and country, too, come to that – seeing death and carnage all around, and then be knocked for six by a death in the house. It was in the house, Inspector?'

'It was, sir, yes.'

'Good lord, not in here?'

'No, sir, in the library.'

'I see, I see.' He looked around, still somewhat befuddled. 'Who was it?'

'One of the musicians, sir,' said the inspector. 'Mr Nelson Holloway, the trumpeter with the band.'

'Good lord. Music wallah, eh? They were good. I mean, that's what everyone kept telling me. Not entirely my cup of char, if I'm completely honest with you, but... I mean... a chap doesn't deserve to die for playing American music.'

'I don't think he was killed by a music critic, sir. It's almost certain it was a robbery.'

'A robbery? Good lord. Good lord. What would a trumpeter have worth stealing?'

'That's precisely what we're currently wondering, sir. Did you see anything last evening? Anything that might help us piece together what happened?'

'"Us"?' he said, looking around at Lady Hardcastle and me.

'I meant the Police Force, sir, but yes, Lady Hardcastle and Miss Armstrong are helping me.'

Captain Summers looked blankly at us. 'Helping?'

'Yes, sir. They're by way of being amateur detectives. They have an enviable record of success around these parts. We shall be working together.'

'I see. I see. Jolly good.'

'Would you mind telling us about last evening, sir? Did you see or hear anything unusual, for instance?'

'Not a thing, Inspector, no.'

'Perhaps you could take us through the evening as you remember it?'

'Of course, of course. I'd been staying at The Grange for a couple of days, d'you see. Friend of Sir Hector. So I was one of the first at the party. Bit early for my taste, but I tried not to fuss. So many things have changed here since I've been away.'

'Here, sir? You've been to The Grange before.'

'No, I mean yes, I have, but I meant Blighty. Gone to the dogs if you ask me. But there I was, best bib and tucker–'

'Military dress, sir?'

'What? No, mess jacket still in India. Travelling light, what? Be back there soon. No point hauling all me traps halfway round the world then hauling them all the way back.'

'Quite, sir. Please, continue. What did you do?'

'I was trying to circulate, do the sociable thing, what? Trying to get back into the swing of it all. Society, and all that. Hoping to be married soon, want to start a new life back in Blighty in a year or two. Doesn't hurt to make a few friends.'

'Oh, congratulations, sir,' said the inspector, amiably. 'Who's the lucky lady?'

Captain Summers smiled ruefully. 'There's the rub, what? Not quite asked her yet. Colonel's daughter and all that. Got to play it a bit carefully, what? Need to woo her. Impress her, what? Can't rush at these things like a bull at a gate.'

'I see, sir, yes. Were you in the ballroom all evening? You didn't nip out for some fresh air?'

'Can't say as I did, no.'

'And did you notice any of the other comings and goings? Did anything strike you as odd?'

'Not really, Inspector. Folk come and go all evening at a shindig like that.'

'Did you see Mr Holloway leave the room?'

'The dead chap?'

'Yes, sir.'

'Can't say as I did.'

'So you wouldn't have noticed, say, if someone followed him out?'

'No, Inspector, not at all. I'm not really much help, I'm afraid, am I?'

'Everything is helpful in an investigation like this, sir,' said the inspector, patiently. 'I can see you've had a shock, though, so I shan't detain you further. Thank you for your time.'

'Free to go, what?'

Inspector Sunderland laughed. 'Free to go, sir. Although I should be obliged if you were to stay at The Grange until this is cleared up. We may need to ask you some further questions when we know a little more about the events of the evening. We might be able to jog your memory a little.'

'Certainly, Inspector, certainly.' He stood to leave. 'Lady Hardcastle,' he said with a bow, and walked round the table to the door.

As he closed the door behind him, Inspector Sunderland rolled his eyes. 'What a buffle-headed ass,' he said. 'Nice to see the Empire is in the hands of such bright and brave individuals.'

'He'd had a shock,' said Lady Hardcastle reproachfully.

'A shock, my Aunt Fanny. Man's a soldier; he's seen death before. Said so himself.'

'Maybe so. But as a friend of mine pointed out not so long ago, there's a difference between chaps dressed up as the enemy pointing their guns – or spears, or what have you – at you across a battlefield, and some ne'er-do-well sneaking about in the night doing folk to death in an English village.'

'You're right, of course, my lady. I shouldn't be so harsh. But the man's a buffoon.'

'Oh, he's a buffoon of the first water, no question about it. And so terribly old fashioned with it. Quite the relic. But we should perhaps make allowances. England isn't all he remembers it to be. I think he has a rather romantic notion of what "Blighty" should be like, and all this has quite shattered his illusions.'

'I dare say,' said the inspector distractedly as he made some notes in his notebook.

There was a knock on the door and Jenkins entered with a tray of coffee, sandwiches, and some shortbread biscuits.

'Your luncheon, my lady,' he said, pointedly ignoring the inspector. 'Mrs Brown thought you might appreciate some biscuits, too.'

'She's very thoughtful, Jenkins,' said Lady Hardcastle. 'Please thank her for us.'

'Yes, my lady. Will there be anything else?'

'No, Jenkins, thank you.'

'Very good, my lady,' he said with a slight bow. He left as quietly as he had entered.

Inspector Sunderland seemed to be on the verge of another tirade, but Lady Hardcastle's warning glance forestalled him. He went to pour the coffee.

'Please,' I said, stepping forward. 'Allow me.'

'Oh, I... er... yes, miss. If you insist.'

'Thank you, Inspector,' I said as I poured coffee for the two of them. 'Just doing my duty.'

'Don't show off, Armstrong,' said Lady Hardcastle. 'Pour yourself one, too.'

I curtseyed. 'Thank you, m'lady. You're very generous to a poor servant girl, you are. Very kind and generous. I doesn't deserve it, m'lady, really I doesn't.'

'Are you two a music hall act?' said the Inspector.

'No, Inspector, we're just good friends,' said Lady Hardcastle and motioned for me to sit with them at the table.

'Well that told us nothing we couldn't have guessed for ourselves,' said the inspector, still gazing thoughtfully at his notebook.

'I wouldn't say that, Inspector,' said Lady Hardcastle. 'I think it gave us quite an insight into the man's character.' She rose and made a few quick notes of her own on the Crime Board.

'Showed us that he's a buffoon, you mean? I suppose it did at that.' He snapped his notebook shut and tucked in to the coffee and sandwiches.

We ate together, making small talk. We'd all noticed that the house had seen better days, that there was a shabby air of faded opulence about it, and Lady Hardcastle explained the rumours about the Farley-Strouds' shaky financial state.

'They're not exactly impecunious,' she said, 'but there doesn't seem to be a lot of spare cash around for decoration and modernization.'

We finished the sandwiches and moved on to the biscuits.

'I say,' said the inspector. 'These are rather nice. Mrs Sunderland makes a lovely shortbread, but nothing like this.'

'I'm sure Armstrong could get you the recipe if you like.'

The inspector laughed. 'Tell me, my lady, if you were a policeman's wife, waiting anxiously for him to come home, never knowing what danger he'd got himself into that day, and you'd made some delicious shortbread for him to have with his cup of tea by the fire, how would you feel if he came home and said, "Here you are, my beloved, I thought you made the finest biscuits in all the land, but I have found a far better recipe. Take these inferior things back to the kitchen and make me some of these others, as prepared by a servant in a manor house I've been visiting."?'

'You build a convincing argument, Inspector,' she said. 'Armstrong, keep that recipe a secret. Do not divulge it to anyone, most especially not the inspector.'

'Right you are, my lady,' I said.

'You two...' said the inspector, sipping his coffee. 'Now then, to business. Let us cleanse our investigatory palates by interviewing someone who might actually tell us something. What do you say we talk to someone else from the band. I got the impression that Miss Montgomery wasn't all that close to them. Let's see what one of his fellow musicians has to say.' He consulted his notebook. 'Let's go straight to the top; let's try Roland Richman. He might be able to tell us a little more.'

'He might, he might,' said Lady Hardcastle.

The inspector nodded. 'There's another reason for talking to Mr Richman.' He flipped back a few more pages in his notebook. 'One of the servants says she saw him in the passage outside the library. She can't remember when and didn't think much of it at the time because the musicians were supposed to be there, but it does place him near the scene of the crime.'

'Would you like me to fetch him, sir?' I said.

'That would be grand, miss, thank you.'

I had found Roland Richman in the ballroom, tinkling away on the piano. Actually, that's not entirely fair; he had been playing a rather beautiful piece which had turned out to be one of his own compositions. He had followed me somewhat reluctantly to the dining room and after the usual introductions, Inspector Sunderland had plunged directly into the questioning.

'You'll forgive my directness, sir, but I do need to get to the bottom of all this as swiftly as I can. I have a witness who says she saw you...' he flipped ostentatiously through his notebook, '...."hanging about in the corridor outside the library". She can't remember when, but perhaps you can?'

Mr Richman laughed. 'I suppose it did look like I was just hanging about, yes. I was waiting for someone.'

'Who, sir? And when?'

'I was waiting for Nelson. I don't know the precise time, there are so damn few clocks in this place. But it was during our break.'

'..."during the break",' said the inspector, making a careful note. 'And did you meet Mr Holloway?'

'No, he never turned up. And now I know why.'

'Perhaps, sir. Did you look for him at all?'

'No, we were to meet in the corridor; I didn't want to go wandering off in case I missed him.'

'And you didn't think to look in the library? That's where he told you he was going.'

'That's what he told the others, Inspector. I knew where he was going; he was going to the corridor to meet me.'

'I see, sir. Did you see or hear anything else?'

'No, there was the usual hubbub of a party, I saw that servant girl–'

'Rose, sir,' interrupted the inspector.

'Really?' I blurted in surprise. 'Good for her. I'm glad she escaped from the kitchen to see a bit of the party.'

'Lucky girl,' said Mr Richman unenthusiastically. 'There were a few others but I was keen to get my meeting over with and get back to work so I didn't really pay much attention.'

'What was your meeting about, sir?' asked the inspector.

'Band business, I expect. He didn't say. Just said he needed to speak to me in private. Probably after a rise if I know Nelson.'

'How long did you wait for him?'

'Again, Inspector, I have no idea. No clocks.'

'Quite so, sir. But you eventually went back to the party and played your "second set", I believe you call it.'

Mr Richman smiled. 'Our second set, yes. Then off for a nightcap and an early night.'

'Early night, sir?'

'We usually turn in about six in the morning, Inspector. We entertain people at night for the most part.'

'Indeed you do, sir, one forgets that others lead such different lives.'

'Were you and Mr Holloway friends?' asked Lady Hardcastle.

'Friends, my lady?' said Mr Richman. 'We got on well, if that's what you mean. He'd been with the band a few years and we're a small group. It wouldn't work if we didn't get on.'

'Of course,' she said. 'But what I meant was were you close friends, or just colleagues?'

'I'd say we were friends, yes.'

'And did you have anything to do with one another outside your work?' she persisted.

'What do you mean?' said Mr Richman. 'We had a drink now and again, maybe met for a meal or two. But we work quite a lot, Lady Hardcastle, we spent a lot of time together.'

'You had no other interests outside your work, then? No shared business interests?'

'I'm sure I have no idea what you're on about,' he said, blankly. 'What manner of business do you imagine we'd have time for?'

Lady Hardcastle smiled. 'Forgive me, Mr Richman, my mind wanders sometimes. I was just trying to find out a little more about Mr Holloway.'

'Oh, I see,' he said. 'He was a thoroughly decent chap, that's all you really need to know. An excellent musician, a good friend, and a proper gentle man. Not a gentleman as you'd know them, my lady, he came from the same backstreets as the rest of us, but he was a proper gentle man. I shall miss him.'

'Of course, Mr Richman. Forgive me for intruding on your grief.'

He nodded sadly.

'I've been asking everyone to remain at the house until this matter is resolved, sir,' said the inspector, wrapping up the interview. 'I trust that won't be an inconvenience.'

Mr Richman took a look round the library. 'The place could do with decorating,' he said, 'But I suppose I could slum it for a while.'

'Thank you for your patience, sir. I'll send for you if I think of anything else I need to ask.'

Mr Richman stood. 'Thank you, inspector.' He left quietly.

'Do you have something on your mind, my lady?' asked the inspector.

'Just probing, Inspector. I was trying to find out if he and Holloway were up to anything else. Something illicit, perhaps. Did I spoil things for you?'

'Probably not, my lady,' he said, kindly. 'It's not the way I should have chosen to play it, but it was illuminating to see him so rattled when you asked him. Perhaps they were up to something after all.' He consulted his notebook. 'Let me see now... whom shall we see next?

Ah, yes, Mr Clifford Haddock. Let's see what happens when we get him on the hook.'

'It's certainly the plaice for it,' I said.

'Cod we just get on with it,' said Lady Hardcastle, wearily.

'I... er... oh, oh, I shall salmon him at once.' I left in a hurry.

I found Mr Haddock with Sir Hector in the corridor outside the library, keenly examining what I thought was a rather revolting clock which sat atop an ornate Chinese cabinet.

'Ah, now then, Sir Hector,' the dealer was saying, 'this is a lovely piece. To be honest I'd only give you a few bob for the cabinet – reproduction, you see – but this clock is a very handsome piece indeed. Eighteenth century French. I'm sure I could find you a buyer for this one, yes indeed.'

Sir Hector noticed my approach and rolled his eyes at the dealer's continuing prattle. He seized the opportunity to interrupt. 'Yes, m'dear? Is there something we can do for you?'

'Sorry to interrupt, Sir Hector,' I said deferentially. 'But Inspector Sunderland would like a word with Mr Haddock.'

'Good lord,' said Haddock. 'My turn for the Spanish Inquisition, eh?'

'In the dining room, please, sir,' I said.

'Well, I'd better not keep the Old Bill waiting, eh?' he said. 'This way?'

'Yes, sir, I'll take you.'

He set off in the direction I had come from and I turned to follow, but Sir Hector grabbed my elbow.

'Something fishy about that chap,' he said. 'Oh, I say. "Fishy". Well done, Hector. You heard what he was saying about m'whatnots? Totally the wrong way round. The cabinet's the genuine article – picked it up in Shanghai in '92 – and the clock's a cheap imitation made by a chap from Bournemouth. Either he hasn't got a clue or he's trying to cheat a chap, what?'

'I wouldn't rule either one out at this stage, Sir Hector,' I said.

'The old detective's nose twitching, what?'

'Something like that, sir. That and the fact that he's an oily little tick.'

He laughed a delighted laugh. 'Nail on the head, m'dear. Oily tick indeed. You'd better catch him up before he pilfers anything, what?' He laughed again and waved me on my way.

I hurried along the corridor and caught up with Haddock just as he was passing the dining room door.

'This way, sir,' I said, opening the door for him. He doubled back and entered the room.

'Ah, Mr Haddock, I presume,' said the inspector as I closed the door behind me. 'I'm Inspector Sunderland and this is Lady Hardcastle.'

'Pleased to meet you, I'm sure,' said Haddock. 'And a pleasure to meet you again, Lady Hardcastle. We had all too brief a time together last evening. I should have liked to have got more acquainted. Sir Hector tells me you're a widow. It's a shame for such a beautiful lady to be all alone.'

Lady Hardcastle simply nodded a greeting but made no further response.

'Take a seat, please, Mr Haddock,' said the inspector.

He did as he was asked.

'Well, then, Inspector,' he said. 'How can I help you.'

'I'm sure you're more than well aware of what happened here last evening,' said the inspector. 'So I shan't bore you by restating the details. As you can no doubt imagine, we're anxious to try to build a picture of the events surrounding Mr Holloway's death. I gather you're a guest of Sir Hector?'

'Yes,' he said, with a smarmy smile. 'He invited me down to appraise some of his *objets d'art*. I believe he's looking to sell a few pieces.'

'And since you were here anyway, you were invited to the engagement party.'

'Yes, that is correct.'

'How did you come to be first introduced to Sir Hector?'

'Through a mutual acquaintance.'

'Who might that be, if you don't mind my asking?'

'Mr Roland Richman.'

'So you know Mr Richman?'

'Yes,' said Haddock. 'We bump into each other from time to time in London. I'm quite a devotee of this new American music so we frequent some of the same nightclubs.'

'I see, sir, I see. And were you at the party all evening?'

'I was, Inspector, yes.'

'Mr Holloway was last seen alive when he left the stage during the band's break at around ten o'clock. Did you see him leave the ballroom?'

'Not as such. They finished "The Richman Rag" and then they all got down from that little dais they were playing on. I went to have a word with them all to tell them how well they were playing but he wasn't there. I suppose he must have left the room before I could get to them.'

'I see, sir. Did you notice anyone else missing?'

'It was a crowded party, Inspector. People were coming and going all the time.'

'And did you come and go at all, sir?'

'I... er... I left the room to...' He looked around the room at Lady Hardcastle and me. 'To... er... you know...'

'"Use the facilities", sir?'

'Just that, Inspector.'

'During the break?'

'Yes. It seemed as good a time as any. It meant I'd not miss anything.'

'And did you notice anything out of the ordinary while you were wandering about the house?'

'I didn't "wander", Inspector. I went straight to the... er... you know... and came straight back.'

'And you were there the rest of the evening?'

'Yes. Sylvia usually starts the second set with "I Can't Get Enough of You" and that just gets me hooked for the rest of the night.'

'I see, sir. And can you remember seeing or hearing anything out of the ordinary at all?'

'Not at all, Inspector, no. As I say, it was quite a lively party and what with the wonderful music and the beautiful ladies–' He leered at Lady Hardcastle again. '–I was quite distracted.'

Inspector Hardcastle Sunderland finished making his notes. 'Thank you, sir, you've been most helpful. I take it you're staying at The Grange for a few more days?'

'I've been invited till the weekend, yes.'

'Very good, sir. If I need to ask you any further questions, I shall send for you.'

'Right you are, Inspector. So may I go?'

'You may indeed, sir. Thank you again for your time.'

'Think nothing of it,' said Haddock, and left the room, closing the door behind him.

Inspector Sunderland made a few more notes and then looked up. 'What did you make of that, my lady?' he asked.

'Aside from his being an oily tick, you mean?' she said, disdainfully.

'I called him that a few minutes ago,' I said with a grin.

'To his face, miss?' said the inspector.

'No, Inspector, though it shan't be long before I do. I found him with Sir Hector, talking about some furniture outside the library and Sir Hector buttonholed me as Haddock set off for the library. Apparently Sir Hector isn't impressed with Haddock's knowledge of antiques and wondered if he's a fraud or a swindler.'

'Probably a little of both would be my guess,' said the inspector. 'I'll cable Scotland Yard and see if they have anything on him.'

'And that was when I passed my opinion of Haddock.'

'And what was Sir Hector's reaction?' he said.

'He laughed, of course.'

'Yes, I suppose he would. Not the sort of thing he expected a respectable lady's maid to be saying, I shouldn't suppose.'

'He's known me a few months now, Inspector. I think he long since gave up any misconceptions about my respectability.'

It was the inspector's turn to laugh. 'I should imagine he did, miss, yes.'

Lady Hardcastle had a pensive look about her as she examined the links forming on the Crime Board. 'Oily and shifty, then. And probably not quite as straight and above board as one might hope,' she said. 'And by his own admission he was out of the room during the time we surmise the murder might have been committed.'

'And known to Mr Richman, too,' said the inspector. 'That might lead us somewhere. He was lurking about during that time, too.'

He took a handsome pocket watch from his waistcoat and glanced at it.

'I imagine this is the sort of place that serves tea at four o'clock,' he said.

'On the dot,' said Lady Hardcastle. 'And if I know Sir Hector, he'll still call it "Tiffin".'

The inspector sighed. 'It's another world. And that means that most of the house guests will be occupied.' He consulted his notes. 'Let's see if we can find someone else from the band, then. How about the bass player, Mr Bartholomew Dunn.'

'Why not indeed,' said Lady Hardcastle. 'Do the honours, Flo, would you, dear?'

I got up and went in search of Mr Dunn.

I found Dunn at the foot of the servants' staircase chatting up Dora, the housemaid. He was stroking her hair with the side of his index finger and she was giggling coquettishly when I breezed up and said, 'Afternoon, chaps. How are we all getting along.'

Dora glared at me. 'We were getting along just fine, thank you.'

'Glad to hear it. Mr Dunn? Inspector Sunderland would like a word with you in the dining room if you can spare him a few moments.'

Dora's look suggested that she had much more entertaining ideas for Dunn's next few moments and that if I were to fall down dead there and then, she'd not waste even one of those precious moments mourning my parting. Dunn, though, was evidently a more pragmatic man who recognized that a summons from the police, even one expressed with such casual politeness, couldn't be ignored. He also seemed confident, as he tenderly kissed her cheek, that he would be able to reignite Dora's passions as soon as he'd finished with this Inspector Sunderland, whoever he turned out to be.

'I'll find you the instant I've finished with him,' he whispered.

Dora looked at me again, a smug grin replacing the angry glare.

'You'd better,' she said, and set off upstairs.

He watched her go and then turned to look at me. 'The dining room, you say? Would you be a poppet and show me the way? I'm new round here.'

'New round here, but pretty experienced everywhere else, from the look of things,' I said. 'Follow me.'

He chuckled and I led him through the house to the dining room.

We found Lady Hardcastle and the inspector deep in conversation, but they stopped abruptly as we entered. After the usual introductions and the usual preamble, there followed the usual series of questions about the events of the evening which elicited the usual, "I didn't really notice anything. It was a party. Parties are busy places." It was apparent, though, that Dunn was quite a sociable sort of a chap and Inspector Sunderland decided to exploit this as he moved onto more personal matters.

'Tell me a little more about the band, Mr Dunn. Paint me a picture of the characters.'

'Blimey, really? Well, there's Rolie, of course, Roland Richman, our beloved leader. He's a pretty decent musician as it happens, and he's got very strong ideas about where he wants the band to go. Ambitious, you know? He's quite a sharp businessman, too, for a musician. We never lack for work and we always seem to get paid. I've been in plenty of bands where neither of those were true. Then there was Nelse. Nice chap. Easy going, if a little easily led. Beautiful tone to his playing, too. Trumpets can be a bit brash in the wrong hands, but he had a delicate touch. He could make it cry if he wanted to. We used to have a fiddle player, but there was a falling out and it turned out we didn't need him anyway – Nelse covered that side of things beautifully. We missed him in the second set. I suppose we'll be missing him for always now.' He lapsed into silence.

'You seem very fond of him,' said Lady Hardcastle.

'I'm fond of them all, my love,' he said. 'Skins is quite a lad.'

'Mr Maloney?' asked the inspector.

'The very same. We work together most closely; the "rhythm section" they call bass and drums. He's tight. Technically excellent player – I think he trained with one of the big orchestras. But he has a feel for the music, too. He's a dream to work with. Bright lad. Lots of fun. Always the life and soul. It's always a laugh when Skins is around.'

'And what about Miss Montgomery?' asked the inspector.

'Sylvie? Not so sure about her. She's only been with us a couple of months. I've not quite worked her out yet. She seems friendly enough and she sings like an angel. Or like an angel in a brothel… beg pardon ladies. She has this earthy quality to her voice, like… well, you know. Not the sort of pure, trained, precise sound you get from most ladies. She's got a voice like smoked honey served on warm bread by a naked serving wench while you're reclining on a velvet couch.'

'Steady on, lad,' said the inspector, who was blushing again. 'Ladies present.'

'Pish and fiddlesticks,' said Lady Hardcastle. 'Don't be such a fusspot. I'm just sorry I didn't pay more attention while she was singing. It sounds like quite an experience.'

'It is, my love, it certainly is. But as for her character... I'm not so sure. I don't think anyone's managed to get close to her. She's quite... hard. I've met lads like it, but never girls. The lads have been toughs, you know? Petty villains.'

'Are you saying you think she's a criminal?' asked Lady Hardcastle.

He seemed genuinely taken aback. 'Blimey no, nothing like that. I was just trying to give you an idea of how she makes me feel. She can take care of herself, that one, that's for sure. But criminal? Have you seen her?'

'She is rather beautiful,' she said.

'Exactly. How could someone that looked like that be a criminal? Criminals have a look, don't they. It's science. You can tell.'

'So they say,' said the inspector, finally looking up from his notes. 'Well, sir, that was quite comprehensive. Thank you. Is there anything else you think we ought to know. Anyone else you noticed?'

'Not really.'

'What about Clifford Haddock?'

'Old Fishface? What about him?'

'I believe he's known to the band,' said the inspector.

'He's a pal of Rolie's. Seems to be quite keen on the music so we see him about quite a lot.'

'He's an antiques dealer I understand.'

Dunn laughed, a genuine, heartfelt laugh. 'Is that what he's been telling you? Well he's got some neck, I'll give him that.'

'So he's not, then?' said the inspector, looking up once more from his notes.

'He owns a junk shop on the Old Kent Road. Antiques dealer. Wait till I tell Skins.'

'His story is that he was invited to The Grange to appraise some of Sir Hector's "knick-knacks".'

'Fishface is more likely to nick his knick-knacks, I'd say. On the plus side, he wouldn't know a Chippendale Whatnot from a bowl of peonies so he's unlikely to pinch anything of real value except by blind chance.'

'He was introduced to Sir Hector by your Mr Richman,' said the inspector.

'Then they've got something cooked up between them,' said Dunn. 'But appraising Sir Hector's prized possessions won't be part of it, I can tell you that.'

'Well, Mr Dunn, you've given us a lot to think about. I'm asking everyone who is still at The Grange to remain here for the next few days, but I understand from Mr Richman's reaction that that won't be too much of an inconvenience.'

'Indeed no, Inspector.' He gave me a conspiratorial wink. 'I've got a little something to be getting on with right now, in fact.'

'Then please don't let us keep you,' said the inspector. 'Thank you for your time. We'll find you if we need you again.'

And with a cheery wave, Dunn all but bounded out of the room.

'I wonder what he's so eager to be getting on with,' said the inspector when he had gone.

'Her name's Dora,' I said. 'I think he's hoping to comfort her after her shock this morning.'

'Poor thing,' said Lady Hardcastle with a grin. 'I imagine that experiencing something like that would require a lot of comforting.'

'I think I interrupted them before any proper comforting could begin,' I said. 'But from the look of her, I'd say she was more than ready for a serious comforting.'

'Which would account for his haste,' she said. 'Sometimes comforting cannot wait.'

The inspector laughed. 'You two have a way about you that I find most refreshing in this rarified world of ballrooms and tiffin.'

'Thank you, Inspector,' said Lady Hardcastle graciously. 'I'm greatly enjoying your company, too.' She consulted her wristwatch. 'I say, it's getting on, isn't it. I really ought to be going or I might get stuck here for dinner. You don't mind if I toddle off, do you, Inspector? You know where I am, after all.'

'By all means, my lady. I shall be leaving here soon myself, but I shall be returning tomorrow morning at about ten o'clock. Perhaps you might join me?'

'I should be delighted,' she said.

'And please allow today's events to percolate through your mind, in the meantime. I should be most grateful for any insights you might have.'

'Of course, Inspector. And what are your initial thoughts?'

'At the moment, my mind is entirely open. Richman and Haddock are up to something, I'm sure of that. I'm less certain of Miss Montgomery now that we've spoken to Dunn, too; I think I might make some more enquiries about her. But beyond that, I'm rather stumped.'

'Oh dear.'

'Oh, no, nothing to worry about,' he said with a chuckle. 'It's always like this at the beginning of a case.'

'That's a relief,' she said, standing up. 'Come, servant, let us away.'

'Yes, my lady,' I said with a curtsey, then with a friendly bob in the inspector's direction, I followed her out into the passage.

We walked through the hall and out of the front door. Lady Hardcastle had wondered briefly about saying goodbye to her hosts, but reasoned that since they'd not been the ones who invited her in the first place and that they'd been keeping themselves very much out of the investigation so far, it would probably be just as awkward to seek them out as to slip away without a word.

As it turned out, her deliberations were redundant. As we started on our scrunchy way across the gravel in front of the house we were intercepted by Sir Hector who had been out walking the dogs.

'What ho, Emily, m'dear. Leaving us already? Won'tcha stay for dinner? Cook's already making such a fuss about having to feed the band and a few unexpected stragglers that another mouth won't hurt. Be honest with you, it would rather amuse me to see if I could make her turn a new shade of purple. She's an angry woman, what? Very angry.'

'It's a lovely invitation, Hector,' she said, 'and ordinarily I'd love to take you up on it, not least for the effect it might have on Mrs Brown. But I fear we have matters to attend to back at the house. Another time, perhaps?'

'I shall insist upon it, m'dear,' he said, jovially.

'And we shall see you tomorrow, anyway.'

'You shall? How so? Visitin' Clarissa?'

'No, didn't you hear? We're helping Inspector Sunderland.'

'Are you, by jove. Well I never. Tryin' to keep out of it m'self.'

'He must want to speak to you, though,' she said.

'Oh, he's had a word or several with me and the memsahib, and I don't doubt he'll want a few more, what? But I'll keep out of his way until then. Sufficient unto the day, what?'

'Quite so, quite so.'

'But listen to me prattlin' on, m'dear. Mustn't hold you up, what?'

'Thank you, Hector, we ought to be on our way. And I'm sure we shall bump into you again tomorrow.'

'Lookin' forward to it, m'dear. Toodle-oo for now.' And with a cheery wave, he was off across the gravel towards the door.

'So much for us being involved in the investigation,' said Lady Hardcastle when he had gone.

'My lady?'

'Well, he never said anything about speaking to the Farley-Strouds. He's not sharing everything with us, is he?'

'Perhaps they didn't say very much. Sir Hector would have been cheerfully oblivious to pretty much everything that went on, and Lady Farley-Stroud was so busy trying to make a good impression that she wouldn't have noticed much, either. I doubt there was anything very much worth sharing.'

'Hmm,' she said, doubtfully. 'Perhaps.'

We were walking along the grass beside the long, winding drive, enjoying the late afternoon sunshine and Lady Hardcastle was wondering, now that we'd turned down the offer of dinner, just exactly what we were going to eat. I reminded her that there were some pork chops that needed eating, and some of the last of the new potatoes. As we walked out of the gate and down the hill, she remembered that there was a bottle in the recent delivery from her newly appointed Bristol vintners which would complement such a meal very nicely.

Back at the house and with gloves and hats removed, Lady Hardcastle rummaged in her voluminous handbag and produced duplicate sketches of the people involved in the case.

'I thought these might come in useful,' she said, and set about replicating the crime board on her own blackboard in the dining room while I prepared an early dinner.

Less than an hour later we were tucking in to our meal, which also included peas which Mr Jenkins had kindly given us from the Farley-Strouds' kitchen garden, and sipping at the newly delivered wine which did, as promised, complement the simple food perfectly.

Between mouthfuls, Lady Hardcastle gestured at the crime board with her knife.

'The thot plickens,' she said.

'It does at that,' I agreed.

'The inspector seems to be focussed very much on the friendship between Richman and Haddock.'

'You have to admit that Haddock sounds like a right rum 'un,' I said.

'He does, but I can't quite see how he fits into all this. If he's here to case the gaff or lift a few of the Farley-Strouds' more portable knick-knacks, what was he doing going through the band's instrument cases? And if he was caught mid-rummage, why the scuffle? Holloway knew him. There might have been stern words but no one would have been smacked on the back of the head and left for dead.'

'It might have been an accident,' I suggested.

'It might, but my money's on Sylvia Montgomery.'

'Really, my lady? Why?'

'It's always the one that the police least suspect.'

'In the stories, my lady. But you're saying that because she's the new girl and because Dunn thinks she's a street tough, you think she's a killer?'

'Well...' she said, doubtfully

'There she was, rummaging around her own band's cases, looking for... for what?'

'Looking for somewhere to stash the jewels she's just pinched from the party. She's an international jewel thief, you see, who has joined the band because of the opportunities it gives her for sneaking about in posh houses.'

'And why did she make such a mess of all the cases and then hide the trumpet case?'

'She was looking for somewhere to hide the jewels and Holloway disturbed her. She clobbered him in the struggle, then had to make it look like something else was going on, so she made a mess and then slipped out with the trumpet case.'

'What did she do with it?' I asked, doggedly.

'I haven't the foggiest notion,' she admitted.

'Well,' I said, thoughtfully. 'What if she stashed the stolen jewels in the trumpet case and then clumped Holloway, and then someone else came in–'

'Haddock,' she said, excitedly.

'For instance,' I said. 'And then Haddock tries to loot the place, because he knows Sylvia has just been in there and he knows she's a jewel thief because he fences stolen goods through his junk shop and she's one of his major suppliers? Oh, oh, that was how she got the job with the band in the first place: he introduced her.'

'So Haddock knows Sylvia was there to steal, and he thinks he can save himself a few bob by stealing from her instead of paying for the stuff. He suspects she hides the loot in the instrument cases so he's the one that rips them up, looking for the sparkle.'

'"The sparkle", my lady?'

'The very same. They both assume that Holloway is merely out cold – neither of them even suspects that he has a fatal head injury – and they both get back to their business hoping that they'll be able to explain everything away later. It was Haddock that you saw disappearing into the library, I'll bet.'

'It all sounds like a bit of a stretch to me, my lady,' I said. 'But it's nice to have something to show for our first day on the job.'

'We've made it fit all the known facts, though,' she said. 'That puts it part way to being an actual scientific theory. If we can make our theory predict something we don't already know–'

'Like perhaps that Sylvia has the trumpet case in her room with stolen jewels in it,' I suggested.

'Oh, I don't think a seasoned professional thief who was trying to conceal things in other people's baggage would keep the loot in her own room, but if we can find the case with stolen jewels in it, that would help to strengthen our theory.'

'We're proper detectives after all,' I said, with no small delight.

'We're certainly getting there,' she said.

'And do you think we ought to share our thoughts with Inspector Sunderland in the morning?' I asked.

'I think we ought. But for now, I think we ought to clear our minds completely and indulge in some of the finer things in life. I seem to be in the mood for some ragtime. Fetch your banjo and we shall drink cognac and syncopate the night away.'

I cleared away the plates and the evening passed most agreeably.

The next morning we found ourselves at something of a loss. The early-to-bed life of the country meant that we were both also early-to-rise, and while that might very well have seen a consequent increase in our levels of health, wealth and wisdom, it did rather mean that we were kicking our heels waiting until it was time to go up to The Grange.

We were both dressed, breakfasted and ready for the day before half past seven, but we had no real need to set off much before half past nine if we were to be there by ten o'clock. I had left Lady Hardcastle dealing with some urgent correspondence and was just finishing the washing-up when she appeared at the kitchen door.

'I say, Flo,' she said. 'What with your efforts at the party and your general charm and easy-going nature, do you think your stock is reasonably high at The Grange at the moment?'

'How do you mean, my lady?'

'Well, if you were to pop up there right now, slip in through the servants' entrance and say you'd been sent on ahead to meet the inspector and me, would they smile and greet you, or would they turn you away?'

'Oh, I see,' I said. 'I imagine I'd get a warmish welcome. Possibly even the offer of a cup of tea and a bun. There's a camaraderie among the serving classes that the likes of you shall never know.'

'It is very much my loss, I feel. But if you declined their kind offer and said you'd been asked to wait in the dining room, would they think it odd or out of place?'

'I shouldn't think so, my lady, no.'

'I hoped as much.'

'Is that what you'd like me to do, my lady?'

'No, silly, I'd like you to go snooping. They're used to seeing you about the place and you'd have an excuse to be wandering about above stairs if you were challenged, so I'd like you to have a good old explore. See what you can see. Find what you can find.'

'Oh, what fun,' I said, suddenly rather taken with the idea of some proper detecting. 'May I take your deerstalker and Meerschaum? Perhaps the large magnifying glass?'

She raised an eyebrow. 'Just be as nosy as possible. Look under rugs and into plant pots. Open a few cupboards.'

'What shall I be looking for, my lady?'

'I genuinely have no idea. Anything out of the ordinary, I suppose. Anything that shouldn't be there. I'm sure you'll know it when you find it.'

'Right-oh, then, my lady. I shall discreetly snoop and then meet you and the inspector in the dining room at ten o'clock as though nothing has happened. Or as near to ten o'clock as I can manage in a house with so few clocks.'

'That's the spirit. Good girl.'

And with that, I hurried off to get my hat and gloves and set off at a brisk pace up the hill to The Grange.

It was another beautiful late-summer's morning and the walk along the lane and up the hill was a delightful one. The hedgerows were alive with twittering birds which I was still unable to identify and I saw at least three rabbits and a squirrel, though I met no humans. I found the gates of The Grange already open and made my way as quietly as possible round to the servants' entrance at the side of the house. That door was open, too, and once inside I heard the first signs of life. Mrs Brown was already berating poor Rose and I could just make out the sound of Mr Jenkins's voice as he tried to calm things down and cheer things up.

I poked my head round the kitchen door.

'Morning, all,' I said breezily. 'The door was open, do you mind if I come in?'

Mr Jenkins looked mightily relieved. 'Of course, Miss Armstrong, do come in. To what do we owe the pleasure? Can we offer you some tea?'

Mrs Brown looked irritated once more that I had interrupted her in mid-rant and that my being "company" meant that she would have to tone down her bullying of her kitchen maid. She looked as though having to make me a cup of tea as well would be just about the last straw, so it was fortunate that I had other things to be getting on with.

'Thank you, no, Mr Jenkins, I'm under orders,' I said. 'But perhaps a little later? My mistress is due to arrive in a while to continue the investigation with Inspector Sunderland, but she sent me on ahead to make a few things ready in the dining room. Do you mind awfully? I shall try not to get in the way.'

'Of course, Miss Armstrong. It's never an inconvenience to have you about the place,' he said with a smile. 'Is there anything we can do to help? The room has been swept and dusted, but I gave strict instructions that the blackboard should not be touched. I trust that was the right thing.'

'Absolutely perfect, Mr Jenkins, thank you. I think I shall be fine, but I shall come and find someone if I require anything further.'

'Please just ring, Miss Armstrong,' he said with a smile. 'There's no need for you to come all the way down here.'

Mrs Brown glared at us both and I could only imagine her boiling indignation at the thought of another servant ringing the bell in her mistress's house. My mind was working overtime trying to think of ways of irritating her further, but I had other fish to fry, and there would be time later for me to think of a way to take the bullying Mrs Brown down a peg or two.

'Thank you, Mr Jenkins, you're most kind,' I said.

'Think nothing of it, my dear,' he said. 'You know your way by now, I'm sure. Please feel free to do whatever you need to do.'

I nodded my thanks once more and left the kitchen through the door that led to the "secret" servants' passage which led directly to a concealed door opposite the dining room.

Once above stairs, though, I didn't go directly to the dining room; if we wanted to search that, we'd have all day. Instead, I walked down the corridor to the entrance hall, and then down the opposite corridor to the library. The library was where it had all started and I was certain that it was the place for me to start, too.

There were two doors into the library, one at either end of the room. Most of the traffic in and out of the room so far had been through the door nearest the hall, but the musicians' cases were at the other end of the room and it seemed to me that anyone leaving the room in a hurry after a struggle would come out of the far door. It was nearer to the cases they'd been searching through and it was farther from the entrance hall and wandering guests.

I decided to try to put myself into the mind of the killer, to see what he or she saw, to retrace his steps and perhaps find what he might have tried to conceal. I went into the library through the nearer door and took a look around.

The cases were still where we had found them yesterday, but now covered in a thin dusting of fingerprint powder. I stood among them, imagining myself in the role of the burglar, searching frantically through them, terrified that I might be interrupted at any moment. Was I looking for something? Or was I looking for somewhere to hide something? In the present, the real me had no idea. I'd picked up the trumpet case when the door behind me opened. I had turned. It was the trumpet player himself. He had challenged me, then saw what I was doing and charged. We struggled and I hit him… with the trumpet case. He fell. He was out cold. I could hear the door handle again, so I fled out through the nearest door and into the corridor just as someone came into the room behind me. Had they seen me? I had to get rid of the trumpet case. Perhaps I'd had time to conceal something in it, or perhaps what I was looking for was still in it. Either way, I had to put it somewhere I could find it again so I could search it properly and retrieve the mystery item. Somewhere it wouldn't be seen. Somewhere easy to reach. I had to hurry.

Back in the present I stood in the corridor and looked at the ornate Chinese cabinet opposite the library door, the one Haddock had misidentified as a reproduction yesterday. I'd seen that cabinet several times before and it had never struck me as particularly interesting until Sir Hector had told me a little of its history, but now, in my imaginary panic, it stood out as my potential salvation.

A vase of dried flowers stood on top of the cabinet, next to the revolting clock that Haddock had been so excited about the day before, and there was a tantalizing gap between the clawed feet beneath, but it was the brass handle on the intricately inlayed doors that caught my attention. I reached out and opened one of the doors, and there inside was the missing trumpet case.

I rushed into the dining room, almost bowling the inspector over in my haste.

'Inspector,' I blurted. 'I'm so sorry. I–'

'Calm down, young lady,' he said, kindly. 'What's troubling you?'

As succinctly as I could I told the story of my morning's adventures.

'Well bless my soul,' he said. 'I shall have to have words with the local uniformed boys. How on earth did they miss that? I'd been assured that everything had been thoroughly searched.'

'It's an anonymous little cupboard, sir,' I said. 'I only noticed it because it's directly opposite the door. It's in a little alcove so it's easy to ignore it otherwise.'

'That's as may be, miss, but it's a policeman's duty to notice everything. No matter. What did you do with the trumpet case?'

'I left it there. I was already feeling a little stupid for touching the door handle so I didn't want to get my fingerprints on the case as well.'

'Quick thinking,' he said, encouragingly. 'We'll make a detective of you yet. Now then, would you mind waiting here in case your mistress turns up, and I'll go and take a look at this trumpet case for myself.'

'Of course, sir. Is that tea fresh?'

'Dora brought it in a few moments ago,' he said. 'She seemed a little put out that you weren't here as a matter of fact, looked like she had something on her mind. I told her you were running an errand for me.'

'Thank you. I expect she wanted to gloat about being so thoroughly comforted by Mr Dunn.'

He chuckled. 'I don't doubt it,' he said. 'Why don't you help yourself to some tea and I'll be back in a few moments.'

And with that, he left the room.

I poured myself a cup of tea and tried to sit quietly to wait for the inspector's return or Lady Hardcastle's arrival, but I couldn't settle. I was too excited. I'd made an actual discovery. A real piece of detection. It was all far too thrilling to be sitting quietly drinking tea in someone else's dining room.

At length I heard voices in the corridor and as I rose to find out what was going on, the door opened and Lady Hardcastle came in.

'Thank you, Jenkins,' she said with her head still turned towards the corridor. 'You're a sweetheart. I don't suppose you could magic up a pot of coffee? And perhaps some of Mrs Brown's delicious biscuits?'

There was a muffled, 'Certainly, my lady,' from the corridor and then the sound of Jenkins's unhurried footsteps on the wooden floor.

Lady Hardcastle closed the door.

'Hello, pet,' she said, putting her bag on the table. 'No Inspector Sunderland? How did your snooping go?'

Once more I described my search, and the unexpectedly easy discovery of the missing case.

'Oh, I say, how exciting,' she said.

'I should say so. In the words of Sergeant Dobson I was "all of a pother".'

'I'm not surprised. Actual detecting. Well done you. We have even more to tell the inspector when he turns up.'

'Oh, sorry, my lady, I neglected to say that he's already here. I told him about the case and he's gone to look for himself.'

'Splendid,' she said, and sat down to await his return.

We didn't have to wait long. We'd only just begun to chatter excitedly, speculating on what the significance of the discovery might be, when the inspector came in, carrying the trumpet case.

'Aha,' he said. 'Good morning, Lady Hardcastle. I trust you're well.'

'Splendidly well, than you, Inspector,' she said. 'And rather proud of dear Flo, too. What a find!'

'Quite a breakthrough, my lady, yes. Well done, Miss Armstrong. This should help things along nicely.'

'How exciting,' I said. 'But don't we have to wait for... what did you call him? The "fingerprint man"?'

'Ordinarily, miss, yes, but see the brass catch here?' He indicated the locking clasp that held the case closed. 'Bright and shiny. Not a mark on it, nor anywhere else on the case as far as I can see. The whole thing has been wiped clean. Work of an experienced thief, I'd say.'

'Oh,' I said, disappointedly.

He smiled. 'Not to worry, though, miss, it's still an important part of the puzzle. And who knows what we might find inside.'

He made to open the case, but Lady Hardcastle laid a hand on his arm.

'Before you do, Inspector, would you mind indulging us a little? Flo and I have a little theory about what might be inside and it will be so much more impressive if we tell you before you open it.'

'By all means, my lady. I'm all ears.'

'It relies,' she said, 'on our supposition that Sylvia Montgomery, the newcomer to the band, is actually a notorious jewel thief who is using the band as a cover to get herself into rich houses and steal from the families who live there. Rather than take the jewels out in her own luggage, she conceals them in her fellow musicians' instrument cases without their knowledge. On the evening of the party, she was caught by Mr Holloway as she attempted to hide her spoils in his trumpet case. A struggle ensued and she left him unconscious on the floor as she fled.'

The inspector smiled indulgently. 'I see, my lady. I suppose your theory also has room for Mr Haddock?'

'It does indeed, Inspector. He's her fence.'

'Well, well, well,' he said, producing a telegram from his jacket pocket. 'Either you have a source of your own inside Scotland Yard, or you're a psychic. Take a look at this.' He handed her the telegram.

She read in silence for a few moments and then handed the telegram back to the inspector. 'I say,' was all she said.

'Well?' I said, impatiently. 'What does it say?'

'It says, miss,' said the inspector, 'that Sylvia Montgomery is better known to Scotland Yard as Olive Sewell, a notorious sneak thief with a particular fondness for diamonds, and that Clifford Haddock, junk shop owner and oily tick, is currently under investigation for fencing stolen goods, most particularly a diamond necklace owned by the Countess of Teignmouth. The necklace in question was last seen before a party at which Roland Richman's Ragtime Revue provided the musical entertainment and Superintendent Witham is even now on an express train to Bristol and asks that we detain our songbird until he can make his way to The Grange to ask her a few questions of his own.'

'Gracious,' I said.

'Indeed,' said the inspector. 'How on earth did you two manage to find all that out before I did?'

'Ah,' said Lady Hardcastle. 'Now... well... you see...'

'I think,' I said, keen to help her out, 'that Lady Hardcastle is trying to find a way of saying, "We just made it all up in a flight of fancy," that makes it sound much less like two women indulging in brandy-fuelled whimsy, and more like the work of two keen detective brains hard at work.'

'Thank you, dear,' she said. 'Though I think you might have let the cat out of the bag a little there.'

The inspector laughed. 'Well, you certainly came up with a version of the truth, however you did it, and there's always room for imagination in the world of professional detection. And now we can test the other part of your theory. If you're correct, we ought to find something interesting inside this case other than a bottle of valve oil and an old duster.'

Almost ceremoniously, the inspector flipped open the two catches and slowly lifted the lid. The lining was of red velvet, slightly padded to protect the instrument in transit. There was a lidded compartment along the side nearest the handle and the inspector opened it by lifting a small leather tab. The compartment did indeed contain a small glass bottle of some oily substance and a rag, as well as the "stick thing" that Miss Montgomery had described. The inspector lifted these few items out and it was obvious that the red velvet base of the compartment was slightly askew. A false bottom. Inspector Sunderland pried it loose.

'Oh,' he said. 'That's terribly disappointing.'

We peered closer. There was nothing there.

'It looks as though there was something in there at some point, though,' said Lady Hardcastle. 'That's definitely a secret compartment.'

'I can't disagree, my lady,' said the inspector. 'But it opens up a few holes in your theory. Mr Holloway would most definitely have known about his hollow case, so if Miss Montgomery – Miss Sewell as I should say – was using his case to smuggle her swag, he would have been well aware. Which makes it rather unlikely that she and he would have struggled had he caught her hiding her stuff there.'

'Harrumph,' said Lady Hardcastle.

'It was a most inspired thought, though,' said the inspector. 'And we still need to speak to Miss Sewell again now that we have a little more information about her.'

'I suppose so,' she said.

'May I have a look at the case, Inspector,' I said.

'By all means,' he said.

I flipped down the cover of the storage compartment and closed the case, latching the lid shut. I picked it up and hefted it; it would make a passable weapon in a scuffle. The edges of the case were reinforced with leather, with a double layer on each corner. I imagined myself swinging the case to strike someone and pictured one of those corners making contact with his head. I looked closer at the corner farthest from me.

'Look here, Inspector,' I said. 'Blood. I should say this is the murder weapon.'

He looked where I indicated. 'I should say you're right, miss,' he said. 'Chalk up one more win for the amateurs. Even I'd missed that.'

Lady Hardcastle beamed at me.

'Well done, Flo,' she said. 'Does that make up for our foolish whimsy, Inspector?'

'It more than makes up for it, my lady,' he said. 'And as I said before, there was truth in the fancy. We shall find out more when we get her in here again. But I'm afraid you shan't be here, Miss Armstrong.'

'Oh,' I said, disappointedly. 'Shall I not?'

'Indeed you shall not, miss. While Lady Hardcastle and I apply the thumbscrews in here – you did remember to bring the thumbscrews, my lady?'

'Sadly no, Inspector. Thumbscrews and coshes are entirely Flo's province.'

'No matter, we shall improvise. But while we do that, Miss Armstrong, you shall be putting your newfound searching skills to good use in Miss Sewell's room. I'm not at all sure that she has anything to do with the murder but I'll be extremely surprised if she's not up to something.'

I brightened at once. 'Oh, goodie,' I said. 'I shall turn the place over good and proper, guv, you see if I don't.'

'That's the spirit,' he said with another of his throaty chuckles.

'My maid, the bloodhound,' said Lady Hardcastle.

'You flatter me, my lady,' I said. 'You couldn't have given it a few moments' more thought and come up with a more attractive dog?'

'Pish and fiddlesticks,' she said. 'You know full well what I meant by it.'

'Pfft,' I said, eloquently.

'I think I'd better ring for that Jenkins character to go and find Miss Sewell,' said the inspector, but as he reached for the bell, there was a knock at the door and Jenkins appeared with the coffee.

'My dear Jenkins,' said Lady Hardcastle. 'What a propitious arrival. Set the coffee down over there, if you please, and then might I ask another favour of you?'

'Of course, my lady,' he said. 'Whatever you need.'

'Would you dispatch one of your minions to Miss Montgomery's room, please. Present our compliments and ask if she would be good enough to join the inspector and me in the dining room.'

'Certainly, my lady. I shall send Dora, if that suits; a run up and down stairs might do her some good. She's being insufferably cheeky and mischievous this morning, I don't know what's got into her.'

There was the briefest of pauses while Lady Hardcastle stifled her giggle and composed herself before she said, 'That will be splendid, Jenkins, thank you so much.'

He bowed respectfully, showing no sign of being discomfited by the smirks his innocent comment had provoked, and left the room.

'You'd better get going, pet,' said Lady Hardcastle. 'Lurk somewhere for a few minutes to give them time to get down here, and then slip up to the attic rooms and do your snooping.'

I left the dining room and headed for the library, reasoning that there would be no one there, and waited for my chance to be a proper detective once more.

I hid out in the library for what I considered an appropriate length of time which I passed by leafing through a few of Sir Hector's books. He had an impressive collection, comprising everything from history and biography, to poetry, plays and quite a few novels, including some published surprisingly recently.

But I couldn't linger, no matter how interesting the reading matter, though I did make a mental note to ask Lady Hardcastle to ask Sir Hector if I might be able to read some of them at a more convenient time.

I managed to get all the way to the top of the servants' staircase without meeting anyone, but that wasn't really a surprise at that time of day. During the working day, all the servants would be hard at work (surreptitious comforting notwithstanding) but the musicians were self proclaimed late risers and might still be in their rooms.

There was a brass cardholder on each doorframe, holding a small white card bearing the occupants' names written in a scrupulously neat hand. The rooms nearest the stairs belonged to the household servants so I kept going down the passageway to the smaller rooms at the end. Roland Richman had his own room, as had the late Mr Holloway. Skins and Dunn shared a room which meant that the last one must be Miss Sewell's.

I opened the door and entered quickly, not wanting to linger outside lest I be spotted. I closed the door.

There was a bed – slept in and unmade; a washstand – jug empty, bowl full, face towel scrunched up on the floor; and a small wardrobe – door open, clothes strewn on the floor. Miss Sewell had the voice of an angel, but she lived like a pig.

I stood with my back to the door, trying my imagining trick again. I'd stolen something from the house. I had just a few moments to stash it and get back to the party before I was missed.

I looked around. There were stockings on the floor, a dress over the back of the chair. A suitcase stood open in the corner. Time was running out, what was I going to do with this stuff? My eyes fell on the makeup case standing on a small chair near the looking glass hanging on the wall. It was the only thing in the room that was in any way tidy and ordered.

I opened the case and lifted out the top tray of neatly arranged powders, lipsticks and creams. The compartment at the bottom was slightly less well ordered, but it contained a few items of interest: a pair of diamond earrings which I'd seen Lady Farley-Stroud wearing a few weeks earlier, a double string of pearls, and, at the very bottom, a beautiful diamond pendant which matched the earrings perfectly. I replaced the top tray, closed the case, and took it with me as I left the room and returned to the dining room.

When I returned to the dining room, the interview was in full flow.

'...and I'm telling you that I've never heard of this Olive Sewell character.'

'A case of mistaken identity, then, miss?'

'I should say so, yes.'

'I see,' said the inspector, acknowledging my arrival with a nod. 'Perhaps Miss Armstrong has found something that might shed a little light on the matter.' He noticed what was in my hands. 'Another sort of "case" entirely, it seems. Is this yours, Miss Montgomery?'

'It looks exactly like mine, certainly,' she said.

'You won't mind if I take a look inside?'

She sighed. 'Be my guest, Inspector. Be my guest.'

He opened the make-up case and looked inside, taking in the neatly arranged items in the top section. Then he lifted the tray and removed it.

'Well, well, well,' he said. 'And what do you suppose we have here?'

She sighed again. 'If there's not a pair of diamond earrings, a pendant, and a string of pearls, then your bloodhound has got stickier fingers than I have,' she said, glaring at me.

I confess I was getting a little weary of the bloodhound references by this point, so I glared back.

'So it's not a plant, then? Not some sort of police fit-up?' asked the inspector, holding up the jewellery.

'Well, I could deny it, but I'm sure you consider your little Welsh maid here above reproach, so what would be the point? It's a fair cop. You've got me bang to rights, guv, and no mistake.'

'I have indeed, and you're under arrest for theft. But you're being remarkably flippant for someone accused of murder, Miss Sewell. You were seen leaving the scene of a particularly cowardly killing and here you are in possession of a few items of rather expensive jewellery. I'd say you ought to be taking things a little more seriously.'

'*Mrs* Sewell, if you insist on using that name,' she said, coldly. 'I lifted a few of the lady of the house's less revolting items of jewellery, Inspector, and it would be a waste of all our time to deny that now. But I didn't kill anyone. You already know I was seen in the library while Nelson was still on stage.'

'So tell us exactly what happened.'

Another sigh. 'Well, Inspector, I'm reasonably sure I told you before that I left the stage during the instrumental numbers and went off in search of some decent booze. I started in the library but there wasn't a drop to be had, so I left there and decided to explore the rest of the house. That was when Blodwyn Bloodhound here saw me.'

That earned her another glare.

'And there was no one else in the library?' asked Lady Hardcastle.

'No one,' replied Sylvia. Olive.

'And you noticed nothing out of the ordinary in there?'

'Nothing. I've told you all this before. Just a big library with the band's instrument cases at one end and absolutely no booze anywhere. I mean, really. Not a drop.'

'I know,' said Lady Hardcastle. 'Whoever heard of such a thing?'

'It's not like they couldn't afford it,' said Montgomery. Sewell.

'Well, actually–' Lady Hardcastle began.

The inspector ostentatiously cleared his throat.

'Sorry, Inspector,' said Lady Hardcastle. 'Do, please, continue.'

'Thank you, my lady, you're most kind,' he said. 'Mrs Sewell?'

'What?'

'You left the library, and...'

'Oh, yes. Pretty much everyone was still in the ballroom so I took the opportunity to have a bit of a poke round upstairs. And... well... you know... on thing led to another...'

'And Lady Farley-Stroud's best jewels accidentally fell into your pocket as you walked past them?' said the inspector.

'In a nutshell. I didn't plan it, but it was too good a chance to miss.'

'Didn't plan it? You came to a country house with no plans to rob it? I have it on the best authority that that's your MO.'

'Oh, I can't fault your sources, Inspector,' she said. 'But on this occasion, there was no plan. I had nothing to do with this booking. In fact I didn't know anything about it until I was given a train ticket and told I had to be here by six o'clock with a bag packed for an overnight stay. I had no time for any of my usual research, no time to plan anything at all.'

'You usually have a say in your bookings?' said Lady Hardcastle.

'Yes. Rolie makes the bookings, but we all have a vote. This one came out of nowhere.'

There was a knock at the door and the redoubtable Sergeant Dobson peered in.

'You sent for me, sir?'

'Ah, Sergeant, yes. Mrs Sewell here will be off to the cells soon, but she's expecting a visit from Superintendent Witham of Scotland Yard first. Please keep her secure until he arrives.'

'Right you are, sir,' said the sergeant. 'Handcuffs, sir?'

'No, Sergeant, that shouldn't be necessary. Just take her shoes and don't let her out of your sight.'

'Very good, sir. I can take her down the cell in the village if you likes, sir.'

'No, the superintendent is coming here. Find a quiet room somewhere and make yourselves comfortable until he arrives. We can arrange less comfortable accommodation later.'

'Righto, sir. Come along, madam, if you please.'

Mrs Sewell rose from the table and followed the sergeant.

'Just to be sure, inspector,' she said from the doorway. 'I didn't kill Nelson and I'd like five minutes alone in a room with whoever did. He was a good man, and a damn fine trumpeter.'

She closed the door behind her.

'Another dead end,' said Lady Hardcastle, staring dejectedly at the Crime Board.

'I shouldn't say that, my lady,' said the inspector. 'We've eliminated one of our possible suspects, I think. She's a talented sneak thief who prides herself on leaving no traces. The sort where the victims don't even realize they've been robbed until days, weeks, sometimes even months later. I've heard of cases where it's been up to a year before someone notices that a special item of jewellery has gone missing. She's not the sort to go tearing instrument cases to pieces; too calm and cool, that one.'

'But where do we go from here, Inspector? How does that help us?'

'We now know that the performance was arranged by Mr Richman without consulting the rest of the band and that he didn't tell them about it until the last moment. I think Mr Richman wanted to get out of London in a hurry and didn't want a lot of loose talk about where he was off to.'

'That certainly makes sense,' she said, thoughtfully. 'But why would he be in such a rush to get away?'

'I'm pretty certain that he won't tell us himself,' said the inspector. 'Unless we can kid on that we know a little more than we actually do. And to do that we need to find out a bit more about the band and what they were up to. Miss Armstrong, will you resume bloodhound duties and try to track down…' He consulted his notes. 'Mr Ivor Maloney, known to his friends as Skins.'

'Drummer of this parish. On my way, sir,' I said, and left the dining room.

I found Skins sitting on the low wall outside the French windows which opened from the ballroom. He had his back to the house and was looking out across the grounds and down into the valley of the River Severn. I coughed politely.

'Mr Maloney?' I said.

He turned and smiled. 'Call me Skins, love, everyone does. What's your name?'

'I'm Armstrong, sir,' I said.

'And that's what your mother calls you, is it?'

'As long as she calls me in time for supper, sir, I don't mind. Inspector Sunderland would like to speak to you.'

'No problem, darlin', you lead the way.' He stood up. 'But seriously, what do they call you?'

I went back into the ballroom through the open French windows and he dutifully followed as I led him through the house towards the dining room.

'Seriously, Mr Skins, they call me Armstrong.'

He chuckled. '"Mr Skins". You are a caution.'

'So I've been told, sir. My name is Florence. My mother calls me Flossie, my friends call me Flo, and you... I shall make up my mind about you presently.'

'You can't say fairer than that, Miss Armstrong. I eagerly await the results of your deliberations. But please don't call me "sir"; I ain't nobody's superior. 'Cept when it comes to the drums, then I'm the absolute cake, second to no man, and all shall bow before me.'

I smiled and we walked on.

'Nice gaff this,' he said, admiring the oak panelling in the passageway. 'Must be nice working here.'

'They tell me it is, sir, but I'm afraid I don't work here.'

'Oh, right,' he said. 'So how come you're dressed up in all the clobber, and running errands for this inspector geezer? The detectives round here have maids or something?'

'Something like that, sir,' I said and opened the dining room door. 'Lady Hardcastle, Inspector Sunderland, this is Mr Maloney.'

I gestured for him to enter and he walked in grinning.

'Call me Skins, guv,' he said, reaching out to shake the inspector's hand. 'Everybody does.' He waved a salute across the table. 'Lady H,' he said, and sat down before anyone could say anything. I took up my unobtrusive place in the corner.

'Thank you for agreeing to speak to me, Mr Maloney,' said the inspector, pulling out his own chair and sitting down. 'My sympathies on the death of your friend. Were you close to Mr Holloway?'

'Close enough, Inspector,' said Skins. 'We'd been working together for maybe... I don't know... maybe three years. Travelling and that. You get close to a bloke when you work together like that, don't you?'

'You do, sir, yes. And what about the rest of the band, are you close to them?'

'Again, guv, close enough. Me and Barty get on best, I'd say, and Rolie's all right for a manager, I s'pose. So, yeah, not bad.'

'What about Miss Montgomery?' asked the inspector, careful to use her alias.

'Odd bird, that one. Sings like a nightingale, mind you.'

'Odd, sir?'

'Oh, you know. Bit stand-offish. Like she's always got something else on her mind. Other fish to fry. Know what I mean?'

'Actually, sir, I think I do, yes. Now then, this Engagement Party engagement, sir. It's your normal line of work?'

'Our bread and butter, guv, yes.'

'So it must have been reassuring to know it was coming up.'

'Do what, guv?'

'Good to know there was a nice little earner on the horizon, takes the pressure off paying the bills, eh?'

'It would have been grand, guv, yes. 'Cept this one was sprung on us.'

'Oh?'

'Yeah. Train ticket and "Pack your bags we're on the three o'clock train and if you miss it, you're sacked." Not really time to look forward to it.'

'I see, sir. Was that usual?'

'With Rolie, everything's usual. He's a bit of a fly one, our Rolie. Like Sylvie; always got an iron or two in the fire what we don't know about. Usually we know about bookings weeks, even months in advance, plan them together, like. But every once in a while...'

'What happens every once in a while, Mr Maloney?'

'Every once in a while, Inspector, he takes a whim and we scarper off dead quick like.'

'Scarper, sir? Is it like that? Running away?'

'Or running towards. I never know for sure.'

'But you have your suspicions?'

'You can't help but have suspicions, guv.'

'And what were your suspicions this time?'

'Nothing I could make sense of, that's for sure, but I've heard what happened in the library and I've been wondering about a few things.'

'I've been closeted away in here for the most part, sir, so I've not heard the gossip. What have you heard about Mr Holloway?'

'Coshed and left for dead they told me,' said Skins

'Indeed, sir, yes. At first we thought it was a robbery.'

'A robbery? Nelson?'

'Is that unlikely, sir?' asked the inspector.

'We're musicians, Inspector, only one step out of the gutter – not even that to hear some people talk about us. We ain't got nothing worth nicking.'

'Meaning you no offence, sir, but that was my thought at first. I presumed he'd stumbled upon a burglary and had been walloped for his troubles. But then we discovered his missing trumpet case, and that got me thinking,' said the inspector.

'Thinking someone was there to nick his trumpet case, you mean? An empty trumpet case?'

'Again, sir, you leap straight to the heart of it. Was it empty?'

'Was it empty? Hmmm.' Skins sat a moment in thought. 'Here's the thing, Inspector, right? See, I don't like talking out of turn, and I ain't the sort to go dropping no one in it, but there's a chance – I mean, just a chance, right? – that there was something in that case. That's what I mean about my suspicions.'

'What sort of a something, sir,' said the inspector, leaning forwards slightly.

'That's the thing, see, I ain't at all certain. I just heard some things, that's all.'

'What sort of things?'

'Well, see, our Roland, he's a bit of a sly one, like I say. Always got a fiddle going, some scheme or other. So anyway, last month we was playing these dates in Paris – there's some lovely clubs there, they love a bit of the old ragtime, the Frogs – and one night we was in this little dive in Montmartre. And we're sitting there in the break, you know, me, Barty, Rolie, Nelson and Sylvie, all together, like, but round two tables. So we're sipping some rough red wine or other, and this bloke comes over and whispers in Rolie's ear. Then he and Nelson gets up and goes to sit at another table and they're chatting away, all secretive like.'

'Could you hear what they were saying?' asked Lady Hardcastle.

Skins turned towards her. 'That's just it, my lady. I could and I couldn't.'

'What do you mean?' she said.

'Well, I could hear snatches of it, like, but I couldn't suss out what they was on about. So this bloke what come over, he's saying, "I've got it, but I'll never get it past the English Customs." And Rolie says, "Don't worry about that, we can take care of that, can't we Nelse," all chuckly and smug like. And Nelson, he chuckles back.'

'So you think they were smuggling something?' said the inspector.

'Well, that's what it sounds like, don't it.'

'It does. And if Nelson was involved, that means it could have been in his trumpet case. But why get Nelson involved at all? If Richman was the schemer, why share the proceeds?'

'He doesn't have an instrument case, does he,' said Skins. 'He plays piano so he don't carry nothing but his music. Our bags sometimes gets checked, but never our instrument cases. Never figured that one out, but that's the way it happens. Rolie must've needed someone with a case he could hide something in.'

'It would have to be something small,' said Lady Hardcastle. 'But that doesn't narrow it down much. It could be money, jewellery, documents... anything—'

'Quite so, my lady,' said the inspector, cutting her off before she could reveal too much of what we already knew. 'Did you get any hint as to what it might be, Mr Maloney?'

'No, nothing. There was more mumbling and then we was back on for the second set.'

'Did you get a good look at this chap that came up to speak to them? Had you ever seen him before?'

'No, like I said, it was a bit of a dive. Dark, candles in old wine bottles, you know the sort of thing. Oh, actually, come to think of it, you most probably don't. But anyway, they ain't the sort of places where you can get a good butcher's at someone if he fancies keeping out of sight.'

'What about his accent,' asked Lady Hardcastle. 'Could you tell where he was from?'

'You're a shrewd one, my lady, I can see why he wants you in his team. Yes, I was going to mention that. He spoke English, and the few words I heard seemed normal, like, like he was comfortable with the language, but a couple of words didn't seem to come natural, like it wasn't his own language. Know what I mean? He sounded posh, like, but foreign with it.'

'But no idea what sort of foreign?' asked the inspector.

'Do I look like a language professor, guv?'

'No, sir, but you have a musician's ear. You hear tones and rhythms that the rest of us might miss. It's like second nature to you. And you travel. You must have heard many dozens of accents.'

Skins sat a while in contemplation. 'All right, then. So I don't reckon he was English. Nor French – you can tell them, even the ones what's really good at English. He was like... I tell you what, there was some sounds like the Lascar sailors up the East End.'

'Indian?'

'Yeah, but not rough like them, more like he was an educated man.'

'Was there anyone else there, Mr Skins?' I said.

'Anyone else, love?'

'You know, anyone that the Indian gentleman might have spoken to? Anyone else suspicious? Anything that might give us a clue as to what was going on?'

'Oh, I see. No, darling, it was a regular Paris nightclub. Mix of people. Some rough, some smart. Everyone from street toughs to music aficionados to military types and posh ladies and gents out for a bit of adventure.'

'Oh,' I said, disappointedly. 'So no one stood out?'

'Not really, love, no. Just your average Saturday night crowd in Paris.'

I nodded.

'Thank you, Mr Maloney, this is all most helpful,' said the inspector as he made yet more notes. 'I appreciate that it's inconvenient, but could I prevail upon you not to leave The Grange for a few more days. I might need to talk to you again.'

'Inconvenient, guv?' said Skins with a grin. 'Free lodgings, free meals, and fresh air? You're kidding, right?'

'Well, when you put it like that, sir, I suppose you could treat it as a holiday.'

'Too right, guv. Anything else I can do for you?'

'Not for now, sir. Thank you very much for your time.'

'My pleasure, guv.' He stood to leave. 'Lady H, Miss Armstrong.' He bowed. 'Don't forget, love, I'm still waiting to hear what I can call you.'

I smiled and bowed in return and he left the room.

'What can he call you?' asked Lady Hardcastle after Skins had closed the door.

'I've not decided yet, my lady.'

'Is it a difficult decision?'

'No, my lady, but one can't take such things lightly. There's power in a name.'

'There is, there is,' she said. 'Well, Inspector, what do you make of all that?'

'If he's not spinning us a yarn, it seems Mr Holloway and Mr Richman were up to no good. There seems to have been someone else involved who was...' he consulted his notes, '..."posh but foreign" who might have been Indian and might have been paying them to smuggle something small into the country. Or it could be a load of old nonsense. But there's some correlation between what he says and what Mrs Sewell said, so I should say it's worth talking to Mr Richman again as soon as we can; at the very least he might give the lie to Mr Maloney's tall tales.'

'Would you like me to fetch him, Inspector,' I said, but before he could answer there was a knock at the door.

It was Jenkins.

'Begging your pardon, Inspector, but a telegram has arrived for you.' He presented the telegram on a silver tray.

'Thank you, Jenkins,' said the inspector.

'May I clear the coffee tray, sir?'

'Yes,' said the inspector distractedly as he read the telegram. 'Please do.'

'Very good, sir,' said Jenkins, and went unobtrusively about his business. 'Luncheon will be served in half an hour on the terrace, sir, my lady. Shall you be joining us?'

'Would you think me very rude,' said the inspector, looking up from the telegram, 'if I asked for a plate of sandwiches in here? I really do have a lot of paperwork to get through. Notes and such like.'

'Of course not, sir, my only intention was to make certain that you felt welcome. I shall have lunch sent here for you presently.'

'Thank you, Jenkins.'

'And you, my lady?' said Jenkins.

'Actually, Jenkins dear, I have one or two errands to run in the village,' said Lady Hardcastle. 'So if the inspector is busy, I shall be slipping out for a while. I can get out of your way for a while, Inspector.'

'Please don't leave on my account, my lady,' he said. 'But if you need to be elsewhere, please do. Shall we reconvene at three?'

'That will be splendid. So, no, Jenkins. Thank you for the kind offer, but I shall be away for an hour or two myself.'

'Very good, my lady. Perhaps an early tea when you all return to work?'

'You, Jenkins, are the very model of a modern... ummm... something or other,' said Lady Hardcastle. 'Whatever would we do without you? That would be splendid. Thank you.'

Jenkins left, beaming.

'What's in the telegram, Inspector? Anything juicy?' she said as Jenkins closed the door.

'Quite possibly, my lady. Quite possibly very juicy indeed.'

'And...? Is that all we get?'

'For now, my lady. I think this afternoon's interviews should prove very nearly conclusive.

'I say,' she said. 'How exciting. But for now, we must away. Servant, neither shilly, nor shally. Let us leave the good officer of the law to his deliberations and hie us to the village.'

And with that, we were gone.

We left the house through the front door and set off for a walk into the village in the warm, late summer sunshine. The grounds were clean and tidy, but not luxurious, with the same air of faded opulence that clung to the house itself. The whole place was charming, comfortable and welcoming. I had succumbed to snobbishness when I first encountered the Farley-Strouds and had dismissed them as pretentious lord-of-the-manor types who were clinging to memories of their wealthier past and trying desperately hard to be something they were not. But the more I got to know them, the more I succumbed instead to their geniality and charm. They couldn't afford to maintain The Grange as once they could, and they should probably have sold up and bought a nice little flat in Bristol or Gloucester. But that would have meant giving up the life they knew and loved, not to mention putting at least a dozen servants out of work, so instead they made do. I decided that I very much liked the competent and capable Lady Farley-Stroud and her charmingly baffled husband. The village was very much enriched by their presence.

We were walking along the grass beside the long, winding drive, enjoying the late afternoon sunshine and Lady Hardcastle was wondering aloud about some unusual bird she'd just seen, when I saw a strange movement out of the corner of my eye. I touched her elbow to alert her and turned to face whatever was approaching us.

It was Mr Bikash Verma, running at an impressively athletic pace and obviously trying to catch us up. Lumbering behind him, much more slowly and clearly none too happy about having to move even that quickly, was a gigantic, muscular man in what I took to be Nepalese garb. He looked like he could lift a horse above his head if only he could catch up with one.

'I say!' shouted Mr Verma. 'Lady Hardcastle! Please! Wait a moment!'

She turned to face him and we waited for an awkward few seconds while he closed the distance between us.

Panting and laughing, he finally caught us up. 'I say, that was invigorating. Thank you for waiting.'

Mr Verma, too, was dressed in loose-fitting clothes of an unfamiliar style, but made from a much more luxurious fabric. The man-mountain was still lumbering towards us and was still some way distant but Mr Verma paid him little attention.

'Good afternoon, Mr Verma,' said Lady Hardcastle, warmly. 'How lovely to see you again.'

'You too, my lady,' he said with a small bow.

'Did you enjoy the party?' she asked. 'Did I miss too much fun after I left?'

'It was very enjoyable, thank you. And no, you didn't miss much unless you would have enjoyed our ill-advised game of croquet by candlelight.'

'Oh, I say,' she said, delightedly. 'What larks.'

'There was certainly more larking than playing,' he said, ruefully.

'Wonderful, wonderful. Well, now then, Mr Verma, what is it that brings you careering across the grass at such a pace? What might I do for you?'

The muscle man had finally caught up and Mr Verma indicated that we should resume our walk. 'Clarissa was telling us at the party that you are something of an amateur sleuth,' he said.

'Indeed I am,' she said proudly. 'With my faithful assistant Armstrong, I have solved many a mystery.'

'Two, my lady,' I said. 'You've solved two mysteries. And one of those more or less solved itself.'

'Very well,' she harrumphed. 'Yes, Mr Verma, I have solved one mystery and my maid here has helped me enormously by being a Dreary Dora and spoiling all my fun.'

Mr Verma laughed. 'Well that's one more than I have managed. I am in a spot of bother.'

'"A spot of bother"? Would you think me awfully rude if I were to ask you how it is that you speak such wonderful English?'

'Not rude at all, my lady. I studied at Cambridge.'

'Really? Goodness me. Which college?'

'King's.'

'Well I never. I was at Girton.'

'It's a wonder we never met,' he said graciously.

'Oh, you charming young man. I fear I was there long before you were born, dear boy. And now you're the King's emissary?'

'I am, my lady, and that is why I was especially keen to come to Clarissa's party and why I most urgently need your help.'

'Gosh,' she said, rather nonplussed. 'What on earth can I do that might be of help to the King of Nepal?'

'The tale is a long one,' he said. 'But I shall try to keep it brief. If doing so makes anything unclear, please stop me and I shall try to elucidate.'

Lady Hardcastle nodded and gestured for him to continue.

'My country,' he began, almost as though reading from a prepared script, 'has a rich and complex religious history. Over the centuries, many gods have been worshipped and many sacred idols have been fashioned. One such idol was presented to the King as a gift on the occasion of his coronation. It was cast in pure gold, decorated with precious jewels of exquisite colour and clarity, but the most magnificent of them all was the emerald which formed its single, all-seeing eye. It was of the deepest green and the size of a hen's egg, nothing like it had ever been seen in the kingdom before or since.

'The idol was given a special place in a temple to the north of our capital and the people would come from miles around to see it. It was once a sacred object, but it was also a creation of rare beauty, and even though the religion it represented had long-since faded away, it was still revered. At first it was guarded day and night by the Royal Guard, but after a time it became apparent that it was so beloved by the people that no one would dare steal it, and soon the guard was stood down.'

Mr Verma paused for a moment and Lady Hardcastle seized the opportunity to interrupt.

'Let me guess,' she said. 'It was stolen?'

'It was stolen, my lady,' said Mr Verma. 'There was a public outcry and everyone, young and old, rich and poor, joined the hunt for the thief. After a month of searching and more than one unfortunate false accusation, a gang of Indian thieves was apprehended at the border, attempting to smuggle the statue into Bengal. The members of the gang were hanged on the spot and the statue returned to Kathmandu, but during the month it had been missing, there had been some damage. Several of the jewels had been prized loose from the idol, including its magnificent emerald eye. Over the following months, many of the jewels were recovered and the rest replaced with similar stones, but the Eye was never found.

'For nearly ten years, the King's agents have been searching for the Emerald Eye, but every time they picked up a new trail, fate intervened and once more it slipped from their grasp. Early this year I was appointed the King's Royal Secretary and as one of my many duties, I inherited the task of finding the Eye. We heard that it had surfaced once more in Calcutta, and then in March we heard a rumour that it was being offered for sale by a sailor in Marseille. From there we managed to follow its trail to Paris, where the story was circulating that it was in the hands of an Indian antiquities dealer who had found a buyer in England and that the Eye would soon be making its way to London.'

'My goodness,' interrupted Lady Hardcastle. 'I think I might have heard that part of the story this morning.'

Mr Verma stopped dead. 'Really?' he said, apparently somewhat shocked.

'One of the members of the band told us what we thought was a tall tale about something being smuggled from Paris. We had no idea what it might be.'

'But why on earth would he tell you such a thing out of the blue? Do you know this man?'

'I'm sorry, Mr Verma, I thought you knew. Armstrong and I are helping Inspector Sunderland with the murder investigation.'

'I see,' he said, warily. 'And you were questioning this musician?'

'Yes. Mr Maloney, the drummer,' she said, and then briefly recounted his story of the Parisian bar and the mysterious Indian stranger.

Mr Verma's mood shifted subtly but noticeably. 'Ah,' he said. 'Then I fear I might put you in an awkward position. I had hoped to enjoin you in my quest for the Eye, but if you are already involved in the investigation of the murder... You cannot serve two masters.'

Lady Hardcastle bridled. 'I serve no master, Mr Verma.'

'An expression, my lady, nothing more. I merely meant that my aim is solely to recover the Eye and return it to my King. I have no interest in any of the incidental crimes that follow the jewel wherever she goes. Whereas you... you wish to find the killer and solve the mystery like someone in a detective story, and for you the Eye is merely a colourful detail. The Eye is recovered... the Eye is not recovered... it would not matter to the solving of the murder. You see? You have made your commitment to the police inspector and I cannot ask you to help me if it might mean betraying his investigation.'

'And might it mean that?' she said.

'It might, Lady Hardcastle. It might. I shall trouble you no further, but all I ask is that if you come upon any information regarding the whereabouts of the Eye and you can share that information with me without compromising your own investigation, that you do so.'

And with that, he turned abruptly on his heels and strode back towards the house, the Man Mountain puffing along behind him.

'Well that was abrupt,' said Lady Hardcastle.

'I'm at something of a loss to understand what it was that he wanted from you,' I said.

'Well, he told a romantic tale of a cursed jewel–'

'"Cursed", my lady?'

'Sacred, beloved, stolen, cursed... It's all the same. He told us the tale to appeal to our innate girlish romanticism and to get us snooping round The Grange on his behalf. That's how I read it.'

'I don't think I unpacked my girlish romanticism, it might still be in that trunk we put in the attic.'

'I thought it seemed a little heavy. But now that he knows that we're already involved, perhaps he thinks we might not be so amenable. In fact, we might actually make things more difficult for him.'

'How so?' I said. 'You think he had something to do with the robbery in the library?'

'Oh no, I think our Mr Verma is far too shrewd an operator to soil his own hands with something as sordid as rifling through instrument cases, but that body guard of his seems built for dirty work. And one could imagine him sloshing someone round the head and leaving him for dead without a second thought. And I think I know of someone who might have a particular interest in an Indian jewel.'

'Nepalese, my lady.'

'What? Oh yes, Nepalese. Not far from India.'

'Should we go back and tell the inspector?'

'Not straight away, no. He can wait until later. He wasn't at all keen to share the contents of his telegram, was he. Well, if he can have his little secrets, then so can we. Speaking of which, we need to get to the Post Office. I've had a rather splendid idea and I have a telegram of my own to send.'

With our errands run and a sandwich eaten in the Dog and Duck, we were back in the dining room at The Grange with Inspector Sunderland. To judge from the wreckage of his own lunch on the sliver tray on the table, he'd been very well looked after, and I wondered if we were going to have trouble keeping him awake after such a handsome meal, but he seemed as alert as ever.

'So, ladies, to business,' he said. 'I'm sorry if I seemed distracted before lunch but I'd had some interesting news and I was keen to get one or two things confirmed before we resumed this afternoon. Sir Hector was good enough to let me use his telephone and I've had confirmation from Scotland Yard and, through them, from our colleagues in the *Sûreté* in Paris, that Mr Roland Richman is indeed a known smuggler. He's been picked up a couple of times at Dover with bottles of cognac in his duffel, but never anything more. The French lads were sure he was responsible for moving some diamonds that had come down from Amsterdam last year but nothing was proven.'

'That does seem to square with what Skins told us,' I said.

'It does, miss, yes. But there's more. It seems that acting on information from customs officers in Marseille, the *Sûreté* has just picked up one Praveer Sengupta, an English-educated Indian gentleman from Bengal. They have strong evidence against him on a number of charges of smuggling antiquities out of the Subcontinent and into Europe.'

'Well, well,' I said. 'So he's "posh but foreign". This is all very encouraging.'

'Very encouraging indeed, miss.'

'We've just heard something even more encouraging, Inspector. Something that fills in yet another of the gaps,' said Lady Hardcastle.

'I'm all ears, my lady,' he said.

She repeated Mr Verma's story of the Emerald Eye with surprisingly few of her usual embellishments and when she had finished the inspector let out a low whistle.

'And Verma just ran up to you and blurted this out?' he said

'He did, Inspector. Which is odd, don't you think?'

'Most peculiar. Most peculiar indeed. What did he hope to gain? Surely he knew it would implicate him or his servant in the murder.'

'He's a bright chap,' she said. 'That wouldn't have escaped him. But he was genuinely surprised that we were involved in the investigation and I'm afraid I might have rather played up the "dizzy old biddy" routine at the party so he might not have had too high an opinion of my capacity for deduction.'

'You, my lady?' he said. 'A dizzy old biddy?'

'Oh, come now. Lots of bright young things, a few glasses of fizzy wine and some very reasonable cognac...? Everyone loves a bit of flattering attention, Inspector, and I thought I might get more as a disreputable aunt figure than a disapproving civil servant.'

'Civil servant?'

Lady Hardcastle paused very briefly. 'Figure of speech, Inspector. Someone boring and official, let's say. But it seems I played my part well and he thought I might be exactly the sort of dizzy old biddy who would go trotting off round The Grange looking for his missing jewel without a second thought for how it might be linked to other events.'

The inspector looked thoughtful. 'Perhaps, my lady. Perhaps. And if he's looking for the jewel, it might mean that neither he nor the... the, er, "Man Mountain" are involved. If one of them had pinched the case, they'd have the jewel.'

'Unless,' I said, 'it was still in the trumpet case when they hid it but someone else found it before they could retrieve it.'

'Are you two sure you wouldn't like a job on the Force?' said the inspector. 'I've got detectives on my squad that can't see things like that.'

'You're a shameless flatterer, Inspector Sunderland, and we see right through you,' said Lady Hardcastle. 'But I suppose it's my fault for revealing my weakness for such blandishments.'

I, on the other hand, was keen for more of any sort of flattery and blandishment and rather fancied being compared to a proper detective again.

'What's our next move?' I asked. 'Do we rattle Richman's cage? Thumbscrews and Chinese water torture till he squeals?'

The inspector laughed. 'Or we could just sit him down and ask him a few more questions. All calm and polite, like.'

'Or that,' I said. 'But I know a few ways of hurting him that'll leave no marks if you want.'

He gave me a puzzled frown. 'I'll bear that in mind, miss. But if you could just fetch him without causing him any damage, that'll do for now.'

'Righto, sir,' I said, brightly. I turned to Lady Hardcastle. 'He's not nearly as much fun as I thought, you know.'

They both laughed.

Once again, Roland Richman was sitting in the dining room at The Grange, but he didn't look nearly so comfortable and self-assured as he had last time.

'Well, then,' he said, almost nervously. 'To what do I owe the pleasure of this second meeting? Has something happened? Do you know who did it?'

'Not quite yet, sir,' said the inspector. 'But a couple of things have come to light which need some clarification.'

'If I can help, Inspector, you know I shall.'

'Thank you, sir. I wonder what you can tell us about Mr...' he consulted his notebook. 'Mr Praveer Sengupta.'

'Praveer Sengupta,' said Richman, thoughtfully. 'Name rings a bell. Indian gentleman, I take it? Have we performed for him? I vaguely recall playing an engagement at a do in Cheltenham with some ex-Raj types. Was that it?'

'Not quite, sir, no. This particular gentleman has just been arrested in Paris. Have you ever been to Paris, sir?'

'More than once, Inspector. But I don't recall–'

'You see, sir, I've been in communication with my opposite number in the *Sûreté* in Paris. I've been told that you met Mr Sengupta in a bar in Montmartre last month.'

I'd been wondering how he was going to reveal what we knew without dropping Skins in it. And without actually lying, too. Clever chap, that Inspector Sunderland.

Richman, meanwhile, didn't seem nearly so delighted.

'Ah,' he said, at last.

'"Ah" indeed, sir. Shall we start again? What business did you conduct with Mr Sengupta?'

'It was some… ah… some courier work,' said Richman.

'Delivering messages around Paris, sir? Was the music not paying so well?'

'Not as such, Inspector, no. It was more, ah…'

'To put you out of your misery just a tiny bit, sir,' said the inspector, 'perhaps I should tell you that I've also been in contact with my colleagues at Scotland Yard. They, in turn, have close contact with His Majesty's Customs to whom you are well known on account of your occasional smuggling exploits. Once again, sir, your dealings with Mr Sengupta?'

'Oh, very well,' said Richman, impatiently. 'Sengupta paid me to bring a little something into England.'

'And would that "little something" be a Nepalese emerald, by any chance?'

'Good God, Inspector, how did you–?'

'I believe the customary response is, "I'm a detective, sir; it's my job to know."'

Richman looked defeated.

'There are some other things I know, too, sir, but there's a dismaying number of things which still elude me. I know, for instance, that you brought the gem into the country in a secret compartment in the late Mr Holloway's trumpet case. I strongly suspect that there was some sort of trouble in London – a rival gang, perhaps – which necessitated your sudden flit to Gloucestershire. I know that Mr Haddock is a fence and so I suspect that he's involved in the deal somewhere. But I still don't know who rifled through your traps and bludgeoned your friend, and I don't know where the gem is now. I have more than enough to charge you with some serious offences, Mr Richman. Will murder be one of them?'

Richman sat in silence for a few moments, gathering his thoughts. Finally he spoke.

'You must understand, Inspector, that I never for a moment anticipated that any of this would happen. I've known Praveer for a long time; he's another ragtime enthusiast. I knew he was a dealer in, shall we say, "unusual" Indian *objets*, and he knew of my lack of squeamishness concerning moving things across borders. When he approached me in Paris I thought it was just going to be a simple matter of bringing a gemstone to London and passing it on to his buyer. Nothing to it. Easy money. And so it seemed. At first. We got it past Customs without a hitch and I was waiting in London for Praveer's man to contact me. But that was when it all started to become a little unpleasant.'

'Unpleasant how, sir?' prompted the inspector.

'My flat was broken into. Twice. At first I thought, as you did, that some London gang had got wind of our venture and had decided to try to acquire the gem for themselves. But then I met The Giant.'

'And who is "The Giant", sir?' asked the inspector, though I suspected he had guessed as well as I.

'No idea what his name is, but he's a huge Indian bloke. And I mean really, really huge.'

'And what happened when you met him?'

'It was during the third burglary. I came back from a rather successful night at a club in the West End to find the door to my flat wide open. By this time I was a little spooked, I can tell you, so I'd taken to carrying a cosh in my pocket. If someone was going to try it on, I was going to make sure I could give hime what for. So I crept cautiously in, holding the cosh ready to strike, and there he was, in my front room, larger than life and twice as terrifying. I said, "Now listen here, what do you think you're doing," and brandished the cosh at him. He just put down the cigarette box he'd been looking in, and sort of lumbered towards me. I went to strike him but he just brushed me aside like I was a rag doll and lumbered out.'

'He didn't say anything?'

'Not a word. He didn't look especially concerned, either. He just went out, down the stairs and out into the street. I looked out of the window and saw him just casually waddling down the road.'

'And you've no idea who he was?'

'None whatsoever, Inspector. But I can put two and two together as well as the next man. I'd smuggled a jewel on behalf of a man known for dealing in those "unusual" items—'

'Shall we stop being so coy and just admit that they're stolen, sir?'

'If you like, Inspector,' said Richman. 'Although they're not always stolen, as such. Sometimes it's just that their removal from their country of origin is prohibited, even by their legitimate owners. Praveer isn't averse to shifting the odd bent item, and I'd be lying if I tried to paint him as some sort of saint, but he's more often an agent for people who find themselves unable to liquidate their assets because of some interfering local laws about removing national treasures.'

'As you wish, sir. So you knew you were in possession of an "interesting" item...'

'Yes. But I hadn't twigged until that point who might be interested in it. It looked for all the world like the gem's original owners might be wanting it back.'

'Why not just pass it on to the buyer in London?' asked Lady Hardcastle. 'Then it would be his problem.'

'That was exactly what I was going to do. But the buyer in London, or his agent at least, had gone to a party in Gloucestershire. At the house of a family that I'd introduced him to.'

'The redoubtable Mr Haddock,' said the inspector. 'And so you called Clarissa Farley-Stroud, offered your services, and got down here as quickly as you could.'

'It seemed to kill two birds with one stone,' said Richman. 'I could get out of London and away from that monster, and I could offload the gem to Fishface and make it, as you said, his problem.'

'And all this time the gem had been in Mr Holloway's trumpet case?' I said.

'Seemed the safest place,' said Richman. 'I managed to get in touch with Fishface and we arranged to meet in the interval; you know, try to keep it casual, like an incidental meeting if anyone saw us. I was going to take him into the library, get the gem, give it to him, collect the rest of my fee and try to forget all about it.'

'So what went wrong?' asked the inspector.

'No idea. He never showed up.'

'I've asked you this once before, sir, but I think we both know I didn't get an honest answer. Would you now tell us, please, exactly what happened when you left the ballroom that night.'

'I went round to the library and waited outside—'

'Did anyone see you?'

'Couldn't say, Inspector. There was a man in the corridor, up by the far door of the library by that ghastly Chinese cupboard, but he had his back to me and was walking away so I don't imagine he noticed me. I hung around for as long as seemed safe, but there was no sign of Fishface or Nelson, so I got back to the ballroom before anyone wondered why I was hanging around in the passageway.'

The inspector made a few more notes, but he seemed to be done for now.

'Right you are, then, Mr Richman. There's a superintendent from Scotland Yard on his way to interview Miss Montgomery, but I'm sure he'll want a word with you, too. You can go, but stay in the house.'

'Interview Sylvia?' said Richman.

'Oh, yes, sir, sorry, more bad news. Your songbird is well on her way to being a jailbird. She's a jewel thief.'

'She's a what?'

'She's Olive Sewell, a well known jewel thief, sir. She lifted some of the hostess's jewellery while you were trying to offload your stolen gemstone. You might consider a name change for the band. How about Roland Richman's Reprobates' Revue?'

'Very droll, Inspector, very droll. I'll be in the ballroom.'

He left, looking very dejected.

'I wonder how keen he'd be to stay if we told him the "Giant" was here in the house?' I said.

'Just as well we didn't mention it,' said the inspector. He sighed, looking suddenly very tired. 'I suppose we'd better speak to Haddock again,' he said, wearily. 'Although I don't feel we're getting any closer.'

'Nonsense, my dear Inspector,' said Lady Hardcastle. 'We're nearly there now. Just one or two more things to iron out and then we can nab our man.'

'We can?' he said, doubtfully.

'Indubitably.'

'My breath is duly bated,' he said, still without conviction. 'Miss Armstrong, would you do the honours, please?'

'Certainly, Inspector. One grilled haddock, coming up.'

I found Mr Haddock on the terrace, playing backgammon with Captain Summers. There were drinks on the table and they seemed to be enjoying themselves.

'Aha,' said Captain Summers, catching sight of me. 'The daring lady's maid. I say, Haddock, did you know this one threw an Irish prize fighter to the ground? Tiny little thing like that. Don't know what the world's coming to.'

Haddock leered at me. 'What can we do for you, my dear?'

'Inspector Sunderland would like to talk to you, Mr Haddock,' I said.

'What a shame,' he said. 'I was rather hoping you'd come to join us.'

I said nothing and waited for him to rise and follow me.

'Well, Summers, my lad,' he said at length. 'Time and Inspectors of Police wait for no man. We shall finish our game presently, but for now I have to accompany this delightful girl to the dining room.'

He rose unsteadily to his feet and followed my in through the French windows of the ballroom. As we neared the door he caught up with me and put his hand on my behind.

'I'm sure we have time to get a little better acquainted before I see the inspector,' he said. 'What a pretty little thing you arrgggghhh.'

There were only two punches and a kick, and quite gentle ones at that. As I helped him to his feet I said, 'I'm so sorry, Mr Haddock, it's this ballroom floor. Very slippery. I must have lost my balance a little. Are you quite all right?'

He glared at me.

Still grasping his hand I leaned in close and spoke very softly in his ear. 'Please don't touch me again, sir. The floors are quite slippery throughout the house now I come to think about it. Who knows how disastrously I might lose my balance the next time.'

He said nothing for the rest of the short walk to the dining room.

'Ah, Mr Haddock,' said the inspector as we entered. 'Sorry to have to drag you in here once again, but there are still one or two matters to clear up. Oh, I say, you look a bit bedraggled, sir, are you quite all right?'

'Slipped in the ballroom,' he said, glaring at me.

Lady Hardcastle caught the glare and gave me a questioning look of her own. I grinned and she smiled.

'Treacherous things, ballroom floors,' said the inspector, though I think he caught the silent exchange between me and Lady Hardcastle and had his own idea of what might have happened. 'But to business. Would you mind telling us again why you came to The Grange?'

'I came at Sir Hector's invitation to appraise some of his *objets d'art*.'

'And nothing else?'

'I'm sure I don't know what you mean, Inspector.'

'If I were to mention the names Roland Richman and Praveer Sengupta in conjunction with the Nepalese jewel known as the Emerald Eye, would you have a clearer idea of what I might mean?'

'No, Inspector,' he said belligerently. 'Not a clue.'

I took a half-step towards him and he flinched.

'Keep that vicious little harpy away from me,' he whined.

'I'd love to,' said the inspector, 'but she doesn't work for me. I've tried to keep her under control, but you know what it's like with women these days. Law unto themselves, they are.'

'Just keep her away from me and I'll tell you what you want to know.'

'Good lad. She's quite reasonable. I'm sure she'll not harm you. At least not while there's anyone watching. So tell us again about your visit to The Grange.'

'It's true that I was invited down here by Sir Hector,' he said. 'But on the day of the party I got a telegram from Richman saying that he was going to be playing and that we should complete our business down here.'

'Your business being the sale of the Eye,' said the inspector.

'Yes,' he said, resignedly. 'I have a buyer lined up in London but Richman was getting into some hot water over it all, so we decided to make the transfer here, then I'd complete the whole deal when we got back. No one would be looking for it at my place.'

'And you arranged to meet him in the interval.'

'You seem to know all about it, Inspector. I don't really see why I have to go through it all.'

'Indulge me. You arranged to meet in the interval, but you didn't show up.'

'I got delayed, that was all. I went to the... er... you know. I told you before. When I got back to the library Richman wasn't there.'

'So you just left it at that?'

'No... I... er...'

'You, er, what, sir?'

He sighed. 'I went into the library.'

'And what did you see?'

'Chaos, Inspector. Chaos. The band's things had been torn apart.'

'Did you see Mr Holloway?'

'No. No, I stayed long enough to see what had happened and got out. Richman had told me about The Giant and I was afraid he'd followed him down here, so I wasn't going to hang around for him to tear me apart, too.'

'I see,' said the inspector. 'Did you see anything else?'

He paused. 'I think I heard the far door clicking shut as I came in, but I can't be certain.'

'And it never occurred to you to mention this when we questioned you before?'

'Oh, come on, Inspector. It wouldn't have taken you long to find out my reputation. And then how would it look? I reckoned it would all blow over and I'd be long gone before you sussed who I am and then there'd be no awkward questions and no unpleasantness.'

'I see. Well, if what you say is true, then aside from being a lying little toe-rag, I've got nothing to hold you on, but don't leave The Grange until I say you can. On your way, Haddock.'

'Charming,' said Haddock.

'Don't push your luck, "sir",' said the inspector.

I shifted my weight slightly and he was out the door like a startled rat.

Inspector Sunderland slumped in one of the dining room chairs and massaged his temples.

'I just can't seem to piece it all together,' he said, dejectedly. 'The jewel is the key, but no one involved seems to have had cause to pinch it and kill Holloway in the process.'

'Apart from Mr Verma's servant,' I said.

'He was my main suspect for a while,' he said. 'But then I asked myself why Verma would have come to you and told you the story if he already had the gem. He'd have done a moonlight as soon as they had hold of it and would have been heading east before the sun was up. Richman and Haddock are a couple of chancers out of their depth. Montgomery-Sewell is a tricky little thief but seems genuinely fond of her colleagues so I can't believe it's her. The – what did he say they were – the "rhythm section" seem like pleasant young blokes with nothing on their mind but girls and music. No one saw anything. No one knows anything. We've got a murder weapon and a motive, but no real suspects. I don't mind telling you, ladies, I'm stumped.'

'Well,' I said. 'When you put it like that—'

There was a knock at the door and once again the cheerfully respectful face of Jenkins peered round. Lady Hardcastle waved him in.

'Come on in, Jenkins,' she said. 'What can we do for you?'

'It's more a matter of what I may do your you, my lady,' he said, proffering his silver tray. 'Another telegram has arrived.'

'Good show!' she said and took the telegram from him.

'Will there be a reply, my lady?'

She read the message, which seemed rather a long one, and a minute passed before she said, 'No, Jenkins, there's no reply. This is everything I needed.' She looked at her watch. 'It's coming up to teatime, Jenkins. What are the arrangements today?'

'We were planning to serve it on the terrace again, my lady. Shall you be joining us?'

'Today, Jenkins, we all shall. But would you mind delaying it for a short while?'

'That would be a matter for Sir Hector, my lady. He's rather particular about serving tea promptly at four o'clock.'

'No matter, then. But perhaps you could make discreet efforts to ensure that all the house guests are present and that no one leaves before I arrive. Would that be acceptable?'

'I shall do my utmost, my lady.'

'Thank you. And do you by any chance know where Miss Clarissa is?'

'I believe she's in her room, my lady. Grace, her lady's maid, has just gone up to her.'

'Splendid, splendid,' she said. 'Thank you, Jenkins, your help is greatly appreciated, as always.'

'Thank you, my lady. Will that be all?'

'More than enough, thank you.'

'Thank you, my lady,' he said with a bow, and left.

'What's in the telegram, my lady?' asked the inspector.

'All will be revealed in the fullness of time, Inspector,' she said. 'I need to confirm one or two things with Clarissa Farley-Stroud, and then I believe you shall have your man.'

'Well I have nothing of my own,' he said. 'So I suppose I should allow you this one indulgence.'

'I promise you won't be disappointed, Inspector,' she said as she made her way to the door. 'But if you are, I promise to be properly contrite and to eat as much humble pie as possible.'

She swept out of the room, leaving the inspector and me equally bemused and bewildered.

'What do you think she's up to?' asked the inspector.

'Blowed if I know,' I said. 'She's a woman driven by whim and caprice, but usually also by perspicacity and insight, so I generally tend to let her get on with it.'

'All in all, miss, I'd say from my brief experience of her that that's probably wise. Have you worked for her long?'

'About fourteen years now,' I said.

'And is it a life that suits you?'

'Very much so, Inspector, yes.'

'My sister is in service,' he said. 'But I'm not sure if I could do it. I like being my own man.'

'Sadly, I'm not in a position to be my own "man",' I said. 'But you still have to answer to your superiors, you still have to do someone else's bidding from day to day.'

'True enough, miss. But I do have a certain amount of freedom to conduct myself as I please in the execution of my duties. A certain amount of autonomy, you might say.'

'As do I, Inspector. More, perhaps, than most servants. Ours is a… I hesitate to say "unique" working relationship, but it's certainly unusual. We have shared adventures over the years which most could scarcely imagine. It broke down some of the traditional barriers between an employer and a servant.'

'I've noticed the way you speak to each other,' he said with a chuckle. 'It's rather refreshing, to tell the truth.'

'It causes quite a few raised eyebrows and more than a little disapproving tutting, but we carry on regardless.'

'Well, you seem happy in your work and there's not many as can say that in this day and age,' he said. 'When this case is wrapped up – and I'm rather coming round to the idea that your mistress might well wrap it up this afternoon – I should like to treat you both to a drink or two and hear the stories of your adventures.'

'That would be delightful, Inspector, thank you. Perhaps Mrs Sunderland would like to come, too?'

'Actually, miss, I rather think she would. I think she'd like you.'

'Then I shall put you in the mistress's appointments book and we shall sup together as friends one evening before the weather turns.'

'I shall look forward to it.'

I was about to ask the inspector about his own family, but there was another knock at the door and Dewi the footman came in.

'Begging your pardon, sir, but there was a telephone call for you,' he said. 'Gentleman couldn't stay on the line so he asked me to say…' He screwed up his face in concentration, trying to remember the exact words. 'Tell the inspector that Superintention Wickham has been delayed at Swindon by a fallen tree on the line and has had to return to London. Hold Sewell locally until someone from the Met can pick her up.'

'Thank you… Doughy, is it?' said the inspector.

'Close enough, sir,' said the young man, followed by some rather harsh words in his native Welsh.

'Watch your tongue, lad,' I said in the same language. 'You never know who might be listening.'

He blushed crimson. 'Sorry, miss.'

The inspector looked puzzled and said. 'Right, well, can you please find Sergeant Dobson and ask him to bring Miss Montgomery to me.'

'Yes, sir. Right away, sir.'

He hurried out.

'What was all that about?' asked the inspector.

'He cast doubt on your parentage, suggested what he imagined your mother did for a living, and then expressed his contempt for the English in general.'

'The cheeky little beggar,' he said, slightly hurt. 'My mother was a schoolteacher.'

'It's just his little act of rebellion, inspector. Like a safety valve on a steam engine.'

'I understand that, miss. But, I mean. Really.'

A few minutes later there was yet another knock at the door and a very flustered Sergeant Dobson peered in.

'Ah, Dobson, good man,' said the inspector. 'There's been a slight change of plan and I'm going to need you to take Miss Montgomery to the police station after all. But I suppose you might as well both come out onto the terrace for Lady Hardcastle's announcement before you go. We'll see if we can snag you some sandwiches.'

'Ah, now, see, I've got some bad news on that score, sir.'

'What sort of bad news?'

'It's the lady, sir. She's… ah… she's done a bunk, sir.'

'Oh for the love of–'

'I'm most dreadfully sorry, sir.'

'How, sergeant?'

'Well, Sir Hector let us use his upstairs study, sir. It's out of the way, like. So we was up there and she starts fidgeting with her… with her underthings, and she says, "Sorry, sergeant, but my corsets seem to have got a bit twisted. Would you mind popping outside while I straighten myself out. Just for a minute, there's a love." So I did. I went out and sat on a chair on the landing, like.'

'How long did you leave her?'

'She was ages, sir. A good few minutes.'

'And you didn't think to check what she was up to?'

'Well, no, sir. Not at first. She was… you know… she was… rearranging herself.'

The inspector sighed.

'But after a few minutes I did knock on the door, but there was no answer,' said the sergeant.

'And when you went in, she'd gone.'

'She had, sir. Out the window.'

'But you took her shoes?'

'Well, no, sir, didn't seem much point. We was up on the first floor. Where was she going to go?'

'Out the window and down the blessed drainpipe,' said the inspector with no small amount of exasperation.

'Yes, sir,' said the sergeant, sheepishly.

'Did you look for her?'

'I had a run round the house, sir, but she'd vanished.'

The inspector sighed again. 'Oh well, she'll not get far on foot. Get word out, sergeant, and we'll see if we can pick her up before she manages to catch a train.'

'Right you are, sir. Sorry, sir.' He hurried out.

'I despair,' said the inspector, but unfortunately I was laughing so I couldn't commiserate. 'Really?' he said. 'We're laughing now, are we?'

'Oh, come on, Inspector. You've got to admit it's rather funny. And poor old Dobson. He wants so much to get things right. He offered to take her to the cells and we knew she was a slippery customer.'

'So it's my fault?'

'Well, if the shoe fits…'

'Don't mention the shoes,' he said. 'If he'd taken her blasted shoes, she'd still be sitting up there in her wonky stays.'

I laughed again.

'I suppose we ought to get out onto the terrace,' he said. 'At least Superintendent Witham won't be here to take the rise out of me in person.'

'Come on, then, Inspector, take me to tea.'

There was already quite a gathering on the terrace when the inspector and I arrived. Dunn and Skins were sitting together, with Dora hovering around trying to look like she was supposed to be there, but obviously trying to flirt with Dunn. Richman and Haddock were together, deep in whispered conversation. Verma was sitting with Summers and trying to look interested as the empty-headed captain finished off some dreary tale of life in the Raj. Theo Woodfield, Clarissa's affianced, was hovering near the low wall, looking down into the valley. Sir Hector and Lady Farley-Stroud were in what I presumed to be their usual places at the head of the table, both looking rather subdued and anxious.

The inspector and I stood with our backs to the house, where we could watch them all.

Jenkins was fussing with the tea things on the large table and had just signalled to Dora that they should withdraw when Lady Hardcastle arrived with Clarissa, and Verma's servant.

Richman was halfway out of his chair in fright when he saw the Man Mountain, but the inspector signalled that he should stay where he was. He sat down, but his eyes never left the imposing figure of the Nepalese servant as he made his way round the table to his master's side.

When the murmuring had died down a little, Lady Hardcastle spoke. 'I expect you're wondering,' she said with evident glee, 'why I've asked you all here.'

I couldn't resist a grin of my own at the detective story theatricality of it, but no one else seemed impressed or amused.

'Oh, please yourselves,' she said. 'Now we're all aware of the terrible events of the night of the party. Or their consequences, at least. But until just now, only one among us knew exactly what happened to Mr Holloway.'

I watched the assembled group for any sign of a reaction, and I could see that the inspector was doing the same. To my disappointment, no one betrayed anything other than curiosity.

'Armstrong and I have spent the past two days in the company of Inspector Sunderland as he questioned most of you, trying to establish just exactly what happened on that fateful night. Until a few moments ago we had all the pieces of the puzzle, but no key to fit them together. With so few clocks, no one could remember when anything happened, and no single person seemed to have a clear idea of all the comings and goings. But then it struck me that the one person we hadn't yet spoken to may well have been paying a great deal more attention to who was at her party and where they were during the evening, and so I spoke to Miss Clarissa. It seems that she does indeed have a very clear recollection of the events of the evening.'

Lady Hardcastle continued, 'She's a—'

We didn't find out what she was, though, because at that moment, with much huffing, puffing, and the inevitable Welsh swearing, Bert and Dewi struggled onto the terrace with Lady Hardcastle's Crime

Board. At her instruction, they turned the board round on the easel to reveal the blank reverse. With their task complete, they should probably have returned to their other work, but instead they hung about, hoping to hear what was going on. No one said anything, so they joined Dora at the far side of the table.

Lady Hardcastle began sketching a plan of the ground floor of The Grange on the blackboard. When she was done, she pinned a piece of paper in the top corner of the board and turned to face the assembled residents and guests.

'There we are,' she said. 'That's the ground floor of the house, and that piece of paper was recovered from the stage. It's a running order, or "set list" as I believe the musicians call it.'

The musicians sat up a little straighter and nodded their agreement as all eyes turned towards them.

'Now Miss Clarissa doesn't wear a wristwatch, she thinks them rather vulgar,' said Lady Hardcastle, looking at her own watch. 'But she has a marvellous memory for tunes, and so we've managed to piece the events together using the songs to mark the passing of time.'

There were murmurs of appreciation, but still no signs of fear nor of a guilty conscience.

Lady Hardcastle continued. 'Now, the early part of the evening proceeded much as it might at any other party. People arrived, drinks were served, guests mingled, circulated, chatted, and congratulated the happy couple. And the band played. They were all on stage together until they reached this song,' she said, tapping the set list. 'This is "Standing Room Only" and is an instrumental number which meant that Sylvia Montgomery wasn't required. She left the stage and, by her own testimony, went off to the library,' she drew a little circle in the library with the letters SM in it. 'Where is Miss Montgomery, by the way?' she said.

'She went for a little walk, my lady,' said Inspector Sunderland. 'I'll explain later.'

'Oh,' said Lady Hardcastle. 'Ah well, no matter. Miss Montgomery spent a few minutes in the library and then left, whereupon she met Miss Armstrong, my maid, in the corridor.'

I nodded.

'They parted company and Miss Montgomery returned to the ballroom.' She rubbed out the SM circle in the library and redrew it in the ballroom. 'Armstrong continued with her errand in the servants' section of the house, and when she returned, she thought she caught a glimpse of someone else going into the library, but she couldn't be certain and had no idea who it might have been, even if there had been someone there. And that's significant because during the next song...' She tapped the set list again. '..."The Richman Rag", Miss Clarissa had noticed one of the guests leave the ballroom.'

There was another murmur from the assembled guests.

'No one knows for sure where this person went, but if they had walked in the direction of the library, they might well been the person that Armstrong saw going into the library through the door nearest the hall.'

'Who is this person?' asked Mr Verma.

'We shall come to that in good time, Mr Verma,' said Lady Hardcastle. 'When "The Richman Rag" ends, the band take their well-earned break, and Nelson Holloway goes off to the library, ostensibly to retrieve a bottle of scotch that he had hidden among his things, but actually to check that the secret contents of his trumpet case were still safe and sound.'

'And what were these "secret contents"?' said Verma.

'I think you know, Mr Verma, but let me explain for the few people here who might not. Mr Verma is an emissary of the King of Nepal and he has been sent to England in pursuit of a precious gemstone known as The Emerald Eye. The Eye was stolen from a temple north of Kathmandu a number of years ago, and it recently arrived in Europe. A ragtime bandleader was paid to smuggle it into England, which task he accomplished with the help of his trumpeter who concealed the gem in a secret compartment in his trumpet case.'

By now, all eyes had turned to Roland Richman who simply stared at the ground, refusing to meet anyone's gaze.

'Mr Richman had arranged to meet another accomplice here at The Grange to hand over the gem, and so during the break in the band's performance, Mr Clifford Haddock left the ballroom, followed a short while later by Mr Richman. Haddock went straight to the bathroom, believing he had time before the planned rendezvous, but he was delayed there, so that Mr Richman, who was waiting for him outside the library, thought that something had gone wrong and abandoned the meeting.'

She drew a series of lines on the plan, indicating Haddock going upstairs in search of the bathroom, Richman waiting outside the library, Richman returning to the ballroom and Haddock coming back downstairs.

'At this point,' she continued, 'Mr Haddock, seeing Richman's absence, decided to check whether he had gone into the library. He went in, just as the missing guest came out through the other door.'

She drew a new line showing the missing guest leaving the room.

'What Haddock saw in the library shocked him. The instrument cases stored there by the band had been ransacked and there were signs of a struggle. He left the library and then he, too, returned to the ballroom where his arrival was, again, noticed by Miss Clarissa during the first song of the second set, "An Angel Fell". The band was without Mr Holloway at this point but while some people noticed a slight change in the sound, few noticed the absence of the trumpeter.

'Now, the reason for the chaos in the library was that the missing guest had been searching for the Eye. He was caught in the act by Mr Holloway, and in the ensuing struggle, Mr Holloway sustained his mortal head wound. As the missing guest left, he concealed Holloway's trumpet case – the only case he hadn't managed to search – in the Chinese cabinet in the corridor. He hid for a while until the coast was clear, then returned to the ballroom just as the band struck up the next number, "My Heart Belongs to You".'

'But who was this person?' demanded Mr Verma again.

'All in good time, Mr Verma,' said Lady Hardcastle. 'All in good time. Some time between hiding the trumpet case and its discovery two days later by Armstrong, Mr Holloway's assailant retrieved the Emerald Eye from the trumpet case, wiped the case clean of his fingerprints and concealed the Eye in his own case which was safely stored in his room.'

'And how the devil do you know that,' said Verma, clearly now rather agitated.

'Because when Miss Clarissa and I searched Captain Summers's room just now,' she said, producing an extraordinarily large emerald from her jacket pocket. 'we found the Eye wrapped in a sock and tucked into one of his dress shoes at the bottom of his suitcase.'

The terrace was in uproar. There were shouts of disbelief and of outrage, and Lady Hardcastle was bombarded with questions. Only three people remained entirely impassive: Mr Verma, his servant, and Captain Summers himself.

When the hubbub had died down, it was once again Mr Verma who led the questioning, while Captain Summers remained silent under the extremely watchful gaze of Mr Verma's mountainous servant.

'One presumes you have an explanation for this blackguard's actions, Lady Hardcastle,' he said. 'And how did you uncover his perfidy?'

'I have both, Mr Verma,' she said. 'To be honest, I'm rather annoyed with myself for not thinking of it sooner, but Captain Summers actually gave us his motive the very first time we met him. He told us he intended to propose to his colonel's daughter back in Bengal, but said that he needed to "impress" her. That should have set my mind racing at once as soon as I found out that the whole affair revolved around a gem which had been stolen from Nepal but which had passed through Bengal on its way to Europe. But I didn't manage to put two and two together then, nor would I have if desperation hadn't made me ask an old friend for information about one of the house guests. We had reached a dead end with our investigations and our main suspects were becoming less suspicious by the moment. And so I decided to contact my dear friend, Colonel Dawlish. Do you remember Dawlish, Captain? I believe you met in Calcutta early last year, just before he returned to England.'

The captain said nothing.

'He certainly remembers you. I got his telegram this afternoon and he has quite a bit to say about your relationship with Lavinia Isherwood.'

At this the Captain looked up, his face scarlet with indignation. 'How dare you!'

'How dare I indeed,' said Lady Hardcastle, calmly. 'But let me tell you what I know – or surmise – and you can tell me whether it's true. Lavinia is the eldest daughter of your regiment's colonel, Sir Basil Isherwood. You have been besotted with her ever since she and her mother travelled to Calcutta to join the colonel two years ago. You pursued her relentlessly, but it seems her own affections were directed elsewhere, towards a dashing young subaltern. According to Colonel Dawlish, you bullied this young lad remorselessly until he requested a transfer to the North West Frontier, but even with your way clear, Lavinia still rejected you.'

The captain was still fuming, but offered no dissent.

'The story of the Emerald Eye was well known throughout northern India, and earlier this year rumours began to circulate that the Eye was once again on the move. The barracks was alive with chatter about the gem and many of the men, enlisted and officers alike, began talking wildly about recovering the Emerald Eye, and what they'd do with the handsome reward offered by the King of Nepal for its return. You dismissed all this as foolish nonsense until you overheard a remark made by Lavinia to one of her friends at dinner. She's a silly, romantic girl of the sort that has read much but experienced all too little, and it seems she had become enchanted by the notion of the "cursed" gemstone. She said that she would surely marry the man who was brave and resourceful enough to recover it for her.'

Still the captain said nothing, but his expression softened somewhat, presumably as he recalled the fair Lavinia.

'Somehow – and perhaps you might one day explain how, since it seems to have eluded some of the most diligent and well-motivated investigators in the region – you managed to find out not only where the Eye was, but also where it was going. You arranged a leave of absence based on a fabricated family crisis and set off in pursuit, following the trail of the gem all the way to Paris where it was now in the hands of a shady antiquities broker named Praveer Sengupta. You witnessed a meeting in a Paris nightclub and guessed that the band leader that Sengupta was talking to was going to bring the gem into England. I confess I'm a little hazy on the next steps, but you ended up here at The Grange. I believe you were here entirely by chance, but when you found that the band you'd seen in Paris were playing here, you saw an opportunity perhaps to finally lay your hands on the Eye. It was by no means certain that they would have it with them, but what a stroke of luck if they did. You could steal the Eye and then return to Lavinia a hero. How am I doing so far, Captain?'

'Pretty damn well,' he said, coldly. 'Some of the details are missing, but you've captured the essence of it. I never meant to kill Holloway.

And if he'd not tried to play the bally hero, none of this would have happened.'

'One might say, though,' said Lady Hardcastle, 'that it also wouldn't have happened if you hadn't travelled halfway round the world on some romantic quest to impress a silly girl who cares nothing for you.'

Suddenly the captain was on his feet, a revolver in his hand. 'Have a care, *my lady*,' he said, menacingly. 'I've listened to altogether too much impertinence from you as it is. How dare you judge Lavinia! A woman like you who doesn't know her place and imagines she can behave like this? You're a disgrace to your sex, you vicious old harpy.'

He advanced on her and I was powerless to help, trapped as I was between the inspector and the table. He took the gem from her outstretched hand and stared coldly into her unblinking eyes as he cocked the revolver. She held his gaze and the terrace held its breath.

But then there was movement. Sudden, violent movement. I had entirely misjudged Mr Verma's servant whom I had thought a clumsy, lumbering, muscle-bound lump. He moved with the silence and grace of a man a quarter his size and before Summers had even noticed him, much less had time to react, he had grasped the captain's wrist, angling the pistol upwards and away from Lady Hardcastle as his other hand punched him forcefully in the back. Summers fell, the pistol fired, and the Man Mountain bent and retrieved the Emerald Eye from Summers's left hand. He backed away from the fallen captain, holding the gem in one hand and, as we all now noticed, a dagger in the other, wet with blood.

Lady Hardcastle knelt to try to assist the captain, but it was clear that he was dying.

'Tell darling Lavinia that I loved her always,' he whispered, but then the fight left him as he breathed his last, rattling breath.

It was as though we had awakened from a trance and suddenly there was uproar once again. The inspector was struggling to reach the Man Mountain but everyone was on their feet and he couldn't get round the table.

Another shot rang out and Dora and Clarissa screamed in unison. We all turned to see Mr Verma brandishing a square-looking automatic pistol of his own.

'Ladies and gentlemen!' said Verma, loudly. 'Take your seats, if you please.'

Those that had seats meekly sat, while those of us that did not, stood stock still.

Mr Verma ushered his servant behind him and began to back away from the table towards the steps leading down to the expansive back lawn.

'I have my King's gemstone, and your murderer is dead. Justice has been served.'

'It has not, Mr Verma,' said Inspector Sunderland forcefully. 'Your servant is under arrest for the murder of Captain Summers and you are under arrest for threatening these people with a firearm.'

'I can see at least two problems with your arrests, Inspector,' said Verma, still backing away. 'The first is that I'm still holding the firearm in question and if anyone makes any attempt to stop us, I shall make good on that threat and shoot them. The second is that, as emissary of His Majesty, the King of Nepal, I have diplomatic status. I'm sure you can imagine the sort of pressure which would be brought to bear at the highest levels if you attempt to bring charges against me or my servant.'

The inspector sighed and shook his head, an almost comical gesture which I confess did make me smile a little.

'I knew you'd see reason,' said Verma. 'You all seem like intelligent people, so I'm sure I don't have to issue any more melodramatic warnings about the consequences of attempting to stop us. Sir Hector, Lady Farley-Stroud, thank you for your generous hospitality. Miss Clarissa, long life and happiness to you and the charming Mr Woodfield. Lady Hardcastle, thank you for returning the gem to me, I knew you'd manage it.' And with that, he set off towards the front of the house where his motorcar was parked on the drive.

For a few moments no one seemed quite certain what to do until Lady Farley-Stroud spoke up. 'Jenkins,' she said, calmly. 'Telephone Doctor Fitzsimmons and tell him there's been another death. Inspector Sunderland?'

'My lady?'

'I'm sure you'll want to make one or two telephone calls of your own. Please use the instrument in Sir Hector's study. Dewi and Bert, you can clean up out here as best you can, but don't disturb the body. Dora, fetch fresh tea and bring it to the drawing room.'

Her servants immediately went about their appointed tasks, glad, it seemed, for something to do.

'The rest of us, I feel, are in need of a stiff drink. There's brandy in the drawing room.'

'I couldn't do without my brandy, my dear,' said Lady Farley-Stroud conspiratorially to Lady Hardcastle. 'I keep some hidden away in here where Hector can't find it.'

She opened her large sewing box and rummaged around, eventually producing a bottle of very fine cognac which she proceeded to pour into the teacups as Dora filled them with tea.

The inspector came into the room and beckoned Lady Hardcastle and me over to him.

'I've got some boys coming up from Bristol to help dot the Ts and cross the whatnots, but I think that more or less wraps things up,' he said.

'Have you put out an alert for Mr Verma and his servant?' asked Lady Hardcastle.

'I have, but to be perfectly honest, my lady, I can't help but think that Verma was right: there's not a lot we could do even if we did manage to catch him.'

'Hmm,' said Lady Hardcastle.

'At least the murder was solved,' I said.

'Again, miss, if I were being properly honest, I'm not completely sure that we'd ever have got the poor chap for murder at all. A decent brief would talk that one down to manslaughter, I've no doubt. And if he played up the "romantic quest" angle, a sympathetic jury might even have gone for self defence. But the mystery has been solved, at least. I do hate loose ends. Thank you for that, ladies.'

'It was entirely our pleasure, Inspector,' said Lady Hardcastle.

'I am slightly puzzled, though, my lady,' said the inspector. 'You say you got all that from a telegram from your friend Colonel...?'

'Dawlish, Inspector. Yes. Or, more properly, no.'

'No?'

'Well, I might have embellished a little. Indulged in a tiny bit of imaginative speculation.'

'So what exactly did Dawlish say?' he said with a grin.

She produced the telegram from her jacket pocket and read it aloud. '"Remember Summers from Calcutta. Stop. Bit of a rum un.

Stop. Rumours he loved the colonel's daughter. Stop. Almost court-martialled for fighting with a subaltern who then transferred to NW Frontier. Stop. Will contact Isherwood for more if needed. Stop. Love George."'

The inspector laughed. 'And from that meagre cloth you embroidered the whole tale?'

'And from all the painstaking interviews you conducted, my dear Inspector,' she said, laying a hand on his arm.

He laughed again. 'You're very kind, my lady, but still…'

'Oh pish and fiddlesticks, Inspector. He didn't contradict me, and it does all fit with the facts that we know of.'

'I suppose it does at that, my lady. And he's not in a position to contradict anyone, now, so I expect that yours shall become the official explanation.'

'Oh no, Inspector,' she said, slightly horrified. 'That will never do. I shall contact Colonel Isherwood for confirmation so that the official explanation is as true an account as we can make it. I can't leave it like that.'

'As you wish, my lady,' he said. 'But as far as Bristol CID is concerned, this one is over and done with. I'm afraid I have a lot to attend to, though, so I shall leave you to your tea. It's been a pleasure working with you both. Till next time.'

He shook us both warmly by the hand and went out to the corridor where I heard him say, '…at Chipping Bevington station? Thank you, Sergeant. Tell them to cuff her this time and get her down to Bristol.'

Skins came over to us.

'Thanks for that, Lady H. I know it was still all a bit of a mess, but at least we know now. And what a story. I met a bloke once up North. Milton, his name was, Milton Hayes. He writes poems and that. He'd love this one. I might write to him.'

'Oh, I say,' said Lady Hardcastle. 'What fun.'

'Yeah,' he said. 'But thank you. It was awful not knowing who killed Nelse. He was a good lad.'

'It sounds as though he was,' said Lady Hardcastle. 'What will you do now, though? With poor Mr Holloway gone, and Richman and Montgomery facing charges for theft, smuggling and who knows what else, there's only you and Mr Dunn left.'

'Don't worry about us, Lady H,' he said, cheerfully. 'There's always work for the likes of us. Best rhythm section in London, us. We'll be all right.'

'That's reassuring,' she said. 'And your immediate plans?'

'Well, I don't suppose the Farley-Strouds will want us hanging about now the case is closed. Not sure, really. We could get a train back to London tonight, I suppose, but it's a bit of a schlepp with just the two of us and all our clobber.'

'Oh no,' said Lady Hardcastle. 'That will never do. I have two spare bedrooms and you shall be my guests for the night. There's certain to be someone in the village who will lend us a cart to get your instruments to the house.'

'That's very generous, Lady H. Very generous indeed. Thank you very much.'

'It's purely selfish, Mr M. I've become rather fond of your ragtime music and we could do with some proper musicians to accompany our poor efforts.'

'You're on, my lady,' he said, cheerfully. ''Ere, Barty,' he called. 'Put that maid down and come over 'ere a mo.'

Barty Dunn disentangled himself from the Dora's flirtatious attentions and joined his friend, who explained their good fortune. Dunn, was as effusively grateful as his friend and they both left to get themselves packed.

Skins had only taken a few steps when he turned back and said, 'There is just one thing that never got resolved.'

'What's that?' asked Lady Hardcastle.

He turned to me. 'Did you ever decide what I can call you?'

I smiled. 'You, Mr Skins, may call me Flo.'

'Righto, Flo,' he said, and hurried off to join his friend.

'I suppose, my dear Flo,' said Lady Hardcastle, 'that we probably ought to get going, too. Leave the poor Farley-Strouds to try to get things back to normal.'

And so we said our goodbyes and slipped away.

Our evening with the two musicians had been an unqualified success. They had arrived with all their traps just as I was putting the finishing touches to dinner and they had joined us for what they both proclaimed was the best meal they had eaten for weeks.

We had adjourned to the drawing room where we pushed the

furniture to the walls so that Skins could set up his drums and we had the most enjoyably entertaining time. They proved themselves extremely versatile musicians and managed to turn their hands to almost every musical style that Lady Hardcastle threw at them. By the time we had finished, following a spiritedly syncopated version of Chopin's *Nocturne No. 2* which had left us all laughing with the joy and silliness of it all, Skins had assured us that if ever times were hard, we should get in touch with them. He knew a few clubs, he said, that would "love a bit of that".

We had managed to secure a carriage to take the boys and their instruments to the station at Chipping Bevington and they had left with our good wishes ringing in their ears and a few rounds of sandwiches in their pockets.

And now we were back to normal. The mystery was solved, the culprit was dead, the Inspector had returned to Bristol and we… we were once again at something of a loose end.

There was plenty for me to do, of course – we'd not been in the house for a few days and there were chores aplenty simply waiting for the attentions of a diligent maid – but it all seemed a bit mundane after the excitement of the past few days.

'What we need, Flo dear,' said Lady Hardcastle as I tidied up around her. 'Is to take a holiday. We should get away for a few days, take the air.'

'Is there not sufficient air here, my lady?' I said.

'There's an abundance of air, and it's as fresh and clean as one could wish. Apart from the dismaying smell of dung when one ventures too close to a farm. But I was thinking of the seaside, perhaps. Brighton? Or a nice spa. Harrogate? We haven't been to Harrogate for simply ages.'

'It sounds lovely, my lady. Will there be hotels with cooks and waiters and chamber maids?'

'I should think so. Or we could rent a little cottage.'

'Hmm,' I said. 'I'm not sure that your idea of "taking a holiday" quite matches mine.'

'Oh pish.'

'And fiddlesticks, my lady. Yes, I know.'

The doorbell rang.

I returned with a telegram which she read with growing alarm.

'Pack, Flo. Now. We need to get to London on the next train. Harry will meet us at Paddington.' She scribbled a reply on the reply form and handed it to me with some change for the boy.

When I came back she showed me the telegram.

HONEST - MAN - ARRIVED - SOUTHAMPTON - YESTERDAY - STOP - SEEN - BOARDING - TRAIN - BRISTOL - THIS - MORNING - STOP - GET - OUT - STOP - WILL - MEET - YOU - PADDINGTON - STOP - HARRY

We packed in a rush, stuffing a change of clothes and some toilet things into two Gladstone bags and were out of the door in less than twenty minutes. We hurried into the village and managed to catch Constable Hancock in the police station. Lady Hardcastle explained that we were going away for a few days and asked him to keep an eye on the house for her. She didn't tell him where we were going, nor why, though she did say that a German man might arrive in the village looking for us. If he did, she said, it was imperative that the constable say nothing about our having left.

'Right you are, m'lady,' he said, somewhat uncomfortably. 'Is this fellow dangerous?'

'Extremely dangerous, Constable,' she said.

'Oh. Right. Do you need a carriage? I think Ned's back from taking those two lads to the station earlier.'

'Oh, Constable, that would be marvellous,' said Lady Hardcastle, and within ten more minutes we were on our way to Chipping Bevington.

FOUR

The Half Death of Günther Ehrlichmann

I was born on the 23rd of March, 1877, in Aberdare in South Wales, the youngest (by 20 minutes) of seven children born to Gwilym Armstrong and his wife Marged (whom everyone knew as Meg). Ours was a happy childhood, on the whole. We had little, but we had enough, and amid the chaos and the rough-and-tumble, the hand-me-down clothes and the making-do, we enjoyed a carefree life.

Aberdare was a mining town and my father, my six uncles (on both sides of the family) and two of my brothers all worked in the pits. My father lost his left leg in an accident in 1873, but he had a quick mind and a facility with numbers which, combined with his long experience at the coal face, made him a useful man to have in the office, and so by the time I was born he worked above ground. My mother, meanwhile, somehow managed to raise seven children as well as working long days in the grocer's shop. She had been a housemaid when she met my father, so she was no stranger to hard work, and she always managed to keep us clean and happy with a smile on her face. There was always food on the table, clean clothes on our backs, and laughter filling the little house that we all somehow managed to cram into.

We played on the street whenever we could, but my favourite summers' days were spent exploring. With my twin sister Gwenith and as many friends as we could round up, we would make our way to our mother's home village of Cwmdare where "Mamgu" (our grandmother) would give us a greaseproof parcel filled with Welsh cakes to sustain us on our adventures on Craig Rhiwmynach, the mountain above the village. The climbing was never arduous but it

218

was the highest and most exciting part of our young world and we felt like gods as we looked down the valley to the town, the villages, the railway, and the mines below.

I loved school. Most of my friends merely tolerated it, and Gwenith positively hated it, but I found something magical even in the mundane and boring work of copying letters and working out sums. But those tedious tasks enabled me to do something that really captured my imagination: to read. I read everything I could find, which in Aberdare wasn't much. There was no public library in the town and so, with my parents' reluctant permission, I would regularly walk the seven miles over to Merthyr Tydfil and spend the day in the library there. The librarian came to know me well and occasionally even let me borrow books, even though I wasn't strictly allowed to.

At thirteen years of age, my schooling was done. There was little work for girls in a mining town, but my ambitions lay further afield anyway. I loved the town, I loved the mountains, I loved the valley, but I knew there was more, and I wanted to see it. We had been on a day trip to Cardiff once, and in my young mind, that bustling city was the height of sophistication and glamour.

I knew that my mother had worked in service and in my naïveté I thought that it would be an excellent way to see more of the world than just what was visible from the top of the mountain. My mother, of course, well knew how misguided my romantic ideas of life in the big city were, but she also knew that there was little for me at home and that there was more of a chance for me to make something of myself if she indulged my fantasy.

'You can try it, my love,' she had said. 'And if it's too awful we'll have you home quick as a wink.'

And so, with the help of one of her old friends, I managed to secure employment as a scullery maid to a well-to-do family by the name of Williams in a prosperous area of the capital. I begged Gwenith to come with me. I couldn't imagine life without her and tried desperately to convince her that we would have the most wonderful adventures together in Cardiff, but she was adamant that there was more than enough adventure for anyone in Aberdare and steadfastly refused to budge.

And so I went alone. I missed my family, most especially my sister, but there were other young children among the servants and I soon made friends.

The hours were long, the work was hard – and most often dull – but as well as teaching me to read, school had also taught me a tolerance for drudgery that saw me through. I did as I was told, learned my duties well and managed to stay out of trouble. For the most part. There were the usual tellings-off and chastisements, but on the whole I got on pretty well.

Theirs was a mining family, but unlike my own they didn't work in the mines, they owned them. The house was large and lavishly appointed and it was possible, when they were away, for even the junior servants to explore. Mr Evans, the butler, would huff and bluster if he caught us, but we were careful enough and managed to get away with it for the most part. One girl was fascinated by the music room and would try to sneak in to play the piano whenever she could, and the boys, of course, loved the billiards room. But for me there was only one room worth the risk of being at the wrong end of one of Mr Evans's lectures on correct behaviour: the library.

When the family was away, I would spend every possible moment of my spare time (of which there was, admittedly, precious little) hidden away in the library, working my way through their impressive collection of books. The best possible times were when one of my rare days off coincided with the family's absence and I would manage to spend a whole day reading. I would usually sneak into the library, snaffle a couple of choice volumes and spend the rest of the day in my room, making sure to sneak back and return them later that evening.

One such Sunday I had done exactly that and was just about to leave when a copy of *Emma* caught my eye. I had discovered Jane Austen earlier that month and I couldn't help opening up the book and reading the first few pages just to give myself something to look forward to the next time I was free.

I sat down on the floor by the tall bookshelves and crossed my legs. It wasn't long before I was completely engrossed and lost track of time so that I was still there, avidly devouring page after page of Austen, when the door swung open and in walked Mr Williams.

There was a moment of mutual shock, but then to my immense relief, he began to laugh.

'Well, well, well. What have we here?' he said. 'It's Florence, isn't it. We don't see much of you up here.'

I stammered an apology and hurried to put the book back on the shelf.

'What are you reading?' he said kindly, taking the book from me. 'Ah, Austen. A girl of impeccable taste. I find her a little fussy at times, but she sees the truth of people. A keen observer, don't you think?'

I wasn't completely sure what he meant, but as he gently coaxed answers from me, I found myself beginning to gabble excitedly about not only Jane Austen, but all the books I'd read. He seemed both amused and impressed and invited me to come to the library any time I wanted to, as long as I treated the books carefully and always put them back in the correct spot.

I was dumbfounded. When he had first walked in I had been sure that my illicit reading would be my undoing, but it turned out that it was an important turning point. Over the months that followed I had many more conversations with Mr Williams about literature, poetry, history, politics... everything, in fact, that his library contained. I was, I now think, his pet project, an attempt to make something of the poor little waif from the Valleys. Whatever his motives, though, I shall be forever in his debt.

Life in Cardiff had settled into a comfortable routine and before I knew it, two years had passed since I first left home. I had visited Aberdare at Easter during my first year away and it was wonderful to see them all, but even at fourteen I already knew that my life was going to be elsewhere.

I had taken to reading the newspapers as well as Mr Williams's books, and on the 12th of July 1892 (I still have the clipping) I saw an advertisement for an agency at London. London! Cardiff had much to offer, but... London. I applied at once.

Mr and Mrs Williams wrote me the most excellent references and within a month I was on a train bound for Paddington.

Lady Hardcastle kicked the sole of my boot.

'Daydreaming, pet?' she said.

'Actually, yes, my lady. Just reminiscing about the first time I was on a train to London.'

'Ah, yes, your first big adventure. Actually, the start of the whole big adventure, if you think about it.'

I was still lost in thought.

'Any regrets?' she asked.

'What? Oh, no, none. Well, there are the death threats, obviously. And the drudgery. And the years of running for our lives in strange countries. And the other death threats. And your complete inability to put on a corset without choking yourself. And being chased from my home by a dead man. Other than that, it's been wonderful.'

'Oh.' She seemed genuinely dejected.

'You goose!' I said. 'I wouldn't have swapped it for the world. In fact you and Sir Roderick gave me the world.'

'Thank you, pet. I couldn't have done any of it without you. But I could really do without the being-pursued-by-a-dead-man part of it myself. He really is dead. I saw him.'

'I did, too, my lady. Could Harry have made a mistake? Is it really him?'

'We shall find out soon enough. Is this Reading?'

It was, indeed, Reading. We'd soon be at Paddington and Harry should be waiting for us. I'd not seen Harry for a few years and, despite the unnerving circumstances, I was rather looking forward to it. He had been in London when we first returned from India in 1901 and we had seen him often for the first six months. He had been the most excellent fun to be around but then he had been posted abroad somewhere (I never did find out where). He and his sister shared a mischievous sense of humour and a sideways view of the world which never failed to amuse me and I don't remember ever having laughed so much as I had when the two of them got together. I didn't imagine there would be a great deal of laughter this time, though.

The London suburbs seemed to stretch out much farther along the railway line than I remembered, which made the last part of the journey seem to crawl by. I felt that by the time we reached the built-up areas we should be just moments from our destination, but it took an absolute age before we were finally drawing into Brunel's magnificent Paddington Station.

With only a single bag each, we had no need of a porter and we were already making our way hastily down the platform while others were still gathering their traps. I had had an eye open for pursuit since we boarded the branch line train at Chipping Bevington, but there had been no obvious signs there, nor at Bristol Temple Meads. If anyone had boarded the train between there and London I judged they would have been among the first to alight and would now be loitering on the platform so as to catch sight of us. But there were no obvious candidates and everyone I saw was simply going about their business, completely oblivious to the two women heading towards the station concourse, carrying their own bags.

Harry was waiting for us next to W H Smith, exactly as planned. If you were casting the role of Dashing Spy for a play, you'd pick Harry. Tall, as dark-haired as his sister, and with a way of carrying himself which somehow conveyed authority. He also had a smile which could brighten anyone's day and he turned it upon us as we approached.

'What ho, Emily,' he said, reaching out to take her bag. 'You found the place all right?'

'Yes, dear,' she said. 'Apparently the train drivers all know the way. It's as though they come straight here.'

'Good-oh. Oh lord, I see you brought that blessed servant again. I thought you said you were going to get rid of her.'

'Good afternoon, Mr Featherstonhaugh,' I said, with a curtsey. I made my usual point of mispronouncing it as "Featherston-huff" which in turn drew his usual raised eyebrow and rueful smile.

'It's "Fanshaw", you silly girl, as you very well know,' he said, indulgently playing along. 'And how are you, Miss Strong-Arm? Beaten up any sailors lately?'

'No sailors, sir, no. A couple of civil servants who got too lippy, but no sailors.'

He laughed and motioned for us to follow him.

'Let's get a cab,' he said. 'Not too keen on hanging about in the open just now.'

As we walked, I said, 'But I thought you told us Ehrlichmann was on his way to Bristol.'

'And so he is, dear girl, but friend Ehrlichmann is not a "lone wolf", as they say. He is – or at least was – an agent of the Imperial German government and they, let me tell you, have people absolutely everywhere these days. We've got our eye on most of them, but you never know. Better to be safe than sorry.'

There were three motor taxis waiting on Carriage Road in the station and Harry ushered us into the first. He gave the driver an address in St John's Wood and we set off.

Harry's flat was on the third floor of a mansion building and once we were inside, he took a careful look out of the window at the street below. He seemed satisfied and at last seemed to relax. He asked if we'd like some tea and ambled out to the kitchen. I offered to do it, but he would have none of it.

'It's a fine state of affairs when a chap is incapable of making a simple pot of tea for his guests,' he said.

Lady Hardcastle had been examining the books on the shelf. She seemed to be still on edge, but she, too, was calming down a little now that she was back on familiar territory and in the company of someone who had some power to help.

'So you're still refusing to hire a valet?' she said as she settled into one of the armchairs.

'There's a woman who comes in a couple of times a week and runs a duster over the place,' he said, coming back in from the kitchen with a tray. 'But it's too much of a fag to go through all the hiring business. Will I like him? Will he keep out of the way? Will he be discreet? And then I might find that no matter how useless and annoying he is, I can't get rid of the blighter.' He winked at me and set the tray on a low table in the centre of the room.

'I know how you feel, dear. I mean look at me,' she said, pouring the tea. 'I hired this one fourteen years ago and I'm still stuck with her.'

'I can hear you, you know,' I said.

'And they're always earwigging,' said Harry.

I harrumphed and sipped my tea.

'Tell me, darling,' said Lady Hardcastle. 'What are your Foreign Office sources saying about this chap? This supposed Ehrlichmann. The real one really is dead. It was all in my statement. Even the German government confirmed it.'

'I've not seen him myself, Sis, but I trust the chaps that have. Chaps that encountered him in the '90s have reported seeing him large as life.'

'What do Customs say? What's on his passport?'

'We've had a watch on him, but obviously he's not using his own name. His passport says he's Hans Schneider, a salesman from Düsseldorf.'

'This is all most perplexing,' she said.

They began discussing all sorts of increasingly fanciful explanations for his reappearance but my mind began to wander.

Work as a parlour maid in London was less grimy but no less arduous than work as a scullery maid in Cardiff. The hours were still long and the work was still hard, but I had a nicer uniform and I spent more time above stairs. And I had a room in the attic which I shared with one of the other parlour maids. I was moving up in the world.

The family lived in Kensington so my afternoons off often included a walk in Hyde Park, and I found myself rather pleased with how things were turning out for me. Here I was, a fifteen-year-old girl from the Valleys, and already I was living in a big house in London and taking walks in one of the most famous parks in the world. Admittedly it wasn't my own house and I only managed to get to the park once a fortnight, but it still seemed like an enormous step up the ladder from a mining town in South Wales.

I kept in touch with my family, writing at least once a week, and they seemed pleased that things were going so well for me. I missed Gwenith most of all and begged her to come to London and join me but she was working with Mam in the shop and was still, I think, at least partly convinced that I had lost my mind. Why would anyone want to move to somewhere so crowded and dangerous when they had the Brecon Beacons on their doorstep. And everyone "talked funny", too. I knew for a fact that she'd never set foot on the Brecon Beacons, having never ventured farther from our house than the mountain above Mamgu's cottage, but there was no persuading her.

I was greatly enjoying my new life in London. My accent softened and I began to think myself quite the sophisticated girl about town. Time passed quickly and, once again, I found that two years had flown by without my really noticing. It was 1894, I was seventeen, and just as before I was getting itchy feet and beginning to look around for new opportunities.

As a parlour maid, I not only had more frequent contact with the family, but occasionally with their guests, too. Sir Clive Tetherington, the owner of the house, was a Permanent Secretary to the Foreign Office which meant that a number of rather important people came to call. This, in turn, meant that as "the well-read one" I often found myself wheeled out when the family wanted to impress guests with the high quality of their staff. If I'd known a little more about the world I should probably have found it a little condescending, but as an ambitious seventeen-year-old, eager to impress, I relished the chance to show off.

One of Sir Clive's particular friends was a colleague of his from the Foreign Office by the name of Sir Roderick Hardcastle. He and his wife Emily visited often and whenever I was around, Lady Hardcastle made a point of talking to me, asking me interesting questions about what I was reading, what I thought about the events of the day and, for the first time in my life, treating me as though I were an intelligent adult.

One summer's afternoon, I was folding napkins in the laundry room when John, one of the footmen, came to find me to tell me that I was to go to Lady Tetherington's study at once. He and I had never got along and there was an evil smirk on his pointy face as he implied as heavily as he could that I was in trouble.

I straightened my pinafore and pushed past him, making my way calmly upstairs to the Mistress's study. I knew I wasn't in trouble, despite Evil John's leering insinuations, but I was very curious as to why I might have been summoned in the middle of the day.

I knocked on the door and entered to find Lady Tetherington and Lady Hardcastle seated on the armchairs beside the oak desk. They were drinking tea and chatting, but they stopped as I came in.

'Ah, Florence,' said Lady Tetherington. 'Thank you for coming up. I hope we're not interrupting your work.'

'No, my lady,' I said. 'Just some linen folding. I can catch up any time.'

'Splendid,' she said. 'You know Lady Hardcastle, I think.'

'Yes, my lady. Good afternoon, my lady.' It was going to get confusing with all these ladies about.

I could see that Lady Hardcastle was amused, too. 'Good afternoon, dear,' she said with a smile. 'Your mistress and I have been having a little chat, and she's given her consent for me to make you an offer.'

'My reluctant consent,' said Lady Tetherington.

'Her reluctant consent,' agreed Lady Hardcastle. 'You see, I am in somewhat urgent need of a new lady's maid. My own – a lovely girl – has fallen in love with a soldier and will be moving to… oh, I can't remember where. Wiltshire somewhere. But anyway, once she's gone, I'll be entirely without help. And we can't have that, can we?'

'No, my lady, I don't suppose we can,' I said.

She laughed. 'Quite. Now we've met a few times and we seem to get along, and I'd really rather like to offer you the job.'

I was somewhat taken aback. I had imagined that all this was to be an elaborate way of saying that she was reorganizing her staff and would I be prepared to fill a parlour maid vacancy in her household, but here she was offering me the position of lady's maid. It was unheard of. To my eternal embarrassment, I just stood there with my mouth open.

Lady Hardcastle looked disappointed. 'Oh, I'm sorry, dear. I shouldn't have asked.'

'No, my lady,' I eventually managed to stammer. 'I should be honoured. I just...'

'Well that's a relief,' she said. 'I thought I'd horrified you.'

'No, my lady. You surprised me, to be sure, but I'm thrilled.' I looked towards Lady Tetherington. 'Are you certain that this is all right, my lady? I don't want to let anyone down.'

It was Lady Tetherington's turn to smile. 'I shan't pretend that it will be easy to lose one of the best parlour maids I've ever had. One of the best I've ever heard of, in fact. I seriously thought of telling Emily to shove off if I'm honest. I mean. The blessed cheek of the woman. But it's a remarkable opportunity for a girl of your age, dear, and I honestly couldn't live with myself if I thought I had stood in your way.'

I paused for just a moment to make it at least appear that I was giving it serious, mature thought, but I couldn't keep up the pretence for long and abruptly I blurted, 'Yes, please, my lady. Please can I?'

They both laughed.

'I think that's settled, then,' said Lady Tetherington. 'I shall leave you two to work out the details. But don't let her bilk you, dear. Lady Hardcastle is a notorious cheapskate and I have it on the best authority that she underpays her servants and makes them work under the most appallingly harsh conditions.' She winked.

'Out, Jane, before I take my hunting whip to you, you impudent knave!' said Lady Hardcastle, pointing imperiously to dismiss Lady Tetherington from her own study. 'Actually, dear I can't mean knave, can I. What's a female knave? But out! Out, I say, you foul slanderess!'

I knew we were going to get along famously.

We talked for quite a while about what she would expect of me and, to my surprise, what I should expect of her. I'd never known such a thing. My two employers to date had been perfectly wonderful, but I'd never been told I should expect them to be polite and considerate, or that I should speak up at once if I thought I was being treated unreasonably. This was going to be a new life indeed.

We agreed that I should start work in the Hardcastle household in a fortnight's time and she said that she would make all the necessary arrangements with Lady Tetherington. Once she had gone, I wasted no time in rubbing John's stupid beaky nose in it, but with the others I was more circumspect, playing down the promotion and trying not to appear too full of myself.

Having just watched two years fly past almost unnoticed, I was dismayed by how slowly the next two weeks crawled by. My few possessions were packed on the first night and I found myself willing the hours to pass. On my final day, the staff gave me a most splendid farewell lunch and each of them wished me well. The family, too, gave me a warm send-off and Sir Clive presented me with a journal and a beautiful pen.

'I know you like to read, my dear,' he said. 'I wonder if you might find the time to write, as well.' I didn't know what to say. I just stood there with my little bag in my hand and burst into tears. Parlour maids came and went and we weren't treated like this. I had no idea how to react.

Eventually I managed to mumble my thanks and went out through the front door – the front door! – and got into the waiting Hansom that the Hardcastles had sent to collect me.

The Hardcastles were younger than the Tetheringtons, though no less wealthy, but they lived a much simpler life. The house itself was run by just a cook and a housemaid, while Sir Roderick was tended to by his valet, Jabez Otterthwaite, and I, obviously, looked after Lady Hardcastle. I was more than a little out of my depth at first and more than once I thought I'd made a terrible, arrogant mistake in accepting the job. But I had been carefully watching the senior maids ever since I entered service and had persuaded one of them to teach me some dressmaking skills, and the rest of my duties I picked up slowly as I went along. Eventually I began to feel as though I was living up to the confidence Lady Hardcastle had shown in me and after a few months began to properly enjoy myself.

If I thought that the last four years had been pleasant enough, the next twelve months in the Hardcastle household were positively idyllic. As lady's maid I was expected to attend my mistress almost wherever she went and I found myself traveling all over the country and even, once, to Paris. It was the most fun I had ever had.

There were times when I was left behind. She disappeared for days at a time and on her return, refused to speak about what she had been up to. I'm embarrassed to say now that it never occurred to me to be nosy enough to find out what she'd been doing, nor clever enough to work it out for myself. But in my defence, I was only seventeen and I'd led a somewhat cloistered life in servants' quarters where the sort of things that I subsequently discovered about her were never dreamed of, much less spoken of.

She was the best possible company and although there was never any doubt that we were employer and servant, she treated me with the utmost respect and always talked to me as though my opinion mattered.

Sir Roderick was something of a rising star in the Foreign Office and one day in 1895 he came home with the news that he was to be posted to Shanghai. Better yet, Lady Hardcastle was to go with him and I would be accompanying her. Everyone else was being left behind, but I was going to China. China!

I felt yet another kick on the sole of my boot.

'Florence!' said a voice sharply.

I struggled awake.

'Sorry, my lady. I was just resting my eyes,' I croaked.

'And your mouth, pet; you're drooling,' said Lady Hardcastle.

I wriggled upright in the chair and tried to come to.

'Come along, up you get. Harry wants us to meet someone.'

I pushed myself out of the surprisingly comfortable chair and straightened myself out. Harry was already wearing his hat and was putting on his gloves. I tried to see if he were armed but there were no obvious signs.

'Looking for this?' he said, drawing a tiny pistol from his waistcoat pocket. 'Latest thing from America, an update of a Belgian weapon. We're trying them out.'

'Very impressive,' I said. 'Though I confess I'm more impressed that you noticed me looking.'

'A gentleman always notices when a woman is looking at him, Miss Armstrong,' he said with a wink. I blushed.

'When you've finished admiring my brother's weapon, Flo, perhaps we might go?'

I hurriedly put on my own hat and gloves and followed them out.

We quickly found a motor taxi and Harry instructed the driver to take us to Whitehall. I was almost surprised by the comfortable feeling I had in the familiarity of the London streets. We had lived there for five years before moving to Gloucestershire, of course, but I'd spent much more of my life living elsewhere so it shouldn't have felt so much like being home. Nevertheless, that was how it felt.

The journey was a short one and when we arrived at the anonymous Regency building, the uniformed man just inside the door acknowledged Harry with a nod and allowed us in without further ceremony. Harry led us briskly to an office on the first floor and knocked on the door.

'Enter!' said a muffled voice from inside.

Harry opened the door and ushered us in. A silver-haired man in an impeccably-cut suit was sitting behind a large oak desk, and he stood as Lady Hardcastle entered.

'Emily,' said Harry once we were all inside. 'Allow me to introduce Sir David Alderman. Sir David, this is my sister, Lady Hardcastle.'

'How do you do,' said Sir David.

'How do you do,' said Lady Hardcastle. 'And this is my maid, Florence Armstrong.'

'Ah, yes. I'd heard that you and she were a team,' said Sir David. 'Welcome, Miss Armstrong.' He gestured to two chairs in front of his desk. 'I'm embarrassed to say that I have only two chairs. I'm not used to entertaining crowds.'

'Please don't worry, Sir David,' I said. 'I'm more than happy to stand.'

'Very well. Thank you,' he said. 'I hope you don't mind the peremptory summons, as it were, but I felt I needed to introduce myself and reassure you that we're doing everything we can to track down this man, whoever he might turn out to be, and to keep you safe.'

'Thank you, Sir David,' said Lady Hardcastle.

'Although I must say, I've been wanting to meet you for some time.' He tapped a buff folder on his desk. 'Your file makes most impressive reading.'

She inclined her head slightly in acknowledgement.

'But as I'm sure you'll understand, events over the past couple of months have turned that idle curiosity into something more urgent.' He flipped open the folder and riffled through the pages. 'I have copies here of the statements you gave to the Governor-General's office in Calcutta in 1901, and the one you gave to this office on your return to England in 1903. They're entirely consistent with each other and you are adamant that when you left Shanghai in 1898, Günther Ehrlichmann was dead.'

'As a dodo, Sir David. I saw him with my own eyes.'

'Quite. But now I also have reports from some Special Branch officers in the field,' he said, looking at another sheet in the file, 'which are equally certain that Ehrlichmann is in England and is looking for you.'

'Is there no chance that they might be mistaken?' she asked.

'There's always that chance, Lady Hardcastle, as I'm sure you're aware. But the officer in question, one Hugh Waring, was in China in the '90s and knew Ehrlichmann well.'

'Ah, yes,' she said. 'I remember Waring. Able young chap. I'm glad he's doing well.'

'Quite. And Waring maintains that the man he saw most assuredly is Ehrlichmann. He might have aged ten years, he says, but he would... let me see... "stake my pension on this being the self-same Günther Ehrlichmann as I knew in Shanghai in the '90s."'

'Well that's one mystery,' said Lady Hardcastle. 'The other is why he should be after me.'

'Really?' said Sir David. 'I should have thought that was obvious. You're a loose end. The Imperial German government doesn't like loose ends. They had hoped to remove you and Sir Roderick from the field of play in '98 and thought they had. But you pop up like a bad penny in Calcutta and then come home to make a royal nuisance of yourself to them and their plans in London. If I were them, I'd have wanted you bumped off long since. Damn glad you're on our side, to be honest.'

'I could understand it if they had tried to kill me as soon as I cropped up in England again,' she said. 'But why now? And why Ehrlichmann? And why isn't the blighter still dead?'

'I can't answer any of those questions for certain, but we do know that German militarization continues apace and their new fleet is close to becoming a nuisance. My presumption is that they imagine you know something they don't want us to know, something which might disrupt their current plans.'

'Or perhaps,' I said, 'it's just personal. Perhaps Ehrlichmann has been imprisoned or in hospital all this time and is only now free to pursue us.'

Sir David appeared irked by this impudent interruption from a servant. 'Quite,' he said, looking quickly away from me and back to Lady Hardcastle. 'Can you think of anything you discovered in Shanghai that you might have previously neglected to mention? Anything at all?'

'No, Sir David, everything I discovered during my time in Shanghai and Tsingtao is in the reports.'

'Hmm,' he said. 'Very well. Still, at least we have you here in London now where we can keep you safe. Where will you be staying?'

'With me, sir,' said Harry.

'Splendid,' said Sir David, making a note on a large notepad. 'I'll have a man from the Yard pass by once in a while to make sure everything is tickety-boo, but you just leave everything to us and we'll have this cleared up in no time.'

I decided that on the whole I'd rather be disliked for asking impertinent questions than simply for the outrageous crime of being a servant in a public place. 'Is there a reason,' I said, 'why you don't just pick him up and ask him?'

'I beg your pardon?' he said, clearly trying to restrain himself.

'Well,' I continued, 'here's this chap that you believe, however improbable it may be, to be a long-dead German agent. You don't really know who he is nor what he's up to, but you strongly suspect that whatever it is, it isn't for the good of King and country. So why don't you just lift him and find out? At the very least you could warn him off.'

He smiled an insincere smile. 'I see,' he said. 'Yes. Yes, I suppose we could, but I prefer to let the game play out. If he really is Ehrlichmann, he'd not give anything up without us applying... pressure. And that would invoke the wrath of the Germans. And in the end we'd still be as ignorant as ever but we'd also need to be on the lookout for retaliation. And having tipped our hand, we might hamper our broader efforts to keep an eye on what the blighters are up to.'

'We might stop the blighters from blowing holes in our heads, though,' I said.

He looked briefly as though he might do the job for them, but he recovered quickly. 'I can assure you, Miss Armstrong, that your mistress is in no danger now that she's under our protection.'

I'd made my point so I decided to let it lie.

'Thank you, Sir David,' said Lady Hardcastle. 'I'm sure that now we're with Harry, we can deal with any eventuality. I appreciate your concern.'

'You're quite welcome, Lady Hardcastle,' he said. 'Unless there's anything else you wish to ask me, I've covered everything I needed to.'

'No, I feel suitable reassured. It was good of you to take the time to talk to us.'

'Think nothing of it,' he said. 'Featherstonhaugh, can I leave you to show Lady Hardcastle out?'   *Fanshaw*

'Yes, sir, of course.'

We rose to leave. Harry ushered us back out into the corridor and I cast one last look over my shoulder as I left. Sir David's answering smile was slightly more disconcerting than the glare I was expecting.

Out on the street, Harry was beside himself with glee.

'What's amusing you, brother dear?' asked Lady Hardcastle.

'It's little Flo here telling the old man off like that. I can't tell you the number of times I've wanted to ask him exactly the same question. Why the blazes doesn't he just pinch the chap and put his heels in the fire?'

'And why haven't you asked him?'

'Politics, mainly, sis. And craven careerism. No point in upsetting the apple cart. But he's a good egg, Sir David, and if he thinks this is the right course, I trust him. But I've been itching to get him to spell it out. Good on you, tiny lady.'

'It was nothing, sir,' I said. 'I don't think I made him very happy, though.'

'Oh, he'll get over it. Just not used to being challenged by the lower orders, that's all.'

'Lower orders, is it? I'll be sure to remember my place the next time you're being roughed up by Hungarian toughs in an alley in the East End. Wouldn't want to involve myself improperly in the affairs of the toffs.'

Harry laughed. 'Don't you dare,' he said. 'I'm pretty sure I owe you my life for that one. Now, what say we adjourn to the Ritz for a slap-up tea. My treat.'

'Your treat, dear boy?' said Lady Hardcastle. 'In that case, you're on.'

He hailed another cab.

I'd seen enough atlases and read enough travel memoirs to know that China was a devil of a long way away, but it's one thing seeing it on a map, quite another thing is to spend the best part of three weeks travelling there on a P&O ship. And I used to think it was a long way from our house to the top of the mountain.

Sir Rodney had been posted to the British Consulate in Shanghai and he and his wife were billeted in a pleasant little house in the British Settlement. The city had been carved up by the Western powers and it was possible to live one's life there without ever really feeling one had left Europe. The climate was different, and obviously it was China if you chose to look, but there was so much Britishness in our part of town that we might as well have been living in Kensington.

Sir Roderick worked normal office hours which left Lady Hardcastle free to do much as she pleased during the day. There were calls to be made and received, of course, and luncheons to attend, but there was plenty of time to explore Chinese life. She had employed a local woman as a housemaid and we spent many hours learning each other's languages (apart, that is, from my own first language – neither of them showed much inclination to learn Welsh). And once we had mastered a few basics, we prevailed upon her to show us around.

With our local guide we were introduced to the Chinese area of the city where we would often shop and eat. The ladies of the Consulate were horrified at this behaviour and cautioned Lady Hardcastle most sternly against "going native" but this spurred her on even more. She even bought some Chinese clothes for us both, complete with the little pillbox hats that some of them were wearing.

Life had suddenly begun to far exceed even my wildest imaginings and at just eighteen years old I was living an adventure I had never even dreamed of.

Life settled into a sort of routine for the first few months, but then Lady Hardcastle resumed her periodic absences, leaving me for days at a time in the company of the housemaid. Sir Roderick usually dined at his club during those times and I had little to do but practice my Mandarin.

During one such absence, I was awakened not long after dawn by the sound of the front door being stealthily closed. I thought at first that it was Sir Roderick returning from one of his rare all-night card games, but as I came to I remembered that he had arrived home shortly before I had retired for the night.

Curiosity was never much good for the long life and happiness of moggies, and it could well have proved my undoing, too, but I just couldn't stop myself from going to find out what had made the noise. I crept towards the hall as silently as I could manage and was startled to see a plump Chinese man standing there with his back to me. I must have let out a gasp, for he turned round and there, large as life, was Lady Hardcastle.

'Ah, Florence, there you are, dear. Help me out of these togs and prepare me a bath, would you? I'm quite done in.'

I had thought that the the most exciting thing that could ever possibly happen to a girl from the Valleys had been when, at thirteen and against everyone's advice, I had left home to start my life in service in Cardiff. But life had topped that when I had left Cardiff for London at fifteen; surely nothing could be more exotic than that. Except that then I had left London for China and I absolutely knew that nothing could ever be more exciting. And then, on that morning in Shanghai, I had a conversation with Lady Hardcastle as I helped her get ready for bed.

Emily Charlotte Ariadne Featherstonhaugh was born on 7 November 1867, the younger of two children born to Sir Percival

Featherstonhaugh, Permanent Secretary to the Treasury, and his wife Ariadne, known to her friends — of whom there were many — as Addie. She and her brother Henry Alfred Percival Featherstonhaugh – who had never been anything other than Harry – had a childhood as far removed from my own as it was possible to imagine. There were toys and outings and friends who came to tea. When their parents entertained, they would sneak to the top of the stairs where they would almost always be "accidentally" caught and indulgently introduced to the guests by their doting parents. For five years, Emily's life had been idyllic, and then one day, it had come crashing down around her ears. Harry, now aged seven, was sent away to school.

Emily was devastated. Not only had her childhood companion and confederate been taken away from her, but he was off on an extra special adventure that she couldn't share. He had gone to school. He was going to be learning things that she felt she would never be allowed to know. It just wasn't fair.

She had made such a fuss that her parents, as indulgent as ever, had engaged a governess several years before they had planned and Emily, determined to prove herself every bit as clever as her brother, had taken to her lessons with a determination that surprised everyone. It wasn't long before the first governess, whose specialism had been teaching simple reading and arithmetic skills to the very young, was forced to admit that the young girl had long since passed the level at which she felt comfortable teaching, and another had to be engaged. And then another. And another.

The years passed and Emily's academic prowess showed no sign of peaking. It had been expected that she would follow her parents' friends' daughters who were attending an assortment of finishing schools around Europe before being presented at coming out balls and beginning the search for suitable husbands. But when Harry came home and for Christmas 1883 and told her that he was about to sit the Cambridge entrance examination, Sir Percival and Lady Featherstonhaugh's plans were changed again. Harry intended to study at their father's old college, Kings, which meant that Emily would be unable to follow him, but there was a women's college now, and Emily set about persuading her beleaguered parents that they should support her newfound ambition.

And so it was that in October 1884, Emily Featherstonhaugh had gone up to Girton College, Cambridge.

It was at Cambridge that she met the charming and handsome Roderick Hardcastle and where, almost as significantly, she had come to the attention of certain dons who had long been on the lookout for people such as she; well-connected people with sharp minds and the ability to use them. People who could gather information useful to Her Britannic Majesty's government about the activities and intentions of its allies and enemies. People who could spy.

Of course, they usually recruited men. Men up at Cambridge who were bound for the Foreign Office or the Diplomatic Service were ideal, but there were women, too. Most often they were society women, wives of diplomats and businessmen, but there were lone adventurers, too, and it had recently occurred to the "certain dons" that there were now, among the university's students, a number of young women who might be of great use to them.

And so in her final year, Emily was recruited. She was trained in the use of codes and ciphers, and in such rudimentary espionage techniques as had been developed at that time (she later confided in me that the essence of this was "blend in and keep your eyes and ears open, dear girl") and by the time she graduated (with a double first, naturally) she was ready for her first posting. Or she would have been had not something not happened which her new masters found even more useful: she married Roderick Hardcastle.

Two years her senior, Hardcastle had already made quite an impression at the Foreign Office by the time he and Emily wed, and they formed the perfect intelligence team. They were young, charming, elegant, and fun. They had access to all the right people and, more importantly, all the right people were keen to be in their company. They played the role of dizzy socialites, all the while gathering information from the foreign dignitaries, businessmen and industrialists who were so delighted to be part of their orbit.

Short postings abroad followed, to Europe, the United States and to India, earning Roderick promotion and a knighthood and Emily a reputation as one of the finest spies of the age.

I sat dumbfounded. I had managed to piece much of the story together for myself during our many conversations over the past months, but I had never in my wildest imaginings even dreamt of the full extent of the truth. And just when I was beginning to think I was able to come to terms with it all, Lady Hardcastle said something even more extraordinary.

'The thing is, you see, my dearest Armstrong, that I am in the most desperate need of an assistant. There are places I find it difficult to go, places where I cannot blend in and keep my eyes and ears open. And a lot of these are places, my dear girl, where you could pass entirely unnoticed. I've mentioned you to my superiors and they are impressed by what I've said and what they've surreptitiously observed for themselves. How would you like to take a second job? As well as serving as the most excellent lady's maid a woman could ever wish for, how would you like to be a spy?'

'I swear, Flo, it's as if you're hardly with us today at all,' said Lady Hardcastle.

As promised, Harry had treated us to a most magnificently indulgent tea at the Ritz. There had been sandwiches, pastries and the most extravagantly gooey, cream-filled cakes, and even before we had finished, a feeling of overfed contentment had washed over me. As Harry and Lady Hardcastle began to speculate in hushed tones about the Ehrlichmann affair, I had found it harder and harder to concentrate and had, indeed, drifted off into a world of my own. But now it seemed that my opinion was being sought.

'I'm sorry, my lady,' I yawned. 'It must be this delicious tea that Mr Featherston-Huff has treated us to. Thank you, sir.'

'Think nothing of it, Strong-Arm,' he said. 'It was entirely my pleasure. Although I am a few bob short, so I've volunteered your services in the scullery for a couple of hours. I hope that's all right.'

I treated him to my most disdainful look and he laughed.

As did Lady Hardcastle. 'What I was saying, dear, is that until Sir David's wheels have ground a little finer, there's very little we can do but wait. I was suggesting a day out tomorrow.'

'That sounds very jolly, my lady,' I said. 'Did you have anything specific in mind?'

'I thought perhaps the National Gallery in the morning, a light lunch somewhere, then drop in on an old friend of mine in the afternoon and perhaps a concert in the evening.'

'Or a show, my lady?' I said, eagerly.

She chuckled. 'Something low and vulgar, with dancing girls, and a handsome fool in tennis whites falling in love with a girl from the tea rooms?'

'If such a thing exists, my lady,' I said, 'then I absolutely insist that you buy us tickets at once.'

It was Harry's turn to chuckle. 'I think I know just the thing. Leave it to me. You see to the highbrow stuff, Sis; Strong-Arm and I will take care of the real entertainment.'

We had tried our best to be entertaining guests, but by nine o'clock Harry had given up the unequal struggle and declared that it must surely be time for countryfolk to be in their beds.

I slept the sleep of the just, or the just-too-exhausted-to stay-up-any-longer, at least, and awoke next morning refreshed and alert. I had quite forgotten how draining it was to be on the run, but with Harry to help, and with Sir David's men out searching for Ehrlichmann, everything seemed a great deal more manageable.

I persuaded Harry to let me help with breakfast and also to take a walk to the baker's. And this had meant that we had had fresh toast with the omelettes I made, instead of the stale crumpets and mouldy jam that Harry had previously been contemplating.

The morning was spent, as promised, at the National Gallery, where I was treated to one or two more depictions of classical and biblical scenes than I was comfortably able to feign interest in. Lunch was somewhere near Park Lane, then we set off to see Lady Hardcastle's old friend.

I was quite prepared for an afternoon of discreet invisibility as she chattered to one of her socialite friends in a fashionable flat somewhere, and so I was both intrigued and delighted when we ended up in Marylebone, outside Madame Tussaud's famous waxwork museum. We went to the ticket desk and after a brief conversation with Lady Hardcastle, the young man there called over one of his colleagues who then disappeared through a door behind the desk and into a back office.

Nearly ten minutes later, a woman of Lady Hardcastle's own age appeared through the same door. She was wearing overalls and had a pencil tucked behind her ear.

'Oh my goodness gracious. Emily, it *is* you,' she gushed. 'Jacob told me Emily Hardcastle was here to see me and I said, "She can't be, dear, she's hidden herself away in Yokelton in the West Country, or Bumpkinshire or somewhere. She couldn't possibly be here in civilization." But here you jolly well are. Darling! How are you? It's been simply ages.'

Amid the cheek kissing, several more "Darling!"s and quite a few more than the necessary number of declarations of surprise and delight, Lady Hardcastle managed to explain that she was in town for a few days visiting her brother and thought that it would be an ideal opportunity to catch up with some old friends.

'Joan, dear, you remember Florence Armstrong, my maid?'

'I do indeed. How are you, my girl? She's not working you too hard?'

I remembered Joan now, we had met several times shortly after our return from Calcutta. She was one of the sculptors here at the waxworks.

'She treats me cruelly, madam, as you might remember,' I replied.

'I said you should come and work for me, my girl, but you wouldn't listen. Could do with someone like you about the house.'

I curtseyed, Harry laughed and Lady Hardcastle rolled her eyes.

'Now then, Joan darling, don't encourage her.'

'She'd never leave you, darling, never in a million years. You've been through altogether too much, you two. But let's not get maudlin, what can I do for you? Have you finally come to take me up on my offer of a "backstage" tour?'

'As a matter of fact, my darling,' said Lady Hardcastle, 'that's exactly why we're here.'

'And it's about time, too. Come with me, and I'll show you where we do the magic.'

After a morning of Old Masters, seeing the work of the sculptors close-up was a joyous treat. We saw heads being modelled in clay, wax heads being finished with hair and makeup, and complete figures being dressed. They were working on a new tableau and it was utterly fascinating to see the care and skill that went into putting it all together.

We moved on into the public areas, including a free tour of the Chamber of Horrors, and the afternoon was an absolute delight. Call me shallow if you will, but I'll take waxwork models of the famous and infamous over "A Doctor Tending a Patient's Foot in His

Surgery" (no, really), any day.

To close the day, and true to his word, Harry had managed to secure tickets for the most enjoyably silly show in the West End. As promised, there were songs, dancing, and the most preposterous love story you could possibly imagine. We had a late supper at the Ritz and then home for brandy and bed.

We were with family so, of course, there was nothing untoward about my sitting there with them both, enjoying Harry's cognac and joining in with the continuing speculation about what could possibly be going on' with the man who appeared to be the late and unlamented Günther Ehrlichmann and how it might involve the spies of the Imperial German Government.

'It seems to be a most intractable puzzle,' said Lady Hardcastle, polishing off the last of her cognac. 'But I have the most awful feeling that I'm going to be terribly disappointed by the solution. Let's just hope that we manage a satisfactory resolution, no matter how prosaic the answer turns out to be.'

Breakfast the next morning was interrupted by a ring at the doorbell. Reflexively, I began to rise to answer it, but Harry put his hand on my arm and went himself. He returned a few moments later with a telegram.

'It's for you, Sis,' he said, handing it over.

She tore it open and read. 'Oh bother,' she said presently. 'It's from Inspector Sunderland.'

'Your tame policeman in Bristol?' said Harry.

'The very same. I asked our tame constable in Littleton Cotterell to keep an eye on the house and watch out for strangers. It seems Sunderland has news. He wants me to telephone him. I don't suppose you could let me use the telephone at your office, dear?'

'I can do better than that, Sis. I have one here.'

'I say, you are quite the terribly modern man about town, aren't you, dear. No sign of a valet, but you have a telephone.'

'I'm frightfully important, Sis. I need to be reachable at all times.'

'Of course you are, darling. May I call the inspector? Or do you need to keep the line clear in case your masters need you urgently? There might be envelopes to lick, or paper fasteners to count.'

'Place your call, Emily,' he said, 'before I change my mind about helping you at all. It's in the hall by the door.'

Lady Hardcastle motioned for me to follow her and we went into the small hallway where, sure enough, there was a telephone on an old aspidistra stand beside the door. She lifted the earpiece and waggled its cradle a few times. We put our heads together and she positioned the earpiece between us so that we could both hear.

'Operator,' said the disembodied voice. 'Which number do you require?'

'I should like to place a trunk call to Bristol,' said Lady Hardcastle, with the exaggerated diction usually reserved for use by aristocratic ladies when speaking to foreign waiters. She gave the number and there was a prolonged series of clicks, pops and crackles before we were eventually connected.

'Inspector Sunderland?' said Lady Hardcastle.

'This is he,' said the distant voice. 'Is that you, Lady Hardcastle?'

'The very same. I received your telegram.'

'Ah yes,' he said. 'Thank you for telephoning. I trust it wasn't too inconvenient but I thought it better to explain events in person, as it were.'

'Not inconvenient at all, my dear inspector. It turns out that my brother has a telephone all of his very own.'

'How the other half lives, eh, my lady? I contacted Constable Hancock as soon as I received your telegram the day before yesterday. He said you left in something of a hurry.'

'There was an element of haste, yes Inspector.'

'I do wish you'd just come straight to me, my lady. But no matter. Hancock kept me informed. It seems that a tall, fair-haired gentleman in what Hancock described as "foreign-looking clothes" was seen snooping around your house late that first afternoon.'

'Oh dear,' said Lady Hardcastle. 'I do hope no one gave him cause to harm them.'

'No, my lady. He was discreetly observed and left to go about his business unmolested. When he had satisfied himself that there was no one home, he went to the pub and made enquiries about you, saying that he was an old friend of yours from London who just happened to be in the area. According to the landlord there...'

'Joe Arnold,' suggested Lady Hardcastle.

'That's the chap. He said the gentleman had a peculiar accent, but he couldn't place it. But apparently that meant that he didn't trust this fellow at all and with the admirable tightlippedness of village folk, spoke to him at length while revealing absolutely nothing of any use.'

'What an absolute darling,' said Lady Hardcastle.

'Quite so, my lady. It seems you've made quite a favourable impression in your little village. The foreign fellow paid for a room for the night and then left early in the morning after a hearty breakfast. Hancock says he hung round your place for a while and then set off around noon in the direction of Chipping Bevington, at which point Hancock telephoned me to let me know he might be coming my way. I put a couple of boys on Temple Meads station and sure enough he got off a local train and went to the London-bound platform.'

'So he's already back in London?' asked Lady Hardcastle.

'He is, my lady. My lads saw him get on the London train at four-fifteen. but not before he'd had a long conversation with two men in dark suits he met in the buffet.'

'Two men?'

'Two men. They chatted earnestly for about twenty minutes but my lads couldn't get close enough to hear what was said.'

'That's a shame,' said Lady Hardcastle. 'I should very much like to know what passed between them.'

'I thought you might, my lady,' said the inspector. 'And so did my lads. Which is why they pinched the two blokes in question as soon as chummy had left on the London Express.'

'Gracious me,' she said. 'That was bold.'

'Bold, my lady, and as it turns out, not as helpful as I should have hoped. In some ways, at least. In other ways, very informative indeed.'

'How so?'

'The two men said nothing to my boys. They were brought down to the station where they continued to say nothing. I'd left them in the cells for a while, let them cool off, see if they might be a bit more talkative if they thought they might be staying a while, when I get summoned into my governor's office. He didn't look best pleased. A little rattled, in fact. And he says I'm to release the two men immediately. Obviously I asked why, and he just said, "Because I said so, Inspector."'

'Well, well, well,' said Lady Hardcastle. 'Most instructive. Is all well with you, Inspector? Are there any repercussions?'

'None for me, my lady. I shut my mouth and did as I was told. But please be careful. I don't know what you're involved in – though there's some talk, and I can draw my own conclusions pretty well – but this blond chap isn't working alone and he seems to have friends who have powerful friends.'

'Thank you, Inspector. I'll not forget your help. Keep yourself safe and I shall tell all when we return. Or as much as I can, at any rate. Goodbye for now.'

'Cheerio, my lady.'

More clicks and pops and the line went dead.

'Bother,' she said. 'Harry! We have problems.'

We went back into Harry's small drawing room and Lady Hardcastle recounted the conversation with succinct precision.

'The problem with you cloak-and-dagger types,' he said when she had finished, 'is that you always find yourselves mixed up with other cloak and dagger types. We don't get chased around the country by dead foreigners in the FO. It's all very grown up and civilized.'

'The foreigners I can deal with for the most part,' said Lady Hardcastle. 'But those two that Sunderland picked up weren't foreign. And they weren't released on the say-so of a weary desk sergeant who can't be bothered with all the paperwork. Someone ordered their release. Someone high up.'

'I know, Sis, I know. That's the trouble with you cloak-and-dagger types, you're always dragging your nearest and dearest into your murky world with you.' He paused, realizing what he had just said. 'Oh, Emily, I'm sorry. I didn't mean…'

She put her hand on his arm. 'Don't worry, darling, I know.'

I had accepted Lady Hardcastle's offer of a life of espionage without a moment's hesitation. My training had begun almost as quickly, and she spent many hours patiently passing on her knowledge of the mysterious arts. She had already supplemented her own meagre training with several years of field experience and I was given the full benefit of her hard-won skills long before her methods found their way into the official training guides (which they assuredly did).

The next few years in China provided many tales to tell, and one day I promise I shall make an effort to share those that are not still classified as Top Secret. But for now, the story that concerns us takes place some four years later in 1899.

The Hardcastles had become something of a fixture in the social life of the British Settlement in Shanghai. They were still young and beautiful, and with Sir Roderick's stellar career in the diplomatic service and his wife's charm and grace as both hostess and guest, their company was sought by senior officials from Britain, France, America, China and even Germany. No one suspected their true motives for such far-reaching social connections and simply accepted them as delightful young people who were fun to be with. In the stuffy world of international business and diplomacy they were a breath of the freshest possible air.

The previous year had been a pivotal one in the history of China, with formal treaties establishing a Western presence along the coast, including the Germans in Tsingtao and the British in Hong Kong. Elsewhere in the world, Imperial Germany was beginning to flex its industrial and military muscles and the other Great Powers were more eager than ever for information about their activities.

With that aim in mind, Sir Roderick and Lady Hardcastle had been dispatched northwards to Tsingtao, ostensibly as representatives of Her Britannic Majesty's Government to wish the new German port continuing good fortune, but also, of course, to gather whatever information they could while they were there. There was a rumour that the German Navy was testing a new vessel out there on the western edge of the Pacific, far from the prying eyes of their European neighbours, and their European neighbours were devilishly keen to find out what it was.

The trip was an uncomplicated one for the Hardcastles and they fell into a practised routine. Together they attended parties and balls, meeting the great, the good and the eager to impress. A few days into the visit, Sir Roderick would manoeuvre himself into being invited to a card game, a billiards evening or some other men-only activity and his wife, pleading a headache or some other non-specific malady, would regretfully decline the corresponding ladies-only event and take to her bed.

Once the evening was well under way, she and I would slip out and engage in some thoroughly improper snooping. It was ordinarily quite difficult for us to go unnoticed in China, but at night time, with a little makeup and our Chinese garb, we could pass casual scrutiny. From a distance. In the shadows. As long as nobody looked too closely.

And so on this trip, while Sir Roderick was gambling with the gentlemen, Lady Hardcastle and I were tasked with exploring the docks in order to try to find out just exactly what the Kaiser's navy was up to.

Fortunately the docks and the naval yard were full of activity even at night and we managed to get close enough to the secret pens over the course of the long night to see exactly what we had been sent to see.

I had heard about submarines, of course, and now they are all too familiar, but to see an early prototype then, dark, sinister, and clearly designed for no other purpose than to kill, was rather unnerving.

Hiding in the shadows, further concealed between wooden crates and metal drums, Lady Hardcastle made sketches of the sinister vessel while I made notes about the personnel and equipment we had seen. A few hours before dawn we had left as quietly as we had come, and made our way back to the Residence.

Nothing had happened, nothing had gone wrong. It had all been a thoroughly ordinary and successful reconnaissance and we were back in our rooms before the servants stirred.

No, whatever it was that went horribly wrong happened later.

We compiled a thorough report from our joint recollections, Lady Hardcastle's sketches and my copious notes and sealed them in the usual way for dispatch to London in the diplomatic bag. A brief précis was encrypted and sent by telegram and our work in Tsingtao was done.

Two days later, we set off once more for Shanghai and we were soon back in our regular routine. Things in China were becoming increasingly unsettled and the Boxer Rebellion was bringing danger from the countryside into the cities on the coast, but we were safe for the time being and we tried to continue as normal.

We had been back for two weeks and Sir Roderick was at the office as usual while Lady Hardcastle lunched with a friend. The friend in question always took her own lady's maid and so we were able to sit and gossip together while our mistresses sat at a separate table.

With luncheon over, we made our way back to the house. I didn't know at first why I felt so sure that something was amiss, but as we approached the front door, I knew that it was. Lady Hardcastle clearly felt it, too, and as she went to unlatch the door, we both saw at once that it had been forced.

With a finger to her lips, Lady Hardcastle gently pushed the door open and stepped silently into the hall. The Chinese maid was lying on the floor, a trickle of blood from her temple forming a tiny, shocking pool of crimson on the otherwise pristine tiles. I knelt close and found that she was still breathing, but clearly deeply unconscious.

Lady Hardcastle crossed stealthily to the hall table and slid open the well-waxed drawer. She drew out the revolver that was stored there "just in case" and motioned for me to follow her.

Now that the initial shock had passed, I became more aware of things beyond the hall and I could hear voices coming from Sir Roderick's study. We approached as quietly as we were able and listened at the door.

'...tolerate your spying any longer, Hardcastle,' said a voice with a heavy German accent.

'I'm sure I have absolutely no idea what you're talking about, Herr Ehrlichmann. I am a representative of Her Majesty's government here in China. The very suggestion that I have been involved in "spying" is impertinent in the extreme. I should go so far as to say that it is slanderous.'

'I would find your indignant denials much more convincing and much less amusing had we not intercepted your report. We know you were in our naval dockyard, "Diamond Rook". Not the most impenetrable of code-names.'

'And where was this supposed "report", Herr Ehrlichmann?'

'In the diplomatic bag, exactly where you put it.'

'You expect me to believe that you intercept and search diplomatic bags now?'

'To be honest with you, Hardcastle, I don't care what you believe. Nor what you're currently planning to report to your masters. I'm here to kill you. You've been a... what is the expression you use...? A "thorn in our side"? Yes, you've been a thorn in our side for far too long. It is time we plucked you out.'

'Now, look here...'

Somehow, the quietness of the gunshot made it all the more shocking. It was followed by the sound of a body slumping to the floor, knocking something off the desk as it fell.

The door was pulled open sharply and Ehrlichmann burst out, stopping almost comically in his tracks as he was confronted by Lady Hardcastle who was levelling a revolver at his chest. His own weapon, a small, easily concealed, single-shot pistol, hung uselessly at his side.

Ehrlichmann smirked. 'Ah, the lady wife. And with a gun. How charming. Get out of the way, you stupid woman.'

Calmly, and without taking her eyes from his, Lady Hardcastle pulled back the revolver's hammer with her thumb. Unnecessary on a gun of that sort, but surprisingly threatening for such a tiny movement.

'I think,' she said, coldly, 'that you might have made one or two mistakes.'

He laughed. 'I don't think so, your ladyship. I am not the sort to make mistakes. Now get out of my way and I might forget how foolish you are being. You do not, I think, wish to join your husband.'

He took a rapid step towards her, reaching for the revolver, but without flinching, she pulled the trigger and shot him in the shoulder. The shock of the bullet's impact made him flinch away and he fell backwards against the doorframe.

'Go and check on Roddy, please, Florence,' she said, still covering Ehrlichmann with the revolver.

I did as I was asked and returned quickly, shaking my head. He had been shot through the eye.

'At least two mistakes, you Teutonic nitwit,' she said. 'In the first place, Roddy was not a spy. I am Diamond Rook, you dunderhead. Second, you came armed only for a single shot. What kind of inept assassin are you?'

Almost too fast to see, a knife appeared in his uninjured hand and he threw it at her with a force I would scarcely have believed possible from such a position. Somehow, though, Lady Hardcastle had anticipated this move and was already stepping aside, even as the knife left his hand.

'Third, you allowed yourself to be goaded into disarming yourself. If you're the best weapon Imperial Germany has at its disposal, the world is safe. Fourth, you killed my darling husband.'

Ehrlichmann was still defiant. 'And why was that kartoffelkopf's death a mistake?'

'Because of mistake number five. For reasons I can't fathom, you still don't actually believe that I'm about to kill you.'

He did, indeed, look genuinely shocked as she pulled the trigger again and ended his life.

'See to Mrs Lee, would you, dear,' she said as calmly as though nothing had happened. 'It looks as though she's taken a knock to the head.'

I did as I was bidden and slowly brought the terrified Mrs Lee round. I bandaged her head and offered her brandy while Lady Hardcastle called the consulate. Or tried to.

She returned as Mrs Lee was trying to apologize for letting Ehrlichmann in. We both told her not to be so silly and that no blame could possibly attach to her. Lady Hardcastle had more pressing concerns.

'I managed to speak to the duty officer,' she said. 'But not for long. The consulate is under attack and he said we should get out of the city as fast as we can. "Take a boat to anywhere," were his exact words. Then we were cut off.'

'Under attack, my lady?' I said.

'It seems a local group of Boxer rebels has taken it upon itself to attack European targets in Shanghai. No Westerner is safe and we are to flee as fast as possible.'

Our first concern was that Mrs Lee be able to get home from the British Settlement unmolested. We had no idea whether there would be consequences for locals who were working for Europeans, but it seemed a possibility. Lady Hardcastle gave her a month's wages and sent her on her way. Mrs Lee protested, but the look in Lady Hardcastle's eye convinced her that things were serious and she eventually left with promises to return to work as soon as things were calm again.

And then we, too, fled. We changed into practical travelling clothes, packed a few essentials and set off for the docks.

It didn't strike me at the time, but Lady Hardcastle didn't grieve. Not then anyway. There was much to be done and the safety of others (even though it was only me and Mrs Lee) to consider. She just seemed to push the grief to one side while she got on with more pressing matters. It came out eventually, of course, and nearly destroyed her, but for now there was no sign that she had lost the love of her life.

I was devastated and frightened, but not as frightened as I was about to be – the next two days were among the most terrifying of my life. There were near riots in the streets as armed Boxers went from house to house rounding up Europeans. They were happy enough to leave the docks alone, content that we were leaving the country, but for us there were other problems. We had struggled to make contact with British representatives, the majority of whom were trapped in the Consulate, but the trouble came from the German intelligence service. Ehrlichmann's death had been discovered and investigated when he had failed to return, and we soon learned that they had a reasonably good idea who to blame.

Whenever we tried to book ourselves a passage out of Shanghai we found ourselves dogged by German agents and eventually we came to the horrifying realization that nowhere in Shanghai was safe.

Under cover of darkness, we fled inland.

I, for one, slept uneasily knowing that the man we were all assuming was Ehrlichmann was back in London. How good was his information? Did he know Lady Hardcastle had a brother? Did he know that that's where we'd go?

I finally gave up the unequal struggle against wakefulness and got up from my troubled dozing not long after dawn. I dressed quickly and went through to the tiny kitchen to make myself some tea.

Harry's "housekeeper" had been in while we were out the day before and there were eggs, bacon, cheese and butter in the little larder so that I knew that by the time the milkman had been, there would be plenty for breakfast. There was almost no bread left, and it was stale anyway, but that was all right because I knew where the baker's was now and could pop out for a fresh loaf before the others were up.

Still feeling jumpy and paranoid, I took the precaution of having a quick butcher's through the curtains before I went out, just to get the lie of the land. London was coming alive, and a coalman's cart was already clattering along the street. I could see the milkman carrying his cans a few doors down, while a well-dressed man in early middle age, carrying a furled umbrella and briefcase – the sword and shield of our modern age – hurried towards the tube station.

It all seemed perfectly normal and perfectly safe, until the young loafer who had been leaning against the lamppost opposite the building, looked up. And by "looked up", I actually mean "looked directly at the window I was looking out of". I had barely cracked the curtains, only enough to take a look at the street, yet he most definitely saw me. He gave an impudent grin and an ironic salute and sauntered off.

I woke Lady Hardcastle.

'I'm so sorry to wake you, my lady,' I said as she struggled to wakefulness. 'We're being watched.'

'Watched?' she mumbled. 'By whom?'

'By a young lad in the street. He's gone now.'

'Blast and bother,' she said, finally becoming fully alert. 'Harry!' she yelled. 'Get up!'

There was grumbling and mumbling from the next bedroom, followed by a thud, a crash and an extremely colourful oath. Harry appeared at the bedroom door, tying the cord on his dressing gown.

'What is it?' he said. 'What's the matter?'

'The flat is being watched, dear,' said Lady Hardcastle.

Harry sighed. 'I know.'

'You know?'

'Yes, Sis, they're my men. Or "our" men. I got some security chaps from the FO to keep an eye on the place for us.'

'Oh,' said Lady Hardcastle and I together.

'Sorry,' I said. 'I thought…'

'No, I'm the one who should be sorry,' said Harry. 'I should remember that you two are in the game.'

Lady Hardcastle chuckled. 'Sometimes I wonder if our lives might be simpler if we were *on* the game. But do try to keep us informed, Harry dear. Flo might have hurt the poor lad if he'd spooked her.'

'Little chap?' said Harry. 'About five-foot-three in his socks? Tatty cap, cheeky grin?'

'That's him,' I said. 'You put your best man on the job, then? Someone who could really look after us?'

Harry smiled. 'You of all people should know better than to judge a chap's abilities from his size. Yes, Eric is one of our best men. Observant, bright, quick-witted, light on his feet and absolutely terrifying in a close-quarter scuffle. He's you in breeches, Strong-Arm.'

'Fair enough,' I said. 'But he's not quite the steadfast and true-type. He took one look at me and strolled off.'

Harry let out a little snort of a laugh. 'Just ringing the changes, I expect. There will be three of them working shifts. Don't want to spook the natives by having idlers hanging about the street all day.'

'So I'm safe to go to the baker's then?' I said.

'My dearest Strong-Arm, I suspect you'd be safe walking through the darkest alleys of Limehouse with five-pound notes pinned to your hat.'

'Don't do that, dear,' said Lady Hardcastle. 'But do please nip out and fetch us some bread. There's something about not sleeping that makes me really very hungry indeed. Is there any chance of a cup of tea before you go?'

'There's some in the pot, my lady,' I said.

'I'll get it,' said Harry. 'You just get the bread and try not to hospitalize any of our men on the way.'

The trip to the baker's was thoroughly uneventful and I believe I clocked Eric's replacement reading a newspaper on the street corner. Now I knew that these idlers were on the side of the angels, I felt just that tiny bit safer in Harry's flat.

Breakfast was as magnificent as breakfast in a bachelor's flat can be, and we were onto extra toast and a third pot of tea when the doorbell rang. Harry went to answer it and returned a few moments later with a large envelope.

'What have you got there, brother dear?' said Lady Hardcastle.

'Treasure,' he said.

'It's awfully thin treasure, sweetheart. Don't you have anything more substantial?'

'This is quite substantial enough, old girl,' he said, carefully opening the flap. 'I contacted one of our chaps in Berlin to get the lowdown on Ehrlichmann.'

'I thought Sir David was one of your chaps,' I said. 'I thought he was researching Ehrlichmann.'

'He's Home Office, old thing, different department. He just expressed an interest in your case one day and offered to help. I'm never one to turn down an ally, and it never hurts to make new acquaintances in Whitehall.'

'It's all positively Byzantine,' said Lady Hardcastle. 'But what have your chaps found?'

'Let's have a look, shall we?' he said, and began to read the documents he had taken from the envelope. 'Tum-te-tum...' he said, as he scanned for items of interest. 'Ah, here we are. It seems there is no Günther Ehrlichmann on the payroll of German intelligence. He simply doesn't exist.'

'No, dear, he doesn't,' said Lady Hardcastle, testily. 'I killed him nine years ago.'

'No, sorry, I paraphrased badly. I should have said that there never has been a Günther Ehrlichmann. Ever. The man never existed.'

'Then who...?'

'Let me have a read, this is fascinating stuff.' Harry sat down distractedly and began to work his way through the long memorandum. It seemed to be taking him ages so I went and made some more tea.

While I was in the kitchen, the telephone rang and I heard Lady Hardcastle say that she would answer it. It was clearly a brief call, though, because by the time I brought the tea tray through, she was back in her chair.

'Who was that on the telephone, my lady?' I said as I set the tray on the small table.

'Sir David,' she said quietly, trying not to break Harry's concentration.

'What did he want?' I said.

'It was very sweet. He just wanted to check that all was well and that we were still comfortable at Harry's.'

'How odd,' I said.

'A little odd, certainly. But quite charming. Who would have thought that the Home Office had real gentlemen in it?'

I remained unconvinced that Sir David was either charming or a gentleman, but I said nothing. Meanwhile, Harry had finally finished reading.

"Righto, Sis, let's see if I can get this straight. It seems that the man who killed Roddy and then met his own end in the hallway of your rented house in Shanghai, was called Jakob Gerber. He and his brother Karl – his twin brother Karl, it says here – were, "the German government's most feared assassins. They carried out their international mischief-making under a shared alias: Günther

Ehrlichmann." Apparently Ehrlichmann's true double-identity was the best-kept secret in recent memory at least partly because the possibilities it opened up were both lethal and terrifying. He was a killer who could seemingly be in two places at once. He could distract with his left hand and kill with his right.'

'Well I'll be blowed,' said Lady Hardcastle. 'And so the man pursuing us now is twin brother Karl.'

'So it would very much appear,' said Harry. 'You only half-killed Günther Ehrlichmann; you left the other half very much alive.'

Lady Hardcastle turned and looked at me. 'I said I was going to be disappointed. Twins! How terribly ordinary.'

'Ah, but ordinary goes out the window with the next bit. Our chaps in Berlin have been all of a flap since all this came out and have worked like devils to find out what they can. They couldn't figure out why he should suddenly come after you now, after all these years. And it's been puzzling me, too. As much as trying to work out why a dead man should be after you, why now? I know a fair few people capable of holding grudges, but to hold one for nine years without making the slightest move… And then when you consider that Karl was alive and well all this time, why did no one see him until early this year? The identity of Ehrlichmann died with his brother, and Karl Gerber hasn't been seen at all from that day to this.'

'And do we now know what happened?'

'Naturally, Sis. There was some amount of chaos in Shanghai at the time of the… incident.'

'There was a certain degree of local unpleasantness,' said Lady Hardcastle drily.

'A few days of spontaneous Boxer activity, yes. Not quite the main event, but enough to make life disagreeable for Westerners and an ideal opportunity for the Chinese to round up undesirables.'

'Undesirables?' I said.

'Anyone they didn't much like, essentially. One class of person they most especially didn't like was the European spy. Word had reached them that Ehrlichmann was already targeting Diamond Rook, so they left them both to it and positioned themselves to pick up whoever was left standing. Sorry, Sis. But you know what I mean.'

She waved his concern aside.

'They saw Karl Gerber later, walking healthy and free, and they and recognized him at once as being Ehrlichmann. They presumed he had eliminated Diamond Rook, and so they seized him. Ehrlichmann had taken care of one of the key European spies and now they had the other. Obviously they missed the fact that you were Diamond Rook, and that they only had half of Ehrlichmann, but it gave them something to play with. And play with him they did. Even after they worked out the truth of what had happened and you were long gone, they held on to Gerber. The Germans had disavowed him, and with his brother dead, there was no one to come looking for him. He disappeared into a Chinese gaol in 1899 and was never seen again. Until earlier this year.'

'And what happened then?' asked Lady Hardcastle.

'No one is quite certain exactly what happened, nor how, but one day an older, thinner Gerber turned up in Berlin and asked to be taken back into the fold.'

'And did they? Take him back, I mean.'

'That's all a bit hazy,' said Harry, thoughtfully. He leafed through the memorandum again, but didn't seem to find anything helpful. 'I can't believe they would find themselves able to trust an operative who had been under the control of a foreign power for almost nine years, but they do seem to have found a mutually beneficial purpose for him: they let him loose on you.'

'It does make a little more sense now,' said Lady Hardcastle. 'Even just knowing that he's not a ghost. And revenge is understandable, especially if the thought was what was keeping him going in that Chinese gaol.'

'But what are we going to do now?' I said.

'That, my dear Florence, is a very good question,' she said, and lapsed into silence.

We got nowhere the previous evening after the revelations from Harry's contacts in Berlin. It was obvious that Lady Hardcastle was rattled and was just putting on a brave face, and the anxiety was blunting her usually sharp mind. The conversation just went round and round in circles and I'm ashamed to admit that I got a little testy with it all and went to bed early.

The principal consequence of that little outburst of petulance was that I was also awake bright and early. I had persuaded Harry to have his grocer deliver more provisions and I was all set to make a lavish breakfast to atone for my peevishness. All that was required was a fresh loaf, so I set off once more for the baker's round the corner.

London in the early morning is unlike anywhere I've ever been. The city never seems to come to complete rest, but there's still a feeling just after dawn of momentum building again. The clatter of the delivery carts, the first omnibuses taking the early-starters to their work, the dustmen and street sweepers making everything fresh again. And then there are the smells. The harsh, oddly dirty smell of bricks and paving stones damp with dew, the hundreds of fires lit by bleary-eyed servants, and of course the bread.

The woman behind the counter at the bakery recognized me and chattered cheerfully as she made up what had already become my "regular" order.

'And look, love, he's just brought out some lovely Chelsea buns. They'll go lovely with a cup of tea, they will. You'll be well and truly in your mistress's good books if you serves her one of them.'

I should have liked to have made my own (I make a wickedly good Chelsea bun, if I do say so myself) but the facilities at Harry's flat can be most charitably described as "rudimentary" and so I allowed myself to be persuaded to buy three. And some rolls for lunch.

Something nagged at me on the short walk back, but I couldn't for the life of me put my finger on what it was. Was there something I had forgotten to do? Somewhere I should have gone? I knew there was something, but try as I might I couldn't work out what. I tried to put it out of my mind in the hope that I might sidle up on it unawares in a little while and trap the errant thought.

I met the milkman as he struggled up the steps to the entrance to Harry's building and offered to take Mr Featherstonhaugh's milk up to the third floor. He was most grateful and flirted half-heartedly as I took the can from him. His heart wasn't really in it but I laughed appreciatively and we each felt that we'd played our parts.

I met no one else on my way up to Harry's flat and mused on the fact that I had left and then returned entirely unobserved.

Entirely unobserved. That was what had been niggling me. Where were our watchers? Unless they had grown a great deal more adept in the past twenty-four hours, and had managed to remain completely concealed as they kept us safe from harm, there were no longer any of

Harry's Foreign Office agents outside the flat.

I let myself in and found Harry already up and about. I took off my hat and gloves and put on my pinnie and resumed my breakfast making. Harry hovered, trying to be useful, but it wasn't long before I pressed a cup of tea into his hands and asked him ever so nicely to please sit down and get out of the way.

'You do make me laugh, Flo,' he said. 'I'm sure I've never met a servant quite like you.'

'I'm a one of a kind.'

'That you are. I've never really had a chance to thank you for taking care of my little sister, you know.'

'It's just my job, sir.'

'Harry,' he said. 'After all that you've done for her, I think you really can call me Harry.'

'I'll try, sir, but it doesn't come naturally.'

'No, no, I've noticed that. But I mean it. If it weren't for you, I think Emily would have gone doolally tap years ago.'

'Or strangled herself with her corsets,' I said.

He chuckled. 'Or that, certainly. Not the most practical girl, my sister. But you keep body and soul together and I really don't know what she'd do without you.'

'Thank you, sir. You're very kind. I don't know what I'd do without her, either. Have you ordered our watchers to stand down, sir?' I asked.

Harry laughed again. 'That was quite a change of subject,' he said. 'There was I trying to be all gracious and offer you my heartfelt thanks and appreciation for your years of hard work...'

'And I'm touched, sir, really I am. But it's been bothering me.'

'No, Flo, they're not stood down.'

'Where are they, then?'

'Outside on the street,' he said. 'Why?'

'Take a look, please, sir. There's no one there. There was no one there when I went to the baker's and no one there when I came back.'

'Well I'll be blowed,' he said, getting up to take a look for himself. 'You're right you, know,' he called from the drawing room. 'Not a soul in sight.' He came back to the kitchen. 'And you're sure you saw no one? Of course you are. You'd know how to spot a tail.'

'I have a little experience in that area, sir. That's why I was so

257

annoyed that it took me so long to work out what was wrong.'

'How do you mean?' he said, puzzled.

'Just now, on the way back from the shop. I knew there was something missing but I didn't know what. Fat lot of good I am as a protector of people's little sisters.'

'And whose little sister are you supposed to be protecting?' asked Lady Hardcastle, emerging from her bedroom, tying up her silk dressing gown.

'Mine, Sis,' said Harry. 'Sleep well?'

'Not badly, certainly. Is anything the matter? You two seem to be in conspiratorial mood.'

'Your tiny protector has noticed that my men are missing.'

'Missing, dear?' she said, yawning.

'Vanished. Scarpered. Done a bunk. The old moonlight flit. In short… they're gone.'

'Hmm,' she said. 'Well perhaps that's all to the good. It does rather precipitate things, doesn't it. I should be most intrigued to know exactly why they have, as you say, "done a moonlight", but by leaving us exposed they rather force us to action, do they not? It was terribly easy just to sit here waiting for Ehrlichmann–'

'Gerber,' I interrupted.

'Yes, dear, sorry… waiting for Gerber to turn up and be arrested, but now we have something of an incentive to take matters into our own hands.'

'Do you have a plan?' asked Harry.

'As a matter of fact, I believe I do.' She produced a book from her pocket. 'Your library is a little limited, dear thing, but you do at least have some taste.' She showed him the book.

'*The Return of Sherlock Holmes*,' he said. 'And this has given you your plan?'

'Well, quite,' she said, yawning again. 'Little point in thinking up one's own plans when Conan Doyle has already done all the hard work.'

'And what do we do?' I asked.

'I have assignments for both of you,' she said. 'But first, breakfast. Harry, darling, you're a wonderful host, but your cooking is woeful. Thank goodness for Flo. I don't know what I'd have done without her all these years. I'd have gone doolally. Or starved to death. Or strangled myself with my corsets.'

Harry laughed, I blushed, and we all settled down for a slap-up nosh.

We had been given our assignments and had each set off on our separate missions. There was one tiny grain of comfort: at least whoever had stood Harry's watchers down hadn't replaced them with his own. Unless they were very good indeed – and I sincerely doubted that they were good enough to stay that well hidden for that long without slipping up – I, for one, spent my day entirely unobserved. The obverse of this cheery coin was that it was a good bet that Ehrlichmann/Gerber knew where we were, but even that was something that we intended to take advantage of.

Harry's task had been the most straightforward, but perhaps the most difficult. He had been dispatched to the Foreign Office to try to find out why the watchers – placed there under his own orders – were now missing and why no one had troubled to consult him on the matter.

My own part in the affair was more pleasurable and after completing the first part of my tasks for the day, I was the first one to return to the flat. I made myself a sandwich and set about rearranging the furniture in the way Lady Hardcastle had described, paying particular attention to the placing of the large armchair and the lamp.

With that done and my sandwich eaten, I left once more to make some more arrangements. We had all managed to convince ourselves that Ehrlichmann would make his move soon and that he would be most likely to wait until after dark. The disappearance of our watchers seemed to indicate that tonight might be the night and so there was some degree of urgency in putting Lady Hardcastle's plan into action.

It was dusk by the time Lady Hardcastle and I reconvened at the flat and put the finishing touches to her plan. We set everything up together, but once the dummy was in place, she was careful to keep the light between her and the window blinds so that her shadow was not seen.

By now, you've probably surmised that Lady Hardcastle's plan, taken as it was from that particular Sherlock Holmes book, might have involved a waxwork dummy sitting in a chair near a window.

And you'd be right. *The Adventure of the Empty House* had provided the inspiration, and Joan from Madame Tussaud's had provided an old head that looked very similar to Lady Hardcastle along with a generic body of about the right size. It had been delivered in a large packing crate which two porters from the waxworks had very kindly brought up to the flat.

'Are you sure this is going to fool him, my lady?' I said as I put the finishing touches to the dummy's costume.

'Fool him? I can't see why not. Dear old Joan made some hasty adjustments to this old head with her trusty sculptor's tools and it does bear more than a passing resemblance to yours truly. I should think it will make him believe that I am sitting alone in the flat and lure him into this room where we can spring our trap.'

'I do hope you're right, my lady,' I said. 'Did you ever imagine it would come to this?'

'Come to what, dear? Setting traps for murderous assassins? I don't suppose I did, no.'

'I meant being pursued by murderous assassins in the first place,' I said. 'I'm not sure it crossed my mind when you casually said, "I say, Flo, do you fancy spying for the Queen?" It seemed like a fantastic adventure, but not a dangerous one. When we fled through China, into Burma – oh my goodness, do you remember that terrifying trip down the Irrawaddy? – I thought we were going to die most days. But even then I thought the danger was behind us. We had more than our fair share of run-ins with people who wanted to kill us, but so far none of them managed to get up and pursue us halfway round the world after we had dealt with them.'

'No, we've been quite fortunate that way. Due in no small part to your prodigious skills, dear. For your part, did you ever imagine you could kill a man with your bare hands?'

'I was quite a scrapper back in the Valleys.'

She laughed. 'I don't doubt it. But you see what I mean. We none of us can predict the future.'

'My Auntie Bronwyn could see the future. Or so she claimed.'

She chuckled again 'So you said, pet, so you said. But now let us conceal ourselves and prepare to spring our trap. You know your duties?'

'I do indeed, my lady,' I said, and set about my own preparations for the final phase while she concealed herself in the shadows in the corner of the drawing room.

It was a long evening. Just as in *The Adventure of the Empty House*, the Lady Hardcastle dummy had to be surreptitiously moved at regular intervals to simulate the appearance of a real woman spending a quiet evening relaxing with a good book.

Time dragged on.

Just after midnight there was a scratching at the lock on the front door as though a drunk were fumbling clumsily to get his key to fit into the impossibly tiny keyhole. Then, with a click, the door opened and stealthy footsteps crept along the short passage to the drawing room door. Slowly that door opened and there, silhouetted in the light that had spilled in from the landing, stood Günther Ehrlichmann (or Karl Gerber as we now knew him). He held a silenced automatic pistol in his hand.

Unexpectedly, he didn't enter the room.

'Lady Hardcastle, Miss Armstrong,' he said from the doorway. 'Please step into the centre of the room with your arms raised above your heads.'

We didn't move.

'Come, ladies, I too have read *The Adventure of the Empty House*. It is much better in German, I feel. Did you think to fool me with your dummy and your shadow show? Please step from your hiding places now before I lose my patience.'

The plan appeared to be falling apart. If he had stepped into the room we would have jumped him but standing there in the hallway with gun levelled, there was little we could do to break the stalemate. Reluctantly, Lady Hardcastle stepped from the shadows and I stood from my hiding place beside the armchair.

'That is so much better,' said Gerber. 'Now we can talk.'

'Talk?' said Lady Hardcastle, incredulously.

'Of course, talk,' said Gerber. 'We are civilized people, we should talk.'

'Before you kill us,' she said.

'Yes, of course you must both die. But first I should like to talk. I have spent a lot of time imagining this moment, and I should hate for it to pass without some... ceremony. Yes, I think there should be ceremony. We should make a moment of it.'

'Perhaps you should come in, join us in a drink. There's no need to be so formal if we're to die anyway,' said Lady Hardcastle, icily. 'Let's at least make our last moments pleasant ones. Come in, do.'

'I think not, Lady Hardcastle. I have heard much about you in recent months and I do not intend to put myself within reach of your deadly servant. We shall talk as we are.'

'As you wish, Herr Gerber. You're the one with the burning desire to talk, so what is it that you wish to say?'

'I have wondered about this for many years, Lady Hardcastle. When you killed my brother, I wondered what I should say. You killed a part of me and I wanted to kill you, too. You do not have a twin, so you cannot know. But you took my life as surely as you took his. And then the Chinese rebels captured me. Took my freedom as you had taken half my life. I spent nine years in a Chinese gaol. Abandoned by my own government and left to rot. Nine years alone to contemplate just one thing: revenge.'

'Oh, so you're completely mad, then?'

'Have a care, Lady Hardcastle. Remember who has the gun.'

'Oh, I remember. I remember that your brother had a gun, too. I remember that he used it to kill my husband.'

'It was our job to kill enemy spies.'

'Roderick was no spy.'

'No, that was the mistake of our masters in Berlin. They learned afterwards that you were the spy. But now I have the chance to put everything right. I can complete the job that Jakob and I were given, I can avenge my brother's death and the theft of nine years of my own life. Two bullets, to give so much satisfaction.'

'Two bullets? Whatever happened to the famous German efficiency?'

'One each, Lady Hardcastle. Of course I have to kill you both. You left me alive to seek revenge for the murder of my brother, you do not think that I should be foolish enough to leave someone behind to avenge you.'

'If you put it like that, it does make sense,' she said, casually.

'With you both dead, I shall retire to my family's home in the Tyrollean mountains, and I do not intend to spend the rest of my days looking over my shoulder. It will be nice there. I dreamed for many years of seeing the sky.' He seemed momentarily to drift off into a world of his own.

It is at this point that I should reveal a fresh deception of my own. The trap in *The Adventure of the Empty House* was just the starting point for Lady Hardcastle's plan and I have glossed over my activities earlier in the day, entirely failing to reveal just exactly what I was up to. I thought it would help to convey Gerber's sense of frustrated bewilderment at the immediately ensuing events if you, too, were in the dark and believed (with some irritation, I shouldn't wonder) that she had simply reused Holmes's plan in its published form.

As far as Gerber was aware, I was standing in the drawing room beside my mistress. And I have deceitfully written this narrative to make it appear so to you, too. But that is not precisely what happened. The first of my tasks that day had been to travel to the other side of London to visit the Royal Artillery barracks at Woolwich where Staff Sergeant Daffidd Evans was stationed with his wife, Gwenith. It had been my job to enlist the help of my sister in our risky undertaking.

And so it turned out that the woman standing in the middle of the drawing room with her arms raised, dressed in a maid's uniform, was not me at all, but Gwenith, my dear twin sister. We thought it would add an extra dimension to the Sherlock Holmes trap and give us a safeguard against Gerber seeing through the clumsy ruse. I would also, we thought, add a pleasing symmetry to the whole twin-filled affair.

While Gwenith had been "me" in the drawing room, I had been in the kitchen, and as Gerber drifted off into his Tyrollean daydream, assuring Lady Hardcastle that he had no intention of spending his remaining days looking over his shoulder, I was tiptoeing up behind him in stockinged feet, hoping with all my heart that he had started as he meant to go on and didn't plan to look over his shoulder now.

What a foolish and empty thing it is to hope. As I positioned myself to strike, something, some movement of mine, perhaps, some tiny sound I made, caused Gerber to turn his head. He spotted me.

Things weren't going at all the way I'd imagined them, but I did notice that some good had come of it all. As he turned his head in surprise at my approach, his body turned as well, shifting his aim away from Gwenith and Lady Hardcastle. While the clockwork in his brain was still whirring, I struck out at his gun hand, knocking the pistol from his grasp and sending it skittering across the floor. I should have been growing used to it, but I can't deny that I was beginning to get more than a little fed up with people pointing guns at me.

I shifted my weight slightly, readying myself for another blow but was forced instead to block a terrifyingly fast counterattack from the white-haired German.

'I wasn't entirely idle during my nine years in China,' he said, aiming a shatteringly painful kick at my knee. 'My captors encouraged me to keep active and learn some new skills.' I managed to partially deflect a blow to my face but he still caught the side of my head and left my ears ringing.

He easily caught my next two strikes and was positioning himself for another attack when both our attentions were caught by an oddly quiet and polite cough from the drawing room.

'I'm sorry to interrupt while you seem to be having so much fun,' said Lady Hardcastle. 'But I thought I ought to point out that I now have this rather handsome pistol.' She waggled the gun which was now aimed steadily at Gerber. 'A Luger, isn't it? It's rather striking, don't you think? Very modern looking.'

Rather unexpectedly, Gerber placidly raised his hands in surrender and allowed me to limp past him into the drawing room.

Gwenith helped me to the sofa where I gratefully sat down. It had been a while since I'd been bested in a fair fight and my knee was going to be reminding me of my near defeat for quite a while.

'Right then, Herr Gerber,' said Lady Hardcastle. 'Now that I have the gun, perhaps we can get things back on track. Would you be good enough to lie on your front with your hands behind your back, please?'

He meekly complied, the hint of a smirk on his scarred face.

'And Gwenith, dear, if you would be a poppet and secure his wrists with the cord as I showed you, that would be grand.'

Gwenith took a length of cord from the bookcase and went over to the supine Gerber. There was a knock, and a voice called through the still-open front door.

'I say, is there anyone at home?' It was Sir David Alderman.

'In here, Sir David,' called Lady Hardcastle. 'Thank goodness you've arrived. I find myself a little short-handed what with... Oh, I say, how dismaying.'

Sir David stood in the drawing room doorway with a revolver levelled at Lady Hardcastle.

'Get up, Gerber, you idiot,' he said. 'I should have known you'd botch this.'

Gerber stood.

'Give him his gun back, Lady Hardcastle, there's a good girl.'

Lady Hardcastle handed the pistol back to Gerber who moved to stand beside Sir David, covering Gwenith with it as she moved to sit beside me on the sofa.

'I wondered who had stood Harry's men down,' said Lady Hardcastle, calmly. 'I thought it might have been you but I really hoped it wasn't.'

'That buffoon Featherstonhaugh thought so, too,' he said, taking a couple of steps into the room, Gerber moving faithfully with him. 'He came sniffing around me this morning all please-and-thank-you and three-bags-full-sir, trying to get some information out of me. Your family really are the living end. I sent him on a fool's errand on the other side of town so he won't be bothering us if that's what you were hoping for.'

'Ah well,' she said. 'We'll just have to make do as best we can without him.'

'Don't worry, you won't have to cope for too long. We'll soon put you out of my misery.'

'Your misery, Sir David?' she said, showing surprise for the first time. 'What have I ever done to you?'

'You have been a thorn in my government's side for a very long time, Lady Hardcastle.'

'Your government?' she said, still perplexed. 'Oh, I see.' The penny had dropped. 'Well I never. Fancy there being a German spy in the heart of the Home Office. How about that, eh, girls?'

Gwenith and I just looked at each other.

'But why now, Sir David? Why blow your cover now?'

'My cover won't be blown, Lady Hardcastle. Herr Gerber here will kill the three of you and then he shall disappear into the night like an avenging angel. My office will be called, of course, and Featherstonhaugh's, but really, I'm so sorry, there was nothing I could do to stop him.' He chuckled. 'As for the timing... let us just say that you saw some things in Tsingtao which we should rather you hadn't seen. Your report was quite useful to the British all those years ago, and you set us back a little, but there still might be details deep within your memory which you didn't include at the time, some little titbit about the submarine or its pen. We would really rather there was no one left around who has seen even the early prototypes of our submarines before we start sea trials of the latest version. Surprise is everything in warfare, dear lady.'

'Warfare? There's no war.'

'Oh, give it time. War shall come sooner or later. And when it does, Imperial Germany shall be very much the side to back.'

'When did you decide to betray your country?' asked Lady Hardcastle.

'Betray my country, my lady? But I've been serving my country all along. My family name is Haltermann, not Alderman, we are originally from Hannover. My parents moved to England when I was very young. A little change of spelling, a white lie or two about my ancestry… gaining access to the British establishment was all very easy. And no one looked terribly hard once they heard I was a Cambridge man. Being the "right sort" opens so many doors, don't you find? But of course you do. You were at Girton yourself.'

'I was, it's true. Ah well. It's a shame it all has to end like this. I rather imagined myself growing old and irascible, surrounded by irritated relatives and dying in a comfortable bed after saying something profoundly witty.'

'You're breaking my heart,' said Sir David, coldly. 'Well, I've had my fun. Gerber, do what you do and let's get out of here.'

I've always been terribly fond of Harry Featherstonhaugh, but at that moment I could have kissed the fellow. Sir David's last words were almost drowned out by the sound of three more pistols being cocked in the doorway behind him and there stood Harry and two uniformed soldiers.

'Hello, Sis,' said Harry. 'Sorry I'm late. I was halfway to the other side of town when I realized I probably ought to be here instead. Luckily I found a couple of chaps milling about nearby who were able to come and help.'

'Hello, love,' said the soldier with three stripes and a crown on his sleeve. 'You all right?'

Gwenith nodded.

'Guns down, hands on heads,' said Harry to Gerber and Sir David. 'Captain, if you could do the honours with the handcuffs, the staff sergeant here can go and see to his wife. Looks like she's hurt her knee.'

'That's Florence with the damaged knee, you dolt,' said Lady Hardcastle.

'Is it, by crikey,' he said. 'Well I never. You two do look awfully alike, you know.'

'It's being twins that does it, sir,' I said.

'Harry, darling,' said Lady Hardcastle, 'it's a relief to see you all. Where did you find our new friends?'

'Long story, Sis, but the short version is that when Flo went over to the barracks this morning to fetch her sister, Staff Sergeant Evans didn't want her to go alone. He enlisted the help of his captain and they came looking for us. I found them near the tube station.'

Meanwhile, the artillery captain had handcuffed the two Germans while Staff Sergeant Evans hugged his wife and then took a look at my knee.

'The rozzers are on their way, too,' said Harry cheerfully. 'I put in a call to Scotland Yard but since I already had these chaps with me I thought I'd come straight over. Good thing I did by the looks.'

'Timely, darling, timely,' said Lady Hardcastle. 'I thought our goose was most definitely stuffed, basted and in a medium oven with only the potatoes still to be done.'

'Oh do for heaven's sake shut up, you twittering old harpy,' said Sir David. 'I've never met a more aggravating woman in all my—'

His childish rant halted abruptly when Harry's fist made contact with his nose.

'Sorry, *Dave*,' said Harry. 'You were saying?'

Sir David simply glared at him.

Gwenith took over from Daffidd in fussing over my knee and soon declared it "bruised but not badly damaged" and bound it tightly with a bandage which Harry had produced from a cupboard in the bathroom.

'There you are, Floss, good as new,' she said.

'Thanks, Gwen bach,' I said. 'When did you learn to do that?'

'Training to be a nurse, I am. With the army.'

'You never are,' I said. 'Since when?'

'Easter, I started. I'm a lot older than the other girls, but I loves it. Wish I'd done it years ago.'

'Good for you. What does Daffidd think?'

She looked over at her husband. 'Oh, he thinks I'm just doing it for the chance to see men in their underwear.' She winked.

'I don't mind that so much, bach,' said Daffidd with a grin. 'It's when you has to get them out of their underwear that I worries.'

Sir David tutted and sighed theatrically.

'Shut up, Dave,' I said. 'No one's talking to you.'

'Why you impudent little—'

I never got to find out what I was an impudent little one of, though I had some pretty good guesses. At that moment there was another knock on the still-open front door and a commanding male voice said, 'Police! Mr Featherstonhaugh, are you there?'

'Come on in, Superintendent,' called Harry, jovially. 'The party's in the drawing room.'

Harry's drawing room, already rather full, was soon made yet more crowded by the addition of a bowler-hatted detective and three uniformed constables.

'Crikey, sir,' said the detective. 'You have got a full house.'

'Just a little soirée, Superintendent, a few close chums, you know. We had a couple of gatecrashers, though. Would you mind awfully?'

'Be my pleasure, sir. Come along Alderman. You, too, Ehrlichmann.'

'That's "Sir David" to you, you jumped up little—'

'Was, sir. It was "Sir David". It won't be come tomorrow morning so you'd best get used to it. Can't have German spies as knights of the realm. That wouldn't do at all.'

Two of the constables laid hands on Gerber and Sir David and manhandled them towards the door.

What happened next has haunted my nightmares from that day to this. I remember that once, a few years before, Lady Hardcastle had managed to borrow a moving picture projector which she set up in the London flat for a party. Her guests were greatly amused by the flickering images, never more so than when she cranked the handle at the wrong speed. Winding it too fast made the people on the screen jitter about comically, while winding it too slowly made them move about with a ponderous elegance, as though struggling through treacle.

In my memory, the events of those next few moments move with that same terrible slowness, each tiny movement etched on my mind forever, with me unable to move quickly enough to do anything but scream.

Gerber had learned more than just the Chinese fighting arts in his prison cell, he had mastered the skills of Harry Houdini himself. No one had noticed, but while we were all congratulating ourselves on our brave capture of the nefarious German spies, Gerber had freed his hands from the cuffs that bound them. As the constable pushed him past Harry, he grabbed Harry's revolver and began to race towards the door. As he crossed the threshold on his way to freedom he turned. The projector in my memory stops here every time as I see him level the gun and point it straight at Lady Hardcastle. There was a bang, the loudest single sound I had ever heard. The flash was blinding. And then he was gone. He fired two more shots over his shoulder as he fled down the stairs, keeping his pursuers at bay as he bolted for the door and freedom. He was gone.

And then the awful moment of realization. Lying on the floor, blood pulsing from a wound in her stomach, was my Emily.

Autumn had arrived and the view from the window of the small hospital room was bleak and grey. And although everything inside the room was bright and white and antiseptically clean, the view in there was bleak and grey, too.

Lady Hardcastle had been unconscious for six days.

While the constables had hared off into the darkened streets in search of Gerber, Daffidd and his captain had taken temporary charge of Sir David in the flat while the superintendent had driven Harry and me, with the wounded Lady Hardcastle propped between us, to a surgeon on Harley Street. The streets were slick with drizzle and the car had slid more than once as the superintendent drove at incautious speed towards the hospital.

She had been in surgery for five hours as the doctors removed the bullet and tried to repair the internal damage. It had taken all their considerable skill, but they had eventually stemmed the bleeding and stitched her back together. Days passed, and although she remained mercifully free of infection, she had not regained consciousness. She had lain there in the crisp, white linen sheets, her dark hair framing her face, neither moving nor uttering a sound.

Harry and I took turns in staying with her, reading her the telegrams and cards that arrived every day from her friends. We read from the newspapers, too, especially the unfolding story of the fall of disgraced Home Office official, Sir David Alderman. Investigations were ongoing, it seemed, but a network of spies and agents had been uncovered and the German Ambassador had been summoned to explain the actions of his government. Diplomatic tensions were high.

Of Gerber, there was no sign. Harry's men had been on the lookout and all ports and railway stations were on alert, but he had not been seen. I didn't mention this in my reports to the comatose Lady Hardcastle.

I turned away from the window and sat in the armchair beside the bed to read. Harry had brought me a brand new book by Mr E M Forster and I found myself childishly pleased to keep reading my own name as Lucy explored the city of Florence. After a few minutes there was a gentle knock at the door and Harry came in.

'What ho, Flo,' he said, bending to kiss my cheek. 'How's the old girl?'

'Oh, you know,' I said, putting down my book. 'Gabbling away as usual. Complaining about her lunch, joking with the staff. She even…' My voice cracked a little and Harry put a comforting hand on my shoulder.

'I know, Flo, I know.'

'The stupid old biddy,' I said with a sniff. 'Just careless and rude, she is. Standing in the way of a bullet and then not even having the decency to wake up and tell us she's all right.'

'She will,' said Harry. 'The doctors say it can sometimes take a few days for the body to recover from a shock like that.'

'She'd better,' I said. 'I don't know what I'd do without her.'

'There'll be no need to find out, old thing,' he said with another reassuring pat. 'She'll be right as rain in no time.'

There was a rustle of linen and a croaky voice said, 'I bally well will as well.'

Harry and I looked over in shock at the slowly awakening figure of

Emily Hardcastle.

'Now do stop being so maudlin, there's a dear. And would you be a pet and fetch me a cup of tea? I'm absolutely parched.'

The End

Lady Hardcastle and Florence Armstrong will
return in

The Spirit Is Willing